Fiction
£3.99

ISLAND SONG

Pepsi Demacque-Crockett enjoyed a long and fulfilling career within the entertainment industry through the 1980s and 1990s, as part of the pop phenomenon Wham! and later in the singing duo Pepsi & Shirlie.

Pepsi's parents arrived in Britain from the island of Saint Lucia in the mid-1950s and settled in West London. *Island Song*, her debut novel, is inspired by their story.

Pepsi grew up surrounded by a vibrant Caribbean community with music as her backdrop. She now lives in Saint Lucia, the country of her parents' birth, with her husband, James, but is still a London girl at heart.

To find out more about Pepsi:

@pepsidemacquec
@PepsiDemacqueC

PEPSI DEMACQUE-CROCKETT

ISLAND SONG

HarperCollins*Publishers*

HarperCollins*Publishers* Ltd
1 London Bridge Street,
London SE1 9GF

www.harpercollins.co.uk

HarperCollins*Publishers*
Macken House, 39/40 Mayor Street Upper
Dublin 1, D01 C9W8

First published by HarperCollins*Publishers* Ltd 2025

1

Copyright © Pepsi Demacque-Crockett 2025

Maps of St Lucia and London:
Antiqua Print Gallery / Alamy Stock Photo

Pepsi Demacque-Crockett asserts the moral right to
be identified as the author of this work

A catalogue record for this book is available from the British Library

ISBN: 978-0-00-859875-4

This novel is entirely a work of fiction.
The names, characters and incidents portrayed in it are
the work of the author's imagination. Any resemblance to
actual persons, living or dead, events or localities is
entirely coincidental.

This book is set in Sabon by HarperCollins*Publishers* India

Printed and bound in the UK using 100% Renewable
Electricity by CPI Group (UK) Ltd

All rights reserved. No part of this publication may be
reproduced, stored in a retrieval system, or transmitted,
in any form or by any means, electronic, mechanical,
photocopying, recording or otherwise, without the prior
permission of the publishers.

This book contains FSC™ certified paper and other controlled
sources to ensure responsible forest management.

For more information visit: www.harpercollins.co.uk/green

*I dedicate this book to those who came before me
In loving memory of my sister, Tecia*

And to James for taking me home

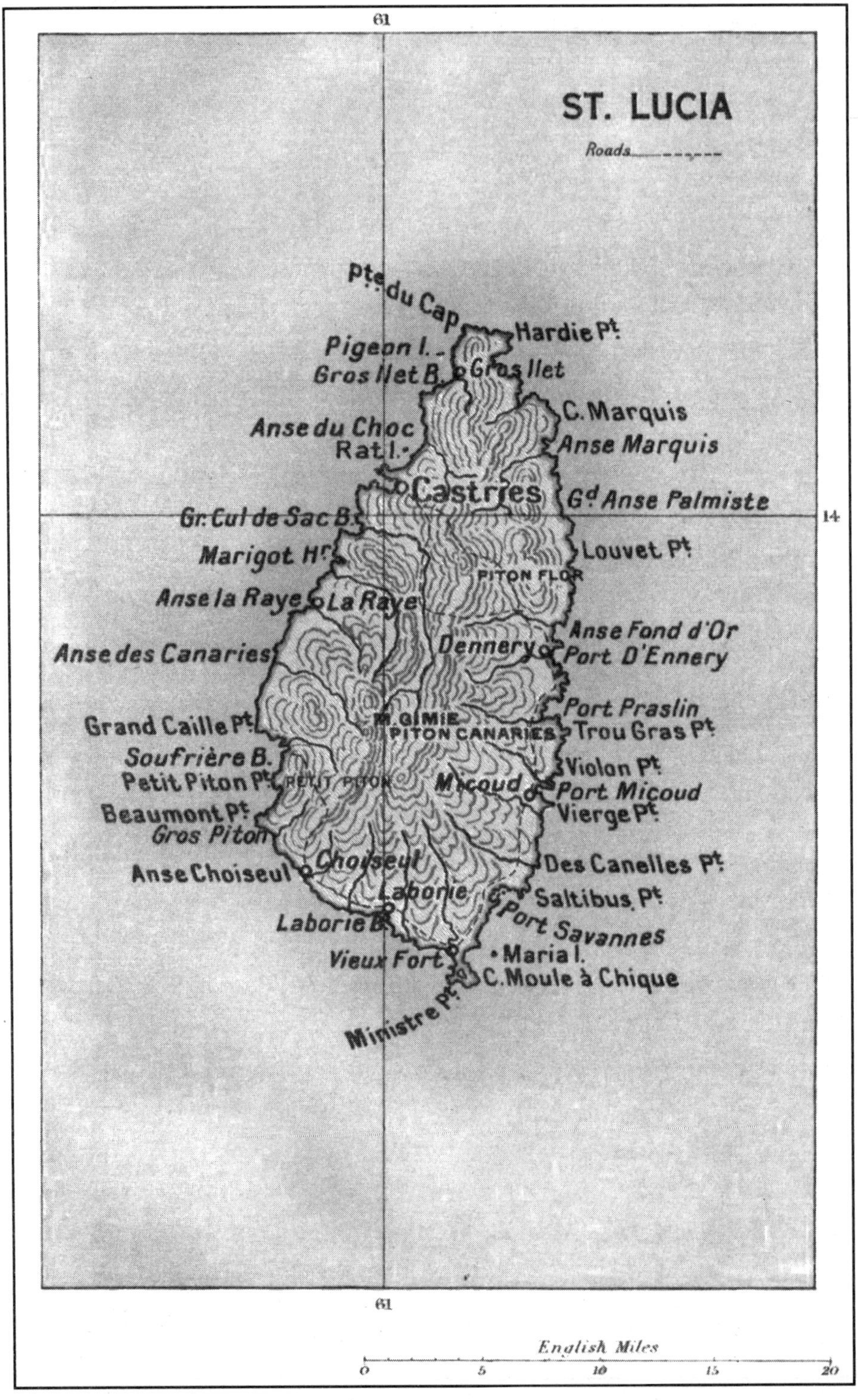
ST. LUCIA
Roads
61
14
Pte du Cap
Hardie Pt
Pigeon I.
Gros Ilet B.
Gros Ilet
C. Marquis
Anse du Choc
Anse Marquis
Rat I.
Castries
Gd Anse Palmiste
Gr. Cul de Sac B.
Marigot Hr
Louvet Pt
PITON FLOR
Anse la Raye
La Raye
Anse Fond d'Or
Anse des Canaries
Dennery
Port D'Ennery
Port Praslin
Mt GIMIE
Grand Caille Pt
PITON CANARIES
Trou Gras Pt
Soufrière B.
Violon Pt
Petit Piton Pt
PETIT PITON
Micoud
Port Micoud
Beaumont Pt
Vierge Pt
Gros Piton
Choiseul
Des Canelles Pt
Anse Choiseul
Laborie
Saltibus Pt
Laborie B.
Port Savannes
Vieux Fort
Maria I.
C. Moule à Chique
Ministre Pt
English Miles
0
5
10
15
20

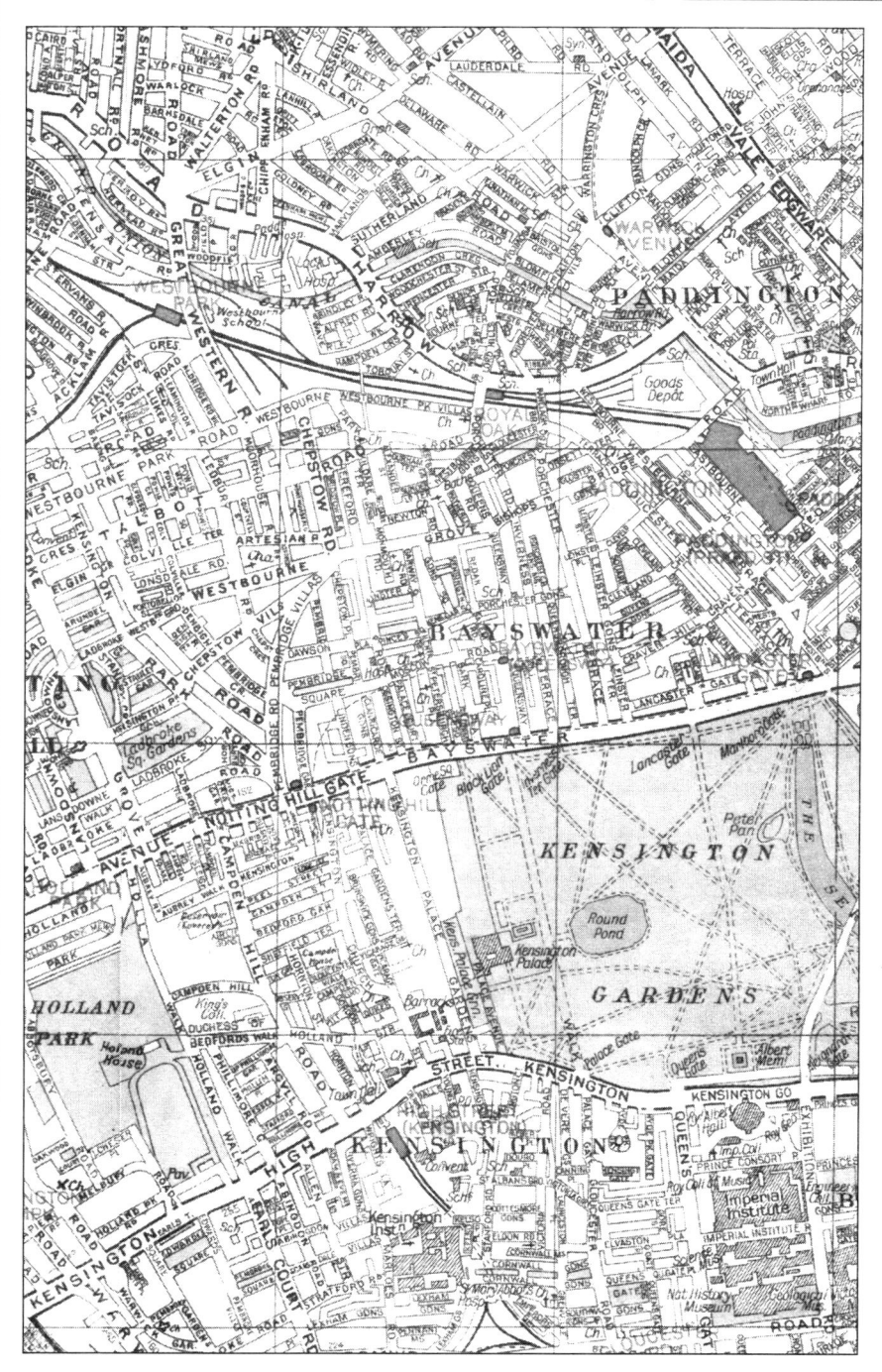

LONDON

Part One

PROLOGUE

It was a summer morning in 1940. The sun would rise and bring with it the news that Canaries had lost many souls with the sinking of the *Blue Belle*.

Of course, there were the souls of the people who died, twenty-five passengers and three crew members who drowned when the island ferry capsized. But the accident took something more from that remote coastal village in St Lucia, something many of the villagers hadn't realised they'd lost. It took the hopes and the dreams of a generation, and replaced them with nightmares and a new folklore that made them wary of the waters that surrounded them. A terror that urged warnings on their children to steer away from any place they might find themselves lost. The village children believed the myth that the water could consume them.

Ella and Agnes Deterville were no different.

Ella had been ten at the time of the disaster, Agnes, seven. Young, but old enough for the inconsolable lamentation that overtook their community on the West Coast to imprint itself on their young minds. A heavy melancholy enveloped the villagers for weeks after the sinking, the usual bawdy jokes and loud laughter exchanged between passersby in the narrow streets conspicuously absent. Though most adults didn't speak about the tragedy in front of their children, the Deterville girls' father, Herbert, often did. A local boatbuilder and fisherman, he was a masterful storyteller who could conjure up the spirits within his tales.

He enjoyed seeing his daughters' astonished faces as he did, their mouths open in rapt attention as his deep expressive voice would rise and fall dramatically. Ella's favourite fable was about the escaped slaves known as The Brigands or 'Neg Mawon', who made a home in the sanctuary of the steep and inaccessible plateaus high above the river.

'When I was young, I climb up dat mountain with my frien' Franklin. You know what we saw, Ella?'

'What did you see Papa?' Ella loved it when her father focused solely on her.

'There was small caves where the slaves hide out and you could see markings on de walls but we couldna make sense of dem. Dere was stones and broken conch shells scattered everywhere. And we could see clear as if it was yesterday de places dey make fire, the black smoke was on de wall and above. De energy up dere was powerful, not a place you want to stay once it got dark, and Franklin got scared when he thought he saw somefing move in de darkness, so we move fas' back down de mountain.'

His eyes would move off into the distance as he spoke.

'It our people history up dere Ella, we are born of fighters, slaves who wanted to be free.'

After his favourite meal of fried fish and breadfruit roasted on the coal pot, he would push his plate away and lean back in his chair, exhaling with a long sigh of contentment.

By the light of two kerosene lamps, sitting at the back of their house with the soundtrack of the river flowing close by, their father would retell the story of the *Blue Belle*. 'You know de boat sink because someone spot a whale and cry out. All de passengers stand and press up in de front of de boat to take a look.' Herbert would pause every time he got to this part of the story and take a swig of his drink, as if bracing himself against the story's inevitable outcome.

'So much weight up front, and dey hit a big wave off de point where de current does run strong against wind and waves. Well, dat wave swamp de boat, and in de confusion, she capsize.' Some nights when funds had allowed, he would reach into the cupboard behind his head and pull out a bottle of white rum while he told the story.

The sisters would sit and listen, Ella relishing the few moments in the day when her little sister, Agnes, wasn't dancing or running around causing havoc. Agnes loved to dance for no reason, a little melody humming in her throat as she twirled and spun in the cool beneath the breadfruit tree outside their house. This annoyed Ella no end, as she sat waiting to comb her younger sister's hair, a responsibility that had fallen to her after their mother, Maryann, had died two years prior from tuberculosis.

'Agnes, why you can't keep still and quiet, stop moving your waist so, stop making noise!'

Agnes would hum her tune louder to annoy her sister even more, but would be shocked into silence by a sharp tap on the back of her leg with the big comb, before Ella dragged her to a sitting position on the bottom step, worn down by generations of Deterville feet belonging to those who had lived in the small wooden house since the end of the plantation era a century before.

The *Blue Belle* had sailed hundreds of times before, Herbert told his daughters. On the fateful day of its last voyage, he had been out on the water with the other fishermen. They had seen the whale breathing air and spraying spume from its blowhole far in the distance in the early hours of the morning as the sun began to rise. At first, they hadn't been concerned. 'But den we fin' flotsam in de water off de point at Anse Cochon. Den we hear dat de *Blue Belle* never arrive in town.'

'Papa, how you know it was de boat?' Agnes sat looking at her father, wide-eyed and waiting for the answer.

Herbert took another shot of rum, then squeezed his face tight to take out the bite of the alcohol. He focused his gaze on his older daughter. 'I know your sister don't like to hear dis, but we fin' hats an baskets in de water as well as some pieces of de boat dat come loose an float.'

Agnes relished the details. 'So, Papa, all de people are at the bottom of de sea?'

Her sister Ella however imagined bodies swaying in unison with the back and forth of the ocean's motion, arms reaching and grasping for the surface, tortured faces upturned from the seabed seeking sunlight and fresh air from their final resting place in the cold dark blue of the deep Caribbean Sea.

'Why you ask Papa such nonsense, Agnes? Stop asking such fings,' Ella would always chide in an effort to drive her own fears away. It was as if the words themselves could summon up the ghosts of those lost, and Ella dreaded the idea of them lingering in the house long through the night after they all went to bed.

In truth, no one knew for sure where the bodies came to rest. Without a drivable road connecting it to the rest of the island, Canaries existed in a small world of its own, only a simple wooden cross on the clifftop serving as a remembrance of the tragedy.

The fastest way to the capital of Castries or to the old French capital of Soufrière to the south was by boat, and for many years, when the villagers sailed past, they would see the memorial that marked the spot.

For those naturally fearful like Ella, the sinking of the *Blue Belle* anchored them to the island, and nothing – not the passage of time, nor curiosity about what existed beyond the island – could sway them. It rooted Ella to her village, leaving her with no desire to travel; she could appreciate the beauty of where she lived without taking to the sea or the road.

But for Agnes, like her father, the water and what lay beyond it beckoned like a siren's call, an island song chiming in her heart. She watched her father eagerly set out for the ocean in the early hours of each morning, six days a week to catch fish.

He was grateful to be able to provide for his daughters and every day, good catch or not, he would drink a shot of rum, also encouraging his fellow fishermen to do the same. He became known as 'Mayor-One-Shot', the villagers turning to him when there were any disputes, and he would start his mediation by encouraging those in disagreement to take a shot of rum together. '*Bwè kòm a kanmawad*, drink rum as friends.' Herbert would raise his glass in thanks for another safe return home.

'Canaries look so sweet from de water. You live in a beautiful place, my children,' he would tell his daughters. 'Dem tracks across de mountains hard to travel but I know one day you will take to de road.'

When talk began of building the West Coast Road that would finally join the village, Agnes made herself a promise, her feet already itching with excitement.

'Papa, I will be de *first* on de bus.'

CHAPTER ONE

1956 – Ten years later

Agnes stared at her father's best friend, as he stood in the front room of the two-room house she and Ella had inherited when their father died. They had loaned Franklin their father's boat on the condition that the sisters would receive a third of the catch which Franklin sold at the market. But now the man was telling them the boat was no longer seaworthy, twisting and untwisting the fishing hat he held tightly in his hands as he spoke.

'De caulking between de planks need to be replaced. De boat tekkin on too much water. You going to hav to fix it,' Franklin said.

'Fix it?' Agnes said. '*Épi ki lajan?* With what money?' She glanced at Ella who had barely looked up from the work she was doing on the sewing machine their mother had left them. Their mother had been a talented seamstress, and while she had passed on her skills to both of her daughters at a young age, she had also tried to encourage Ella to leave the household chores to go out and play.

'Ella, why you don't go out wit de children like your sister, why you stick by my side so?'

Agnes could almost always be found climbing the coconut trees by the beach, or relishing a swim in the ocean, diving off the jetty, even joining her father on a fishing trip in the pirogue he had made with his own hands on the bank of the Canaries River behind the house. Their father ignored the old wives' tale that it was unlucky to have a female aboard the boat.

'You are my lucky charm Agnes – look how much fish we catch today. De folks in de village don't know what dey talkin' about.'

But Ella had preferred to watch her mother sew, cook and cultivate vegetables in their small patch of red soil that she called a garden. Staying close to her mother's side, Ella had no regrets about missing out on the trivial things her sister occupied herself with.

Now Ella was a seamstress who was always busy. Most weeks there was someone getting measured for a dress for an up-and-coming wedding or christening. She was a perfectionist who took her time with each garment, but even perfection didn't mean she'd get paid on time, and on most occasions there was a delay while her customers scraped together their payment.

Agnes sold fruits and vegetables at the market, but with a son and daughter to care for now and no man in the house to help them, bills were racking up fast. Everything needed paying for, from the kerosene in the lamps, the coal for the coal pot, to the replacement of the corrugated iron sheeting covering up the jagged rusty holes in the roof.

There were many temptations in the Saturday market in the village, things Agnes knew came from places far away. Pretty fabric, household items like stainless steel pots and pans, even earrings and necklaces made with the dark yellow gold from Guyana on the South American coast. All of which were luxuries the Deterville girls could not afford.

'So you use de boat and don't fix it!' Agnes didn't think she could get any angrier, until Franklin's reply.

'It's not my boat to maintain, it your boat. De share you get from de fish is what suppose to pay for de boat upkeep.' Franklin didn't spare a second after his reply, fleeing the house before Agnes had a chance to fashion a response.

It had been nine years since Herbert had died, though the memory of the day it happened was still sharp for the sisters.

It had been Ella, the eldest, who had tried to wake their father after she noticed he was still in bed at six-thirty that morning, an hour later than usual. She shook and shook him until her arms hurt but he wouldn't awaken.

'*Papa lèvè*, wake up, wake up, WAKE UP!'

Agnes had sat up in the single bed they shared and moved quickly to her sister's side.

'What is wrong with Papa? Why he not wakin' up?' Agnes stretched out her hand to touch her father's expressionless face, peaceful as if still in a deep sleep, but Ella pulled her hand away, he was cold to the touch.

'Agnes go an get Auntie Flora an tell her Papa not waking up.'

'No, you go and get her. I will stay with Papa.'

Ella turned to her sister, in a voice more powerful than she had ever heard herself use before.

'*Ou paka tann!* You don't hear! You never listen! Agnes. Go and get Auntie Flora *APWÉZAN!* NOW!'

Agnes's eyes had widened, her face a mask of terror and shock as the truth snaked around her, but she turned on her heel and ran from the house. When she returned, with their Auntie Flora, her lips tight and her usual joyful features absent, she told them immediately that he was dead, before wailing at the top of her voice, summoning folk from the neighbouring houses towards the agonising sound.

Before they knew what was happening, there was a crowded melee within their humble home, bodies pressed close upon one another, the wailing lament rising and falling with the heavy gasps of their grieving. The heat and claustrophobic atmosphere of death overwhelmed the girls. They fought to stay by their father's side, yet slowly they found themselves pushed aside by the throng, driven back towards the rear corner of the tiny bedroom, where they sat in shock.

Herbert's lifeless body, the grotesque centre of attention, was the only still object within the house. Only seventeen and fourteen years old themselves, it was their Uncle Matthew who had taken control of the situation, physically ejecting non-family from the property before standing guard outside the house to stop further invasion.

Since then, they had lived alone and had been piecemealing an existence together in the small house that was now home to a family of four. There was a single bedroom with two beds. Agnes slept in one bed with her son, Charles, and Ella slept in the other with her niece, Tina. In one corner sat a metal bowl on a tabletop where they could wash, and a cloth curtain that hung from the ceiling on a piece of fishing wire to give the barest semblance of privacy. The adjoining room was the kitchen, consisting of a Formica shelf, a cupboard to house dry food provisions, cups, plates and utensils, two stools, and a living area, an old tea chest and a small table with four handmade chairs at which to eat.

There were no pretty ornaments sitting on white linen doilies, their house was sparse, and money was spent only on daily necessities or small amounts put away for a rainy day. There were a few pictures of beloved family members hung on the walls as a reminder of times gone by, including their father standing proudly with his siblings. Absent however, was any picture of their mother; a memento that they would have dearly loved to possess.

The picture that held prime position in their home was a large coloured photograph of the new Queen of England, her Royal Majesty Elizabeth II. Her Coronation in 1953 had been celebrated in St Lucia with as much excitement as in England. The village of Canaries had crowded around the wireless at the church hall to hear the Princess Elizabeth become their queen.

'She now rises from her throne as Queen Elizabeth the Second. She walks to the doors of Westminster Abbey, much to the joy of the cheering crowd.'

The joyous cries of the crowds in London emerged from the radio and the villagers cheered along with them. The death of the queen's father George VI had made Agnes think of the grief the queen and her younger sister Princess Margaret must have experienced, and reminded her of what she and her sister had felt on Herbert's death.

'I feel we are like them, with no father,' Agnes would say to Ella.

'They rich and live in a palace with their mother and maids and servants. We are not de same!' Ella soon burst the bubble of Agnes's mournful fantasies.

They were doing their best, but it was barely enough to get by. And now, with the loss of income from the boat, their situation was going to be even more difficult.

Agnes watched Ella sitting at the sewing machine, the whir of the pedal and the smell of the oil that kept it running calming her frayed nerves. The machine sat in the far corner of their home's living area like a working monument to their mother. Agnes and Ella frequently argued about the household chores, but each eagerly took their turn meticulously dusting the sewing machine's black metal frame and pedal every week. When it was her turn, Ella would wipe it down tenderly singing a prayer to her own melody: 'Hail Mary full of grace, the Lord is with you, blessed are you among women . . .' Agnes would habitually open the small drawers that contained the coloured cotton reels of thread, pull out a spool of yellow and hold it to her nose in hopes of meeting the aroma of her mother. But her fragrance had faded long ago.

Fading too was Agnes's patience with just getting by, drowning in the sameness of her days. *They* were drowning, and for some reason Ella either refused to see it or refused to admit it.

Agnes's frustrations grew stronger day by day. Her wishes and her prayers were always the same. 'Oh Lord hear my prayer, show me Lord what to do, to keep food on my table, clothes on de backs of my children, take away de shackles dat hold me down so I can move in de right direction.'

The children were growing fast. Ella could adjust their uniforms for school for a little while longer, but without the funds to replace Tina and Charles's shoes, Agnes grew more and more worried.

The thought of escape had once seemed like a dream to her, but now it felt more real than it ever had before, and she never forgot her father's words.

'My girl,' he'd said to her once, 'never, ever let anyone take away dat fire in your belly. Let your sister be de sensible one. Enjoy your life with the spirit of adventure. Promise me dat?'

'Yes, Papa.'

But it was at her uncle's house that her future had truly started to form in her mind as a solid plan, around a name that sounded nothing like Canaries and which now filled her thoughts.

England.

Uncle Matthew's head had been buried in the *St Lucia Times*, the front-page headline staring back at her as she sat across from him on one of her regular visits.

Caribbean people leaving for England on ships, like the HMT *Empire Windrush* which had made all the news reels some years before. 'You know dat song we hear a few years back from dat fella from Trinidad?' Agnes watched Uncle Matthew scratching his head trying to conjure up the name.

'Oh you mean de Mighty Sparrow?' Agnes tried to jog his memory.

'Not Sparrow, no, de other fella . . . Kitchner! Dat's him, he was singing the praises of London Town. And now I hear Caribbean fellas driving buses all over dat place and there is so much work and not enough people to fill de jobs. So de British calling for us to come!'

'So, Uncle, why you don't go?'

'I have enough work to keep me here and I don't feel any desire to go, but many have gone already and answered de call.'

Uncle Matthew had told her more about the capital city, London, the place that she had learned about at school, the bustling heart of the British Empire which was filled with millions of people. Words and phrases crowded her mind. 'The Underground', 'Piccadilly Circus', 'Buckingham Palace'. Each time she let her imagination loose they became more real, and Agnes promised herself with every prayer that she would one day leave to enjoy what the outside world had to offer. But it was not just for herself she intended to go. Agnes planned to bring back all the money that she could earn to share with her family. To give her children Charles and Tina more than she and Ella had, or could ever give them if she stayed in St Lucia.

She was *leaving to come back* she told herself.

Agnes was sick of barely scraping a life in Canaries. For all she loved about her life in their pretty village: its colourful roofs, humble wooden homes and rich red soil, it was not enough. England would change everything for the Deterville family, she was sure of it.

But the reality was that before she could leave, she had to find a way to provide what her family needed now. Sending Tina and Charles to school, having food on the table, paying her bills and buying shoes for her children came first. *Then* she might be able to put money away and buy her ticket to England.

She remembered her father's mantra, 'Hard work never killed nobody.' Agnes had to prove to Ella that this was the best way forward for them all, and she was willing to work hard for it.

CHAPTER TWO

1956

Agnes studied herself in the mirror as she prepared to leave for what she hoped was her first day of work. Uncle Matthew had arranged for Agnes to have an interview for a job as a housekeeper for the Chesters, an English couple who lived at Sweet Cinnamon Cottage on top of the ridge overlooking Canaries.

Her new uniform, a white shirt and a skirt she'd taken in that had once belonged to Ella, flattered her figure, and she'd pinned her dark, silky hair into a neat bun.

For nine years the sisters had fended for themselves since their father had passed away, but the daily toll of struggle and worry had not beaten down Agnes's fighting spirit. Her song of hope played loud in her heart. And at twenty-three, she still turned the heads of the boys in the village. With her petite frame and attractive features graced with high cheekbones, she would be referred to as mulatto; light skinned or the Kwéyòl term '*shabine*'. She always walked with a determined stride in her step that gave the impression she was heading somewhere in particular.

'Hey Agnes, slow down my girl, why you walkin' so fas'! Let me walk wit you na, *Ou gade dous,* You look sweet,' the young men would shout out at her.

'I have no time for you and your laziness, I have work to do and your mothers never tell you to respect a woman?' she would reply firmly, hiding a smirk as she did so.

A giggle came from behind her, shaking her from her daydream as she took one last look in the mirror. Agnes turned round.

Tina and Charles lay on the bed watching her, their smiles the spitting image of their father, Vince, who was long gone. Vince, a police officer who oozed confidence and authority, was not like the young men in the village. Boys like Raphael Toussaint, the one with the loudest voice shouting for Agnes's attention, in his phony American drawl, aping the GIs who had flooded the island during the Second World War and left an indelible mark.

No, Vince wasn't like them at all. The way he stood outside the police station, leaning against the wall, a matchstick twirling around his mouth, with his arms crossed in front of him. His uniform pressed sparkling clean and his boots polished bright. He was tall and handsome too, and he knew it.

He would normally tip his hat to the women in the village and carry the bags of the frail grandmothers, but Vince was quietly watchful as Agnes walked past the police station one morning with Ella, both carrying their bags of provisions to sell at the village market in the square. Agnes enjoyed the feeling of his leisurely gaze appraising her as she glanced at him from under her long lashes, a flirtation hinted at in her smile.

'I don't like him,' Ella told Agnes when they returned home.

'The way he just watch you. Dat man look like de mongoose watching de fowl . . .'

Agnes liked the way that Vince gave off authority and kept the other fresh boys at bay. Especially when they got too familiar, like the night she danced with Vince at the church hall.

They had been dancing the night away near the opened doors at the back of the church hall. The breeze was blowing in from the jetty, it made her feel older and more sophisticated to be in his arms.

The fact he was a dashing police officer brought Agnes a lot of attention. She could feel the eyes of the envious women on her, and she got the sense that Vince clearly enjoyed the attention too. When he went to the bar to buy drinks, she had barely been alone for a moment, when she felt a tap on her shoulder. It was the young man from the house up on the hill again, Raphael Toussaint.

'Hey beautiful, you going to dance wit me?' he had asked her. Coming from one of the well-to-do families in the village, Raphael had a reputation for being a spoilt playboy, living off his father's position as Minister of Agriculture in the government. From what she heard, he drank a lot, played around with women and could not hold down a job.

'No! You can't see I am with somebody?'

'Well, he is not here now, I can show you a better time dan him, anyway. Le' we dance na.'

Agnes shook her head, 'Who you fink you are?'

Raphael was lucky not to get a further lash of her words, as Vince returned with drinks.

'Is this man bothering you?'

His scowl was enough and Raphael slipped away, but not without an impudent and suggestive smile flashing his gold tooth, before grabbing another girl by the hand to dance.

Agnes watched as he spun her around. She had to admit he sure could dance.

But Agnes was only interested in being romanced by Vince. And romanced she had been. His reputation as a womaniser had not yet reached her ears. It didn't until it was too late.

At seventeen, she'd succumbed to his charms, ignoring Ella's warnings. Of course, her sister had been right. Despite promises to marry and take care of her, Vince had been absent for the birth of his daughter, having left the village to take a post in a nearby town. She'd allowed herself to believe his promises when he briefly resurfaced a year later, but when she found herself pregnant again, this time Vince was gone for good.

Now, looking at her children on the bed, Tina, six years old, and Charles now four, Agnes knew that she would do anything to give them a better life. Vince had broken her heart, but her anger at him was its equal and it fuelled her ambitions.

She never wanted her children to feel trapped like she did. She wanted them to feel fearlessness and curiosity, just as her father Herbert had encouraged in her. 'Canaries is not de world Agnes, one day you will have the chance to see it all for yourself.'

Agnes held a prayer, and a song of optimism in her heart that maybe, *just maybe*, this opportunity could help change the course of her life. 'I am ready to work hard Lord, I am ready to make my family's life better.'

Yes. She was determined that by knocking on the Chesters' door, it could change everything.

Agnes's Uncle Matthew had been a gardener at Sweet Cinnamon Cottage for a number of years. He maintained the cottage grounds, trimming the grass and cutting back the bushes for the expatriate employees from the British Foreign

Office Department stationed on the island. Matthew was kept busy creating a beautiful sanctuary of tropical flowers, fruit trees, even a vegetable and herb allotment. At the centre of the garden grew a large cinnamon tree, lending the cottage its name.

Sweet Cinnamon Cottage was more than a place of work for Matthew. His family ties to it went back generations. Agnes's great-grandmother Magdalene was an enslaved woman who gained her freedom in 1834 and then worked as a nanny for the Labadie family who had arrived from France. They were the last family to own the Canaries sugar plantation before it was abandoned in the 1860s. After they were gone, the villagers, who were only a few decades out of enslavement, took to unceremoniously dismantling the great house for material to build their own homes, fashioning a future for themselves from the ruins of the past.

Sweet Cinnamon Cottage, an outbuilding, had remained untouched, lacking the same symbolism as the Labadie family home.

Now Agnes found herself at the cottage's back door and smoothed a nervous hand down the front of her skirt.

After a moment, the door opened, and a petite white woman in her mid-twenties answered. She was pretty, with waved bouffant strawberry-blonde hair pinned to the top of her head, and was dressed in stylish red capri pants with a white collared shirt and red lipstick to match her trousers.

'Yes?' she asked, somewhat hesitantly to the stranger at her door.

Agnes cleared her throat. 'Hello, Mrs Ches-tor, my name is Agnes, and I come to clean and cook for you. Matthew said you will need my help, Ms.'

Mrs Chester looked surprised. 'I . . . I haven't yet discussed this with Mr Chester . . .'

Maybe it was the gentle yet firm sincerity with which Agnes had made her offer of assistance, but Mrs Chester seemed to quickly think it over, then smiled and gestured for Agnes to enter the house.

The cottage kitchen alone was the size of the home Agnes shared with her family. It possessed three bedrooms and a large lounge and dining area with wide French doors that opened onto a shaded veranda where one could sit and enjoy the view of the village through the trees, and below that were steps that led down into a lush garden. It also had *two* flushing toilets; no need to go to the tap with a bucket the way Agnes had to do at home. Here they just pulled a chain and it was all taken care of.

Agnes tried to answer Mrs Chester's questions as best as she could. The lady seemed interested in where she lived, and with who, and Agnes nodded politely when Mrs Chester told her what she would be expected to do.

'There'll be some cooking and laundry, and the cleaning and tidying of course, but Mr Chester and I are quite tidy already!' The woman laughed, and Agnes was reminded of the musical sound of the small bell that was rung at the church altar before communion.

At the end of the tour, Agnes seemed to have passed the test and Mrs Chester made it official with a smile: Agnes would be the Chesters' new housekeeper.

Each morning after breakfast and her daily chores, Agnes would leave her home at 7.00 and start her fifteen-minute walk to work.

She enjoyed the work she was expected to do, and was grateful for the regular wage she received in a small brown envelope at the end of each week.

Lillian Chester had an energy Agnes liked. She was never

afraid of getting her hands dirty in the soil in the garden or taking the dried clothes off the washing line. She moved quickly and was expressive with her hands, which fluttered around her like butterflies emphasising her words to make her point. When she was happy, she would clap her hands with joy.

'That looks like a lovely cake, Agnes. Edward's going to enjoy that!' *Clap, clap, clap.*

'Her eyes are so blue, the colour of the ocean and she don't eat much, her waist is so small, but she like to drink tea,' Agnes told Ella as she prepared supper, rolling the floured dough in her hands, then dropping the white dumpling balls into the boiling bouillon on the coal pot, of salted pig tail and red beans. The children's favourite meal.

Ella preferred to focus on the cooking as she sat on the wooden stool stirring the contents of the canawi, the clay cooking pot seasoned over many years of constant use, trying to ignore Agnes's wearing enthusiasm for her new employer.

Mrs Chester had a graceful, gentle manner that Agnes admired.

'Every morning, she always ask after my family,' she told Ella. Agnes would try and mimic Mrs Chester's Queen's English: '"Good Morning Agnes. How are your family?" She say it so nice Ella, all I can answer is, "Fine, thank you, Mrs Chestor!"'

But Ella would only glower at her, and eventually her patience would snap. 'You can't see I'm busy Agnes, I have no time to chit-chat about Mrs Chestor.'

One day, Uncle Matthew told Agnes that he'd heard Mrs Chester sobbing earlier while he'd been tending the hibiscus on the far side of the garden.

'It not de first time the lady of the house in a sad mood,' he told his niece. 'I fink she missing England.'

She and Matthew felt they understood how far away she was from her own country, her people, her family. She looked so lonely when her husband was not around, and never seemed in harmony with her surroundings. There had been occasions when Agnes would stop in her tracks while she did her housework and watch Mrs Chester in the garden just looking off far into the distance, with her arms wrapped around herself as if she was holding herself together. Agnes could see a cloud of sadness around the woman but she didn't feel it was her place to ask the question '*Ki mannyé ou?* How are you?'

Uncle Matthew had spoken quietly to Agnes as they stood in the kitchen. 'We are not her family and dis is not her island. Be patient, kind and do your job well.' Agnes reassured her uncle that she would do her best to make sure Mrs Chester was as comfortable as possible. But she knew it wasn't purely Christian goodwill requiring her to keep Mrs Chester happy. Agnes wasn't ready for the woman to pack up and leave St Lucia yet, she needed her wages for her own future.

Mrs Chester constantly complained about the heat and mosquitoes, and one day said, 'I don't know how you do it, Agnes. The heat doesn't seem to bother you as it does me, neither do the mosquitoes. I suppose you're used to it?'

'I jus' take my time, Ms. And if you get hot, don't fan your hand in front of your face. It will jus' make you more hot. The mosquitoes will soon get used to your blood and leave you alone.'

'I suppose you are right, Agnes. I really should slow down, Mr Chester tells me the same, I just hope those blighters get used to me soon.' Mrs Chester watched Agnes for a moment, and then smiled. 'Your wisdom about the island is much needed around here.'

No one had ever told Agnes she had wisdom. From as far back as she could remember, the villagers referred to her as *'hadi'*, rude. But she knew that was only because she refused to get involved in the gossip and wasn't afraid to tell people to mind their own business. Ella was the one they called wise, the sensible one.

Every day the lady of the cottage praised Agnes for her hard work and she grew in confidence day by day, manoeuvring herself around the house, doing her chores with purpose. There was no doubt that Mrs Chester was a sensitive soul and Agnes decided keeping her employer calm and comfortable was also part of her job.

For Mrs Chester, afternoon tea was the most important ritual she had brought to Sweet Cinnamon Cottage from England.

The tea had to be brewed for no less than four and no more than five minutes. Mrs Chester always said in her sing-song voice, 'Pour the milk before the tea, and always serve at half-past three.' But things were never *quite* perfect for Mrs Chester's afternoon tea routine, because the milk was condensed and the swatting of flies or mosquitoes always interfered with the rhythm of the pouring.

Swat-swat pour the milk, swat-swat jug down, swat-swat pick up the teapot with one hand while the other hand swatted.

Agnes would view this fuss with bewilderment.

Why she can't jus' relax? It not even mosquito season, and the flies don't do her nothing.

The thing that always brightened Mrs Chester's tea ritual was admiring her bone china Minton tea set, the one she had inherited from her grandmother and that had travelled from England all the way to the West Indies intact. Often Mrs Chester's only moment of contentment in her day was taking her first sip from her flowery teacup.

She would usually say, 'It's not perfect but it will do.'

Then her chest would rise and fall and she would look into the distance, seeming to inhabit another place before she shook herself and reached for a slice of the perfect vanilla essence cake Agnes had baked.

This performance would be repeated each teatime throughout the week, a ritual that Agnes came to anticipate as much as her employer, as she learned to hold the teacup in the correct way with her thumb and forefinger.

Sometimes Mrs Chester would explain to her over the tea tray about other things in England she had never heard of.

'I had the privilege of being invited to the presentation of Dior's spring collection at The Savoy. It's a wonderful place Agnes, and the clientele equally so. The pearls and diamonds glittered as the model walked the stage and each garment was utterly exquisite, I will never forget it. You would have enjoyed it Agnes.'

'What is de Savoy Ms?'

'Oh Agnes, The Savoy is THE finest and most famous hotel in London. Its afternoon high tea service is just sublime! All the film stars and aristocracy go there.'

'I would like to go there Ms. When I am in London. Do you fink I could?'

Mrs Chester seemed to brush off the question quickly, and concentrated on straightening the teacups on their saucers. 'I imagine anyone can enjoy high tea should they choose to.' She then proceeded to divulge further details of the event in the most intricate detail, from the decor on the walls to the attention of the waiting staff, the day having been seared into her memory.

One of the things Agnes admired about the lady of the cottage was how fashionable she always looked in the capri pants and short-sleeved shirts she would wear during the day. Then before her husband arrived home from work, she would change into a full circle skirt and pretty top or dress. It was 1956 and feminine sheath dresses or flared skirts pulled tight at the waist worn to emphasise a shapely figure were the fashionable silhouette for the modern woman and the island capital was no exception. Mrs Chester must have noticed Agnes admiring her full swing skirts because one day she said, 'Agnes, one day we will get the sewing machine out to make you a skirt just like this. These swing skirts are all the rage in London.' Her employer smiled encouragingly at her housemaid. 'With your pretty features, I think it would make you look like you were part of the fashionable set.'

'That would be nice, Ms,' Agnes replied. The thought of owning an item of clothing that was fashionable in London brought her great delight.

Agnes would, as often as she could, glance at the well-thumbed *Women's Own* magazines Mrs Chester read. These magazines were like another world to Agnes, who would get lost in the images. She would hold the shapes, length of the dresses and fabric design in her memory. Ladies all dressed up looking like they went to church every day. The hats and handbags, the elegant poise and the subtle smiles of the models pulled her into a fantasy of walking the streets of fashionable London herself. Her stride would be graceful, her feet in dainty leather shoes with no holes in them; the weight of the garment flowing at the hem swishing around her ankles; turning heads of passersby leaving behind the delicious scent of her expensive perfume. It made Agnes giggle at the thought. One day, she thought, I will live this dream for real.

Mrs Chester would cut out the recipes from the back of the magazine that would inevitably never be made due to the paucity of any number of vital ingredients.

'Agnes, can you get mushrooms on this island?'

'Mash-Rooms Ms? I don't know what dat is?'

'Well, they're grown in a mix of manure and soil, you usually find them in a woodland in the autumn when the ground is wet . . . Oh, Agnes, I'm not sure how to describe it . . . I used to get a few pounds from Clive, the vegetable man in Dorset.'

Agnes said nothing, imagining only a muddy mass of earth.

'I'm not doing a good job of describing a mushroom, am I? It's what I use to make stuffed tomatoes for Mr Chester, it's one of his favourites.' A note of distress would enter Mrs Chester's voice and Agnes would feel the burden of trying to assuage her employer's concerns.

'You stoff a tomato, Ms? If you tell me how to do it, I will try Ms.'

This would make Mrs Chester laugh. 'That sounds so funny when I hear you say it . . . "stoff a tomato".'

'Yes Ms.' Agnes could only agree, unsure whether to laugh too, or to feel embarrassed at her own ignorance.

Either way, Agnes soaked it all up like a sponge, and was eager to share it all with Ella.

'Mrs Chestor tell me about *quaint* villages dere with cottages made of stone. People walk in the rolling countryside and along de riverbank. And it gets so cold dere, snow falls, and everything looks so *magical*.'

'Chewps.' Ella kissed her teeth. 'Don't let dat lady put fings or words in your head, sister. Mrs Chestor's world is *not* your world. Every day you coming home with nonsense she saying to you.'

Her sister's words stung, but Agnes wouldn't be swayed. She knelt at her sister's feet. 'Daddy tell us not to give up on our dreams, Ella. De more Mrs Chestor talk about it, de more she make me realise dat England *is* my dream. It's a place I have to go to one day. I could do so much more dere. I could make a good living, Ella.' She took her sister's hand. 'Can't you see?'

Ella pulled her hand from Agnes's grasp. 'One day? *Ou oblige ou ne ti manmay.* You forget you have children. Of course you can dream about leaving me . . .' Ella pointed towards the room where the children slept. 'Leaving dem? Only because you know I will look after dem.' Agnes dug deep inside her to find the right words. 'I know you don't like it when I talk about leaving Canaries. Since we were children you always tell me to *pé la,* shut up, when I talk about going to see the rest of the world. I can't stay quiet about it any more, I don't have de fear of leaving like you.'

Ella could not answer, or look into her sister's face as she spoke. Agnes's eyes were like their mother's. The tender eyes Ella missed so much.

'I won't be afraid like you, Ella. I want to go so I can work and send money back for my family, and, yes, dat includes you, my dear sister.' Agnes took Ella's hand again, and when she didn't pull away, she squeezed it. 'Remember we used to talk about having our own sewing shop, with the best cloth and patterns? How can I do dat staying here in Canaries? Dey encouraging St Lucians to go to England, so I want to take my chance, not just for me but for us.' Agnes tried to look into her sister's eyes, hoping to see that for once, something she had said had allowed Ella to see things differently. But what met her was a wall, the same one she had erected ever since they were children.

Ella stood and began pacing the small room angrily, her lips pulled tight on her face, no longer able stay silent on the matter. 'Don't be fooled by what Mrs Chestor is telling you,' Ella warned, stopping mid-pace and facing her sister directly. 'She different from you. Life is easier for her. She a white woman who can move around de place how she want. Just remember, while she is here you have a job.'

'I know dat. Mr and Mrs Chestor will leave St Lucia one day. She talk about going home all de time. So when dey go back to dere country what am I to do? Go and sell fruit on the side of the road? Dat's not enough for us my sister. Dat's not enough for me!'

Agnes was angry now. 'And you fink I'm stupid? *Mwen pa bèt!* I am not foolish! I know my life is not the same as hers. I know she does not see me as the same as her. Yes, I know she is a white English lady and I am just a coloured St Lucian girl, so, I know I can never walk in her shoes, but still I can try and make something of my life! Something more than what I was born into. Struggle and worry, I am not like you Ella, I am not afraid to try a different life!'

Agnes hated arguing with Ella because with every word she used to stand her ground she could see the pain it caused her sister. Ella's face was a mask of hurt, her skin tight on her face, mouth turned down with eyes holding back tears. And when the words were all said and done Agnes would feel her centre of gravity was off kilter, her anchor to home knocked off balance. Their disagreements left a heavy weight of dejection in her heart at the loss of her sister's support. Their home required unity to function smoothly, as any upset caused the children distress, they always sensed it keenly. The sadness in her stomach could take days to shift, she knew that Ella was not only angry, but afraid of change. Agnes stood to her feet, resigned, but not to the fate Ella had prescribed for her. Nothing she could say would get Ella to change. But she also knew that nothing anyone could say, even her beloved sister, would change her mind, either. Agnes would go to England.

* * *

The days after their disagreements would weigh heavily on both sisters. Each would keep to their own space, and when Agnes was out at work, Ella would busy herself at the sewing machine, working on the small commissions that helped to bring food to their table.

One evening before Agnes had returned home, and while Charles played with his toys on the doorstep, Ella looked up to find Tina standing by her side.

'What is the matter, child, why you not doing your reading practice?'

Tina moved closer and wound her arm around her aunt's neck. 'Why you sad, Ella? Is it because you not talking to Mama?'

Ella did feel a great sadness in her heart.

'Sometimes we don't always agree on fings, you know dat child.'

Tina tilted her head to one side. 'Is Mama going to England, I hear her tell you that, will she take me?'

Why did Ella have to answer this, she wondered with frustration. It was just like Agnes to leave her with the consequences of her actions. Ella felt she couldn't deal with Tina's anxieties now, and Agnes would have to face up to her choices one way or another.

She put her arms around Tina's waist, holding her close in an embrace.

'Promise you and Mama won't fight no more.'

Ella took her foot off the pedal of the sewing machine. 'Come Tina, you and Charles can help me prepare the dinner for when your mama comes home.' She looked into Tina's eyes, seeing her own fears reflected. It wouldn't help the children for them to fight.

'I try to be patient, Tina, I promise, God will help me if I pray to him.'

Ella hoped she was right, but Agnes would never listen to her.

It was just like when she had tried to warn Agnes about Vince.

As the eldest of the two orphans, she had tried, unsuccessfully, for years to shield Agnes from the pain the world could cause. Pain Ella knew first-hand, from losing their mother and father, and from the dread she carried like a lead weight in her stomach, remembering the sinking of the *Blue Belle* and the souls that had perished that day. Sixteen years later, she would still awaken from the awful nightmares, unable to breathe or cry out as the zombie faces of the dead clutched at her clothing and pulled her further into the abyss. Eventually she would return to the living world, crying out for rescue, to find her sister shaking her gently saying, 'ced*Sésé mwen, sésé mwen. Bondous dous li*. My sister, my sister. God calm her,' while her heart pounded in her chest and her body was drenched in sweat.

Every year on the anniversary of the sinking, the villagers sailed in flotillas of small boats from the beach in front of the village to the spot where the sons and daughters of Canaries had perished, and laid wreaths at the foot of the cross on the clifftop. And every year, Ella could not summon the courage to be part of the floating congregation that would offer up prayers to the souls in heaven. Ashamed, she offered her prayers for the dead, not from the site of their watery tomb, but from a pew towards the back of the humble village church.

Her fear of the dark void and its sinister mysteries overwhelmed her. It seemed to cement her to the land, locking her within the village's perimeters.

The villagers had long ago labelled her enigmatic; quiet, but when she spoke her words were wise and she could be kind. Ella was a beautiful contradiction, an elegant swan held together with an innate fear. She was not brave. The thought of going out into the world stole her strength; she would have to prepare herself each time she was required to make a foray into the village. Unpleasant surprises might hide behind every bush, unkind thoughts behind a neighbour's smile, monsters real and imagined lurked in every corner.

With Agnes gone, how could Ella be brave for Tina and Charles if she couldn't be brave for herself?

She could only pray for God to make her strong and hope that he heard her.

CHAPTER THREE

Edward Chester had been adamant that he and Lillian should live outside of the clamour and commotion of Castries to give his wife a sense of village life, which might remind her more of the home they had left behind. Though the reality was that for Edward, the lives of the villagers were more distant to him than the cricket scores from Lord's that came through his wireless on the BBC World Service.

One evening on the veranda, while he perused the now three-week-old news in his copy of *The Times* which was shipped over from England, Lillian shared an idea with her husband. 'Darling, I am thinking of asking Agnes to accompany me down into the village. I want to meet her family and some of the villagers. What do you think?'

Edward didn't lift his eyes from his newspaper and took a moment before answering. 'That's a lovely idea, darling, but I do think you should wait a while longer, don't you? You have been through a lot recently, and I think you should take your time meeting new people. Besides, I am sure they won't have much to share with you, they are simple folk, living simple lives, what would you possibly have in common? They live in another world, and we are just passing through. I am sure Agnes and Matthew could fill you in on the goings on in the village while they are here doing their work.'

Lillian sat still for a moment and took a sip of her drink to compose herself. Edward's response was disappointing, but Lillian decided to persevere. She wanted to avoid the conversation turning into an argument, yet she could not help but give Edward a little dig of her own. 'I just think it would be nice to know the community we are part of. These are real people going about their daily lives, unlike your work colleagues pretending to run the commonwealth over martinis at the British High Commission.'

Edward put his paper down, rather testily, and picked up his drink, running a finger through the condensation on his glass before answering. 'Lillian, dear, we promised each other that we would keep things peaceful and calm to allow you to recover. Plus, there is no one of any importance in the village.'

Lillian flinched at her husband's comments, both the condescending way he'd referred to the local people and his mention of her recovery. It seemed to be the elephant in every room they shared.

When Lillian first fell pregnant, they had been living at their posting in Jamaica. The news that she was pregnant made her feel that she was complete as a woman, to finally be fulfilling her dream of creating a family unit with Edward.

But it wasn't to be. With each subsequent miscarriage, joy had turned to a relentless cycle of pain, bitter disappointment and anguish. Eventually, the thought of meaningless chit-chat over lunch at a white colonial members' club with the overprivileged ladies with whom she had little in common horrified her –

women who preferred their children to be seen and not heard, and who wholesaled out their children's upbringing to Jamaican nannies.

Edward tapped his fingernails on his glass, bringing her back to the present. He continued: 'I'm just reading here in *The Times* that thousands of West Indians have taken up the call to go to England to help rebuild her back to her former glory, but now us Brits are complaining that they're taking all the jobs and housing.' He shook his head. 'It's rather a dilemma. Don't get me wrong, I believe England needs to build up its workforce, and from what I gather, West Indians are willing to learn and advance, but I am not sure if England can handle the influx of foreigners coming in, even if they are part of the Commonwealth,' he said airily. Lillian thought he was looking at her as if she was one of his junior staff at the Commonwealth Office. 'And to add to that, some ministers in government are now asking the question of what to do with them once the job is done. At the end of the day, we *must* be careful who we make friends. I am here to do one job alone, I am trying to advance myself and provide a better life for *us*, not to make friends, but to move on to better opportunities as soon as we can.'

Edward was easily provoked, and Lillian mentally bit down on her frustration, but she couldn't just exist like a butterfly in a jam jar. She'd need to find a way to appeal to his sense of Britishness, of keeping up appearances.

'Yes, I can see that dear, it must be very trying.' Slowly, she took a sip of her drink. 'How about we go to Sunday Mass, then? It will give us a chance to meet the local priest. Agnes tells me he's from Canada. The locals will finally get to meet us – the people who live on the hill – and we'll get to meet Ella, Agnes's sister.'

Edward downed the last of his rum from his glass. 'A sister?'

'Yes. And she has two children. It will give you a chance to meet her family. I spend more time with Agnes than I do with you these days. She is not only a good housekeeper, she has also become a good friend.'

Edward cocked a brow at his wife's use of the term 'friend' to describe her relationship with their housekeeper, and sighed. 'That sounds like a better idea, but you really mustn't fraternise too much with the staff.'

'It will do us good to be seen at church, don't you think?'

He hesitated, giving her another raised eyebrow. 'Next Sunday? You're sure you want to do this?' Edward asked.

'Yes, I am sure.' She rose to refill his glass before he could change his mind. 'Thank you, darling.'

Agnes stood on the steps outside the Church of St Anthony, anxiously watching for Mr and Mrs Chester to arrive. It seemed strange to Agnes that the lady would want to sit in a hot church with a perspiring congregation around her. When on this Sunday morning she could be taking the breeze on her veranda at home.

'Agnes, why you standing there so? You look like you lost somefing and you searching for it!'

Agnes tried her best to be polite with her answer to the nosey elderly lady, but couldn't help but reply, 'Good morning to you, Mrs Fredrick. You're here to mind God's business, not mine.'

Mrs Fredrick's eyes bulged. 'I knew your father and your mother. I'm sure they told you to respect your elders. *Hadi tifi!* Rude girl!'

Agnes responded with a loud 'Chewps.' Feeling satisfaction that she could nip the woman's nosiness in the bud.

Agnes had doubted Mrs Chester's motives for coming to church at first, but now couldn't help but feel excited. She knew that those who brought others to God were blessed, and she felt a frisson of pride in herself for having them join her for Sunday worship. She was also acutely aware that their presence would cause plenty of interest from the congregation, not all of it positive. She did not look forward to the comments that would be muttered in Kwéyòl at just the right volume for her to hear. *Eh eh, Gadé épi jan blan,* Look at her with her white friends.

The church bell rang, signifying the start of Sunday morning mass. Ella and the children were already inside, and Agnes worried that Tina and Charles would be misbehaving and worrying their aunt Ella, so she was keen to get back inside the church. She was about to do just that when she saw the Chesters walking towards her. She waved in relief.

'Apologies, for keeping you waiting, Agnes. Mr Chester was dragging his feet this morning.'

'You're just in time, Mrs Chestor.' She turned to Mr Chester. 'And good morning, Mr Chestor. It's good to see you both. We have to go in now.'

Agnes just hoped Mrs Chester would not complain about the heat and the mosquitoes like she did when she took her tea. This blessed day was her day off from work, so the Chesters would have to take the morning as it came.

As Agnes quickly ushered the Chesters to the bench where Ella and children were seated, she could hear the whispered questions about who these white people were, and was aware of heads turning in their pews to get a better look at the newcomers. Once the Chesters were seated, Agnes sat between Tina and Charles. Charles was seated next to Mrs Chester and he stared up at her transfixed. Lillian's white hat shone in the muted sunlight and her baby blue linen sundress gave a highlight of freshness to her face; she must have looked like an angel from one of the bible stories to Charles. When

Mrs Chester looked at him and winked, he turned his face into his mother's chest, smiling.

Lillian touched her husband's hand to signal that she was happy he was sitting with her in the most simple and delightful church she had ever been in. They were the only white people at mass other than the priest Father Thomas. The last time she had been to mass was in Jamaica; there were many more white expats in the congregation of the local Anglican Church there.

She took in the environment with deep breaths, captivated by the stained-glass window upon which for the first time in her life, she saw Jesus on the cross depicted with dark brown skin. Her attention shifted when the pastor instructed the congregation to stand, giving her a smile of encouragement from the altar. Lillian felt gratified to be part of the community of churchgoers as everyone stood in unison. She took a deep breath and tried to enjoy the feeling of the moment, though she was conscious of the eyes of the villagers on her and her husband. She didn't feel unwelcome, despite being stared at, and she did her best to respond with a polite smile for the people staring at her, but they would quickly look away if there was any suggestion of eye contact. She realised it must be unusual for a white woman to be standing amongst this group of churchgoers.

The small church was filled with women in pretty hats dressed in their Sunday best, fidgeting children, and gentlemen dressed in their clean pressed white shirts, trousers and polished shoes. Everyone sang at the top of their voices, something that amused Edward. Lillian ignored his nudge at her elbow and threw herself into the singing instead. The hymns were sung by the congregation with real vigour, and at times, the melody would be a little out of tune without the accompaniment of a musical instrument, but no matter, it was belted out in good faith.

Prayers were said, and with all windows and doors open, the warm but soothing breeze blew in, adding to the raised joyous spirits of all in attendance. When Father Thomas asked his congregation to welcome each other with a handshake, Mrs Chester turned to Agnes and little Charles, who was too shy to take her hand. Tina shook her hand shyly but politely. Then Lillian stretched a little further and spoke to Ella for the first time. 'It's so wonderful to meet you, Ella.'

Ella gave her a polite, though guarded smile, her eyes watching Mrs Chester, cautiously. 'It's nice to meet you too Ms.'

As Father Thomas gave the finale to his sermon, there was elation in his voice. 'What a fine morning this is, your voices raised to the heavens in celebration of the beauty of Christ's love for us all. Amen!'

The Chesters, along with the rest of the congregation, responded in agreement. 'Amen!'

Once the mass ended, Father Thomas stood outside the church greeting his parishioners and church guests. 'It was wonderful for me to see some new faces at mass this morning,' he said to the Chesters in a Canadian accent. His thinning white hair barely covered his balding scalp, which was turning red in the midday sun.

Agnes was keenly aware of the villagers standing around and eavesdropping, which annoyed her, but she bit her tongue and pasted a smile on her face as she spoke to Mrs Chester. 'Ms did you enjoy de service?'

'Oh yes Agnes it was delightful and what a treat meeting Ella, Tina and Charles. We felt very welcomed.' And in front of all the congregation Mrs Chester gave Agnes an unexpected hug. Agnes knew it would be the talk of the village for weeks to come. *Eh eh Agnes and the white lady are very good friends.* Agnes did feel somewhat surprised herself but enjoyed the kind gesture from Mrs Chester, before she was accosted by one of the villagers, no doubt wanting to hear first-hand all about this new development.

'I hope this will not be the last time we see you at mass,' Father Thomas continued.

Lillian took the father's outstretched hand and smiled. 'I am sure you will see us here again, Father, and we hope you will join us for tea one afternoon at Sweet Cinnamon Cottage.'

The pastor nodded his head in acceptance. 'How often do you get back to civilisation?' Edward enquired. Lillian felt a prickle of embarrassment at Edward's turn of phrase and the patronising edge that was not missed by Father Thomas.

'I find a richness of civilisation within the simplicity of the life here,' he told them. 'As a man of God, this is where I get to focus on my duty of care to my parishioners.'

'Well of course,' Edward said, almost through gritted teeth, 'practise what you preach and all that.' Lillian could see from the sweat creeping across Edward's brow that he'd rather be anywhere else right now.

She felt the ground beneath her feet shift a little, and knew that his patience with their little expedition was wearing thin. She looked around, wishing she could break away from her husband and mingle with the villagers. She caught Ella's eye as she stood beneath the shade of a tree with Tina and Charles.

'Excuse me Father, I must just say hello to Ella Deterville. I'll just be one moment, Edward.'

Her husband frowned but didn't stop her. 'Don't be long darling, we must be getting back.'

* * *

Ella stood quietly in the shade under a palm tree holding Tina's and Charles's hands, as Agnes chattered away to the other worshippers.

As she watched Mrs Chester approach, she could see that Agnes had described her well. She was bird-like, and conspicuous amongst the villagers clustered around her. The village children giggled when she smiled at them. She mopped at her brow with a kerchief as she gestured towards Ella. 'You are in the perfect spot out of the sun, Ella. Can I join you in the shade?' Mrs Chester moved towards her before Ella could answer. 'Tina and Charles have been so well behaved.'

'They are always well behaved, Ms.'

'But I bet they would rather be playing with the children over there.' Tina looked up at her aunt and tugged at her sleeve, hoping she would agree.

Ella frowned, but sensed she had lost that battle already. 'Okay, go and see your friends.'

Charles started to pull himself away from his aunt too. 'Don't dirty your clothes!'

'Oh dear, Ella, what have I done? Here you are keeping the children out of trouble, and then I come along to spoil it.'

Ella took in a deep breath, wishing the lady had remained standing with her husband, instead of bothering her under the tree, but she knew how important this woman was to the fortunes of her family. She felt a growing concern that the influence of Mrs Chester on her sister meant change was coming. The stories that she was putting in her sister's head about England – every notion and idea shared with Agnes was pulling her away from her family and her home. 'It's okay Ms. How did you enjoy mass? You bring a little excitement to the church dis morning. It's not every day we have de people staying at Sweet Cinnamon Cottage walking down de hill to join us in prayer, I fink you mus' be de first.' Ella kept her eyes ahead watching Tina and Charles at play.

'It was a delightful gathering and I will make every effort to walk down the hill again.' Mrs Chester gave a small laugh, wiping the perspiration building on her forehead.

'So, you enjoying living at Sweet Cinnamon Cottage?' Ella asked her question, her eyes still fixed on the children, as she kept cool under the shade of the tree.

'Well, I am *starting* to enjoy it, especially now that we have Agnes working for us. She is a gem. You must be proud of your sister because from what I understand, there is very little employment in the village. How do you make ends meet?' Mrs Chester turned to Ella trying to catch her eye.

'Well, I sew Ms.' Ella felt vexation rise within her at the woman's nosiness. Yes, she was proud of Agnes for getting a job, and thankful for the additional money it was bringing into the family home; however, Ella, like many of her fellow villagers felt a strong sense of pride in her resilience and self-sufficiency living so far from the city and its conveniences. Ella didn't need Mrs Chester to tell her something she already knew.

'How wonderful! You're a seamstress like myself. I promised to show Agnes how to make a swing skirt, which is very fashionable in London at the moment. I can show you too, if you like?'

Though her head was saying *Be polite, don't be rude,* Ella felt an increased heat start to flow from the base of her back, slowly moving up to her neck and chest.

'London is far away from here, Ms. Agnes don't really need fings like dat. She is working to feed her family, dat's de most important fing.'

Before now, Ella did not think she would have had the courage to speak so forthrightly to a white lady. She had been taught in school to respect the English, to always focus upon the glorious history of Great Britain and its Empire upon which the sun never sets. At the corner of her eye Ella saw Mrs Chester's face fall, and she wondered if she had felt the edge in Ella's voice, the edge she couldn't hide. Luckily for both of them, they were saved from the awkward silence by the arrival of Edward Chester, coming to collect his wife.

'Darling,' he said, placing his hand firmly on her elbow and drawing her away. 'I think it's time to walk back up the hill. It is getting very hot,' he said, smiling at her.

'Well, it's been a delightful morning, and it has been so nice meeting you, Ella. No doubt we will meet again.'

'Yes, Ms.' Ella thought Mrs Chester's smile was not as bright as it was and she sank a little herself as the Chesters walked away. She felt deflated after meeting them, despite the glow of upset and irritation that still lit up her chest. She felt she had no influence in keeping her sister with her in Canaries, or even in St Lucia. The Chesters were a shining light for Agnes, the door of new possibilities had opened to her sister, and Ella knew that fighting to push that door closed would only make Agnes more determined.

CHAPTER FOUR

Six months in, Agnes was enjoying working for the Chesters, and had even got a handle on preparing the tea service, just the way Mrs Chester liked it. She had, however, only saved a little more than a quarter of the money she needed to buy her passage to England. There was also the worry that while the Chesters had the freedom to go back to England whenever they wanted to, Agnes did not have the promise of another job.

She knew the lady of the cottage could get lonely when her husband was at work. Her mood would change from sunny to cloudy in an instant, and she would seek out Agnes wherever she was on the property, in the garden hanging the laundry or in the kitchen preparing the evening meal. Always the mention of her husband in every sentence.

'Edward and I would love to dance Agnes . . . Edward and I would love to go walking . . . We do miss going to the theatre in London. When you go to London, Agnes, you should try and go to the theatre.'

'Yes, Ms, I hope to do dat one day.'

Despite feeling more at home in her job, when Mrs Chester called for Agnes one Friday afternoon as she was setting up afternoon tea, she became nervous. *Maybe dey don't like my cooking no more, dey cah afford to pay me no more. Maybe dey going back to England? Oh Lord please I need dis job.* Agnes set the tray down and stood anxiously waiting for Mrs Chester to speak.

'Well, Agnes, Mr Chester and I enjoy your cooking and baking and can see you are thorough with your chores.'

The words provided little relief for Agnes, convinced a 'but' was coming.

'I have discussed this with Mr Chester, and we would like to increase your wages with an extra three dollars a week, as an indication of our appreciation for your service.'

Agnes did the calculations in her head. The increase would bring her weekly wage to 12 Eastern Caribbean dollars. Agnes smiled. It would never be enough to buy fabric and a lease on a shop plus a ticket to board the ship to England, but she was one step closer.

'Thank you, Mrs Chestor. Please tell Mr Chestor that I am very grateful.'

Agnes returned to the kitchen, her smile widening. She was getting closer to fulfilling her dream, and she was growing fond of Mrs Chester, too, who had, on several occasions asked Agnes to call her Lillian. But despite their growing relationship, Agnes found that hard to do.

The legacy of the plantation was not so far in the past. Mrs Chester was the white lady of the cottage, her employer, and as Ella would say: 'De lady is not your friend, she is your boss, she doesn't see you as her equal. And she will be quick to let you know, you mark my words.'

In this case she knew Ella was right, it's how they were

raised. 'Don't cross the line, show respect and know your place.' Despite what Mrs Chester might say, white people on the island expected and enjoyed being treated differently, as superiors. It's just how it was, the order of things.

One morning Agnes arrived at Sweet Cinnamon Cottage at her usual time and was changing into her work clothes. She would usually hear Mrs Chester pottering in the kitchen, but this morning it was quiet. 'Mrs Chestor? Good morning?' Agnes called out. She made her way to the Chesters' bedroom where she was due to start her daily chores and knocked on the door. 'Mrs Chestor, are you dere?'

A faint cough was the only response. Agnes knocked again and slowly entered the room. Lillian was in bed underneath the covers. The curtains were partly closed, allowing only a sliver of sunlight into the dark room. 'Mrs Chestor, it's Agnes.'

Mrs Chester looked up and Agnes could see the blood had drained from her face and her eyes had dark circles around them; she didn't look herself without her rosy cheeks and vibrant energy.

'No, Agnes, I don't feel well. I will have tea in my room later. I will stay here for a while.' Agnes wanted to ask her what was wrong, but instead she did as she was told. When Agnes brought Mrs Chester her tea mid-morning, the room, and Mrs Chester herself, were unchanged. Agnes rested the tray on the bedside.

Mrs Chester sat up, pulling the covers down around her. She was fully clothed. 'You in you bed with your clothes on? What is going on wit you, Ms?'

Agnes could see that Mrs Chester had been crying – her eyes were even puffier than before, and her hair was all over the place.

Mrs Chester reached out and rested her hand on Agnes's. 'Thank you, Agnes. I don't know what I would do without you . . .' She trailed off, her voice breaking as she continued. 'Oh, Agnes, I want to go home to Dorset.' The tears were flowing now as the words rolled from her mouth. 'I feel lost, like I have been fooling myself and living in a dream.'

'Eh eh, this is no dream? We have gardening to do today. You always say you love being in the garden Ms.'

Mrs Chester didn't seem to hear her. 'I want to go back to England. This is not where I want to start a family. I don't think the heat is good for me.'

Agnes fought to find the right words to calm Mrs Chester down. It was her sister's words and wisdom that came into her mind . . .

'Try not to worry yourself, Ms. Ella always say too much worry can make you sick. Just rest yourself now, Ms.' Mrs Chester looked so fragile curled in on herself. 'Stay here and enjoy your tea, Ms, and I will be back to see you in a while. Everyfing will be all right.'

When Mrs Chester nodded, Agnes headed towards the door, pausing to look back at her employer. She was peering into her teacup, exhibiting no sign of the restorative qualities the tea usually offered her.

In the kitchen, Agnes remembered Uncle Matthew telling her that not long after she and her husband had arrived at Sweet Cinnamon Cottage, he had heard Mrs Chester sobbing while he was tending to the hibiscus on the far side of the garden. On another occasion, he had seen her standing in the garden wiping her eyes, looking sad and lonely.

'Then there were times she would not come down for the whole day and times I see she crying. Then you will see jus' before Mr Chestor get home, she all dress up with big smiles.'

Agnes got on with her chores, the whole time worried about Mrs Chester. But when she checked on her again at three o'clock, she was surprised to hear Mrs Chester's voice sounding much brighter than it had earlier. Agnes was relieved to see her fully dressed, with her hair in place, the bed all made and the room flooded with sunlight.

'Ms, you looking much better. Good to see you up!'

Mrs Chester looked at Agnes coyly. 'It was just a little blip, my dear. I didn't sleep well last night, but I feel much better now after a nap. Come on, now, let us head out to the veranda and make the most of the afternoon.'

Whatever had happened that morning, Agnes was glad it had been short-lived. But it had happened, and it unnerved Agnes. The next day, she found Lillian sitting on the veranda, cups of tea growing cold around her, birds picking at the bread crusts that remained after the Chesters' breakfast. Tears were running down her face.

'Mrs Chestor, let me help you,' Agnes said, feeling a knot in her stomach as she used a napkin to gently wipe the tears from Lillian's cheeks.

Mrs Chester turned to look at Agnes, her eyes swimming with tears. 'He doesn't want to go home, Agnes. I don't think I can take it any more.'

'What can't you take?' Agnes was confused.

'It . . . it's my birthday tomorrow, and he is not willing to take one day off and spend it with me. He says it's the most critical part of some big audit of the whole office's affairs, and he will make it up to me as soon as he can.'

'It's your birthday tomorrow?' Agnes asked, shocked she hadn't known. 'Well, I will make you a nice cake and give you a little surprise to celebrate.'

'That would be nice.' Lillian sniffled, then smiled weakly. 'Agnes, you are so good to me.'

* * *

Once back at home, Agnes kept returning to Mrs Chester's sad and lost demeanour, and found herself formulating a plan to make her employer's birthday a special one. She decided to give her the pretty crocheted doily she'd made, and a handkerchief from Ella embroidered with the initials 'L.C.' Without dispute or a frown of disapproval for once, Ella had wrapped it prettily in tissue paper. Agnes insisted that Matthew join her to bring in the cake she had made for Mrs Chester's birthday tea. Lillian fanned her face to hold back tears as Agnes and Matthew presented Mrs Chester with the cake and sang the Happy Birthday song. When they were done singing, Matthew presented Lillian with a perfect red hibiscus flower he had picked fresh that morning. 'Mrs Chestor, all I have is dis flower which Agnes can put in your hair.'

Then Agnes found her mouth speaking before she had fully engaged with the thought. 'Mrs Chestor, when Ella and I have a birthday we always go to the waterfall in Ravine Duval. We would like to take you there tomorrow.' She glanced at Matthew. 'Uncle Matthew will come with us, and we will take some food. Ella, Tina, and Charles will come too.'

Mrs Chester clasped her hands together and nodded, but now it was happy tears that flowed down her cheeks.

CHAPTER FIVE

The next morning, Lillian and Matthew strolled along the village street to the ramshackle bridge over the river holding picnic baskets.

Today, Lillian felt a spring in her step, looking forward to the day to come, spending time with Agnes and her people at the waterfall. They made their way past the river where a small group of village women stopped their scrubbing and slapping of clothes to gaze silently as they walked by. Lillian stopped for a moment to take in what she felt was an idyllic setting and waved at the women, who waved back. Maybe she was a surprising sight to them, in her large hat and lime green summer dress. She could hear them laughing as she walked away and hoped they were not laughing at her, then she decided not to care and enjoy the moment. Some children playing in the river were brave enough to speak to them.

'Hey Mr Matthew, what you doing with dat white lady,

where you taking her? You taking her to Ravine Duval Mr Matthew, be careful my lady dere are snakes!'

'Hush your mouth boy, min' your business!' Matthew said, his embarrassment evident to Lillian.

'They're children having fun, Matthew. It's quite all right, but are there snakes?'

'Don't worry about dat Ms.' Mrs Chester took Matthew's word on the matter.

The sound of birds, rustling trees and bamboo stalks knocking together in the breeze serenaded her as she walked, raising Lillian's spirits. The rainforest was beautiful, green and lush. The gentle breeze had a slight chill to it which cooled and soothed her brow as she walked.

Her delight in the setting was interrupted by the sound of a child calling to her. 'Mrs Chestor, Mrs Chestor!' Lillian looked ahead to see Agnes's daughter, Tina, running towards them. When the girl finally caught up, she paused shyly before saying excitedly, 'Mummy said to come and get you for the picnic.'

Lillian bent and greeted her, her excitement almost matching the girl's. 'Good morning, Tina. It's so nice to see you again.'

'Not far now. We real close, Ms!' Matthew reassured her.

A few minutes later Lillian heard the burbling of the waterfall before it came into view.

The beauty of their picnic spot took her breath away. The cascading waterfall fell into a deep pool surrounded with large stone boulders, the aquamarine water was clear and the smaller rocks beneath added an extra texture of colours: greens, browns and blues. The tiniest of fish darted through the water, their silver fins catching the sunlight. Giant ferns grew in the gaps in the rock. Large-leaved elephant ears, heliconias and palms created a verdant green border of tropical plants.

'Happy Birthday, Mrs Chestor!' they all called out in unison.

'Thank you, all. Ella, it's such a pleasure to see you again. Thank you for the beautiful embroidery on my gift.'

Lillian couldn't be certain, but she was sure she witnessed a blush creep across Ella's face. Lillian turned to Charles next. 'And hello to you, Charles.' Ella watched Mrs Chester's gestures and heard her kind words but she found it hard to succumb to her niceties. This woman was tempting her sister away from her, feeding her fantasy that her own island had more to offer than the beauty of Ravine Duval.

When Charles remained silent, his aunt replied, 'Don't mind him, Ms. He is acting shy, but he will soon be making trouble.' Ella was taking part in the picnic. For Agnes's sake, she would remain polite and cause no drama but she would watch Mrs Chester's every move, hoping to discover what spell she was weaving to entice Agnes to leave her home and family.

Agnes explained that Matthew was going to catch some freshwater crayfish which they'd then wrap in fresh banana leaves and roast over the makeshift fire he'd erect in a circle of stones piled with dead wood and sticks.

After lunch, Lillian was eager to get in the water, and removed her sundress, revealing her swimsuit underneath, and made her way towards the pool.

'Take care, Ms!' Agnes called out to her. 'The wet stones can send you down.'

Lillian stepped gingerly into the water, the cold sending a delicious shiver up her spine. She welcomed the cooling of the water, her torso shuddering from the chill before she submerged her head and swam towards the waterfall. Carefully checking for rocks, she swam under the veil of the cascading water. Once there, she sat herself on a large rock and closed her eyes. Here, away from the familiar surroundings of Sweet Cinnamon Cottage, Lillian could escape her usual thoughts of England and her lost babies.

'This is so wonderful, Agnes. Are you coming in? You must!' Lillian shouted. She laughed at the wide smile on Agnes's face as she removed her dress, and in her cotton underwear and petticoat, swam to join Lillian on the rock.

They sat in companionable silence for several minutes, the only sounds the roar of the waterfall and the children playing beyond it. 'Thank you, Agnes, how did you know this was just what I needed?' Lillian shouted above the sound of roaring water.

'You are welcome, Ms Lillian!' Agnes surprised herself. It was the first time she had called the lady by her name. She was not sure if Lillian had heard it over the sound of the waterfall. It felt good saying it, for a moment in God's beauty, they were just two friends, nothing more complicated than that. But she checked herself, and decided not to make a habit of doing it. Whatever she felt now, Mrs Chester was still her employer after all.

Agnes shouted again much louder above the roaring waterfall. 'I DON'T HAVE MUCH, BUT I HAVE DIS!'

'MAYBE SO AGNES, THIS MAKES YOU RICH AGNES, RICH!'

For the first time Agnes could see that this was Lillian, free, adventurous and happy. Agnes knew there were no waterfalls in London, but she would sacrifice this moment for the value of a ticket to take her across the waters of the Atlantic Ocean.

It was Ella's shouting that changed the idyllic scene. 'Tina! Where is Charles?'

'I don't know Auntie Ella.'

'What you mean you don't know?' Ella fired back, Tina started to cry and Ella cried out. '*Charles kote ou!* Where are you Charles! *Kote ou!*' Agnes and Mrs Chester heard the fear in Ella's voice and were already in the water moving briskly back to land.

Agnes clambered out of the water. 'Ella where is he?'

'I had my eyes on him Agnes but he move so fast!' Everyone started to call Charles's name, trying to raise their voice above the roar of the waterfall. They began searching around the boulders that littered the length of the narrow gorge.

Uncle Matthew had almost reached the mouth of the gorge where the lush green foliage from the surrounding forest high above nearly reached the riverbed, when he shouted the words that everyone had been praying to hear.

'I find him, he is here!'

Charles was armed with a stick, busily poking a dead headless snake that was floating in a small pool of water where a narrow tributary met the river, utterly oblivious to the cacophony around him. Matthew grabbed Charles by the scruff of his cotton shirt and led him smartly back up the gorge to the others. Before Agnes or Ella could chide the boy, Mrs Chester chimed in with a strong note of relief in her voice. 'Thank Heavens, boys can be so inquisitive, he went on his own little adventure.'

Ella, upset with herself for not keeping tabs on Charles, took aim at Mrs Chester, whose comment riled her up further. '*Inquisitive!* He could die from a snake bite but then what do you care for any of us?'

Agnes came to Mrs Chester's defence. 'Ella! She didn't mean it like dat.'

'Oh, now you taking sides Agnes?'

'No, calm yourself sister, I am not taking sides, de lady is jus' sayin' . . .'

'You fink I am stupid Agnes, I know what she is sayin'. It's my fault I should have kept my eyes on him.' When in reality, if only for a minute or two at most she had been busy keeping her eyes on Agnes and Mrs Chester, watching the fun they were having under the waterfall.

Mrs Chester intervened. 'I can see I am not helping; you're right, Ella, I should keep my silly comments to myself.'

Ella did not acknowledge Mrs Chester's attempt at de-escalation; instead, she grabbed Charles from Matthew's arms. 'Tina, hush your crying.' Ella began to move away hastily, raising her voice as she walked. 'Agnes we should make our way back home.'

Not much was said on the walk back as everyone allowed the exhaustion of the day and the upset to wash over them, the other grown-ups and children were striding at an easy pace. Ella walked more slowly, trailing behind while still fuming at Mrs Chester's comment.

Ella's focus had been on Agnes and Mrs Chester's conversation under the waterfall, and not on the children. She knew her sister would lay the blame at her feet for Charles wandering off. Well, maybe Agnes should spend more time watching them and less time trying to be Mrs Chester's friend!

Agnes and Mrs Chester's loud laughter was echoing around the trees and the mountain walls. *Look how they laugh and talk to one another. I should be under dat waterfall with my sister, not dat lady.*

Ella knew the song of adventure had been planted deep within her sister's heart, it was their father's fault. It was always his words that accompanied Agnes's island song.

Follow your heart's desire, don't be afraid . . .

Ella didn't want to see the world, she wanted to stay home, where her heart was. Mrs Chester gave more volume to Agnes's song, and it was getting louder every moment she spent with her sister.

Ella continued to walk behind at a slow pace and with each step she said to herself, '*Mwen* (step) *pa* (step) *enmen* (step) *madanm* (step) *sala*. I don't like that lady. *Pawdonnen mwen senyè*, Forgive me Lord.'

* * *

Byron Clarke was the first and only man who had managed to scale the wall Ella had erected around herself, or allowed her to believe that there was a life for her beyond their island. He was the only one who cracked the veneer of her protective shield.

They'd first met while Ella was volunteering at the newly established village primary school, teaching the youngest how to read. It was a task that put a song in her heart after years of loss and sadness at the death of their father and lifted her spirits.

It was the time some years before when Agnes was pregnant with her first child, and already Ella had noticed that Agnes's partner Vince was breaking promises and showing signs of being unreliable. Ella had no thoughts of romance herself. Although she'd never shared it with anyone, she'd always dreamed of becoming a teacher, but she didn't have the money, or the confidence to seek the necessary training and qualifications. It was her father's sister, Aunt Flora, who had taught her to read. As a child, she would sit on the floor in front of her aunt, alongside her cousin Johnnie, concentrating hard on everything Flora said.

The day she met Byron she was sitting with two children under the palm tree in the schoolyard. 'Yesterday we did our alphabet to H. Let us try it again today,' she said. When both children recited their letters from A to H, Ella beamed a smile, delighted at their progress, 'Now we will learn from H to R.'

The new schoolteacher, Mr Clarke, was standing in the doorway of the main classroom, as the other children filed out for their break, allowing his eyes to adjust to the brightness outside before walking towards them with long confident strides. He was a tall, elegant man, thin in the waist, with his shirt neatly tucked in with a belt pulled tight to hold up his trousers. His clothes billowed in the breeze as he walked towards Ella; everything about him was clean and orderly. His skin was shining with health, his smile was friendly, and Ella liked the gap in his front teeth. She could feel the warmth rising in her cheeks. Pretending not to notice his approach, she continued with her lesson. 'Yes, yes, try again children.'

'Don't let me disturb you, children,' Byron said as his approach caused them to halt their recitation. 'I can see you are getting extra help from Ms Ella. Please carry on.'

Ella felt his masculine presence as they continued, flustering her nerves.

'Well done!' Byron praised the children as they delivered the alphabet perfectly from A to R. 'You must thank Ms Ella for helping you with extra classes. Reading is a great adventure that you will come to love. It offers you the opportunity to travel the world and experience other cultures without even leaving your village! Imagine that?'

The children thanked her as they ran off to play. Ella thought about what Byron had said about experiencing other cultures from the safety of the pages of a book, and when she looked up, Byron was watching her.

He eyed her confidently. 'I understand from headmistress Francis you have assisted many children in learning to read since the school opened last year.'

The urge to hide her face or run away at his attention felt overwhelming for a moment and she hesitated before answering. But he was a teacher, she told herself, and she wouldn't make a very good impression if she couldn't speak up for herself.

'Yes, I am determined that all children from the village will be able to read. Everyone should be able to learn from the bible for themselves, after all!' she told him, trying to hide the tremor in her voice.

His eyes were warm and friendly. 'These children will not

forget you, Ms Ella,' he said. And it seemed that neither would he.

That Friday afternoon as Ella stood under the school's tin-roofed veranda and placed her large sun hat on her head, Byron approached her. 'Ms Ella, that is a fine hat. Wide enough to keep the sun off your beautiful face.'

Ella's heart was racing, and she was happy her hat was hiding the appreciative look in her eyes, though she was sure he could see her coy smile.

'Are you walking home? May I accompany you?'

Ella had never walked in the village with a man at her side before. Being in Byron's presence made her feel exposed to the prying eyes within the village, yet a strong sense of excitement welled up within her. She had never known this feeling before, and she liked it.

As they walked, a small book fell from Byron's hands. Ella picked it up and handed it back to him.

'"For never was a story of more woe than this of Juliet and her Romeo." Have you read any Shakespeare? He is my favourite writer of sonnets and plays and one day I plan on going to Stratford-Upon-Avon in England to visit his home. The very spot where he wrote most of his great works. Do you know of Shakespeare?'

Ella had never read any Shakespeare; her favourite book was the bible and it was pretty much all she had read. Headmistress Francis had recently given her a new parcel of donated books for Ella to review to gauge if they were suitable for the pupils in her classes, and now she searched her memory for one of the titles.

'I have started reading Treasure Island,' *she finally answered.*

'Ah, that is a marvellous book, and possibly Robert Louis Stevenson's foremost contribution to popular literature,' Byron responded.

Ella was eager for Byron to move off this topic so she wouldn't be caught in a lie. If he asked her about Treasure Island, *she would not be able to tell him a thing.* 'What brought you to St Lucia, Mr Clarke?'

Her plan worked, and Byron spent the next hour telling her about the village he'd grown up in in Barbados. He'd won a scholarship to go to a teacher training school and vowed to return to his village after completing his training so he could help establish a school there.

'Travel broadens the mind and raises one's own horizons.'

Ella didn't want to admit to this interesting and cultured man that she was afraid to leave her own village. She had never met anyone like him. Anyone from Canaries with his kind of intellect and education gained it overseas and they rarely, if ever, returned to the village, usually swept up in the excitement and opportunity that lay over the horizon in England or America.

Could she imagine herself travelling across an Ocean? No, not yet, but in the future? With Byron to guide her? For the first time she felt a contradiction in her feelings. Maybe . . .

As they walked, Ella knew Byron was watching her. It made her feel hot in her cheeks. Was this how Agnes felt when she was with Vince? 'Is this where you live?' *Byron asked when Ella stopped at the simple wooden gate on the steps to her home.*

'Yes, I live here with my sister, Agnes.' *She paused, before blurting out something that surprised her more than it did Byron.* 'Maybe you would like to eat with us one evening?' *She couldn't believe she had dared to say such a thing, but still, there it was, out in the open.*

'That will be an occasion to which I very much look forward!' *Byron stated with enthusiasm.* 'I am renting the small house just as you leave the village; cooking is a hobby of mine, *but the facilities there leave much to be desired. A homemade meal would be most welcome.'*

Their walks home after school soon turned into invitations to take slow evening strolls to the jetty on Saturday afternoons before sunset, once the heat of the day had passed. As the sun began to slowly sink into the ocean, Byron would woo Ella with his favourite sonnets and his deep brown eyes. 'Doubt thou the stars are fire, Doubt that the sun doth move, Doubt truth to be a liar, but never doubt I love you,' he began one afternoon, the ocean waves lending music to his words. 'When I go to England and visit Shakespeare's home, would you come with me, Ella?'

He pulled her into a kiss then. Ella enjoyed his kisses, tender, soft and not always demanding. She welcomed the moments of light touches and sweet caresses that brought her deep pleasure. Sometimes she had to stop his hot, heavy hands from searching her body for an indication that she was willing to take their passion further. Byron painted a beautiful picture with them both in the centre of the frame. No one had ever made her feel brave enough to take a journey into the unknown. Caught up in his imagination of the moment, she could not help herself and answered, 'Of course I will come with you.'

Ella believed that she had found her song, and it belonged to Byron.

CHAPTER SIX

When Agnes arrived at Sweet Cinnamon Cottage the day after their visit to the waterfall, Mrs Chester met her at the door, bubbling with excitement. 'Our daytrip has unleashed something in me!' Lillian said as Agnes placed her bag on the table. Lillian's hands gestured expressively. 'Oh, Agnes, I have been inspired to see more of your beautiful island. When can we go out again?'

'Mrs Chestor . . . Mrs Chestor,' Agnes said, following Lillian as she buzzed around the entrance hall, picking things up and putting them down, rummaging around in her handbag and patting at her hair distractedly in the long mirror, while Agnes tried to get her attention.

'I know Ella is not keen on me, is she?'

Agnes had tried to talk to Ella about her attitude towards Mrs Chester at the waterfall, but her sister had refused. Agnes thought she understood the truth that Ella had taken her eyes off Charles, but she was not prepared to admit it or apologise to Mrs Chester. 'Why you say dat Ms?'

'I seem to aggravate her somewhat. I have been cordial towards her but she seems prickly towards me.' Mrs Chester did not give Agnes the opportunity to answer.

'Not to worry, with time I am sure she will realise I'm just trying to be friendly. Now that's enough of that but we must plan our next adventure, we must seize these moments, don't you think?'

'Ms, I don't understand you. Seize?' Agnes shook her head, 'The waterfall is always there, you don't have to seize it.'

But Agnes saw that Lillian's face had fallen a little at her intervention, her shoulders drooped and she looked around the hallway as if looking for something else to occupy her mind, delving into her handbag again with her head bowed.

As she turned to leave the room, Lillian stopped her, now twirling a handkerchief anxiously between her fingers.

'Agnes, why would you want to leave such a beautiful place and go to England? To leave behind all the beauty of the island, your lovely people and your family. I know many have been encouraged to go, to help to rebuild England, but what were the words that Edward used? Oh yes, "It's a great duty to the British Empire." But surely your duty is to your children too, to stay?'

'But, Ms, I am finking about my children, dat's why I want to go, you tell me England is a good place with lots of jobs, Ms. Why would I not want to go?' It was all very well of Mrs Chester to enjoy the picnic at the waterfall and think how pretty the villagers looked in their Sunday best and to appreciate the lushness of the rainforest, but she seemed able to ignore the other reality of life in Canaries. 'I am lucky to be working here, Ms, I know that, but when you ready to go back home what will I do? I am sure you know there is very little work in St Lucia.'

Lillian frowned, appearing to think about this.

Agnes continued, 'You always talk of going back Ms and how you miss your home. I want to work and raise money to look after my children, send them to college. And I hope to have my own dress shop one day. How will I do dat if I stay here?'

Lillian dropped her hands to her side, 'Oh, Agnes, I hadn't thought.'

'So as long as you are here I will work hard for you Ms and save as much as I can to buy my passage.'

They had been standing in the hallway, and Mrs Chester sighed and moved towards the kitchen, motioning for Agnes to follow and sit at the table. When they were both seated, Mrs Chester said, 'It takes courage to leave a place you have always known and your children. You know the saying, "Home is where the heart is"? Well, it's true, Agnes. My heart is in Dorset. The countryside there has a different kind of beauty to the dramatic nature here. And it is a place I hold dear to my heart.' Lillian gestured to the landscape beyond the window. 'This island is beautiful, but you are right, Agnes, I do want to return to my home, my island. This is *your* home. Promise yourself you will return.'

The thought of not returning had never occurred to Agnes. Even though she'd wanted to leave Canaries since she was a child, she couldn't believe that anywhere else could feel like home. 'I promise, Ms. Dis is where my children are. I must come back.'

'This is why I want to go home, so Edward and I can settle and have *our* family there. Edward has promised we will, but with every passing day the yearning to return has become stronger, and well . . . Edward seems . . . not to be in haste to return, if I'm honest.'

Mrs Chester paused then and looked up at Agnes, tears welling in her eyes. 'The two miscarriages I suffered in Jamaica . . . Agnes, I am so afraid I won't get pregnant again.'

Losing a baby could make a woman feel less of one, but the anguish of losing two babies could make any woman crazy and even lose her mind. Agnes was starting to understand Mrs Chester's pain and erratic behaviour. Agnes knew she had to give the woman in front of her hope.

'God is good, Ms,' she said. 'I believe you will be a mother. You must believe it too.'

'I do believe it will happen Agnes, but not here on St Lucia. All the waterfalls and sunshine cannot heal this wound, this homesickness. I believe it's what's stopping me from getting pregnant, the worry of thinking I will not return there.'

Lillian and Agnes regarded each other, both with their dreams just out of reach. Agnes felt her own emotions rise up inside her, all of her unspoken yearning simmering inside.

'Have you decided when you plan to go to England?' Mrs Chester asked.

Agnes shook her head. 'Not yet, my sister would not forgive me for walking away from steady work, and I need her support with the children when I go. I want her to always trust me and not to fink of me as reckless. While you and Mr Chestor are here I will stay.'

'This sounds very selfish, but I am happy you will stay,' Lillian told her, with a small smile. 'How much is a ticket for passage to England?'

'I have saved half my ticket money already and de raise you gave me will help me raise de rest,' Agnes told her with pride.

Mrs Chester nodded. 'Well, I just hope we get to enjoy the island again before we leave for my home. And, Agnes, when you get to England, I will be happy to introduce you to my friends who I know would snap you up as a housemaid.'

This comment shook Agnes out of her daydreams. What did she expect Mrs Chester to offer her in England? Nothing more than any other employer, but Agnes had dreams, aspirations and wanted more out of life than being a housemaid.

'Ms I appreciate you finking of me, but when I go England I want to see if I can do different work from being a housemaid. Maybe I can work in a dress shop or restaurant where I get to meet more people and learn somefing new to help me move forward. I would like to learn how it is dat people manage dere business affairs and I cannot do dat as someone's maid, hidden away in their big house, away from all de excitement on de streets. When I go to England I want to feel dat excitement, which I won't, if I just work as a maid.'

If Lillian felt put in her place by Agnes's directness then she didn't show it. 'Yes, yes you are right, and I admire your passion and desire. After all, you will be going to the land of opportunity.'

But the brightness in her voice was forced and Lillian looked drained suddenly, a shell of the bright, enthusiastic woman who'd greeted Agnes at the door. 'Are you okay, Mrs Chestor?' Agnes asked.

'I think I will go and lie down. I feel exhausted.'

'Yes, Ms, go and res' yourself.' Agnes watched Lillian Chester ascend the stairs to her bedroom, where she stayed for the remainder of the day.

The next day when Agnes arrived at the Chesters', Lillian was in a sombre mood. Agnes found her in bed again, the room as dark as the cloud that seemed to have descended over her. This darkness lasted for several days and lost as to how she could help Lillian, Agnes shared her concerns with Matthew.

'I fink you must talk with Mr Chestor, Agnes. Mrs Chestor

not doing good *i ni chagwen*. She is depressed. I fink she need to see a doctor to help ease her mind.'

After work the next day, Agnes decided she'd wait for Mr Chester to return from work so she could talk with him.

'Hello, Agnes,' Mr Chester said when he met Agnes at the front door on arriving home from work. 'Shouldn't you be on your way home?' He paused a moment, glancing anxiously at the door. 'Is Lillian okay?'

Other than a cordial 'Good morning' or 'Good afternoon', Agnes had very little interaction with Mr Chester. She had hardly spoken to him in the time he had lived at Sweet Cinnamon Cottage. She stood nervously at the door, her mouth felt dry and she hoped the words that came out of her mouth would make sense.

'Mrs Chestor is in the kitchen waiting for you, but she has been in her bed all day. I worried for her.'

'Worried, what do you mean?' Edward said, stepping closer to Agnes, concern etched into the lines around his mouth.

'She stay in bed all day and she get up before you come home. Matthew say Mrs Chestor "depress". Sir, she need a doctor.'

Agnes saw a wariness flit across his face, before the lines around Edward's mouth loosened and he spoke with a lightness in his voice, changing his frown to a reassuring smile.

'Well Lillian has had these episodes before.' He coughed. 'And she did inform me that she told you about her . . . misfortunes. So you do understand the strain she has been under, and we are well used to these . . . spells. You have shown my wife much care, which has gone above and beyond your job as a housekeeper. I do appreciate your concern but all she needs is rest.'

'She don't need a doctor?'

'No, Agnes, just rest. Now do get off down the hill before

it gets dark.' Agnes nodded her thanks and quickly left the house. She was not reassured by Edward's explanation of his wife's state. After all, she'd been the one to witness Mrs Chester's behaviour while he was at work, and she knew it was the pattern for Lillian to put on an act for her husband.

The next morning, Lillian was back to her usual self, bubbly and enthusiastic to get into the garden.

'Good morning Ms. I was worried for you yesterday. I spoke wit' your husband Ms.'

'Yes, Agnes, Edward mentioned your concerns. I appreciate your care for my well-being, but I'm as right as rain now so let's not speak about it any more. Father Thomas is coming for tea this afternoon, and I am sure you have some chores to do. Onwards and upwards Agnes, onwards and upwards!'

Despite Mrs Chester's continued insistence that Agnes call her 'Lillian', Agnes was well aware that Mrs Chester chose when to treat her as her friend. When Father Thomas arrived for tea that afternoon, Mrs Chester introduced Agnes as 'the housemaid', though the priest knew full well who Agnes was and said, 'Bless you child,' when she brought the tea tray out onto the veranda.

At home that evening, Agnes asked Ella, 'Why she can't say my name? Father Thomas know me, he can see me, he know my name. Why she have to pretend so?'

Ella chewpsed her teeth and said, 'I told you about dease people, Agnes. Dey have to let you know who is boss, just remember they will always let you know your place, dat is how dey are.'

Agnes knew that her sister was right, and she knew that her concern for Mrs Chester had blinkered her own wisdom. The reality was she was still seen as a housemaid, who should always mind her own business.

CHAPTER SEVEN

December was Agnes's favourite month. It was the time of year when the rainy season came to an end and the blustery trade winds returned, blowing in cooler, drier weather and banishing the humidity of the previous six months. This change in climate always made Agnes hopeful, anticipating new beginnings. During this time, she would throw open all the windows in her house and let the breeze flow unobstructed through it. A ritual that cleared the air and rid the rooms of whatever bad energy had accumulated over the previous months.

One morning Agnes was doing the same at the cottage, and turned to find Mrs Chester waiting for her at the door. 'Good morning, Mrs Chestor, you okay, Ms?'

'Yes, Agnes I am fine.' Agnes followed her to the kitchen as Mrs Chester began talking at full speed. 'I have been waiting for you because I want you to help me pick out a dress for the Christmas cocktail reception we are to attend at the Governor General's residence. All of Edward's work colleagues will be there with their wives. I'm not usually keen on these gatherings, but I want to make the best impression for Edward, and I trust your opinion. Forget about your chores for a moment . . .' Mrs Chester was walking away as she talked to Agnes. 'Meet me in my bedroom!'

When Mrs Chester was in this mood, everything had to be done with haste. Agnes felt ill at ease. She took a deep breath to prepare herself for the chaotic scene she knew awaited her. When she entered the bedroom, it was as she'd imagined. A mess of clothes and shoes she had carefully arranged in Mrs Chester's closet just days before were spread carelessly around the room. Agnes began picking up all the beautiful dresses off the floor.

'Agnes put that down. I know it looks a mess, but you are not here to tidy, but to help me choose!'

Mrs Chester had already tried on three dresses with an assortment of accessories. They were on the fourth dress now, an emerald-green organza cocktail dress that Agnes fell in love with the moment she saw it. The silver-patterned thread of the full skirt shimmered in the sunlight streaming through the windows, the off-the-shoulder neckline framing Mrs Chester's petite figure perfectly. The glint of peridot stone earrings beautifully complemented her blonde hair, pulled up in an attractive chignon that showed off the elegance of her neck. A pair of silver shoes and handbag completed the outfit flawlessly.

'Mrs Chestor, you look beautiful. This is de one.'

'Will Edward love it?'

'Oh yes, I fink so Ms.'

This process had taken two hours, leaving Agnes drained and relieved that an outfit had finally been chosen.

'We have another request for you, Agnes.'

'A request, Ms?'

'Yes.' Lillian hesitated slightly. 'Will you travel with me to Castries tomorrow and help me get ready for the party? The plan is that Edward will be staying overnight tonight, and I'm to join him in the morning. We are staying at a colleague's house on the Morne. There are maids' quarters, and I am sure it will be quite comfortable for you. You could enjoy Castries for the day and travel back with us on Sunday.' Lillian's eyes pleaded with Agnes, who could plainly see the desperation in them. 'Please say you will come.'

Mrs Chester needed her there – but as an attendant required to stay in the maids' quarters. Agnes felt a flickering fire in her and was suddenly determined not to accept Mrs Chester's offer so readily. She knew she was more than a maid to this woman.

'OK Ms, I appreciate the extra pay, but if I am to come dey have to give me a clean and dry place to sleep and a full plate of decent food. I don't want to leave my children and my bed to sleep in a damp room and eat stale food. I hear some of the workers in dem big houses living in bad conditions Ms.'

Lillian tried to speak, but Agnes continued before she could do so.

'And Ms I will have to leave on de morning boat on Sunday to be sure I can take care of the children and get them ready for school on Monday. Ella would have been with dem all weekend.'

Agnes knew Lillian would be relying on her more than ever, and the requests were not unreasonable.

Lillian Chester looked at Agnes with surprise, but Agnes detected a little admiration too. 'Of course, Agnes. I will make sure you are comfortable and taken care of. So you'll come?'

'Yes Ms, I will go with you.'

The journey to Castries was uneventful except for the looks she received on the boat ride over. Agnes chit-chatted to some of the other passengers from the village, and as usual they were keen to know where she was going with Mrs Chester. This time she did not hold back. '*Mwen ka alé evec madam la pou a gouvènè kay. Yo ne a fètè.* I am going with madam to the governor's house. There is going to be a party.'

Agnes knew that would get tongues wagging in the village, and on her return she would be greeted with jealous eyes. But she wasn't under any illusion. She hadn't been invited to the event; her role was to assist Mrs Chester into her emerald-green dress and to keep her calm, after which she would be left to her own devices in the quarters provided for her.

Cecil, the driver, was already at the dockside to meet them, dressed in a black suit, black cap, white shirt and tie in the heat of the sun. He was standing at the vehicle looking as cool as a cucumber despite this get-up, while awaiting his passengers. This would be the first time Agnes had travelled in an automobile. He held the door open for Mrs Chester and asked Agnes to sit in the front passenger seat.

'Good morning, Cecil. I trust Mr Chester is already at the house.'

'Yes, madam. He is awaiting your arrival.'

Agnes felt as small as a child sitting in the front passenger seat. Her body was engulfed by the leather chair, which she held on to for dear life. As the vehicle moved, she tried to stay as stationary as possible, but it was hard to keep herself in one position as the big vehicle navigated through the busy streets of Castries and made its ascent up Morne Fortune where the big houses were nestled amongst thick verdant foliage and manicured gardens. Agnes could see the pedestrians looking inside the car, hoping to glimpse the passengers. She just kept looking nervously straight ahead.

The crunch of the tyres passing over the well-manicured gravel path came to an abrupt stop as Cecil brought the car to a final halt at the bottom of a stone pathway. Agnes looked

Island Song

through the smooth, thick trunks of several mature royal palm trees towards the formal entrance of the large plantation house. Built in the French Creole style with detailed fretwork along the balcony running the length of the entire building, the house had the appearance of an intricately layered lace dress, like one Ella would have made for a First Communion. She had never seen a house like it.

Mr Chester was waiting at the door to welcome Mrs Chester. Cecil asked Agnes to wait. 'Hold on dere miss, I will take you to your room.'

Agnes felt dizzy from the drive and was grateful for the cool breeze coming through the trees. Cecil guided her round the side of the house, past the large kitchen to the servants' quarters within a smaller, simpler, more functional building at the back. The room was plain but comfortable, just as Mrs Chester had promised. The sheets were clean, the towels smelt fresh, and her bed looked welcoming. But she had no time to sleep, despite her exhaustion from the journey. Agnes rubbed her eyes and headed back to the main house to help Mrs Chester get ready.

It was the shouting that awoke her later that night. The voices belonged to Mr and Mrs Chester. Agnes shot up in bed, immediately wide awake, but not knowing what to do. She had been concerned for Mrs Chester as she assisted her in getting ready for the party. Lillian had been agitated and het up, worrying about her outfit and fluttering nervously about the room. Now, as the shouting grew louder, Agnes knew something had gone terribly wrong. She rose from her bed and made her way through the kitchen and into the hallway. The shouting continued. 'I told you I didn't like parties!'

'Lillian, calm down. You're embarrassing me!'

Agnes made her way towards Mr and Mrs Chester's room. When the yelling stopped, she summoned the courage to gingerly knock on the door. 'Mrs Chestor, it's Agnes. You okay, Ms?'

It was Mr Chester who responded. 'Not now, Agnes. Get back to bed,' he snapped.

His response alarmed Agnes but she tried again, her concern for Mrs Chester overcoming her natural fear. 'You sure you okay, Ms?'

There was another pause, but then Agnes heard Lillian's faint voice. 'I'm . . . I'm all right, Agnes . . . please don't fret. I'll see you in the morning.'

'You sure, Ms?'

The final words came from Mr Chester.

'That's enough, Agnes. Goodnight.'

The ferry ride back to Canaries was a bumpy one. The waves were up and Agnes felt slightly sick to her stomach, although that was as much to do with the events of the night before as anything else. Her eyes ached and she was dog tired, desperate to get home to her children and sleep in her own bed. Mr and Mrs Chester sat silently on the ferry, not exchanging a word, just as they hadn't all morning.

Agnes now tried to catch Mrs Chester's eye, but they were downcast, the brim of her hat shielding her face. Mr Chester sat with his arms crossed in front of himself, his pose stern, his stony face staring straight ahead.

On Monday, Agnes was surprised to see Mr Chester at home, as he would usually be heading to work.

'Good morning, Mr Chestor,' Agnes said softly.

Mr Chester cleared his throat and looked up at Agnes. 'Lillian had another bad night last night. If you could make the mid-morning tea, as usual, I will take it up to her. I will have my tea on the veranda.' Edward looked exhausted. 'And, Agnes . . .'

'Yes, Mr Chestor?'

'I would appreciate your discretion regarding the events of this weekend. You do understand, Agnes?'

'Yes, sir. I understand.'

'Mrs Chester's weekend suitcase is in the laundry room. The evening dress will need some extra attention due to an accident that Mrs Chester had with some red wine.' He looked at her despondently. 'It upset Mrs Chester, and it caused her to leave the party early. I am sure you will try your best to take out the stain.'

Agnes had never seen the man look so wretched. 'Yes, Mr Chestor. I will deal with it.'

'Edward, Edward, are you there?' Mrs Chester called out, her voice sounding worn and ragged.

Mr Chester gave Agnes one last glance and then walked slowly down the hallway to attend to his wife.

Agnes spent the next half hour working at the stain on Mrs Chester's dress, watching as the red wine colour drained into the basin. It was a beautiful dress, one that deserved to be worn again, but she thought about it holding the memory of what had happened that night, and wondered if Mrs Chester would ever be able to wear it again.

Later, as Mr Chester took his mid-morning tea on the veranda, Agnes made her way up to see Mrs Chester. She knocked gently on the door before opening it. Mrs Chester was in bed, her face turned away. 'Good morning, Ms. I have some black cake for you to enjoy with your tea.'

'Is that you, Agnes,' she asked, without looking up.

'Yes, Ms. I come to see how you are.'

'Where's Edward?'

'He is having his tea on the veranda, Ms.'

Agnes moved closer and when Lillian raised her head, Agnes moved to arrange the pillows behind her so she could sit up.

Lillian was an unrecognisable shadow of the woman who had been so beautifully dressed up for the party. Her pale skin sagged and she shivered under the sheets like a little bird.

Agnes decided to be bold. 'What happen, Ms?'

Lillian's face crumpled. 'Oh, Agnes. I was feeling so happy to be at the party being introduced to Edward's colleagues, but I was feeling awfully nervous as well. As you know, I don't like to be around too many people. I tend to get clumsy, and Edward says I "overact". It was a careless accident, all my fault. We'd had aperitifs before dinner and then Edward and I weren't seated next to each other, instead I was seated next to the Governor General, I had the glass of wine in my hand and, and . . .' Lillian faltered and covered her face with her hands as if the memory was all too much to bear.

Agnes eased Lillian's hands down and gently held them in her own. 'What happened den, Ms?'

'My elbow hit the arm of the Governor General as I lifted my glass, and the wine went everywhere, all over him and me. It was so shocking, in my nervousness I screamed at him . . . at the Governor General, Agnes. I just screamed!'

Lillian pulled Agnes towards her and held on to her, big bold sobs racking her chest and making her voice ragged as she continued. 'I made such a scene and was such an embarrassment to Edward. An awful, unforgivable embarrassment, Agnes. A dreadful mess is what I made of it all.' Lillian buried her face in Agnes's shoulder and wept. 'I just want to go home.'

Agnes sat with Lillian as she wept, her body shaking with the weight of her tears and the shame she felt from the previous night's events. Agnes had witnessed Lillian's moods before, but this time was different, and somewhere, deep down, Agnes knew that things at the Chesters' had reached a turning point.

Her feeling was confirmed the next morning when Mr

Chester called Matthew and Agnes to the veranda. The look on his face said it all, even before the words had left his mouth.

'I say this with a heavy heart, but Mrs Chester and I will be returning to England as soon as we can. As you know, Lillian has not been herself, and she is missing home very much. There comes a point when we have to prioritise her health, and I now realise that point has come.'

'Oh, sir. I am so sorry to hear dat,' Matthew said. Agnes remained silent. Though she had sensed it was coming, she had no words to describe the pounding sadness in her chest.

'We will need your continued assistance, as I will be required to spend a great deal of time in Castries at the office ensuring a smooth handover to my replacement. You both will be needed here where you can assist Lillian in the packing up of our belongings.'

'Of course, sir.' Out of the corner of her eye, Agnes saw her uncle Matthew glance at her. She knew he expected her to say something too, but the words wouldn't come.

The following week was a flurry of packing and preparing the Chesters for the move. Agnes was surprised at how little they actually possessed. The cottage had come furnished, so almost all of their belongings fitted into suitcases and small boxes. For Agnes, packing Mrs Chester's clothes was the most difficult task. She paused when it was time to pack the emerald dress. The stain was gone, and the dress looked as good as new. No evidence that it had been a part of the drama that had changed everything. Agnes made sure to place it at the bottom of the suitcase and hoped Mrs Chester would wear it again.

On the day of the Chesters' departure for England, Edward thanked Agnes, the heavy weight in his voice matching Agnes's own sadness. 'Lillian would always say you were the best thing about this place. I am grateful for all you have done for her. You have been very kind. Mrs Chester is in her bedroom and has asked to see you.'

Agnes slowly made her way to the bedroom, aware that this would be the last time she'd enter this bedroom and see Mrs Chester there. Lillian motioned for Agnes to come closer when she lingered in the doorway. 'My dear, I know it has not been easy for you for the past months with my upsets.'

Agnes looked down at her feet, her emotions threatening tears.

'Here are some sewing patterns I never got to make with you, but I'm sure Ella will make a better job of it,' Lillian said, patting at a stack of envelopes by her side as tears rolled down her cheeks. 'I'm also going to leave you my white gloves and this handbag. Don't open it until after we have left this afternoon. Not before, you must promise. And you can expect to receive a parcel soon . . .' Lillian paused and took in a deep, tired breath. She took Agnes's hands in hers. Lillian's voice cracked when she continued. 'You have been a great support to me. I always felt safe and cared for in your company. I will miss you dearly, Agnes.'

Agnes thought of all the things she wanted to say in response. She had never been able to forget that Lillian was her employer. But good things had come with the complications of Lillian's life. She wanted to tell her how this job with the Chesters had come at just the right time, with a regular wage that helped her to pay her bills and bring food to her family's table. How Lillian's stories about England had strengthened Agnes's resolve to get there one day and kept her dream alive. How sorry she was to discover that Lillian had miscarried and how grateful she was to have Tina and Charles. How her time with the Chesters had taught her to remain kind despite others' misgivings, and that she had learned that sometimes what people did was more important than what they said. But Agnes knew if she tried to say all these things, she would have burst into tears. So instead, she simply said, 'I will miss you too, Lillian.'

Agnes was seated in her father's chair at the back of the house beside the river. She pressed a hand to her stomach, trying to calm the butterflies that flitted inside her. She needed a moment before opening the sleek black leather handbag Mrs Chester had given her the previous day. It had been hard to wait until their ship had sailed to open it, but she had promised Mrs Chester. A breeze passed over the cool water of the river, caressing her cheeks, its soothing touch calming her enough to finally open the bag.

The handbag was opened by pushing a golden metal clasp which unfastened the main compartment with a satisfying click. Inside were two airmail envelopes, neither stamped. Written on the first envelope were two words: 'For Agnes'. On the second envelope, one word: 'Gift'. Agnes recognised Mrs Chester's elegant handwriting. She carefully eased open the first letter, so as to avoid tearing the thin paper. Her heart pumped harder in her chest as she unfolded the single sheet.

Agnes, thank you for your kindness and for your friendship.
   You made our time in Saint Lucia very special.
   We will keep you, your family and the village of Canaries in our hearts always.
   England awaits you. Travel well.
   With our heartfelt best wishes for you and your dear family.
   The Chesters,
   Edward and Lillian

A handwritten card with the Chesters' address in England was also included. She touched the page. With the Chesters now gone, she was worried about how she was going to make ends meet. Agnes knew she was industrious and she would find a way but would it be enough?

The second envelope was thicker, as if there was more than a letter and address card inside. She dared not guess, even as she opened the envelope. '*Lèspiwasyon, Agnes. Lèspiwasyon.* Breathe, Agnes. Breathe.' Agnes gasped. To her utter shock and amazement, inside was a bundle of British West Indies dollars in crisp tens and twenties. She had never seen so much money in one place in her entire life, and certainly never in her own hands.

Agnes counted the notes: three hundred dollars. She counted the notes again, faster this time, to make sure of her arithmetic. Three hundred. Agnes slapped a hand over her mouth to stifle the shout of joy that was rising in her throat. Instead she said, 'Praise Mr and Mrs Chester, praise the Lord!'

She fanned the notes in her hands with the face of a young Queen Elizabeth in her jewelled crown staring out at her. Overwhelmed with gratitude, tears flooded Agnes's eyes.

'*Mwen ka alé Langlitè. Mwen ka alé!* I am going to England. I am going!' She placed the money back in its envelope and then wiped her happy tears from her face.

This gift would change her life, she was going to England.

CHAPTER EIGHT

1957

Some weeks later, Agnes received yet another surprise. A parcel wrapped in brown paper and sporting many stamps had arrived from England. Inside were two reams of fabric and a Simplicity dress pattern for a sweetheart neckline dress. Tucked inside the fabric was a letter from Mrs Chester.

> *Dear Agnes,*
> *I have no doubt the money we gifted you will contribute to your passage to England. I also know you will want to look pretty as a peach when you arrive at Waterloo station. So here enclosed is some fabric to make some dresses for your grand arrival. I am sure Ella will do a fabulous job . . .*

Agnes had shown the cloth to Ella. The first roll was a sunshine yellow with pretty green palm trees framed by a baby blue mountain scene with white clouds.

Ella stood over the material, beaming. 'It's beautiful, Agnes. And with the pattern, I will be able to make a dress and a skirt for you.' The other cloth sparkled like glass, with its royal-blue sheen that would bring out the honey colour of Agnes's skin and highlight her dark, glossy hair. Ella held the fabric up against her sister. 'I can make two dresses from dis cloth.'

Agnes could see the delight the fabric brought her sister and that made her even happier. 'Ella, make sure you make one of the dresses for yourself. *Yonn pou ou èvèk yonn pou mwen.* One for you and one for me.'

Ella looked up at Agnes, her eyes signalling the bond between them, the love of a sister. Agnes patted Ella's hand; a silent gratitude for all the two had shared. 'Agnes, I have something for you, too,' Ella said. 'Something that will go with the dresses I will make with this fabric.'

Agnes wasn't sure what it could be. Ella returned from their bedroom with something wrapped up in a brown paper parcel. 'Dis was our mother's, I have kept it all dese years. I don't fink I will ever wear it, but you should have it.' It was a cream-coloured woollen coat.

Agnes could not find the words she needed for the moment, but Ella saved her tears with her encouragement. 'I hear it is cold in England. This coat will keep you warm.'

Agnes stood, as Ella helped thread her arms through the sleeves and put the coat on.

'You look just like Mama,' Ella told her. The coat fitted her perfectly and Agnes felt the love and tenderness of her mother and sister as she hugged the coat around her.

It was not long after that, that Agnes found herself seated aboard the ferry to Castries waiting for her friend, Margaret. The two were going together to purchase their tickets to England.

Margaret was an old schoolmate and the wife of Agnes's

cousin, Vitalis, who had made the voyage to England several months earlier. It had been arranged that on her arrival in London Agnes would be staying with Vitalis and Margaret until she could afford a place of her own.

It was a clear day, and the sun was high and strong. With the breeze coming off the sea, it was exhilarating to be out on the calm water, and Agnes prayed the conditions would be like this when she made the crossing to England. Her stomach began churning at the thought of what the journey across the waters would entail, so she was relieved when a friendly voice interrupted her thoughts.

'*Bel tan jodi-a*, Beautiful weather today.' Agnes looked up to find Margaret smiling down at her. Though Margaret was married to her cousin, Agnes didn't see her very often. Their island was small, but between working and taking care of family, there never seemed to be enough time for visiting.

Agnes stood and hugged Margaret, taking comfort in her embrace. She stepped back and looked at her old school friend. She was older of course, her figure as beautiful, buxom and commanding as ever.

On the first day of school, Agnes had been seated next to Margaret, the brightest student in the class. But their classmates had constantly tormented her because of her deep, ebony skin.

'You so black Margaret, I can't see you!' the children would say. But Margaret always had a response. 'If you can't see me why you talking to me. Jus' because you *shabine*, light-skinned, it don't make you the best. Evil people come in all shades.' Margaret wasn't afraid of standing up for herself. She'd grown up with four brothers, so she knew how to fist fight and had a mother who mentored her with a daily dose of words of wisdom and some home truths. 'You are my beautiful daughter. Goodness is next to godliness and you are good. You are strong, you are wise, and you are loved.'

Though Margaret never needed defending, whenever Agnes heard children taunting Margaret about her skin color, she would yell, 'You so rude, leave my frien' alone!'

Although Agnes never used her light skin as a token of privilege, those around her often did. 'Wit pretty skin like dat you going to find yourself blessed in de world. You *shabine*, you will always get work . . . and a man.' Her shade was like currency, one which she had never exchanged for entitlement because Margaret's struggles were still her struggles too. She was aware her light skin and her 'good hair', as those around her called it, gave her advantages, yet she would exchange it all for Margaret's confidence and some guidance from her deceased mother.

Agnes stood to greet her friend. 'Eh eh, that's you, Margaret! *Asiz*, have a seat.'

They talked about having lost touch once they'd left school, despite living in a small community. Margaret was never seen to be playing at the beach in the sunshine, or by the river, she was bound to the home looking after her ailing mother. When she left school, she held a desire to go on to further education but being the only girl in the household, the responsibility of looking after a sick parent fell to her. It was one of her siblings, who had travelled to England some years before who would show his appreciation for the years of care for their late mother, by gifting Margaret the funds to buy her own ticket to the promised land, where she hoped to finally pursue her betterment and join her husband, Vitalis. The pace of the capital at the jetty in Castries was much faster than the village they had left behind: folks moved with confidence to the background sounds of the city; cars, buses, voices, all at full volume.

Agnes and Margaret walked quickly across town to the building in Brazil Street and climbed the stairs to the small office of the Carib Travel Agency. It was hot and stuffy, but they managed to find two chairs under the wall fan. There was no one at the reception desk, but they could hear voices coming from the office marked 'Manager' on the door.

Agnes took the liberty of letting whoever was behind the closed door know they had customers waiting. *'BONJOU! GOOD MORNING!'*

The office door then quickly opened. *'Bonjou!'* a young gentleman welcomed them. *'Bonjou, Bonjou!* I apologise, ladies, for keeping you waiting, my name is Floyd Henderson. What can I do for you today?'

'We want to purchase our tickets to England, and we were told this was the place to come,' Margaret said, smiling at Agnes.

'And we would like to travel together,' Agnes added.

'Ah, when are you planning on travelling? The ship leaves every two weeks. The next ship leaves on the 23rd of this month. Would dat suit you, ladies?'

'Well yes, if dat is the next ship to leave?' Agnes stared at Margaret, feeling thrilled and shocked by the closeness of the date of departure.

'Yes,' Margaret spoke for both of them. 'We would like to buy two tickets for de sailing on de 23rd.'

Margaret took Agnes's hand, and Agnes wondered if it was because she looked as nervous as Margaret did.

'Dat's wonderful, please both of you come to sit in de seats at my desk, and I will take your details . . . I trust you have your passport and your birth certificates?'

Agnes's words trembled out of her mouth as she gave her details. Margaret was a lot more confident in asking questions and making requests. 'We want to be in de same cabin, you can ensure dat for us, Mr Henderson?'

'Well . . . de class of ticket you are purchasing means dere could be up to six passengers in your cabin.'

'Oh, I see.' Margaret's face fell. 'My cousin told me she was in a cabin with another lady, and it was just de two of them.'

'It sounds like your cousin was very lucky. These are de berths available to you on dis ship. If I had any other options I would offer it to you. So now dat I have all your details can I continue and explain your Itinerary?'

'Itin-erary? What is dat?' Agnes felt foolish asking.

'It's your travel details for your journey to England, Miss Deterville.'

'Oh, I understand.' Though she wasn't sure she did. Agnes's mouth felt dry, and she was feeling hot away from the flow of the wall fan. 'Is it possible to get a glass of water, Mr Henderson?'

'You okay, Agnes?' Margaret asked, eyeing the sweat mark spreading through Agnes's pretty white blouse. 'Go and sit under de fan. Mr Henderson will bring you some water.'

Agnes took a seat under the moving breeze coming from the electric fan. It felt soothing through the material of her blouse onto her skin.

Mr Henderson then headed towards a back room before returning with a glass of water. 'It's a life-changing moment when you come and purchase your ticket for a new life,' he told them as he resumed drawing up their paperwork. 'Not knowing what to expect at de other end. Most of my family are dere now.' He looked beyond Agnes, a wistful expression on his face, as if he could see his family in their new lives across the water. 'My father was the first to leave St Lucia. He was a solider in de war and was keen to go back to England. He now lives in Paddington. They call it Little St Lucia. You have family dere?'

A little cooler now, Agnes took a seat next to Margaret back at Mr Henderson's desk.

She focused on the chilled glass in her hand. It helped to

keep her cool. 'Yes, I will be staying with my cousin, Vitalis Deterville in Ladbroke Grove.' Agnes had tried to imagine what Ladbroke Grove was like, thinking firstly of Mrs Chester's description of London as grand and impressive.

'That's my husband,' Margaret chimed in. 'He will be waiting for us when we arrive.'

'Well, it's always good to know you will have someone to welcome you.'

'*Wi mèsi*, Yes, thank you,' Agnes and Margaret replied in unison.

'Your tickets will take you all de way to Waterloo station in London. De complete journey will take fourteen days, and you will arrive in England on Saturday, the 4th of March. De ship sails from St Lucia to Genoa, Italy, with one stop in St Kitts and another in Antigua for more passengers to board. Once you reach Genoa, you will spend a day in de city before boarding de night train to Paris.

'The next day you will board a train from Paris to Calais where you will get on de ferry to Dover and your last train from Dover to Waterloo in London. All food and sleeping accommodations are included.'

Mr Henderson studied the sheet of paper in front of him. 'The total price for your ticket, including de various taxes, will be 427 EC dollars.' They handed over their bundles of notes to Mr Henderson. Almost a year's wages. Agnes had worked hard for every penny. The gift that Mrs Chester had given her was received with gratitude but at the end of the day she felt she had earned every cent of it.

Agnes looked down at her passport in her hands. The dark blue thick card cover with her five-digit passport number at the top and the words 'British Passport' embossed in gold, her name handwritten below it. A gold crest with two lions and then the words: 'Colony of Saint Lucia'. Agnes opened her prized booklet and read the words on the inside cover quietly to herself. 'We Request and require in the Name of Her Majesty all those whom it may concern to allow the bearer to pass freely, without let or hindrance.' She stopped for a moment to take in what she had just read. 'Dis mus' mean I can go anywhere,' she thought. She continued reading. 'And to afford her every assistance and protection of which she may stand in need.'

Agnes allowed the words to echo inside her head and flow into her body. 'Such assistance and protection . . . de queen will protect me!'

She turned to the passport's next page where it stated her profession as 'Housekeeper'.

Agnes stared back at her passport picture. She was told not to smile by the photographer, so she looked very serious, stern even, with a deep frown, but what brought a smile to her eyes as she stared at the picture now, was the stamp 'British subject: Citizen of the United Kingdom and Colonies.'

CHAPTER NINE

A cockerel crowing in the yard announced the opening of the day, waking Agnes. It was still dark outside. Agnes lifted herself out of the bed carefully so as not to wake Charles who was sleeping beside her. Ella was already awake and Tina lay still in the bed.

It was four thirty in the morning on the 23rd of February 1957 and Agnes had left her children asleep in their beds. She looked at both of them curled up under their sheets. Agnes spoke quietly under her breath as she kissed each child on the forehead. 'I will be brave for you both. God is on our side. I do this for you both.' And then she offered a quick prayer for them. 'Oh, God, keep dem safe. They are in your hands oh Lord.'

It was dark in the house and you could still hear the cicadas in the trees. They would stop once the sun began to rise. Agnes's suitcases, or grips as they were called, had been packed for days and stood at the door. Ella had already been busy making cocoa tea and breakfast for her sister. The making of cocoa tea spiced with nutmeg, all-spice, bay leaf and cinnamon was a daily morning ritual for most of the homes in the village. Ella took her time stirring the liquid, making sure it would not boil over.

Agnes sipped from the cup her sister had placed in front of her. 'I will miss your cocoa tea, Ella.' When Ella didn't respond, Agnes added, 'But I know I make it better than you.'

Ella grinned and said, 'You, see you!'

Agnes chuckled.

Yes, I will miss dis.

Both sisters made themselves busy, filling the quiet with packing and organising, and Agnes took great care in packing the yellow dress Ella had made for her with Mrs Chester's fabric, folding it carefully to avoid the worst of the creases it was likely to accumulate on the voyage.

Occasional soft taps on the front door broke the silence and the edgy mood surrounding it; most of the villagers would have been up and about enjoying the coolest part of the day. Relations and friends came by to wish Agnes bon voyage. They brought letters to deliver to their families in England, small parcels of spices, a few half bottles of white rum, and unripened mangoes in brown paper bags for Agnes for the journey. With Ella's help, she just about made it all fit into her bulging baggage.

When 5.45 arrived, it was time to make the short walk to the jetty. Agnes had been anxious since waking, anticipating the moment she would have to say her final goodbye.

When she entered the front room, Ella stood from the sewing machine and walked over to Agnes.

Agnes let out a long, slow breath before speaking quietly so as not to wake the children. 'Ella, I don't want you to come, I want to say goodbye to you here. De children will wake up soon, and I don't fink I can see dere faces . . .' Agnes's voice cracked. 'They know I am leaving today and it will be hard for me an' for dem.'

Ella stood in front of her sister and took both her hands, then lowered her head and closed her eyes. 'Oh Lord, look after my sister, grant her a safe and happy passage to England. She is de only one I have, so hold her in safekeeping.'

Agnes's head had been bowed, and when she opened her eyes, she could see the tears had flowed onto her shoes. Ella raised her sister's head and looked into her eyes. 'You are braver than me. You have always shown so much more courage than me.' They held each other as long as they could.

They both looked up at the sound of a light tap on the front door. 'Agnes, it's Margaret. You ready?!'

Agnes wiped her eyes, picked up her handbag and grips, and walked out of the house. She and Margaret walked briskly to the jetty. Agnes did not turn round, not even once, for had she done so, she might have lost her strength and come running back to the only home she had ever known.

CHAPTER TEN

The ship was enormous. The chains and the anchor that held it in the bay made the fishermen's boats look minuscule as they passed far below the deck of the huge ocean-crossing vessel. There was so much bustle and commotion at the Castries harbour, it made Agnes dizzy. If it wasn't for Margaret walking alongside her on the pier and the luggage in her hands anchoring her to the ground, she was sure she would have fainted.

Agnes and Margaret stepped onto the companionway to board the ship in line with fifty or more other passengers. Agnes looked ahead up the line. She could see mothers holding crying babes, and toddlers fidgeting, tugging at their mothers' arms in a desperate bid to break free and run around to expend some pent-up energy. It strongly evoked images of Tina as a baby looking up at her as she breastfed, thoughts and emotions of Charles. How she loved watching him sleep in her arms.

I should have waited to save enough money to bring them too.

A deep pang of guilt struck her right in her tummy, doubt and insecurity about her decision pricked at her again, should she go back? But then she remembered Ella's words: *God is on your side, and I will see you soon.* The memory of those words combined with the undeniable excitement around her on the ship, strengthened her, and soon she was absorbed in her surroundings. Boxes and crates being swung aboard the ship and loved ones waving farewell from the passenger deck to those on the wharf. The sounds were overwhelming for someone from a quiet coastal village not used to this level of noise and movement. It was affecting all of Agnes's senses and her eyes darted all around her, as luggage handlers called loudly to each other across their large carts, sailors catcalled pretty ladies dressed in their best for travel and people stood tearfully by the side of the jetty as they said heartfelt goodbyes.

The ladies, instantly closer friends because of their shared adventure, finally stepped onto the deck of the ship from the companionway and quickly made their way aboard in order to find their cabin, continually asking for directions along the way. 'Look Margaret, C cabins, this way.'

Agnes and Margaret navigated a heavy metal door to enter the inside of the ship before descending two flights of stairs and walking along the corridor until they stood outside their allotted cabin – C27. They were the first to arrive, and Agnes and Margaret put their handbags and grips down at their feet and stood and looked at what would be their living quarters for the next few weeks. Eight beds, in four bunks, two to the left and two to the right, one on top of the other, with a ladder to climb up to the top bunk.

'Lord have mercy,' Margaret said upon seeing the bunk beds. 'I am not climbing dat ladder each night to go to sleep, when de ship sitting still, let alone when we rockin' and rollin' in the high seas! Agnes, you take dat bottom bed, and I will take de other one, that way we can face each other.'

As voices came from the corridor, Agnes quickly picked up her luggage and placed it on the lower bunk, farthest from the door and closest to the small porthole. She thought it was their cabin mates about to enter and fight them for the best bunks. However, the sound disappeared as the footsteps continued down the passageway. With a sigh, they placed the larger of their grips under their bunks to give them space enough to sit down for the first time.

'You ever see anything like dat, Margaret? So many people.'

'And de boat big. Let's hope we don't get los' on our way to the toilet.' Agnes and Margaret laughed at this thought, which helped them let go of some of their uneasy excitement.

Their laughter stopped when a voice came over the ship's Tannoy. '*Benvenuti signore e signori.* Welcome ladies and gentlemen. Welcome aboard the *SS Lucania*, Pride of Italy. We are about to cast off from the dock and depart Port Castries. You are welcome to come on deck to wave farewell to your loved ones and the beautiful Island of Santa Lucia.'

The excitement of this statement electrified Agnes and Margaret as they hurriedly made their way to the middle deck viewing platform. At first, all they could see was the backs of the passengers waving to shore blocking the view. Margaret pulled Agnes along and found a space both of them could squeeze into. It felt strange waving to no one in particular, feeling the large ship start to move ever so slowly away from the dock while Castries stayed stationary. The thick hemp dock lines handled by the crew were like umbilical cords being severed, disconnecting Agnes and Margaret from their home, their island, their mother country. A sudden juddering movement surprised them all, hands came down holding on to the railing. The ship's giant propellers had started to increase their revolutions, the extra thrust increasing momentum. They crept perceptibly faster away from the shore. The motion smoothed out, and everyone had the confidence to raise their hands once again to continue waving to those on the dockside who were likewise busy waving back. The emotional weight of hundreds of people saying goodbye to their families, not knowing when they would see them again could be felt in the air.

For some, the experience of seeing faces and bodies start to fade was too much to take and they turned away in their tears. Agnes and Margaret were silent as they strained to stay focused on the dockside until the faces and bodies started to become indistinct. They turned their attention to the landscape of St Lucia as it came into view from a different perspective than they were used to. High up on the ship's deck, they felt like giants looking above the tinned roofs. Surrounded by lush greenery, the houses shone in the sunlight, and the palm trees waved goodbye. As the ship moved farther away from land, St Lucia provided a majestic, panoramic vista that took their breath away and they could see the rows and rows of banana trees in the Cul de Sac Valley beyond which the Piton mountains looked magnificent far to the South. It was a lot for Agnes to take in. She could feel her energy expand as wide as her island as it came into full view. There was excitement for what was ahead of her but also an anxious feeling of the unknown.

'Well, here we are, on our way to England! You crying, Agnes?'

Unaware it was happening, Agnes touched her face and tasted the salty moisture on her lips. She took a deep breath to calm herself. She was on her way to the land of milk and honey: England. Finally, her long-held dream had come true. She was leaving behind her children, but she took comfort that they were in her sister Ella's safe care. Her promise to send money and parcels once she had employment was a vow; a promise she was sure to keep. One day she would return to open her haberdashery shop with Ella.

Agnes had tried to explain her departure to her children, she hoped, in the best way possible, with love and tenderness. It had been Tina who had asked the dreaded question a few days prior: 'Mama, you leaving us?'

The frown on her child's face broke Agnes's heart, but she smiled, trying to ease her pain and theirs. 'Jus' for a little while. Remember I told you I was going on a big ship.'

'Yes Mama I remember. You said it was a ship bigger dan de house.' Charles spread his arms wide to show he understood the size.

'Well de big ship is sailing next week. I have my ticket and I will be sailing on it to England. Your Auntie Ella will be here for you. I will send you toys and clothes, and I will work hard so you can keep going to school.'

Charles's lip quivered when he said, 'Mama, Mama, don't go.'

'Don't worry my boy, I won't be gone so long.' Agnes pulled Charles close and hugged him tightly.

'Will you send me toys, Mama, and books?' Tina asked, seemingly thinking about the benefits this trip would bring her.

'Books for sure!' Ella responded for Agnes, who was seconds away from bursting into tears again.

Ella had pulled them all into a hug, and Agnes had sat, surrounded by her small family she loved so dearly, and hoped that when all was said and done, the risk she was about to take would be worth it.

Oh Lord, please don't let them forget my face and my love for them.

This was Agnes's constant thought as she set sail that day.

The island song, the melody in full volume in her heart. This was the sacrifice she had to make, leaving her children behind, but it would not be forever.

When Agnes and Margaret returned to their room to settle in, they were not the only ones occupying Cabin 27. Delia and Edith St Rose, sisters from Anse La Raye, who also turned out to be Margaret's second cousins, were settling in.

'Eh, eh! Dat's you, Margaret?' It was a great surprise for Edith to see she was sharing the cabin with her cousin.

'Yes, yes, my girl,' Margaret said, pulling her cousins into a hug then introducing them to Agnes. 'This is Agnes. Agnes, meet Delia and Edith, my second cousins on my mother's side.'

Agnes, whose tummy was starting to turn from the ship's motion, said hello from her bunk.

'Well, it look like we all from de South in here, not dem fast-pace Castries folk who so love to look down on us countryfolk. You know how de people in de town fink dey more classy dan us, eh eh we can be classy too!' Margaret said. The women found this amusing and a little laughter helped to clear the air and bring some cheer as they made themselves comfortable in their cabin for the long journey ahead.

Agnes's seasickness continued to get worse, and she had never felt so ill in her life. The morning sickness she'd experienced when pregnant paled compared to the crushing nausea she felt as the ship cut through the Atlantic Ocean waves.

'The worst thing about seasickness, dear, is that you won't die from it!' an English nurse who was travelling back home and was assisting some of the more unwell told her as she checked on passengers settling into the journey. This little joke was something she had obviously relished sharing many times as she chuckled at her own morbid humour. 'Make sure you look at the horizon through the porthole and get as much fresh air as possible. And if you are sick again, you MUST drink plenty of water.'

Agnes was too delirious to take in what the nurse had said but understood that the motion sickness wasn't fatal, which was a relief.

From their first meal onboard, the women would return from the canteen complaining about the food. 'I don't trus' dat meat. It look like horse to me!' Margaret brought Agnes a cup of lukewarm tomato soup, which reminded her of Mrs Chester's stuffed tomatoes. It was the first time Margaret had tried tomato soup, and she said it was hard to keep down, but the dry bread was the sustenance that held Agnes's stomach together. The real saviour, however, came in another cup.

'Agnes, drink dis, it's not only you feeling so,' Margaret said one afternoon, as she sat on the edge of Agnes's bunk and handed her a cup. Agnes sat up and wrapped her hands around the warm mug. 'A woman from Soufrière came with a big bag of ginger root that she was taking for her sister in England. The chef allow her to boil a big pot in the kitchen and she sharing it with those who needs it. One fella tell me it soothe his stomach straight away; drink it, Agnes, it will ease you.'

The first sip felt like home. It not only eased her belly; it soothed her soul. As she drank, Agnes thought about what a blessing Margaret was. Her enthusiasm always surprised Agnes. 'How you so, Margaret? You always happy, and you have so much energy I wish I had.'

'My mother always told me life don't wait for no one. You have to make it yourself.' Margaret was a voluptuous woman, with flesh that oozed out of her clothes. Her hands were large and strong, perfect for kneading bread, and she walked with a slow, even stride, not in haste like Agnes. Her eyes shone bright as she continued to share her mother's wisdom. 'Her words never leave me, Agnes. Every day I feel blessed, so why not be happy and always see the bright side. God does good for those who help themselves, remember dat, Agnes!'

It took Agnes almost a full week at sea before her tummy started to settle and the mix of bile and saliva in her mouth stopped tasting so bitter and acidic. The steep swells of the open ocean, driven by the powerful easterly trade winds, fed the unrelenting roll of the ship but they had settled considerably by the end of the seventh day. During the night the intensity had subsided, replaced by calmer gentler swells. When they awoke to this new motion of the vessel, Margaret encouraged Agnes to leave her bed and make her way to the deck to take in the sea breeze.

Outside, the ocean breeze shocked Agnes's system, but also shook her out of her lassitude. The ocean looked boundless, no beginning, no end. The light had changed, the sunshine of her island home had faded to a powdery blue with clouds that moved alongside the ship, scattered far into the horizon. A blustery wind tried to blow off Agnes's headscarf and pulled her off her feet. She felt small and weightless.

Margaret was holding Agnes's arm with one hand, the other on her hat. They had to talk above the wind. 'YOU OKAY, AGNES?'

'YES, DAT BREEZE STRONG AND COLD! I FEELING HUNGRY!'

'OKAY, LET SEE IF WE CAN GET YOU SOME OF DAT HORSE MEAT!'

The laughter came upon them once again. Agnes was feeling better, what a relief.

The lull in the conditions only lasted for two days before the ship was met by a new swell that rolled out of the northwest without warning. The hard surfaces of the bulkheads and doors bruised many a limb as the passengers fought their way between the mess hall and their cabins, bouncing like pin balls from side to side along the poorly lit corridors. The smell of vomit and strong cleaning fluid was the overwhelming fragrance emanating across all decks. The moan of dread at the return of seasickness rose from multiple throats, along with the retches as stomachs started to churn once again.

Swathes of passengers went back to their bunks seeking solace from the unrelenting sense of sickness that rose from deep within their stomachs. Entertainment in the mess hall organised by the crew went unattended and the prayer went up for the journey to just reach its conclusion before they lost the will to live. Agnes had got over her seasickness, but the odour of anyone else's vomit made her retch and she chose to spend as much time as possible huddled with Margaret on the deck of the leeward side of the ship, out of the wind and spray, but free from the moans of the sick, cries of miserable children and rancid smells of down below. They spoke of what they were looking forward to seeing in England and what the months ahead may hold for them, excitement and trepidation in equal measure.

Every so often, a small cluster of folk would gather, chatting, talking, or praying, they were all talking about where they were travelling to; places like Brixton and Birmingham. Some had excitement in their eyes about being reunited with family they hadn't seen for a long time. Many of them were lone men, some of whom seemed anxious about what would await them on arrival in their new country, and the majority were headed to London like Agnes and Margaret.

Some nights, one of the fellas would pull out a guitar or a harmonica and make some music, which helped to lift the passengers' spirits. If the tune was right, there was even some dancing.

Agnes and Margaret spent many evenings catching up on events that had happened in their lives since they had left school. 'Most of my days were spent looking after my mother, my bruthas were getting on with dere own lives. I was happy about dat because dey was not paying attention to Vitalis and I. He was my rock through it all, he gave me respite from the day-to-day caring of my mother.'

'You were lucky you had known him since you were so young Margaret, you know you could trust him. Vince turned my head with his words, I knew very little about him, and look what he did to me.'

'But you too are lucky Agnes, you have Tina and Charles. What more could you have asked for than two healthy children.' The mention of their names made Agnes close her eyes and place a hand on her heart as she took in a deep breath. 'I miss dem Margaret, I miss Ella. Have I done the right fing by leaving dem behind? I see so many women on de boat with dere children, with time and more savings I could have done de same.' Margaret stood up and looked out of the porthole of their cabin and took a moment to answer.

'I have been pregnant many times, but my body could not hold de babies.'

'Oh Margaret, I am sorry to hear dat.'

'Dat's a long time ago now.' Margaret moved on quickly. Agnes sensed that she should not push the subject.

'I know Vitalis will do de right fing by us and make sure we have a good place to live. He wrote and told me dere is so much work and not enough people to fill de jobs. You will be able to send money for Ella so she can look after your children and then later, once you are settled, you can send for dem.'

Agnes wished she had Margaret's confidence.

'What if it don't work out in England, Margaret?'

'Eh eh, Agnes, of course it will, it has to. We have come too far. But if it doesn't, well, we can always go home with our tail between our legs!' Margaret gave a chuckle at the thought.

'And what is your reason for going?' Agnes probed.

Margaret took a moment to think. 'Not all of us could stay in Canaries, struggling to know when we will eat. I want to wake up in the morning and know what work I do will pay my way.' She turned to look at Agnes. 'The truth is, I want to save and go back to school and become a teacher.'

Agnes was a little surprised by Margaret's response. 'Ella wanted to be teacher and I know how difficult it is. How can you earn money while you sitting in a classroom?'

Margaret answered again, confidently. 'Well, first I will work. I like to cook so I will find a job in a kitchen of a restaurant maybe. There is no one I have to send money home to so I will save and pay for my training.'

She sighed. 'Every day I looked after my mother she had disappointment in her eyes. She knew I wanted to go to college. And you know what she tell me before she pass? Dat she was de one holding me back. Of course dat's not true. I wanted to look after her. Who else would do it? I take dis opportunity to live, to know I have done something with my life.'

Agnes nodded in agreement. 'That's what I want. When I worked for Mrs Chestor, she told me so much about how England need us to do de work. I don't feel selfish for wanting to go, I feel I am going to better the chances of my family.'

'Before you can help anybody, first you must take care of yourself, Agnes. We must trust in God and hope de people of England will welcome us.'

CHAPTER ELEVEN

After almost two weeks at sea, arriving in Genoa was an assault on their eyes and senses. The Italian language was different to their ears, and the industrial port was just as busy as Castries, but on a much larger scale. Agnes and Margaret wanted to look their best as they disembarked. Agnes was happy to discover she had lost weight and the dress Ella had made for her fitted even more comfortably. Mrs Chester's gift, the pretty yellow fabric, felt like a good luck charm, and her mother's cream coat was an added bonus of confidence and comfort. Agnes felt and looked like a ray of sunshine. She loaned Margaret her white cardigan, which despite being a little snug looked lovely over her red dress. 'Look at us Agnes. We look ready for England!'

'Passengers for the train to Paris and onward to Calais,' an employee at the train terminal began. 'Passengers for the train to Paris and onward to Calais. Please follow me to board your train to Paris.'

Neither woman had ever seen a train before. 'This ting look like a long snake,' Margaret observed.

Agnes and Margaret boarded the train as directed and found their designated couchette, a tiny cabin with fold-down bunks. It didn't look much different from the cabins on the ship, but it was much smaller. It left them little room to manoeuvre around each other, but at least this time it was just the two of them. Despite the privacy, they discovered as the train pulled jerkily from the station, that it was noisy.

'I hope I don't get train sick!' Agnes stated with obvious concern.

'That might be two of us if this noise and shaking don't calm down soon,' Margaret agreed.

Bouncing around in their bunks with the motion of the train and the screeching of the metal on the tracks made for an uncomfortable night's journey. The next morning there were scowling faces the length of the train, no one seemed to be in a happy mood. Arriving at the buffet car for breakfast and having to wait in line for a cold egg and cured meat sandwich left a nauseous lump in Agnes's throat. She poured two cups of coffee. 'I hope it will be strong enough to keep us awake and stop my tummy rumbling.' The coffee tasted bitter, but an added spoon or two of sugar made it palatable.

Margaret looked as exhausted as Agnes felt. 'I want to reach England now, Agnes.'

This was the first time Agnes had seen Margaret's enthusiasm wane. 'Go and lie down on your bed, Margaret. Let me see if I can find some juice and water for us.' Agnes went to the serving counter once again and discovered a carafe of water but no juice. She took it back to Margaret, who gulped the drink down, sighing with relief when her thirst was quenched. 'De man in the canteen said we have two hours or

Island Song

so to go before we reach Paris. Let's get some rest,' Agnes said to Margaret.

Agnes found it difficult to relax. She closed the blinds around her bunk but felt claustrophobic, so she got up and left the room, looking for a window to look out, that was near the washroom. It was hard to walk as the train sped forward, the vibration of the wheels on the tracks underfoot running through her. It was if she was inside the snake, moving left to right. She felt a little dizzy, but with every step she found her footing, as long as she didn't try to move too quickly. She soon arrived at her destination, and tried to make out the expanse of the green landscape with the cows in the fields and white-capped mountains in the far distance.

'*Bonjou*, Madame, are you feeling far from home?' The voice behind her was one of the Italian train guards. 'It must be very different for you? I was a steward on a cruise liner for a few years, and I used to enjoy arriving in the Caribbean and meeting pretty girls like you!' He took a step closer towards her.

His comment and his proximity made Agnes feel uncomfortable. 'I have to go and see how my friend is doing.'

'Oh, that's a shame. I thought we could get to know each other?'

Agnes tried to move quickly past him. He put his hand up on the bulkhead of the carriage blocking her way. 'You are such a pretty girl, maybe I can show you around Paris, the most romantic city in the world.' He moved in even closer, so that Agnes could smell his cigarette breath and feel it on her cheeks, she felt a sense of panic rise up in her. She began to speak at the top of her voice, 'NO, LEAVE ME ALONE!' pushing past the man who fell back laughing, amused by her actions. With no one coming to her rescue, she moved quickly past him. Her heart was racing trying to push herself forward on the moving train, it felt like she was moving in a thick liquid along the corridor, bumping into passengers as she went. She finally found herself at her compartment. Agnes stood as still as she could for a moment, out of breath. 'Oh Lord give me strength, I ask for your protection Lord.' She stood for a while longer taking in longer breaths to calm herself down. *Why dat man fink he could talk to me in such a way. Hell no Lord, hell no.*

Agnes thought about what had just happened. *So dis is how it will be? I thought people would be civilised in Europe, men treating women with respect. What he say, 'Meeting pretty girls like you.' Not all St Lucian woman are de same, hell no!*

Agnes looked in Margaret's bunk. The vision of her friend asleep helped to calm the pumping in her chest down. *If I tell her, I know Margaret will go and beat dat man.* Margaret was breathing deeply and gently. Agnes pulled the blanket higher up her body so as not to disturb her. *Dere is no need to trouble her with what happen. I'll leave her to sleep. I'm okay now. You safe now Agnes but seems to me I mus' watch my back, be careful who shows me big smiles and call me pretty.*

Gare du Lyon train station felt as hectic as Genoa. Agnes had never seen so many white people in one place.

'*Par ici pour le train pour Gare du Nord,* this way for the train to Gare du Nord,' repeated the guide who had been assigned to assist the ragtag group of West Indians through this global metropolis. Agnes and Margaret stayed close together and took refuge in knowing they both felt a little scared as the guide led them to the platform.

'Please stay close together,' he said, addressing the group. 'I will keep holding up this flag, so you don't lose sight of me. We will be taking the Metro, which is the underground train.'

Agnes felt like a cow being moved to market as she was

Island Song

guided down to the Metro to board the next train to Gare du Nord then on to Calais.

Bodie, ede' mwe. Oh God help me. Carrying bags and baskets, suitcases and babies, making their way through the Metro, the St Lucian and other small island passengers were a sight to be seen. They were self-conscious under the curious stares of passersby, but no one dared to look anyone else in the eye as they made their way down the steps on to the next form of transport. Agnes felt she was going to the depths of the Earth. Arriving at the platform and feeling the train rush past them gave her a strange sensation, as if a hurricane was passing through her.

Margaret had to hold on to her hat as the warm air lifted her bonnet. Agnes felt the grit in her eyes. She desperately wanted this constant movement to end. At Gare du Nord, the group made their way to the platform for Calais, still under the intimidating glare of other travellers. It was not a friendly stare, there was no welcoming smile on their faces. It was more a look of 'Don't come close, move along'. Agnes felt relieved to board the train to Calais; she just wanted to stay in her seat and not move until they arrived in London.

After spending two weeks at sea, the two hours it took to cross the English Channel was but a blink of an eye. What was evident, however, was how much colder it was. They were not tempted onto the deck to watch the White Cliffs of Dover as they came into view out of the grey gloom. Agnes and Margaret rather chose to stay sitting huddled together so as to keep warm from the chill that only got colder and colder for them. Despite it being a spring March day, it felt like winter to the two women.

Arriving in London in the dark wasn't the joyful fanfare Agnes had imagined. Everyone was rushing around trying to find their belongings; for a moment Agnes felt she did not have the energy to take even one more step forward, and decided to just sit on her grips, the only luggage she had. She sat watching the chaos around her as she waited for Margaret, who went off looking for her other luggage and boxes that they still hadn't located.

When Margaret joined her, luggage in tow, they both stood anxiously scanning the station for Vitalis.

'I haven't seen him in so long,' Margaret said.

It had been quite a few years since Agnes had seen Vitalis. She had corresponded with him via letter informing him she would be arriving with his wife Margaret. On the passage over, Margaret had talked about how often she and Vitalis had written to each other, and how much she'd missed him, and Agnes realised that however nervous she was, Margaret had to be ten times that.

'Margaret! Margaret!' A taller, slimmer Vitalis than Agnes remembered was rushing toward them, a wide smile on his face.

When he reached them, Vitalis picked Margaret up and spun her around, kissing her face over and over again. Margaret laughed with delight, they didn't care if they were making a scene. 'I have missed you, Margaret,' Vitalis said when he finally let go of her.

'*Oh bondyé!* Oh God! I am so happy to see you, you made me dizzy, my love.'

Vitalis turned to Agnes. 'Agnes! It good to see you too. How was your journey?'

'*Bondous!* My God! Vitalis, I am so happy I reach but I never want to go on a ship again!'

'Agnes had motion sickness, and our rooms on the ship and train was very small.'

Vitalis chuckled as he responded. 'Well, dat's okay. The talk is they starting to fly an airplane between England and our islands one day soon.'

Agnes was now on solid ground. It felt that she had been waiting her entire life to make the journey and now she had made it. She was finally on British soil.

Part Two

CHAPTER TWELVE

Six months earlier

Raphael Toussaint didn't take his eyes off the Port of Dover as it came into view. The crossing from Calais had been the worst part of his long sea journey, and even hardened sea dogs who had never suffered the slightest seasickness had been throwing their heads into the tin buckets provided by the crew for just such a necessity. Raphael would later boast how he survived the voyage to England. 'The crossing was easy, man. We either stayed in our cabin or went to the canteen to play cards with the fellas, and in the evening we drank red wine with the Italian crew. I never got seasick.' Which was a lie. Raphael was seasick for four days, but no one in London would need to know that.

But now he'd forced himself to step out onto the deck and welcome the approach of the place that was going to change everything.

He was going to make it *big*.

As the ship approached the port, Raphael had already started to feel the change in the atmosphere, the anticipation of the passengers as they joined him on the deck, the excited chatter, the women holding on to their hats and skirts as they billowed around them in the cold October air.

The sense of new beginnings was palpable, as was the temperature that made him shiver and wrap his arms around himself to contain some of the heat and excitement he felt in his body. The suit and overcoat he wore, hat perched on his head, with a shirt and tie his father gave him, was little insulation from the cold.

He carried a single suitcase with very little in it: an extra shirt, underwear, some dollars in his pocket that his mother had put in his hand and a bottle of white St Lucian rum was the entirety of his earthly belongings. That bottle was what he planned to celebrate with once he set foot on English soil.

Even the drab surroundings of the customs hall, and the long queues that seemed to await him and his fellow passengers at every turn, had done nothing to dent his enthusiasm. In London Town, he could make himself afresh, leaving behind all the chit-chat about himself at home in Canaries.

Raphael was tall and elegant, dark-skinned, with a broad nose and a wide smile that would show off his gold incisor teeth. He was a sharp dresser who looked good in a suit, and he knew it. While he had an eye for the ladies, they had their eyes on his pocket, courtesy of his father's well-paid job rubbing off on him. Even the ones who didn't, well he could guess what the women said about him as he flitted around town.

Raphael spoilt . . . His father was a farmer who grew the best bananas in St Lucia and now he working for the government, his family live well. And you see him with his two sisters at the dance last week, showing off and buying rum for everybody.

When Raphael had alcohol running through his veins,

he imagined himself cut in the same mould as the confident American servicemen who had flooded the island during the Second World War.

He would mimic their accents as he tried his chat-up on the local girls of Canaries:

'Hey man, how ya doin' man? Hey, honey, you wanna go dancin' with me?'

The American airmen, with their cool cowboy accents, strolled around town, with the best-looking girls on their arm. They had dollars in their pockets and Raphael didn't see why some of that panache couldn't be his too, and it stuck with him all the way across the Atlantic to England.

If America had been handing out passports that would have been his first destination out of St Lucia, but no such luck. So, with family migrating to the UK and smoothing the way, Raphael figured it would be easier to find a job and make some money first. Britain would just be the first stop before making his way to the States and glittering success.

Despite his confidence, Raphael was shaking from his toes to the top of his head when he arrived at Waterloo station – the chill had got to his bones. Turning to a fellow passenger to confirm what he was feeling, he shivered as he asked: 'Hey man, you feel dat cold?!'

'Yes my brother, and dey tell me we have to wait for summer, dats when tings heat up!'

Linus, his half-brother on his father's side, came to meet Raphael at the station. 'Hey, Raph! How you doing boy? Welcome to London!'

Linus and Raphael shared the same father and Linus had come to London three years previously. Raphael knew he was fortunate to have a relative who was willing to share his digs with him and show him the London ways. Not only was he excited to welcome his brother, but amongst all the chaos with passengers looking for their luggage and moving in all directions, Linus had noticed a man he recognised standing with some luggage.

'Hey, dat Vitalis, I know him from Canaries,' Linus said, motioning for Vitalis to join them. Linus introduced Raphael to his friend. 'Look, my brother, dis is my friend from home, Vitalis Deterville. We worked together for a while. Where you staying my brother?'

Vitalis smiled, and though Raphael felt weary, he smiled and shook his hand too. 'At a place in Ladbroke Grove. Not sure how it is but it's somewhere to start.'

'Margaret not with you?' Linus asked.

'No, she had been taking care of her sick mother. Unfortunately, she has passed, but Margaret will meet me here once things have been settled back home.'

'Look, once you get settled, check me. I'm living in Paddington, 52 Bravington Road. You have a pencil? Let me write it down.' As Linus wrote down the address on a torn piece of paper from his cigarette box, he encouraged Vitalis to look in the same area he lived in. 'Not just de station. We Lucians call dis whole area Paddington. Dis is where you fin' a whole heap ah Lucians. So, if you in de area check me!'

It was now four o'clock in the afternoon, and the light was beginning to dim. Raphael took in the air, it felt sharp in his nostrils, and it clearly didn't smell of roses. He looked down at his feet. There was no gold beneath his shoes. He had heard the stories about London being paved with gold and while he didn't think he had literally believed it, the grey drabness and the cold was adding to his sensation of anti-climax.

But the noise of Waterloo railway station excited him, commuters rushing to find their carriages, whistles blowing and the sound of trains coming to a screeching stop on the metal tracks. He welcomed the stares of some of the travellers moving quickly past him and he would give a polite tip of his hat as a hello. But, despite what he'd learned was customary with English people, with their 'please and thank yous', there was no polite response for him today, just stern, unamused looks and people quickly averting their gaze.

After they'd joined yet another queue at the bus stop, and then taken their seats on the bus after climbing a narrow staircase up to the top deck, Raphael looked out the window as Linus explained things to him. 'Then you hear about a next place and again another sign "NO BLACKS, NO IRISH, NO DOGS". It's no palace where I living, but it's a place to hang our hats.'

Raphael continued to take in the scene out of the window while Linus spoke; it was very different from the world of colour and warmth he had left behind. The sky was now almost dark, and the London he could see out of the window was filled with lights from the street lamps and the shop windows. The people on the streets hurried by quickly, none of them stopping to chat to each other, and they all seemed to be dressed in varying shades of grey or brown.

Most of the words coming out of his brother's mouth were passing through one ear and out the other, but two words stood out. He interrupted Linus who was chatting away unaware Raphael was not giving him his full attention. 'What you mean "No Blacks", what dat mean?'

'You not bin' listening to me boy!' Linus was irritated now by his brother's lack of attention.

'*Ou pàkà tan!* You can't hear! Eh eh you making me raise my voice on dis bus.'

Linus looked behind them and was happy no one was in the seat to overhear their conversation.

He lowered his voice. 'No Blacks mean you boy. To fin' a place you have to fin' a landlord dat want your money and not care where you from or what colour skin is, is a lucky ting. I was telling you it was hard to fin' dis place. You betta listen good to what I telling you because you gonna soon fin' out how tings are here, you hear me?'

Raphael's illusion of what his welcome would be like arriving in London was slowly being shattered.

An't bin in London for five minutes and Linus giving me all dis chat?

Raphael was hoping for a big city ready to welcome him with open arms. But as the bus moved along the streets, London looked uninviting, just hordes of people rushing around with anxious expressions creased into their faces. 'Eh eh, plus I mus' tell you.' Linus wanted to give his brother some good news. 'You come at a good time, my brother. Fings are getting better for me. I pick up some nightshift work with British Rail.'

'Dat mean we can spend some time in de day to see de sights?'

Linus seemed surprised again by Raphael's question. 'Na, man, me have to rest up. I can't take another day off, I have to go back to my nightshift tomorrow.' Raphael became even more disappointed. *Man, I thought dis was going to be one big welcome an' man, Linus giving me a headache wit all his talk.*

At their stop, Linus and Raphael exited the bus and began walking down the street. The night air had a chill in it that took away any notion that warm weather existed in England. Raphael started to feel cold like he had never before. His teeth were beginning to chatter, his bottom lip was trembling, and he could feel the rawness of the cold start to penetrate his shoes to his toes.

'Wat wrong with you boy, you stop speaking?' Linus asked him.

'Me never know it would be dis cold!'

Linus roared with laughter. 'Cold! Dis not cold, wait till de snow come down, now dat's when you will know cold. Here, take a cigarette, it will warm you. We not far now.'

Raphael hadn't actually known what to expect, but was shocked to see the conditions Linus was living in. When the light switch went on, the single bulb hanging from the ceiling starkly illuminated the ground floor room consisting of a wardrobe, two single beds, one on each side of the room, and a dining table in the centre covered with newspaper spread for use as a tablecloth, and four odd chairs pushed under it. The wallpaper that adorned the room was no longer decorative, the flowered pattern washed out and stained with damp. A two-ringed cooker with a kettle, along with a few pots and pans rested on a countertop alongside some empty milk bottles. Under the only window in the room was a sink, within which sat a bowl to catch the occasional yet constant drip from the tap. Through the window he could see only some dustbins and a rusty wrought iron fence.

The bathroom one floor up was shared, and the whole building had an overwhelming smell of fried food which Raphael found hard to shake off, while the cold and damp were equally hard to ignore.

'Welcome to 52 Bravington Road. It not much, but it home for now. You can take dat side, and you can hang your coat behind the door,' Linus offered.

Raphael didn't move, numbed by what was being presented to him. He found it hard to respond to Linus. He decided to stay in his coat a little longer for comfort.

Linus sighed and then said, 'Tomorrow, you will hav' to go to de labour exchange and get signed up so you can get some money in your pocket, and dey will let you know of any work. You will receive your National Insurance number, dat will allow you to get a job. I will give you all de instructions. I ask my boss if there was any work with British Rail but nuttin at the moment.'

Raphael didn't think this was the moment to explain to Linus that he had no intention of working as a hospital janitor or finding himself trapped underground in one of the Tube trains in England – he wanted to make it rich and become successful.

Then, and only then, he had promised himself, would he return to St Lucia to show the village that he'd made it big. Some of Raphael's relatives had made the journey already, and before he'd left, in his mind he'd had images of them living the sweet life, a pretty girl on their arm and money in their pockets to do as they wished. The last job he'd had in St Lucia had been the Geest Roseau Bay rum distillery, and he'd been sacked for drinking out of the barrels and falling asleep, when he should have been working.

Now, looking at Linus standing under the light bulb in 52 Bravington Road, Raphael wasn't ready for his vision to be demolished.

He had forgotten how much Linus looked like their father. Raphael's mother, Ma Toussaint, took Linus in after his mother abandoned him to follow a lover to Trinidad. The story went that Ma Toussaint had found Linus living in a hole in a wall near the beach, when he was twelve years old and his father and second wife had taken him in and treated him as their own. Raphael had been born when his half-brother Linus was fifteen years old and had never known him as anything other than a big brother.

Linus carried on with his brotherly advice. 'At home in St Lucia, I left school and I help to build the family house. Dat became my job in the village, building houses and soon they hear about me in Castries, and I got work there as well. I save my money because I start to hear about England and take my chances. I send Ma Toussaint something when I can. You should be getting yourself ready to do the same and pay your way here.'

Right now, Raphael was exhausted and felt he was being lectured again with information he didn't want. 'Hey, man, take it easy. I jus' reach. It a lot to take in, man.'

'My brother, you can't sit back like you in the village. You in London now. You mus' make tings happen.'

Raphael sat on his bed rubbing his hands to make heat. 'You can get any heat in dis place?'

Linus pulled out his paraffin heater from the side of the wardrobe. 'Dis gonna give you some heat. Hol' on let me show you.'

Raphael had not seen anything like it. 'Wat you mean?'

Linus explained, 'Well you put the paraffin in here and you open this metal guard on the front and you see dis ting here, you light the wick which pull up the oil, then you cover it over wid dis, close the guard.' He held his hands up to the heater and rubbed them together. 'You feel the heat coming through?'

Raphael put his hand in front of the metal guard. 'Yeah man, the heat coming through.'

'You see this can, it take a gallon of paraffin which should last us a week or so and you buy it at the hardware store on the corner. So, as well as rent, electric and food we need money to buy heat in the winter. Every ting cost money. Dat's why we must work, because the sunshine ain't gonna give us warmth like back home.'

Raphael was starting to feel vexed – he'd only just reached England and Linus was giving him too much reality too soon.

'I can't leave it on too long because everything cost money.

I put an extra shilling in de hot water meter knowing you were coming, and I have a little food here dat I get a girl to cook for me.'

When Raphael raised his eyebrows, Linus said, 'Eh eh, why you look at me so. No, she not my girl. I not serious with anyone yet. When I come from work, I have no time to cook, so she make me a bouillon to last me a few days and other meals in between. The girl can cook man and it nice to pick up a plate cook by a woman. I'll heat up de pot for you when you ready to eat, it will help to warm you up and give you a little comfort.'

Raphael rubbed his hands in front of the heater, which helped to calm him down after Linus's unsolicited employment advice. 'So where dis girl from?'

'Pearl, she from St Lucia. She always looking for work and she tell me when she get a job she cah' cook for me no more. So one day soon, I might have to find someone else to help keep my belly full. We living in a good area my brother. We have a lot of people living around here from back home and de other islands. Dere's a Jamaican fella living on the top floor. He take up two of the rooms with his family and a Grenadian fella living in the next room in de back. We work together, but we sometimes have different shifts. On de middle floor the beautiful Cynthia and Bertha. They both work at de hospital. Both of dem nurses from Trinidad. Me have my eye on Cynthia, but she ain't easy.'

'So where Pearl living?'

'Not far from here on the Portland Road. I will show you where dat is because you will have to pick up de food from her, and when she finds work, you will have to cook for us both.'

Raphael responded to this news sharply. 'I can't cook!'

'Well, you have to do your best, my brother. For now I will work for the both of us until you get a job, which I hope will happen soon, but until den all I ask is dat you pick up the food from Pearl each week. I fink dat's a good deal.'

'I suppose so.' Then Raphael remembered he had some cheer in a bottle. 'I nearly forget!' Raphael opened his case. 'Dis should warm us up, some white rum from St Lucia, my brother!'

Linus grabbed the bottle. 'Now you talkin'.'

The two brothers stayed up until the last drop of rum was extricated from the bottle, reminiscing about times gone by. The one room home slowly warmed up, but not enough to stop Raphael sleeping in his father's overcoat.

CHAPTER THIRTEEN

'Raph, Raph, time to get up man, it 7.30, you have to be at de labour exchange in an hour. I put a cup of coffee by ya bedside.'

Raphael sat up, groggy from the previous night's drinking, forgetting where he was. One look around at the cold, damp room, and everything came back to him. His bladder wanted some urgent attention. 'I need de bathroom, first. Where de bathroom, Linus?'

'De bathroom I show you yesterday.'

'Oh dat de only bathroom?' Raphael was hoping for a bathroom closer by.

'It's on de next floor up. Most of de houses roun' here, de toilet is outside in de back yard, like de houses back home. Except when you home, you don't freeze your *bonda*, backside!' Linus laughed at his own comment. Raphael was not amused. Growing up in an affluent household in Canaries, an inside toilet was regarded as a status symbol, so there was no need for Raphael to pee in the bush in the family backyard.

Island Song

Linus continued with his instructions.

'Make sure ya take all ya need to clean yourself up because it get busy in the mornings with everyone wanting to use it, and de hot water kept in a tank, so you better hurry or it will all be gone!'

In the bathroom, Raphael managed to find the string to put on the light. The damp walls were very unwelcoming, but he was happy to see the steam rise from hot water in the tap. He put his hands in the water and washed his face and then glanced up into the mirror. He looked tired. He spoke to the reflection in the mirror. 'You come so far, you have to make dis work, mon.'

There was a brisk knock on the door, and a female voice spoke curtly: 'Don't use up all de hot water!'

'Oh, I soon done!' Raphael responded, stepping quickly to the door. He opened it to find a lovely brown beauty in her curlers and dressing gown. 'Sorry, Sorry, Miss,' he said, moving out of the doorway to let her in.

'I hope you didn't leave a mess in here. You fellas always leaving a mess.'

Raphael was about to respond when the door closed in his face, and he figured that must be the sweet Cynthia Linus had mentioned.

Raphael and Linus arrived at the labour exchange at 8.30 on the dot. There was already a congregation of brown-faced men standing outside the building smoking and chatting. They huddled close together and Raphael thought it was to help keep the heat between them, as they were yet to get accustomed to the colder climate, like him. Linus seemed to know them all.

'Dis my brother, Raph. He reach yesterday,' Linus said to the group.

One of the fellas spoke up, he was wearing a bright red scarf, and was dressed in a work uniform unlike the others, 'How you find it so far, Raph? It not what you expec', right?'

Raphael felt nervous standing with the six men looking at him for a response. 'Well, I here to work and find my way like de rest of you fellas. I hope we can look out for each other.' They liked his response, and each of them shook his hand.

'Now, Raph, you have your passport, you have your address. I write it down for you?'

'Yes, me have it.'

'Take dat line over dere and wait your turn. Make sure you let dem know you ready for work.' Linus was starting to make Raphael feel even more nervous with his mother hen ways.

'I hope you don't take long because I have to head back home and rest up for my night shift, so no hanging around for nuffin else.'

Raphael answered all the questions asked of him by the English lady on the other side of the counter, although there was not much to tell as yet.

'When did you arrive in Britain? What is your address while staying in the country? What is your trade and are you ready to work?' Raphael did an impression of the woman's English accent. 'Dat's all she ask me Linus, she never look me in my eyes. She jus' ask me questions writing what I tell her on de paper in front of her. An den she tell me come back in the next few days to pick up my National Insurance number.'

'And she tell you about the notice board with the jobs available?'

'Yes. She tell me to check every day.' Linus meant well with all his questions, but he was making Raphael feel like a fool. 'Why you asking me questions like I a child, Linus?'

'Eh eh, what you mean? Let me tell you. You lucky to have me at your side, showing you de ropes because I had nobody show me nuffin' when I reach Waterloo! Me find my own way, and it was hard. Dat's why I helping you because I wished I had a place to stay and a friendly person to give their time to help me. You see dat fella with the red scarf I introduce you to, if it wasn't for him, I would be on my ass! No question. Dat's Scottie, he like to help out de new arrivals with good advice, he got a job already.'

Raphael thought back to the fellow they had met on their way to the labour exchange.

'De next time you see him, you shake his hand good, my brother. He from Barbados. He is one of the lucky ones. He arrive in England wit a job. London Transport recruit him in his home country. He receiving training as a conductor on de buses. He help me out many times and he my other brother now. And you know what, I take care of you for your mother who took me into her house and treat me as her own. So you best be grateful for me because soon enough you will find out how hard it can be.'

Raphael decided to show some gratitude towards his brother rather than prolong the sermon. 'I sorry about dat my brother, it just dat since I reach, all you bin telling me is what I can and can't do. Can you ease up on me man? Dis jus a lot to tek in.'

His brother shook his head and sighed. 'I hear what you saying but you mus' understand you lucky to have me showing you de ropes. Most of us turn up here with nobody to show us de way.'

'I hear Linus, I hear you.'

After six weeks of no work and nothing better to do than try his best with his culinary skills, Raphael was struggling with his new life. He received two pounds per week from the labour exchange; it wasn't much, but a little went a long way.

The funds were enough to buy cigarettes, contribute to putting food on the table and the occasional treat of a shot of whisky at the pub, but not enough for a night on the town. He had become friends with Scottie and would pass the time at his place when he was off work. They would drink coffee and play dominoes while Raphael waited for his brother to get home, but he was beginning to feel restless and depressed.

Scottie soon noticed this. 'My brother, no matter what, you mus' not let yourself despair. Wake up every morning like you preparing yourself for work, you got to keep yourself looking good for de ladies because when you have a job an extra money in ya pocket dem ladies gonna be humming around you like bees roun' honey.' The thought of it put a smile on Raphael's face.

Raphael had slowly realised that he was going to have to make some compromises to his grand plan, and first that would mean getting some kind of job. Scottie was right, but he wasn't ready to give up on his plan entirely.

'I hav' never needed a job as much as I need it now, but I not gonna do any job. I want to learn a skill.'

He could not bring himself to go for the interview for some of the jobs that were suggested to him at the labour exchange. Crossing the Atlantic to become an office cleaner or dish washer was not why he made the journey. He wanted to learn a skill that he could write home about with pride, even if he didn't know what that job was.

Scottie clapped him on the back. 'Something will come up, trust me. You gonna be working hard soon, so be ready for dat. An' for now enjoy the rest you gettin', for when the work come, you better believe it will be tough going.'

The next Monday morning, with Scottie's advice ringing in his ears, Raphael made himself presentable as he got ready to leave the claustrophobic one-room accommodation he shared with Linus. He didn't want to be around to get another lecture on reality when his brother came home from his night shift . . . 'I can take care of de bills, if you make an effort to fin' a job!' He was keen to find a job, but he knew, despite his brother nagging him, he would not be thrown out on the street. All he needed was a little more time.

He just had to believe what Scottie said to him: 'Keep looking, something will turn up.'

As he opened the front door onto the street, he felt the air cold and crisp against his face. It cleared his head and the foggy mist accompanied him on his walk to the labour exchange. The first time he'd experienced the hazy grey smog he had thought the whole of London was on fire. He had felt like his lungs were filling up with the black soot which seemed to cling to everything, the building, their clothes, even the rim of their trilby hats. Linus reassured him, 'All de Londoners call it a pea-souper, cos it so thick. Jus' keep walking, it will soon pass.'

Raphael approached the notice board outside the labour exchange building. One of the female admin staff from the office was pinning up the cards with new job offers. 'You're nice and early. You know what they say – the early bird catches the worm!'

Raphael wasn't sure what she meant, but it sounded like one of those odd British pleasantries that everyone seemed to use. 'Some good jobs today, madam?'

'Well, I shouldn't do this here, I should show you this at my desk.' She looked around to make sure none of her colleagues were watching.

'This came in late on Friday. Have you ever done painting and decorating, it's a skilled job?'

'Yes, I can do dat!' Painting and decorating couldn't be too hard, Raphael told himself.

'It's a job at Morton Construction and Co. They have just

completed a building on the Marylebone Road, just past the Edgware Road. They need painters and decorators to do the final paintwork. Look, if you hold on, I need to take your details at my desk for your file, so we have a record that we sent you.'

'Yes, Madam.' She touched her hair to make sure her blonde strands were in place and Raphael put her blushing down to his politeness and big smile.

The number 18 bus took him right outside the new building, which was part of a noisy construction site. He held the piece of paper with all the information he needed to present for the job tightly in his hands, despite the rain coming down. It felt like a golden ticket, as he repeated in his mind the manager's name that he should ask for when arriving on site. 'Mr Harrison, Mr Harrison, Mr Harrison.' He found the rust- and dust-covered corrugated building that said 'Manager/Foreman' on the door and knocked.

'Yes, Yes, come in.'

Raphael pushed the door open. 'Mr Harrison?'

'Yes, that's me, who are you?'

Raphael gingerly stepped in and closed the door behind him. As he turned to face the manager's desk, he saw sitting behind it the biggest white fella he had ever seen. He was as broad as the desk he was sitting behind, and you could tell he was tall too as his boot-clad feet extended someway in front of the desk.

'You from the labour exchange? Well, I hope you are, as we need some hard-working men. I'm behind schedule. We need to get these offices painted up in three weeks, and we have forty offices. Are you ready to work? Can you start today? What's your name, son?'

'My name is Raphael Toussaint, sir.'

'Don't call me, sir, call me Mr Harrison. Is that your paperwork in your hands getting soaking wet?' Raphael was feeling nervous. Not only were his hands hot and sweating, his forehead and armpits were perspiring too, despite the cold weather.

'Hand it over. Then we'll get you sorted out. Out the door and follow me.'

'Yes, sir. Mr Harrison.'

From the moment Raphael was hired by Morton Construction he got into the flow of work, eat, sleep and repeat. It was the first time in his life he had felt like a working man, and it felt good. Linus was happy too. 'Wit money in your pocket, putting a lickle saving away and sharing the bills will let you know how it feel to be your own man, yes my brother!' Linus was only his half-brother, but in Raphael's mind, Linus represented their whole family and his approval meant more than he knew. Raphael had been in England for nine weeks and the long hard road to reality had struck quick and deep. Life in England had not turned out as he expected and the dreams of making it big had started to diminish.

But as well as somewhere to go each day and some much needed income, Raphael's new job also gave him a mentor, Bernard Thomas from Grenada. His sole purpose for being in England was to work hard, earn, save money, and return home to his family where he would build a house and start his own hardware business. His work ethic and his attention to detail was always noticed by Mr Harrison.

'Great work on the door frames, Bernard, and the paint job in the hallway, excellent excellent.' Mr Harrison didn't have the same praise for Raphael, though. 'Can you please make sure the paint goes on the walls and not on the floor, I'm gonna have to go to the boss and ask for more paint, Raph. You don't want me to tell him about your wastage do ya? He'll want me to throw you off the job, and you don't want that do ya?'

'No, Mr Harrison, sir.' Raphael would always end the day with paint all over his overalls while Bernard hadn't a spot on him.

'Raph, I keep telling you, you always gonna end up makin' a mess when you have so much on de brush. Look, let me show you how to do it right . . .'

As well as showing him the ropes, Bernard would spend time talking with Raphael in their break, giving words of wisdom and reasoning. 'Drinking and running after women, dat's a boys' game. I want to leave England, knowing I have a plan for my future back home. I don't want to end my days in England in de cold with nuttin' in my pocket. I miss my family and my fishing boat. I want to go back to dat, you hear me, Raph?'

Raphael had grown up always being scolded like a child. Now he wanted to leave childish ways behind and become more respected like Bernard. He was determined to keep his head down and build his future, but not with alcohol and women. That was the old Raphael.

The things people said about him were true, he was spoilt and selfish. He was humbled by Bernard and Linus, he admired their courage and how they had turned their lives around. He hoped that the guidance from Bernard and the support from his brother Linus was making him a better man.

CHAPTER FOURTEEN

It was another cold, snowy November morning. Raphael had decided to wear two pairs of socks, plus full body long johns under his trousers, a jumper, his white working overalls, overcoat and a cap for good measure, which were all hand-me-downs from Linus. These were the layers of clothes he had to pile on to keep warm, but he could still feel the freezing cold coming through his boots. It was bearable as long as he kept moving.

The first time he witnessed the snow, he felt like a character in a fairy tale watching everything turn white and pretty, like a picture post card. With one touch though, the fantasy melted away in his hands, leaving a slick of cold water in his palms. As he stood waiting for the bus at 7 a.m., he stomped his feet, marching on the spot and blowing into his gloved hands, steam rising from the wool weave.

He jumped on the bus when it arrived. It was filling up with transport workers heading to the depot in Baker Street. They had gotten to know each other's faces, and the Caribbean courtesy of saying good morning to each other, as well as a polite nod of the head, was always a welcomed tradition.

'Good morning, Raph. You still working for the construction company?' Scottie was already in his conductor's uniform heading to start his shift for London Transport. Raphael had been so busy with work, the two hadn't seen each other for a few months.

'Morning, Scottie. Yeah, man, I been working there a few months now. I learning something new every day, there's always some other work to do. Hold on, dis my stop!' Raphael pulled the string to ring the bell.

Raphael jumped off the bus at his stop. As the bus moved on, Scottie threw a few more words at Raphael: 'How about us go out on de town soon!'

Raphael gave a thumbs up in agreement.

The office building Raphael worked in was already occupied with workers, as an insurance company had taken the lease. Raphael enjoyed watching the girls leave the building at lunchtime. There were a few pretty brown faces sprinkled amongst the workers but not many. Linus and Raphael had had a few dates to the cinema with the Trinidadian nurses upstairs, Cynthia and Bertha. Bertha was a nice girl, a little quiet for Raphael, but Cynthia, she was Raphael's kinda gal, she had personality.

'Raph, me tell you she pretty right, what you fink?'
'Yeah she nice Linus, but she feisty nah.'
'Yeah I like dat!'

Bernard was already on the job when Raphael arrived, and was not in a good mood. His normally calm exterior was gone and in its place, his eyes flashed with anger.

'Look behind you . . . look!' Raphael turned, and saw painted across a six-foot section of wall, the words:
BLACKS GO HOME.
Raphael lifted his hat, his jaw dropping open in shock.
'Who did dis? Dey mean you an' me right?'
'Of course they mean us! Who else they talkin' about?' Raphael had never seen Bernard so angry. Raphael was upset too but knew the best thing to do was to try and keep calm. Before any other action was taken to remove the abusive words he wanted the boss to see it.
'You tell Mr Harrison yet?'
'What he gonna do? I waited to show you, but I ready to paint over it.'
'I want him to see de kind of people he have working around here. Dem racist fuckers.'
'Me tell ya, he can't do nuttin' bout it. He treat us good because we do a good job for him, but deep down, he most probably tink the same.'
'You hold on, don't paint over it, you hear me.' Raphael marched over to Mr Harrison's office.

His manager was poring over bits of paper and plans as usual, and seemed oblivious of any upset on the floor. 'Morning, Raphael. Why aren't you working on that new office by now? You're not on your break yet.'
'Mr Harrison there is something I want you to see.'
He frowned, 'It had better be good, I'm a busy man.'
Mr Harrison raised himself up from his desk, his stature towering over Raphael, and followed him out of the office.

When he saw the abuse painted on the wall, he was halted in his tracks and drew a hand over his face, shaking his head. 'Who did this?'
'We arrive dis morning to be welcomed wit it. We don't

know who it was. But I'd like to know, too, I can tell you dat much,' Raphael said.

Mr Harrison was speechless for a moment. Finally, he spoke. 'You know I will keep you in work because you both get the job done, but this is a first for me. I wouldn't know who did it, and they aren't likely to admit to it, but I will tell you this. My father worked alongside you fellas in the war, the RAF, and he always spoke very highly of you boys. How you got the job done, were brave fighters and bought some cheer to mess hall. Because of that I have always treated you boys fairly. So, if I should discover who wants this kind of trouble they will be off the job, I promise you that. So, let's get that painted over and get on with our work, okay?'

Bernard went over to the wall still cussing to himself, 'Fuck dem fellas, and you hear Mr Harrison? He calling us "you boys", talking to us like we the little fellows. We men!' With fury, Bernard started painting over the words, leaving the smell of paint and indignation in the air. Once the wall was painted, Bernard and Raphael stepped back and took a deep breath for the first time since that morning, satisfied that the hatred was now hidden under the paint work. But it had seeped into them, as well as the concrete, and still lurked unseen, no matter how many coats of paint they splashed on to the walls. It was gone, but not forgotten.

At break time they heard some voices in the corridor, and then two white fellas came into the room. One of them, a hard-faced cockney, with a Teddy-boy quiff who they hadn't seen before, nudged the other one with his elbow, a sly look on his face.

'All right boys? Looks like you've been busy, ain't cha.' He smirked now, an unpleasant taunting tone to his voice. 'Look, Frank, they have been busy, I'm sure that wall looked different earlier, didn't it?' The man rubbed his hands together and both men laughed coarsely as they left the room.

'It was dem, Bernard, me tell you it was dem!' Raphael said in a low voice. Like Bernard, he now felt filled with anger. But his friend seemed deflated and subdued after being faced with their tormentors.

'Look, Raph, me don't want trouble nah. Truth be told, I had worse abuse said to me walking down the street since I been in England.'

With that he turned to his paint and brushes, indicating that the conversation was over, and Raphael did the same, though he didn't know what to do with himself as fury coursed through his veins for the rest of the morning.

CHAPTER FIFTEEN

Raphael had been working with Morton Construction for almost five months. It was now March 1957. The months had passed so fast, even Christmas had been uneventful, just another day to sleep and eat. The job on the Marylebone Road had come to an end, but Mr Harrison had informed Raphael and Bernard that he wanted them on his next contract in Victoria.

'Here are your pay packets boys and inside there's a bonus, which should tide you over the next couple a' weeks, so rest up and see you in a few weeks on the Victoria job.'

Bernard had mentioned to Raphael that he had a few weeks' work with a new housing association and could see if there was any work for Raphael, but Raphael wasn't interested. 'Na man, I gonna enjoy my few weeks off and enjoy laying in my bed a little later in the mornings and take in some the sights of London.'

'Well, you be careful wit yourself and don't get into any foolishness.'

Island Song

'What foolishness? You teach me well, Bernard. I an't gonna do no foolishness, jus' enjoy me time off and relax meself.' And for the moment, Raphael meant it.

With the extra cash in his wage packet and a few late mornings in bed, Raphael was feeling on top of the world, but Linus always had a manner of bringing him right back down to earth.

'You know, even though you off work, me still expect you to buy the groceries and cook, as now we ain't got help from Pearl no more.'

Pearl, who had been cooking food for them both since Raphael started the job with Morton's, had finally found another job, and so Raphael had been doing the cooking for the past few weeks and he was not enjoying it.

'Linus, we have to fink about getting someone else to do de cooking. I too tired when I get home, and I an't a good cook, I don't like the taste of my own food man.'

'But until we fin' someone you got no choice. So don't forget to pick up de shopping today.'

Raphael tutted and grabbed his coat from the back of the door, placed his hat on his head, opened the door and slammed it behind him. As he did so he could hear Linus's voice through the closed door. 'Don't forget, you hear me!'

As Raphael walked, he muttered to himself under his breath, 'He always talking to me like a child. He lucky he have me staying wit him, paying my way. Maybe it time for me to look for me own place.' He mumbled to himself all the way to the betting shop on the Harrow Road where he placed 2 shillings to win on a rank outsider called 'My Future'. For once it was Raphael's lucky day; he won 2 pounds. He wanted to celebrate, and still with his brother's hectoring voice in his head, was feeling a little rebellious.

It was the middle of the week and he had promised himself

that he would stay away from the drink until Fridays, but with every step he justified his next action, talking himself out of the promise he made.

I am a working man on holiday, I got a right to enjoy my winnings. If I want to have a drink I will have a drink!

Raphael purchased a quarter bottle of whisky, but telling himself he wanted to share his good fortune around, he found his feet walking in the direction of Scottie's rooms. Scottie would be the perfect person to share Raphael's bottle of cheer.

Like Scottie say, it's important to have fun, what de hell man, I do 'as I want!

The bottle was wrapped in a paper bag in his coat pocket, and it was calling to him.

The front door to Scottie's house was open and Raphael took the stairs up to Scottie's rooms two at a time, and rapped on the door.

Scottie peeked out warily, bare-chested and with a thin dressing gown wrapped around him, but a wide grin spread across his face when he saw who it was. 'Raph! You lucky to find me home. Me just raise from my bed, and me have a day off today. You want some coffee?'

'Sure, you want a little shot in it?' Raphael asked, smiling as he raised the bottle of whisky.

Scottie looked at his watch. 'It almost 12 o'clock, well why not?'

Raphael enjoyed Scottie's company. As well as being a mean dominoes player, Scottie was another man of reason. He also had a charm and generosity that was hard to find.

After the two men had enjoyed an afternoon of drinking, trading stories of home and playing dominoes, Scottie told him that later on he was going partying.

'You on holiday, Raph, we work too hard already, gotta let your hair down, my friend.'

That was how Raphael had ended up suited up in his weekend finery standing in a dark room under the haze of a single red light bulb, at a party in Ladbroke Grove. The air was thick with the scent of reefer. Girls were looking pretty, with their hair curled up and their dark skin glistening with the heat building in the room. A couple of the fellas were holed up in a corner with some white girls at their side, their blonde hair taking on a pink shade through the glare of the red light. It was one of those rare occasions where Raphael would witness some of his fellow West Indian fellas who were doing well, men with a job and money in their pockets. Fellas looking sharp, in suits and smelling fresh, cologne liberally applied.

'I respect dat you bin trying to keep your head down but man you hav' to hav' a likkle fun sometimes, especially tonight.' Scottie laughed, a deep throaty chuckle.

'Let me tell you what happened at my job a few weeks back.' Raphael said, telling Scottie about the paint incident.

'Dem Teddy Boys causing trouble?'

'Yeah man.' Raphael chewpsed his teeth, feeling the familiar angry sensation tighten his belly.

Scottie shook his head. 'I also hear dem Teddy Boys throw a brick through de window while some fellas was playing dominoes in their own rooms. Dey not making noise or trouble. Minding dere own business. Dey leave de room fast and run outside but de Teddy Boys leg it.' Raphael had heard about other incidents happening in Ladbroke Grove and it made him nervous.

'Raphael, I'll tell you dis.' Scottie lowered his voice and touched his back pocket. 'Now I always walk wit a switchblade and if ever I catch one of dem Teddy Boy's doing any of us wrong, I will cut dem bad, so dey never stand up.' Raphael had no doubt he would.

'But tonight, Raph, my country folk from Trinidad putting dis evening on! Pretty girls, good music, and I help to put together de bar. We got Black Label whisky; I know you like a shot or two of dat! Plus we have some fellas dat gonna be doing security at de door and dey won't be afraid to use a blade if dey have cause to. Dem Teddy Boys not gonna stop us enjoying ourselves tonight! Right Raph?'

It had been a while since Raphael had let loose and had a night of fun, but he didn't want to be getting involved in any trouble. He was trying to take a different route, working hard and laying off the booze. Getting so drunk that he couldn't stand up, those days he wanted to keep in the past. But drink was in his blood, the desire was always there, hidden and waiting for a spark. He found it hard to turn down a shot when Scottie put temptation in his way, it was as if his fire was being lit, and it felt impossible to say no.

Standing here at the party, he felt that familiar excitement, that old feeling of throwing caution to the wind. After being so responsible for so long he felt he had earned a night of fun. The music was being played on a record player with an extra speaker wired up to it, so it was good and loud. The tunes were the rhythm, beat and melodies of home; calypso, good time music, island songs that brought instant joy to everyone in the cramped space.

One of Raphael's favourite records by Lord Wilson got him tapping his feet instantly: 'I buckle up my shoes and I wander'. Scottie handed him a shot glass. 'Here you go pal, de first of the evening. It going to be a good night Raphael, a good night.' His first shot, and it felt good.

Raphael couldn't help noticing Scottie also had the best sweet talk with the ladies. 'I can't breathe, you take my breath away . . .' Scottie would say to a woman, and the next thing you know, he had hypnotised her, and she would be holding on to him wanting to give him the kiss of life. The ladies just loved him, despite his womanising reputation.

Scottie had the looks too, tall, slim, with hazel eyes. He could wear a suit just as well as Raphael, but to top it off he had silky, wavy black hair which he would smooth down with sweet-smelling pomade. He always had a comb in his pocket ready to smooth down any strand that dared come out of place. 'You have to look good for the ladies ya know.'

Raphael had eased up on his philandering since he had been in England. But watching Scottie charm the women at the party had made him miss some of his old ways; he caught the eye of one of the girls on the dancefloor, who returned his smile, openly flirting, and he felt the familiar pull of a drinkie and good time.

As he downed the next shot, he barely registered the realisation that Linus would be arriving home and expecting his dinner, and danced on.

CHAPTER SIXTEEN

Margaret and Agnes had arrived in England, but Vitalis still hadn't found proper housing for them all. The previous morning, he decided to finally take his friend Linus's recommendation and walked the streets of Paddington, trying once again to find a decent place for them all to live. But he'd had no luck, and now as they stood in front of the dilapidated house in Ladbroke Grove, he could feel their disappointment.

Vitalis was a Deterville. Cousin to Agnes and Ella, the son of Felix, their father Herbert's half-brother. He came from strong stock, used to weathering hard times, but these past few months in England had started to wear on him. And as the day of Margaret's arrival drew closer, he felt the strain even more, desperate not to let her down.

He watched the two women who were unable to hide the surprise at the state of the house from their faces. 'I know it don't look like much, but is jus' for a short time. In fact, as soon as we get the luggage upstairs, I goin' back out to find a different place.'

When neither Margaret nor Agnes moved, Vitalis started collecting their luggage and gestured for them to follow him. Unfortunately, inside the house was not much better. The two-storey townhouse accommodated eight other tenants. Ten residents sharing one small kitchen, one outdoor toilet and a single indoor bathroom which had a small sink to wash in. There was a bath that the tenants could use but the landlord gave strict instructions. 'You are only allowed to have a bath once a week. Do you hear me? Once a week!' Vitalis explained all this to Margaret and his cousin as they followed him up the stairs.

Back home in St Lucia, Vitalis was an industrious young man who never sat still; he would either be fishing, farming or assisting Agnes and Ella's father, his Uncle Herbert, with his boat building on the beach where the Canaries River met the sea. He was a loyal husband who provided for his wife and was never tempted by the flirtatious girls in the village. He knew Margaret was proud of him, and that she remained loyal to him too, despite the attention of some of the more forward men in the village.

Travelling to England was not the first long distance journey he had taken. The first time he had to leave Margaret in Canaries was when he worked a six-month contract in Florida on a large orange grove for the picking season. He toiled in the stifling humidity of central Florida alongside Dominicans, Jamaicans and many other Islanders, many of whom then drifted further North to pick tobacco in the Carolinas in the summer and apples in New England in the fall. Six months away, however, was all Vitalis could handle. He missed Margaret too much and with the money he had carefully saved he was determined they should be together, but on this spring day he wondered if he had made the right decision encouraging his wife to join him in London.

'The Lancaster Road bath house is just a half-hour walk away and is where the tenants prefer to go anyway. There we use as much hot water as we like to wash and do laundry for less than a shilling.' He smiled encouragingly at his wife. 'And we can warm our bodies in the piping hot water and defrost dat chill from our bones.'

As they entered the room together, Vitalis saw the room the way his wife and cousin must be seeing it. The three of them sharing the first-floor room. The single bed pushed up tight against a wall for Agnes and a double bed for him and his wife, with very little room to maneouvre in between. A few stacked suitcases served as a makeshift table, with the beds doubling as seating. A south-facing window allowed what natural light there was to illuminate the lodgings and highlight the sheer ugliness of the degraded interior. Through the window they had a view of a broken brick wall, the remains of which were scattered within a chaotic dump site of discarded household items and concrete rubble. Now, Vitalis could hear children's voices as they rummaged through the mess below. He knew he had to find a bigger place.

Margaret moved to the window and watched the children as they played in the dirt. It was a far cry from the Canaries beach he and Margaret had played on when they were younger. Much of London was still a bomb site, large parts of it razed to the ground by the Luftwaffe during the Blitz. With so much destruction it was no wonder that the government wanted help to rebuild their city, but all Vitalis could think of now was the sadness in Margaret's eyes, eyes that were usually optimistic and full of hope. He wondered how long she could sustain her faith in such a ramshackle grey place.

'What is this?' Agnes asked after she joined Margaret at the window. She was pointing to a few containers on the windowsill.

Vitalis smiled and joined them at the window. 'The snow and cold have some use. I use the windowsill as an open-air refrigerator. The chilled air keep a bottle of milk fresh for some days and stop it from turning sour.' Vitalis didn't mention that he had learned the hard way to place a cup over the top of the milk to stop pesky birds from pecking through the foil lid to access the creamy top of the contents.

'Well,' Margaret said, her voice flat, 'we should start unpacking.'

'Not everything,' Vitalis said, hoping he sounded more confident than he felt. 'I going out soon to look for a place, and it won't be long now.'

Margaret laid one of her grips on the bed and opened it to reveal several colourful summer dresses and short-sleeved shirts. Vitalis didn't have the heart to tell her that the clothes were not suitable for the grey skies and cold damp breezes that welcomed them to England. What's more, there was nowhere to put their belongings other than two hooks on the back of the door.

Vitalis knew the living conditions they were in could not continue. The next morning, he left Margaret and Agnes at the lodgings and walked from Ladbroke Grove, past Westbourne Park station and left onto the Harrow Road. He then decided to cross the street onto Portland Road. Before him was a long line of three-storey terraced houses. Some were in a very poor state of repair, others looked well-loved and others something in between. Most had steps up to the ground floor and off to the side a separate stairwell to a dark basement flat. There was a group of young children playing in the street. A handful of them ran past him and shouted, 'Wogs go home, blackie go home.' Vitalis gave a shake of his head and said within himself, 'They know not what they do. Dease people not gonna beat me down wit dere ignorance.'

He knocked on three houses that had 'Rooms to rent' signs on them but was quickly told 'Sorry, no vacancy', as the doors slammed quickly in his face. His resolve fading, he walked up to the next house, ready to knock on the door, but was stopped in his tracks by a sign hung high in the window, handwritten in bold letters. 'No Irish, No Blacks, No Dogs'. He wondered to himself, 'Why no Irish? They're white people, and why not me? Well at least dey save me de bother of having another door slam in me face! Dey regard me as an animal, fuck dem.'

Vitalis's feet were hurting him, his mouth was dry and his belly was rumbling, crying out for sustenance. As he reached the end of Portland Road he looked at his watch. It was 3 p.m., and he had been searching and wandering the streets for hours, with nothing to show for it. He knew Margaret and Agnes were probably getting worried back at the house.

If he came home with no good news, he was almost afraid she would pick up her barely unpacked bags and head back to Canaries. He turned right into Fernhead Road and walked past a few houses. Halfway down, he noticed a small 'Room for rent' sign. He felt despondent, but he owed it to himself and especially to Margaret to give it one more chance. So he knocked on the door.

It was a well-maintained house, with bright dark green paint, a bronze knocker and matching letterbox cover. The glass was spotless with an intricate lead-lined art deco geometric frieze of red, blue and yellow. The polished step and door suggested a house-proud owner. He knocked a few times, but there was no indication of anyone coming to answer. Just as he was about

Island Song

to give up and turn away, he saw the curtain twitch in the window to the left of the entrance. He stood waiting politely on the lower step, wanting to maintain a respectful distance. A click of the latch and the door opened. 'Yes, hello, how can I help you?' inquired a petite grey-haired white lady. Despite her small stature, or possibly because of it, she gave off the air of someone not to be messed with.

Vitalis put on his widest smile and spoke his best English. 'Hello mam, I can see you have rooms for rent? My wife and I, and my cousin, are looking for long-term accommodation.'

The lady stood behind the door and held it in front of her like armour, revealing only her head. 'Where is your wife? You're here alone.'

'Oh, yes, she is not with me this afternoon. She has just arrived in London, and she is very tired, so she stayed behind.'

'Do you have children?'

'No mam, jus' me and my wife. And my cousin, Agnes,' Vitalis quickly added.

The lady squinted at Vitalis, taking in all his features. Vitalis looked directly at her, noticing her patterned headscarf with a grey curl trying to escape above her ear, her pale skin and her searching blue eyes. She appeared to reach a decision. 'Well, the room available is next door. And there's a second room available for your cousin as well. If you bring them along tomorrow, you can have a look at it. Can you do that?'

'Yes, mam. We can come tomorrow morning. What time would you like us?'

'Come tomorrow at ten. That will give me time to put the breakfast things away. I have a lodger staying here, you see. So I got to take care of that. So 10 o'clock.'

'Yes, mam, I will see you in de morning. My name is Vitalis Deterville and my wife is Margaret.'

'Okay, Mr Deterville, I'll see you in the morning. Good day. And don't be late.'

Margaret stood behind Vitalis as he knocked on the door. The cold and travel had left Agnes feeling ill this morning, so they had left her back at the room. Vitalis gave a quick cough to clear his throat. The lady he had spoken to the day before opened the door, wearing a dark blue snood on her head. Wisps of grey hair peeked out at the front of her hairline, and silver clips held her developing curls in place. She was dressed in her overcoat in readiness to take them to the next-door house, a hint of apron showing under the bottom of the coat. Still wearing her slippers, she moved swiftly to lead the way, chatting to them over her shoulder. 'Thank you for being on time. This is your wife, Margaret? Where's your cousin?'

'She is so sorry she couldn't make it, but the cold has affected her. But, yes, mam, this is my wife.' Vitalis turned to Margaret who smiled.

'Happy to meet you too, Mrs . . . ?'

'Fletcher dear, Mrs Barbara Fletcher.

'Mrs Fletcher, thank you for showing us your room.'

'Well that's okay dear, we haven't agreed on anything yet, so let's see shall we? Your husband tells me you just arrived yesterday.' The landlady's eyes sparkled with curiosity as she looked at her prospective new tenants.

'Where are you both from?'

'We are from St Lucia, mam.'

Mrs Fletcher rolled the vowels around in her mouth. 'St Luchar, where is that?'

'St Lucia is in the West Indies, mam.'

'Sounds like a faraway place . . . hot I imagine?'

'It is, mam. We travel here by ship across de Atlantic. It took us two weeks to get here.'

'My, you have travelled far. You can call me Barbara, none of that "mam". I'm not Her Majesty the Queen! The house belongs to my son-in-law who's moved to Australia with my daughter and grandson. He wants to sell the property but wants to make sure they like it down there and get settled first.'

They were now at the front door of number 63. Barbara put the key in the door and pushed, but it would not budge. Vitalis asked if he could assist. Barbara stepped aside and he gave the door a good firm push. It opened with a sharp creak, and eddies of dust in the dark and musty corridor floated up at the blast of air from the street. There were a few letters on the mat that Barbara picked up. The hallway floor had black and white tiles and as they walked their footsteps echoed up the stairwell.

'The house has not been lived in for quite a while, but as you can see it's in good condition. No holes in the walls or damp. Brian, my son-in-law, is very handy, so before he left, he made sure everything was in proper working order. Margaret, I'm sure you will want to see the kitchen. Take a look, dear?' Mrs Fletcher motioned for her to enter through the doorway at the end of the hall.

'Yes, dey look very nice.' Margaret opened a few cupboards. They looked clean inside although they smelled a little fusty. *I can wipe dat down and get dat smelling good.* She admired the doors which were painted dark green with a cream colour frame. There was a sink and cooker, with enough space for herself and Agnes to move around without stepping on each other's toes. *Agnes will like dis.* She had never been in such a kitchen, especially one with a fridge. Her cousins in America had boasted about having one and now she would be able to boast for herself.

'It has all the mod cons, a fridge, but no freezer, and a gas cooker with an oven.' Margaret moved slowly around the kitchen. She opened a few more cupboards.

'You see this is why I wanted you to bring your wife, because the kitchen is the most important place in the house, am I right, Margaret?'

'Oh yes, you are right Mrs Fletcher, it's a lovely kitchen.' A smile appeared on Margaret's face and Barbara smiled back. Margaret liked Barbara Fletcher.

'There's a gas meter and electric meter which both take shilling coins. Before we talk about rent, let me show you the bedroom on the next floor.' Barbara turned on her slippered feet and nimbly made her way up the stairs which creaked on every step. Before following her up, Margaret looked at Vitalis and opened her eyes wide to let him know she liked the place.

'This is the bedroom,' Barbara told them as they entered from the landing. 'There's a lot of space but not much in it. It's a double bed. The wardrobe's a little small I know, you will have to get yourselves some oil heaters. You can feel how cold it is in here.'

Barbara had turned her attention to Margaret once again. 'I only want honest people living in this house. I had to persuade my son-in-law to rent it because I think it's worse to leave a house like this empty and idle. I know some of the neighbours won't like you moving in here, but I have never, ever been one for bothering much about what other people say. You've got use of the kitchen and this bedroom and your own bathroom, which has a toilet, so no need to use the one outside. There is a bath, but you can go to the bathhouse at the Ha' Penny steps off the Harrow Road, too. It's not far, I go there myself. On the next floor up there are two locked rooms with my daughter and son-in-law's belongings, which you mustn't tamper with. There is an attic room on the top floor, with a small kitchenette on the landing, and that one can go to your cousin, if you think she will be interested.'

Island Song

'The rent is a pound a week for your room and ten shillings a week for the smaller room.'

Vitalis was pleasantly surprised. He was paying one pound twelve shillings for the hovel of a room in Ladbroke Grove. Margaret could not hold in her enthusiasm and blurted out almost before Mrs Fletcher had finished her sentence, 'We want to rent it, both rooms. And we can move in tomorrow.'

Vitalis smiled at Margaret. 'If my wife is happy, I am happy. Can we shake on it?'

But the landlady didn't offer her hand. 'Are you both working?'

'Not full time as yet. I have a little something part time at a hotel in Bayswater where I am a porter. I am going to the labour exchange every day until I get a full-time job. I have a friend dat's working at de Paddington General Hospital, and he said he will be able to get me a job there soon.'

'At the hospital? Are you a doctor, dearie?' Barbara asked dryly.

'Oh no, Mrs Fletcher.' Vitalis hadn't registered the jesting of her tone. 'I would be working in the maintenance department. Really, my goal is to train to be a plumber.'

Margaret chimed in. 'I like to cook, so I will be seeking a position in a hotel kitchen or restaurant, and one day to study to become a teacher.'

'I see. It's good to know you have aspirations, but how can you afford the rent?'

'Well, we have savings, mam. We will be able to pay you the first month's rent upfront.' Vitalis had done the maths, he knew he could afford the deposit. Years of working hard and being frugal had paid off, but without a doubt he would have to make sure he got a job at the hospital which would pay far better than his porter job. Margaret wanted desperately to move in. She was prepared to eat only boiled potatoes for a year if it meant they could afford the place.

Vitalis moved closer to his wife. 'I promise you, Mrs Fletcher. I will be working full time by month's end, and if you rent the small room upstairs to my cousin, she will also be sure to pay the rent on time. Can we start renting from tomorrow?'

Barbara stood for a moment scrutinising Margaret and Vitalis, then nodded her head decisively. 'You know what? I like you two. I can see you are decent people. Now, I expect an envelope through my door every week, and I don't want you bothering me every five minutes about this and that.

'This is a good place, not like some of the other rubbish you get around here. Make sure you look after it. My husband and I struggled for many years, bringing up the kids with practically nothing, but we came good in the end, though he's long gone, God rest his soul.'

She looked sad for a moment then continued, 'Be back here at the same time tomorrow and bring your cousin. I want to meet her, and I'll need your help in airing out the place and moving some furniture. Make sure you have some shilling coins in your pockets for the electric and gas because you will need it for the hot water to get some cleaning done. I will give you some baking soda and disinfectant, Margaret, so you can wipe down the kitchen and I have a few old sheets to start you off for bedding.'

The next day, Margaret, Vitalis, and Agnes brought their belongings, just a few suitcases and the clothes on their backs, to 63 Fernhead Road, the place that they would now be calling home.

CHAPTER SEVENTEEN

My Dearest Ella,
I have arrived safely in England and have been here for two weeks now. The journey over the sea was very hard on me. I was sick for days. In the end, Margaret managed to get me some ginger tea. This helped me very much and settled my stomach.

It is very cold here. Vitalis found a nice place for us all to live. I have my own room which I am getting used to. It feels strange sleeping in a bed on my own. Even with all the covers on, it is very cold in the night, so it would have been nice to have Charles sleeping next to me to help keep me warm!

How are the children? I hope they are not too much trouble. I miss them so much, please tell them that for me. I hope to have a little job soon. Vitalis has a friend, Linus, who needs someone to cook for him and his brother, Raphael. Do you remember Raphael? Raphael always seemed like a rascal and could never hold down a job. We know their mother and their father, Claudia and Bertram Toussaint. I wonder if he still have his old ways?

Margaret took me to buy groceries on the main street near to where I am living. It is called The Harrow Road. There are many shops, but none of them sell plantain, dasheen or sweet potato. All they have are Irish potatoes. We manage to find some mutton and vegetables so I will make a big pot of bouillon for them. They will pay me a little something each week, so hopefully it will keep me going until I find a full-time job that pays me more. There is so much I need to get used to, especially being so far from you all. I miss hearing the children's voices and you my sister. By the grace of God I will keep writing and will hopefully soon be working so I can send you some money as I promised.

I miss you all. I will write again soon and I will write to Mrs Chester too to let her know I reach.

Sending you God's blessing.

From your loving sister,

Agnes

What Agnes didn't share in her letter to her sister, so as not to worry her, was that the little she had seen of England was not what she had expected. She definitely did not see the England that Mrs Chester had told her about. No beautiful landscapes, just the same unremitting grey everywhere.

Agnes was disappointed not to see ladies walking around in their fancy clothes, like she had seen in the *Women's Own* magazines. She was surprised to see white men cleaning the streets, two men on a horse and cart calling out for old furniture. Maybe there was a London like the pictures in the magazines, but she hadn't seen it yet and whatever illusion she had was quickly diminishing. Ella was right: 'Mrs Chestor's world is not your world.'

There was little sunshine, no trees to pick fruit, and most people looked miserable and old before their time. Sometimes even children with worn-out shoes sitting on the steps of shabby houses with broken windows and doors off their hinges, or playing marbles or football in the middle of the street. Agnes would never have let Tina and Charles play in the dirt and the dust. There was a house nearby that she often walked past with Margaret with about six men sitting on the doorstep smoking, looking hungry and lost. Brown-faced men who looked tired with no hope in their eyes. Agnes felt sorry for them. She prayed she would never end up with no hope.

Margaret reassured her. 'Agnes it ain't easy. When you and I first arrived, I wanted to go back to St Lucia. But Vitalis told me not to give up, pray for self-belief and he promise me that he would work hard to make sure we stayed together and to find a place to call home. I count my blessings every day, Agnes, and I fink you should do the same.'

It had only been two weeks since she'd arrived on British soil, so Agnes knew she had to be patient, and hoped the feeling of being lost and ignorant at what she was experiencing would dissolve into knowingness. Both Margaret and Vitalis had now found jobs, Margaret in a hotel kitchen and Vitalis full time as a carpenter at Paddington General Hospital. They were patient with Agnes, and her cousin was always reassuring her that proper work would come soon. But for now, until that happened, it was Agnes's responsibility to cook and clean their living space and the bathroom they all shared. It was a fair agreement for Agnes and with the money she received from the labour exchange, and what she earned from cooking for Raphael and Linus, she was able to contribute to buying some groceries. It was hard to get rice, so potatoes were the most regular item on their plates. It was the least she could do, and it also helped to take her mind off her ever-increasing doubts on how she would survive the coming weeks without a proper job.

Agnes knew at some point she would have to pay her full way and she had to keep her promise to send money to Ella and the children.

On the day she began cooking for Linus and Raphael, the clouds in the sky had finally cleared, and Agnes looked up from her pot out of the window, relishing the sun's beams on her face as she waited for Raphael Toussaint to come and pick up the food. Agnes hadn't seen Raphael since she'd been in England, but from what she was told, he was a working man now and had moved on from his troublesome ways. Something Agnes found hard to believe.

Now this playboy would soon be at her doorstep. Agnes was still determined not to be swayed by his arrogant charm and smooth talk, and when the doorbell rang, she was ready for Raphael Toussaint.

'You Raphael Toussaint, right?' she said after opening the door.

He was surprised she knew his full name. She looked familiar. 'Yes, I come to pick up the food.'

Agnes spoke as she turned to make her way to the kitchen. 'My name is Agnes.'

Raphael was surprised by her frankness. Then it dawned on him. 'You must be from Canaries? Oh yes, you live by the river there in the village, you an your sister . . .'

'Yes, my sister Ella.'

'When you arrive in England?' Raphael sensed that she didn't really want to chat, but he was hoping she would offer him a cup of tea.

'I arrive two weeks ago. Margaret married to my cousin Vitalis. You want a cup of tea?'

'Yes, dat would be nice, Agnes, tanks.'

Raphael approached the table and pulled out a chair and seemed relieved to have been offered a cuppa. He looked so different to Agnes, calmer, less of his showing off ways like back in the village. At least he was drinking tea and not rum in the cosy kitchen. Agnes took her time to brew the tea, just as Mrs Chester would have liked it, but this time with fresh milk and not in a china cup.

Raphael took a sip of his tea from a duck-egg-blue cup and saucer. 'Dat's a good cup of tea Agnes, can I smoke?' Agnes pursed her lips disapprovingly, so he put his cigarettes back in his pocket. 'It's okay, I can wait and have a smoke on de way home.'

'Yes, dat would be better.' Agnes gave Raphael a hint of a smile for the first time since he'd entered the house.

'How far you living? Margaret tell me you living with your brother.'

'Yes, I living in Bravington Road not far from here with my brother Linus. Tell me *ki mannyè kanawi*, how is Canaries?'

Agnes pulled out the other chair at the table and they sat and chatted, reminiscing about the village they had left behind. Agnes explained that it would be a few more hours before her cousin was home from work, so she welcomed the company. Raphael was astonished that he had not been round to see Agnes before, considering they came from the same village, but then Agnes reminded him. 'You may not remember, but you ask me to dance once and I said no.'

Raphael scratched his head, but did not recall, even though he wasn't sure how he could have forgotten such a beauty. 'I have been refused a dance many times, so it's no surprise I don't remember you – it's not my fault, I blame it on de rum.'

Raphael had a charm that made Agnes warm to him despite herself, and he seemed unfazed by what could have been an embarrassing moment, he laughed at himself and found his past antics a source of amusement. Agnes was pleasantly surprised how easy it was to talk to Raphael and before she knew it, a couple of hours had passed. The Raphael that was sitting in front of her did not seem the same man she made every effort to avoid due to all the gossip about his drunken foolishness, which she had witnessed for herself.

'Well, I best get going and see where Friday night takes me. Maybe one Friday night I could take you dancing.' He grinned. 'I hope you won't refuse me again.'

Agnes decided not to acknowledge Raphael's invitation. She stood and went to the cooker. 'Here is the food. It's still warm. I wrap the pots with two tea towels. You coming to pick up the food again on Monday?'

'Yes. It's easier for me to pick it up after work,' he answered.

'What kind of work you doing?'

'I have a painting and decorating job. I learning a new skill, you know. Dat's why we are here – to work and better ourselves, right. I feeling lucky to have dis job. It can be tough for us out there.'

Agnes knew they were both in England for the same reasons, and she hoped to be able to one day say she had a job too. 'Don't forget to bring back the tea towels.'

With the tip of his hat and a smile on his face, he reassured her. 'Yes, Miss Agnes, and don't forget one Friday night, I *would* like to take you dancing.'

Island Song

Agnes did not respond, but couldn't help a flush fire up her cheeks and a smile creep across her face unbidden.

After Raphael had left, the thought of him still lingered in her mind, but she warned herself, 'Agnes, you have no time for man, dat's not why you here. All my life I wanted to come to England, now here I am. Ready to work and sen' money for my children. Dat's it!!'

Agnes walked slowly up the stairs back to her small, scant room on the top floor. In it she had a large bed, a small wardrobe, and a side table with a lamp on which she'd laid one of Ella's small embroidered tablecloths. This was usually a comfort to her, but in the past week, looking at the pretty cloth only made her homesick. As Agnes sat on her bed looking at the ugly walls, for some reason Mrs Chester came into her mind. Maybe it was because of Raphael's compliment, 'Dat's a nice cup of tea Agnes.'

She reached under her bed and pulled out her suitcase. She opened it and removed Mrs Chester's parting gift, the black leather handbag. Agnes took a sniff of the leather. Mrs Chester's perfume had faded, but when she opened the metal clasp there was a slight hint of it, now gone stale. Agnes closed her eyes and breathed it in. An image of Mrs Chester's dressing room came into her mind's eye, her dresses hanging up neatly and her shoes all lined up ready for dancing. This made Agnes smile, but she was yet to experience the England Mrs Chester spoke about. Daffodils in the garden, high tea with scones and crumpets, ladies walking around in pretty dresses and the introduction to her friends regarding work. As Ella had said, 'Mrs Chester's world is not your world.'

Maybe you right, but we have to make our own path, sister.

Spurred into action, she picked up the pen and paper she kept next to her bed and wrote:

Dear Mr and Mrs Chester,
I am now in England living with my cousin Vitalis and his wife Margaret. I am not working as yet but by the grace of God I hope to get a job soon. You did mention Mrs Chester when you was in St Lucia that you would tell your friends I was looking for work, it has not been easy so far for me finding a job and I would be happy to be a housekeeper again.
Everything is different in England, and I hope to one day see the place where you live. I am willing to learn the English ways, I remember everything you teach me.
I hope this letter find you both in good health and you are happy being home in your England.
Here is my address and I look forward to your letter – 63 Fernhead Road W9. London.
May the Lord God be at your side, always.
Agnes Deterville

As Agnes licked a postage stamp and stuck it to the top right corner of the envelope ready to be dropped in the post box, she stared at the address which ended with the word 'Dorset'. She wondered where this was and hoped it wasn't far from Fernhead Road. She set the letter aside and took a look out through the single-paned window of her bedroom; a dull haze of light was streaming into the room making everything look dreary, old and in need of colour. The view was over the back garden of the house, which desperately needed some love and attention. It was spring, and some new shoots were emerging from the wooden stems of various overgrown bushes. Old furniture, broken garden tools, unkempt grass and a square shed in which she had been told was an outside toilet completed the scene. It looked like it would be blown flat by a sudden gust of wind that might whistle through the garden.

If it had been her house, she would have cleared the whole space out and grown vegetables like her sister Ella, and some roses just like the house next door.

As the gunmetal grey sky faded to night, she slept fitfully and awoke in the middle of a nightmare, dreaming that she was being chased by the man on the train, as she ran through the carriages calling for Ella and the children.

CHAPTER EIGHTEEN

After leaving Agnes, food in hand, Raphael had made his way home; it was Friday and he was in the mood for a drink rather than food. The quarter bottle of gin he had purchased from the off-licence was burning a hole in his cloth work bag. He had almost had to stop himself from pulling it out as he spoke to Agnes in her kitchen, but knew it would only serve him up another one of her stern looks.

He placed the food that Agnes had provided on the cooker still wrapped in the tea towels. He poured himself a large glass of gin. The liquor slid down his throat like honey. He sat on his bed and poured himself another, then another, before he laid back and fell asleep.

The next morning Linus arrived from his night shift hungry. Raphael joined him at the table, but Linus only spoke after he had devoured the meal Agnes had made. 'Well, dat was one plate of food. It taste a little different, but it good man.'

Raphael's temples carried a hangover from the gin the evening before and he couldn't face yesterday's food for breakfast himself. Linus wanted to know more. 'The girl who made this is Agnes? She from St Lucia? Where she from?'

'Yeah, she a Canaries girl. I fink you know her. She Mayor-one-Shot daughter. She live wit her sister Ella by the river.'

Linus took a moment to think while he used a matchstick to pull the food from between his teeth. Then it came to him. 'Oh yes, yes, I remember her as a pretty young girl. How she now? She still looking nice?'

Raphael felt a little vexed at Linus's response. 'Why you need to know how she lookin'? The food is good. Dat all you need to know.'

Raphael's response made Linus chuckle. 'Well, well, she still good-lookin' then AND she can cook. Me need to pay my bill and pick up the food next time.'

The only response Raphael gave to Linus's comment was a very loud 'Chewps', which made Linus laugh even more. 'Ha, ha. Don't worry my brother, I won't tread on your feet.'

As the weeks went by, Agnes infiltrated Raphael's thoughts when he wasn't expecting it, and his heart beat that bit faster when he was with her. To make her laugh brought joy to him. He enjoyed watching her move around the kitchen as she packed the meals she had prepared for him and Linus. And when she placed a cup of tea at the table, he had to fight the urge to place his hands around her waist and pull her close so he could kiss her passionately. But it would have been disrespectful, and Agnes might be put off him forever if he did.

Agnes always spoke to him frankly, with honesty. 'If only the girls by the river could see you now, you making something of yourself Raph, you not lazy like before. You don't seem like dat spoilt fella everyone used to talk about, always drunk and doing *papicho*, foolishness.'

Little did Agnes know, Raphael was holding a part of himself secret from her. He still needed a drink to feel alive and occasionally, he needed to dance wild. It was part of his nature, and he could no more deny this than he could his growing feelings for Agnes. He knew his drinking could get a little out of hand, a habit he found hard to break despite his efforts. He liked having a good time. But when he was with Agnes, she made him feel that change was possible. She was the one who had witnessed his transformation in England, she was aware of his reputation in Canaries, the thing that the women who sat at the river used to say: 'De only time I see Raphael is when he holding up de bar in de rum shop or dancing drunk at de dance.'

The ladies at the river would find it hard to believe that Raphael was a hard-working man and not as reckless as before. Having to get to work each day was a responsibility he had never taken seriously until now, and he felt closer to becoming the man he knew he could be. Bernard had left his wife and three children in Grenada for England ready to work. 'Raphael, you have to keep your head straight. Dis ain't your country and if you go wrong dey put you in the locker and throw away de key.' Raphael knew his friend was right. He was quickly realising that you only got a few lucky chances, and your luck could run out at any time.

Waking up each morning with a hangover was not a good habit, but on those weekend nights, with no worry about an alarm clock ringing in his ear waking him for work the next morning, he cherished the freedom of being a weekend drinker. Surely there was nothing wrong with that, a working man had to let his hair down? What was it that the English said about all work and no play making Jack a dull boy? At some point

Island Song

he would have to choose between his drinking and Agnes, but until then, he was determined to try to enjoy both.

It was a crisp spring morning and the sunshine was fighting hard to break through from behind the clouds. When it finally did, it put a skip in Raphael's step as he headed towards the bus stop to travel to work. He turned round as he heard a voice hail him. 'Hey, Raph dat you?'

'Scottie?' It had been weeks since he'd last seen or spoken to Scottie. Linus had given Raphael a good dressing down after he'd partied the night away instead of tending to dinner, and now he was trying to keep in his brother's good books. Things had picked up at work, and Raphael was so tired when he got home, he barely had time to visit with anyone but Agnes. Scottie jogged over to him and shook Raphael's extended hand. 'I haven't seen you in a while man. Dat woman keepin' you occupied?' Scottie asked, grinning.

Raphael smiled back, though he didn't like the idea of Scottie thinking he was being pinned down by a woman, even if that woman was Agnes. He shook his head. 'Na, work, man. Dem keepin' me busy there. Plus I wouldn't say Agnes is my girl yet, I jus' like to spend time with her you know, but I hoping she will be more dan a fren' real soon.' Raphael did hope this was true; the last time he had collected his food, Agnes had let him steal a kiss. He'd felt a thrill as she returned his embrace before handing him his food and pushing him out of the door with a coy laugh.

Scottie nodded and chuckled at Raphael's comment about Agnes. 'Yes man, I have no doubt she will be more dan a fren' soon enough my brother, you have de charm for true, you have de charm. Plus dem bosses hav' us working so hard, and yet they still treat us like second-class citizens.'

Raphael thought back to the 'No Blacks, No Dogs, No Irish' signs all over town and the 'BLACKS GO HOME' message he knew those two white fellas had left for him and Bernard at work. The wall that they had to paint over and over again with emulsion. Covering the black paint, the disgusting words. Every brush stroke concealing the hatred now engrained in the brick. The thought of it still angered him.

'We need to do something about it, we gotta get ourselves organised, make sure we ready to look out for each other. We can't depend on de police to protect us so we mus' protect ourselves,' Scottie said, staring off into the distance. Raphael had some idea what his friend was talking about, but wanted to get a clearer understanding of who the 'we' or 'it' Scottie was referring to were. Before he could ask, Scottie continued, 'You should come over next Saturday evening. We can have a drink, play a couple rounds of dominoes. It will be good to get away from work and problems for one evening. Bring Linus too.'

Raphael thought about Agnes and how she wouldn't want him to go. She had planned to cook for him this Saturday night, and Raphael had been looking forward to spending some time with her, but now Scottie was putting some more of that temptation in his way . . . It had been so long since Raphael had hung out with just the boys, drinking and playing dominoes. Maybe he could stop by Scottie's just for one drink and then go over to Agnes's place afterwards.

He nodded, liking the idea of being able to have both the things in his life he enjoyed the most. 'Yeah, man, that sound good,' he finally answered. The two said their goodbyes, and Raphael continued his walk, feeling pleased with himself, and smiling at the prospect of the weekend to come. *Of course I can do both, see Scottie den Agnes. My weekend set, man I a lucky fella.*

* * *

Island Song

On Saturday afternoon, Raphael and Linus made their way to Scottie's place under the familiar grey London sky. But not even the grey sky and chill in the air could dampen Raphael's mood. First, a drink and a game of dominoes at Scottie's, and then a romantic night in with his girl. He had made every effort to look and smell fresh for her. His suit was old but pressed, his shirt was white and new, and for good measure he chose to wear his father's old tie. The unwashed fresh cotton felt prickly against his skin, but he ignored it. He had his trilby hat placed jauntily on his head – it was Saturday after all.

He had high hopes for the night ahead and was feeling optimistic and confident, light on his feet and upbeat as he thought about Agnes. 'I is a lucky man, I ain't going to be alone tonight!'

Linus was all dressed up too, looking forward to the afternoon's social gathering.

'You know what Raph, dis is de first time you and me get all dressed up on a boys' afternoon out, not sure why we all dress up for Scottie, but why not. It's good to be out of my work overalls.'

'Yeah man I realise dat too. You looking sharp my brother.' Linus didn't have the height or flare of his brother Raphael. He looked very much like their father who was stocky with strong shoulders, wide in the waistline, a round friendly face with the biggest smile, that they both inherited from their father.

'You hoping to get lucky Linus, because you know Scottie will have some of his girlfriends over for sure later dis evening.' Just as he said it Raphael was reminded with a stab from his conscience that he had a date with Agnes that he had to keep. 'You know I have to leave early to go and see Agnes.'

'Yeah man, you told me dat already. An' to be honest I wish I had a girl to cook for me and keep me company on de regular, you sure is a lucky man, Raph.'

When the two men arrived at Scottie's flat, Raphael could see that Scottie had already started drinking. Scottie worked hard, but Linus and Raphael knew that he played hard too. Some of the stories he told them of his weekend exploits made Raphael's head buzz. Scottie seemed to have the stamina to do it all: work on London Transport, then party hard in his own time. He was passionate about politics and Raphael knew he spent time with some radical fellas in the Grove. Scottie enjoyed drinking too and Raphael could see that Scottie's eyes had already turned red, as his blood vessels filled with alcohol. Raphael suddenly felt the need for that heady feeling himself. 'You have a shot for us?'

'Always a shot for you, Raph! Come in my bruddas. Good to see you both, come in.'

As they entered the room, Raphael heard laughter coming from inside. 'Eh eh, you have company.'

Sitting on the edge of the bed was a woman with green eyes and porcelain-white skin, her most striking feature her waist-length black hair, and she wore a green dress which matched the colour of her eyes. Raphael and Linus exchanged glances. Raphael knew that Scottie liked girls and a good time, but he hadn't been expecting to see any female company until later that night. Raphael had assumed it would be a game of dominoes and drinks with the boys, and the girls would come later.

'Good to see you both,' Scottie said motioning them over to the table. He poured two shot glasses of whisky. 'Here you go my friends, here's to us.'

Linus and Raphael took the shots and the three men tapped glasses before drinking. Then Scottie turned to the woman sitting on the bed, who seemed be at home in the room, as if she had been here many times before, and very much at ease with three men. 'This is Theresa. I've told her about my friends from St Lucia.'

'Saint Loo-sha? Is that near Trinidad, Scottie?' The woman spoke with the rounded vowels they had come to recognise as what the English people they worked with would have called 'posh'.

When Raphael and Linus shot sidelong glances at each other again, Scottie chuckled. 'Theresa's my girl.'

Raphael had no idea how Scottie had become involved with a high-class girl like Theresa. Everyone knew Scottie, who had an eye for the ladies, and Scottie was known for going from one girl to the next like a rolling stone. There was a time when he'd have been as keen as Scottie to get out on the town and make some new lady friends too. Raphael could hear the voice of his friend and mentor, Bernard, in his head: 'Leave dat recklessness alone.'

Yes, Scottie liked the high life and fast girls at the weekend, why shouldn't he, he worked hard for it. But Raphael was a changed man now, he told himself. Then Theresa spoke and brought his thoughts back to the present. Raphael was intrigued, where did she come from, how did Scottie meet her?

'One day, I want to visit this island of yours,' Theresa said. Her voice was languid, yet rich; minimum effort, maximum effect and Raphael felt temptation tap on his shoulder.

'It's a beautiful place. You'd enjoy it very much,' Raphael said, trying to shrug off the feeling of being overwhelmed by the woman's cool directness, enhanced by the fact that she looked him straight in the eye as she spoke, almost as if she knew the effect she was having on him.

'It's great having you boys over here. You lot have really livened up the place. You should come out with us later. Let's hit the town!'

Scottie reached for the bottle and poured them all another round of shots.

Scottie returned to the table and sat. 'Before we go anywhere, we need another shot and a game or two of dominoes. You ready to get beat? I'm gonna give you some licks.'

Raphael knew it was getting late, knew Agnes would be expecting him soon. But he had time for one more shot, he reasoned. The domino tiles clacked on the table as Scottie overturned the case and began mixing the tiles. One more game couldn't hurt. Agnes wouldn't mind if he was a little late. He made a mental note to stop and pick up some flowers on his way over. The dark liquor slid down his throat like sweet nectar.

An hour later, the bottle of whisky was almost finished. Scottie picked up the bottle and poured the dregs. Scottie's music collection wasn't much to get excited about except for one precious record that Scottie was happy to hear on repeat. It was now being played on a Technics suitcase record player, the mono muffled sound coming out of the lid of the case. 'Man, I never get fed up of dis record, my island song, Trinidad steel pan, Calypso meringue! I would dance wit you Theresa but I tink I have to stay at de table, I got a winning hand to beat Raphael. Hey Linus, I give you permission to dance wit my girl.' Raphael watched Theresa from the corner of his eye as she tried to find the beat of the music, Linus stood unsteadily, moving his arms and his shoulders to the rhythm, standing on the spot and moving his hips side to side. Raphael could see that Theresa was a beautiful woman, her long black hair swaying as she moved. To get up and dance and not care that anyone was looking, showed a confidence any man would find sexy.

Linus eventually held his hand up and shook his head. 'Na, man, I need my bed,' he slurred. Everyone could see Linus had had enough. A good night of whisky drinking, the first in a long time and Linus's bed was calling him. He swayed across the room, retrieved his coat from the bed and headed for the door. 'Hey, what a great afternoon and now de evening brings it to a close my friends! I will join you next time, Scottie, and it was nice to meet you too sweet Theresa.'

'Linus, it was lovely meeting you too and I hope we meet again.'

Theresa walked behind Scottie who was still seated at the table with Raphael. She wrapped her arms around her man and said, 'Scottie why don't we make a move? Our guests and Annie will be waiting for us at the 101.'

Raphael was intrigued. 'What de 101?'

'Raph, how come you don't know the 101, where you bin man? 101 has the best-looking girls and some sweet jive music, and it don't matter where you from in the world, everyone welcome. It's your kinda place. I know you love to dance. When de last time you dance? Come wit us. You would get along with Annie.'

Theresa stood and put on her brown bearskin overcoat, Raphael and Scottie quickly followed. Raphael was excited in a way he had not been in a while. The anticipation of what the night had to offer, along with the alcohol coursing through his veins, made his heart race. He knew Agnes would be upset with him for having too much to drink, plus he was already late. *I bes' stay out, I'll make it up to her.*

'No walking for you tonight, Raphael.' Theresa unlocked the door to her sleek black Wolseley, and Scottie opened the passenger side.

'Jump in the back, Raph.'

Raphael took his hat off so as not to knock it off his head. He eased himself into the back seat feeling like a king as he spread himself out on the leather seat, thoughts of Agnes slipping away.

* * *

The night club was jumping. The live band on the small stage was playing Wild Jimmy Spruill's 'Scratch 'n' Twist'. The drummer was beating his drums like his life depended on it. The double bass, piano player, guitarist and trumpeter were pumping their instruments keeping the music piping hot. Tables were pushed aside to make as much space for the dance floor as possible. It was a wild scene, bodies in motion in all directions, moving as if there was fire under their feet. The dance craze of the moment was The Twist, dancers twisting from side to side, moving up, down around and over each other. Women moving untamed, shoeless, to make sure they got the full spin on their stockinged feet. Raphael had never seen such an orgy of fun on a dance floor, and his feet were eager to join in. As Scottie and Theresa made their way into the crowded space, it was obvious Theresa was a regular at the 101. The maître d' approached and greeted them. 'Good evening, Ms Morrison, we have your favourite table. Your guests have arrived, they are already seated with drinks as you requested.'

'Thank you. Has Annie arrived?'

'Yes, she is with your party.'

'Marvellous!'

The maître d' took them to their table where another girl was chatting to some other white men, who departed as they approached.

Theresa introduced Raphael to the girl who gave him a little wave and a smile. 'This is Annie. Annie, this here is my new friend Raphael. He is from the West Indies too, but a different island, Saint Lucia.' With the tip of his hat, Raphael said hello to the attractive Annie, who had blonde hair and blue eyes. She was wearing a tight scarlet dress with bright red lipstick to match.

They took a seat.

Raphael looked around him, a feeling of euphoria urging

him onto the dance floor, the band now playing a sultry cover of Ray Conniff's 'Twist'. Some couples were dancing close together and others Twisting in a slower more sensual display. Sitting when music like this was playing was making Raphael's feet itch, but he wanted to be polite.

'This place is jumping tonight, Scottie, come on let's dance!' Theresa grabbed Scottie by the hand and pulled him towards the dance floor, where they shimmied together, their bodies close together and perfectly in sync. *Dey make a handsome couple*, Raphael thought to himself, pulling at his tie to loosen it.

His attention was distracted when Annie rested her hand on his leg under the table, leaning in so close that he could smell her musky perfume, 'Would you like to dance with me, Raphael, I'm sure you're quite the dancer yourself?'

Raphael downed the full shot glass in front of him in a single gulp and stood and reached his hand out to guide Annie away from the table.

They made their way to the small black-and-white-tiled dance floor and saw Scottie and Theresa. Scottie grinned at the sight of Raphael's arm around Annie.

For a brief moment, he wondered about Agnes waiting for him to arrive at Fernhead Road, and was momentarily troubled, but Annie tightened her hold on his waist, moving her body close to his and as he wrapped his hands around her waist in turn, he felt the thought loosening from his mind.

Yes, a working man deserves to have a good time.

And as he danced the night away with Annie, Raphael Toussaint didn't give Agnes Deterville another thought.

It was the shaft of sunlight coming through the curtains that woke Raphael the next morning. That and the foul taste in his mouth.

When he felt movement next to him, he turned to his left and discovered blonde hair sticking out above the sheets.

Annie.

She turned away from him, pulling the sheets with her as she did. He flinched when the cold air hit his skin. He raised his head, quickly realising he wasn't wearing any trousers and his underpants were still around his right ankle.

He raised his head and flopped it right down again, using his arm to cover his eyes as the room spun around and nausea rose in his throat. 'Oh man.' His head pounded and he needed a drink of water. He slowly peeled his way out of the bed and looked around the room. It was messy and cluttered, and clothes and shoes were strewn around it, but there were expensive items in it too, a smart dressing table and matching wardrobe with a full-length mirror as well as a velvet-covered armchair.

He found the rest of his clothes and got dressed, then, stepping over Annie's fur coat which was sprawled across the floor, quietly opened the door and left the room, glancing guiltily back at Annie's sleeping form one last time before he closed the door behind him.

He had no idea where he was, but thankfully, the house was quiet when he crept into the hallway. All he could focus on was his parched mouth and fulfilling his burning desire for a glass of water, which would immediately be followed by an exit out the front door. The house seemed enormous; he passed four closed doors before finding the staircase down. There was a door open at the bottom of the stairs. He walked into the room, and it looked like a bomb had hit it, but like Annie's room, it had the air of being owned by someone with money, if not any desire to keep the place neat and tidy.

He noticed Theresa's coat flung over an armchair, and a flashback from the wild night before came to Raphael's mind.

The image of her laughing and cajoling her house guests. He could still hear her voice ringing in his ears. 'Let's get wild, Daddy O. You sure can move, Raphael!' He found what looked like a carafe of water sitting on a table next to an almost empty bottle of whisky. He downed the water straight from the jug. As he put it back down, water dripped from the side of his mouth. He made the mistake of looking at the bottle of Scotch. The amber liquid instantly made him feel nauseous again and he felt the bile rise once more.

He turned and made his way to the front door, which mercifully opened and closed almost silently. As he walked down the steps he recognised Theresa's car parked in front of the house and realised he was on one of the grand Georgian streets in Bayswater that had seen better days. At this hour, the only people on the street were the early morning workers waiting soberly for their buses.

Under his breath he said, 'No Wolseley ride for me today, time to walk home an let de fresh air clear me head.'

With every step home, the journey cleared the fog from his mind and the nausea from his throat. It was Sunday morning, and though he wasn't sure what time it was, he could tell by the level of activity in the streets that most of the residents were still in their beds. He was hoping the same of Linus, still in his bed nursing his own hangover.

As he approached home, Agnes came into his mind. He felt a tight knot of guilt clutch around his being, and he knew she had every right to be furious with him, if not dump him altogether, killing their romance before it had got properly started. He knew Bernard would call him a fool. Getting tangled up with Scottie's drinking and women was a mistake, and Raphael now knew in his bones that he should have left with Linus before things got out of hand. The feeling of regret started to build from the pit of his stomach. The thought of

Annie made him feel uneasy. It was one thing not to show up for his dinner with Agnes, but if she knew he'd been with another woman . . . The thought of her finding out and what it would mean made him feel even more nauseous. He shivered with a cold sweat.

He could go to Agnes now if he could and apologise, but he knew he smelt of booze and sex and he desperately wanted to wash that feeling off himself, almost as if he could wash away his debauchery.

Raphael cursed the drink. He wanted to get back to feeling good about himself, the man that was hard-working and responsible. The man who had some clarity in his life for the first time. He had to find a way of existing without needing to find joy in a bottle of booze and nights spent with women he had no intention of seeing the next day.

As Raphael put his key in the door he said to himself, *I leaving all dat foolishness behind me now.* As the door opened he could smell bacon – Linus was up already and making breakfast. Raphael was happy to be back in his humble surroundings, but first he'd have to face his brother.

Agnes decided not to throw away the food that had sat in the cold oven all night waiting for Raphael to eat it, it had cost money that was precious. She had seasoned the chicken, the potatoes and peas with love. *I am never cooking for dat man again!* She decided to keep the food covered to eat it later. *It might choke in my throat, but I will never throw away a good plate of food.* She felt tired, it was hard to get to sleep, her anger kept her awake. She felt such a fool. *I thought Raphael was different but he's still the same, untrustworthy and unreliable. Dey never change. Vince, Raphael all of dem de same.*

Agnes looked in the bathroom mirror and could see her lips were still tainted by the red lipstick she wore to impress

Raphael the night before, she felt such a fool to have opened her heart to him. *I should be finking about my children not about man!* She took her wet cotton flannel and started to wash her face removing any evidence of her efforts to beautify herself for a man who was unreliable and didn't appreciate her. With every wipe of the flannel her eyes filled with tears. She felt ashamed that she had let herself and her family down in believing Raphael was a different kind of man.

CHAPTER NINETEEN

It was Agnes's first Easter Sunday in England, it had been almost almost six weeks since she had left St Lucia, and she was determined to go to church. Easter celebrated the death and resurrection of Christ, and the period's themes of renewal always gave Agnes a revitalised commitment towards her faith.

Agnes reflected on this as she looked out of her small bedroom window. The sun was not as bright as she would like. The weather was something Agnes never gave much thought to back home, other than the remote possibility of a hurricane in that season. But now, in England, it affected her mood when the cold and damp was in the air.

On this day, however, come rain or shine, nothing was going to stop her from attending mass wearing the bright yellow dress that Ella had made for her. The pretty fabric that Mrs Chester had gifted her still brought her so much pleasure. It lifted her spirits every time she looked at the cloth. As she brushed down the dress's pleats, she observed with great concentration the printed palm trees and lush mountain scene, and it made her smile and brought a warm glow to her chest.

The image of Mrs Chester also came to mind, how excited she would be to see Agnes in her yellow dress. Would Agnes ever receive a letter back from her, she wondered? The enthusiasm that Mrs Chester had shown Agnes about one day arriving in England now felt like an illusion. Agnes was starting to feel it was just words. Words from a woman worlds apart from the life she was experiencing in and around Fernhead Road.

Margaret called out, 'Agnes you ready!' It was more of a statement than a question. Margaret was such a positive addition to Agnes's life. She could be bossy, but her demands were for the betterment and comfort of her living companions: 'Vitalis, always put de toilet seat down, dere are women living in de house! Agnes, make sure you put the pot back in its place so we always know where to find it.'

It was Margaret who helped Agnes snap out of the anger and disappointment she felt about Raphael. '*Gadé mwen*, look at me, Agnes. Take your min' off him and concentrate on getting a job so you can send money for your family and when he comes to the door jus' hand him his food and close de door in his face, he can't treat you dat way! An' he will soon come to realise he did you wrong. You have travelled too far, remember why you here! You hear what I telling you?'

'*Mwen tann ou*, I hear you, Margaret.'

'I comin!' Agnes replied, knocked clean out of her daydreaming by Margaret's booming voice. She grabbed her overcoat, handbag and gloves and made her way down the stairs where Margaret was waiting.

'Vitalis not coming to church?' Agnes asked as she put on her gloves.

Margaret responded with a loud, 'Chewps. My husban, goin to church? Vitalis prefer to stay in bed. He ask me to light a candle for his mother. I say he should do that himself if he want it to mean anything at all, but he said he tired and roll over to show me his back! Chewps.'

As the women made their way to the church, they talked about how they were trying hard to get used to everything about Britain and three things that were on top of their list. Firstly, the weather, secondly, how hard it was to find staple West Indian food and spices and thirdly, the serious matter of work. Agnes had yet to find a job and was still cooking and cleaning for Margaret and Vitalis while also preparing food for Linus and Raphael. This was her way of earning a little cash to keep herself afloat. She had taken Margaret's advice and at first it was satisfying to close the door in Raphael's face when he came to collect his bagged food, as he tried to engage her in conversation with a pitiful look upon his face that just riled her even more. He could be under no illusion how upset she was at him for not turning up for dinner.

Margaret was now working as a cook at a hotel restaurant, but her road to finding work had brought its own set of challenges. Before she'd got the job at the hotel, Margaret had worked at a café for a day and had returned home and announced she wouldn't be returning there. She hadn't spoken of it since.

Now, with Easter's theme of healing and renewal, Agnes wondered if Margaret was finally ready to talk about it. 'What happened with the café job, Margaret, it would be good to get it off your chest today.'

Margaret took a deep breath, 'God knows you probably right,' and began to explain. 'It was the labour exchange dat sent me for de job. Well, when I reach at de café in Victoria, near de station, it was so busy de manager asks me to work straight away. So I was a waitress for one day. I know I did a good job, considering it was my first time working as a waitress.

Island Song

Taking orders, clearing and wiping tables. And by de end of de day, I was washing dishes too. I worked hard to show I could do de job. And as de door closed behind de last customer, de manager thank me for my hard work.'

Margaret paused and shook her head before continuing. 'But she said she would not be asking me back. Agnes, I was so surprised. I ask de lady what wrong with me? I work hard all day, and I do what was asked of me. An' you know what de lady say?' When Agnes shook her head, Margaret continued. '"You are just not suitable for our establishment." Dat's when I have to calm myself because I was starting to get vex. So I ask her again, what is wrong with me, what did I do wrong? Den she said, "Our regular customers were not happy to be served by you. If it was up to me, I would have you stay, but our customers are very important to us." Well, I spell it out for her, Agnes. I say, "Oh, so I too dark for your customers? You prefer I hide in de back?" She tell me not to take dat tone with her and she ask me to leave. Le' me tell you, I take my bag and I slammed the door behind me.'

Agnes was shocked, but kept silent, letting Margaret speak.

'Remember when de boys at school used to call me names just because I was not a *shabine*, not light skinned. My mother used to tell me dey were ignorant. Now I am in England, and the same small-mindedness find me here. And it's worse because I thought people in England would not be as small-minded. That they would judge me on my manners, how hard I work and my character, but dey jus as ignorant as those foo foo boys in Canaries. But I could not give up Agnes, I know someone would give me job, I will never give up on myself and look, now I am working in a hotel kitchen. And you know what Agnes?'

'What, Margaret?'

'I am grateful I didn't do de job in the café because it made me *more* determined and it help build my strength. So never forget Agnes, everything dat don't go right will give you de strength for another day.'

Agnes linked arms with Margaret as they walked. 'Margaret, I'm proud of you for standing up for yourself, I don't know if I could be as brave.' Agnes hoped if she was to experience any prejudice, she would be just as fearless, like her friend. She recollected some of the stories she had heard on the voyage across the Atlantic. Some of the passengers had talked about letters they had received from family members already in England: 'My brother is living in a place call Reading, he write and tell me one day a white man call him a Coon. My brother say he jus' laugh in de man face, he never hear such a word but later he fin' out it was offensive, it's like calling a man an animal. My brother get so vex once he fin' out. Dease people in England can be ignorant, so we need to stay close to our own people to feel safe.' It scared Agnes to be thought of as an animal. This was not the England Mrs Chester spoke about. She could hear Ella's voice: 'I told you so Agnes, it's not as de lady tell you.'

When they finally arrived at the church, Agnes was welcomed with the scent of frankincense. She made the sign of cross and then followed Margaret down the middle aisle to the third pew from the front. Margaret stopped abruptly at the end of the wooden bench and directed Agnes to sit next to her. There was no one else seated in the pew. With a whisper Margaret explained her seating choice. 'It best we sit here, because it's not far to go to line up for Holy Communion.'

Although she did notice a few brown faces scattered among the congregation, all in their Sunday best, Agnes had never seen so many white people in a church before. The altar looked magnificent with a bright white cloth spread across it, crisp without a crease, and adorned with gold candlestick holders along with an array of bountiful flowers in vases. Agnes was impressed. Gracing the back wall was a large gold crucifix. Agnes was humbled by the image of Christ nailed to the cross. She lowered her head and began to pray.

Despite the church service not being as vibrant and joyful as mass at her church in Canaries, Agnes sang the hymns in her usual way, in full voice. Margaret accompanied her with the same spirit and vigour. They soon realised they had the loudest voices in the church hall. When they were sure they heard a 'shush' directed at them, they looked at each other and quickly lowered their volume.

By taking the Holy Communion, Agnes felt she was forgiven for not observing Lent and the fasting she would have done with her sister this year. As she took the bread and her sip of wine from the large gold goblet, her children and her sister came to mind. Agnes prayed every morning, and now in the presence of the cross she communed once again. Holding her rosary tightly she prayed that her children carried no resentment towards her for leaving them behind. This guilty feeling was so hard to shake, and it was the only prayer that helped to soothe her anguish.

After mass Agnes and Margaret were greeted on the steps by Linus. '*Bonjou, bonjou!* Good morning, good morning! It's so good to see you both.'

'Linus you lookin good and a little heavier than I remember. Looks like England suit you!'

'Well, Ms Agnes it's all dat good food you cooking for me and Raphael.' To compliment a West Indian woman's cooking was one of the highest praises anyone could give, but the mention of Raphael's name made Agnes feel instantly uncomfortable.

Margaret decided to ask about his brother. 'Raphael not coming to church?'

'No Ms Margaret, his bed was holding him back.' Linus chuckled at his own comment.

'*Ou ca wi!* You laughing! It's no laughing matter, Linus. Raphael need to come and repent for all his wrongdoing and hurting Agnes,' Margaret said angrily.

Agnes could feel her face turning red, she felt embarrassed but pleased that her friend was speaking up for her.

This wiped the smile of Linus's face. 'I'm sorry to hear dat Ms Margaret but since dat time Raphael ain't bin himself, he knows he did wrong.'

Agnes found her voice. 'Well let him know I am happy he not feeling good about himself. He left me sitting waiting for him, Raphael, *I kouyon!* He's an idiot!'

Margaret, seeing that things were getting heated, attempted to calm down the situation that she had instigated. 'Okay Agnes, it's Sunday and we are good Christian people and we have to show our strength in forgiveness and show him what kin' of woman you are, dat he must not take advantage of your kindness. Look at us all de way in England, we must support each other. Raphael needs to remember what kind of people we are and come and say sorry to Agnes.' Agnes opened her eyes wide at Margaret and turned her head away giving a very loud 'CHEWPS!'

Margaret wasn't finished with her peace mission.

'Agnes made a big pot of pumpkin soup and some accras. Come and enjoy dat with us and bring your brother with you.'

The morning could not get any worse for Agnes. She was so surprised that Margaret had extended the invitation, another loud 'CHEWPS' came out of her mouth. Linus responded with great enthusiasm, mainly at the menu.

In amazement Linus asked, 'You find salt fish for your accras? Ms Margaret, I have not had dat since I bin here!'

'I manage to get it from the hotel I'm working. I see a box

Island Song

looking sad in the corner of de kitchen. I open it and see it salted fish. I ask the chef what he doing with it, he tell me he never use salt fish before on de menu. So, I tell him if I show him how to make accra, will he allow me to take some home for Sunday? He tell me, "Dat's a deal Margaret!" So I make some for him, he tell me he never taste anything like dat but he don't fink he can put it on de menu for his customers, so he tell me to take the box. I have some at home I can give you.'

'Well, well Ms Margaret you making my mouth water!' Linus was rubbing his hands at the prospect of food. 'Dat will get Raphael out of his bed and I will make sure he come and tell you sorry before he put a spoon of food in his mouth Ms Agnes.'

Agnes looked forward to that, but she was annoyed at Margaret for extending the invitation. Linus moved in haste down from the steps of the church, hurrying to give Raphael the good news. Before Agnes had a chance to voice her annoyance, Margaret spoke. 'Agnes you might be feeling upset with me, but until you face Raphael I know you will not feel right in yourself, because since dat time you have bin looking *faché*, upset.'

Margaret was right, she could not get Raphael out of her mind. It had taken her back to her broken relationship with Vince. *Dease men, all dey do is let me down.*

The sun came out for Agnes and Margaret as they walked back to Fernhead Road and Agnes's frustration with Margaret quickly subsided, knowing she meant well in her actions.

Agnes wondered what Ella would be doing on this Sunday. She would be at church with the children, she would have made soup for them. Agnes hoped Tina and Charles would be well-behaved and eat what Ella put in front of them. She was so far away from them now. She was soothed only by the springtime sunshine on her shoulders and the sunlight on her yellow dress.

Not long after, there was a knock at the door. Agnes wanted to go and hide in her bedroom, but she knew she had to face Raphael, and stood her ground at the sink, comforted by looking at the table on which Margaret had placed a new tablecloth, and a new set of drinking glasses and plates. Linus was the first to enter the kitchen. 'Hello Agnes, ah Raphael wants to talk to you outside.' Agnes moved from her safe spot with arms still crossed in front of her. She made her way to the front door to find Raphael standing on the doorstep.

'Hello Agnes, it's good to see you.' Raphael held his hat in his hands, twisting it nervously around by the brim.

She chose not to answer, but looked him straight in the face, her own still fierce, with a look that told him she was still vexed with him.

'I hope you don't close de door in my face dis time.' He fumbled with the hat, but met her eyes with his own, which looked baleful and contrite. 'Um I want to say sorry Agnes, sorry for leaving you waiting for me. I'm sorry I did dat. It was Scottie dat—'

Agnes interrupted him. 'Scottie? You cah blame anyone for your actions. I waited all night. I thought something bad happen to you. I cah trus' you Raphael. I thought you had change your ways? But no you still that same *sakwé kouyon*, damn fool, from Canaries.'

'NO, dat not true, I have changed, I am not de fool you make me out to be Agnes, well not all de time . . . Since dat Friday, I have been working, not drinking or going out. An' . . . I miss you Agnes.'

'You miss me, what you miss? You still picking up your food, what you miss?'

'I miss sitting with you and talking and making you laugh. And I miss kissing you.'

'Kissing me? I only let you do dat once. An don't fink I go

let you do dat again. I am here to find work Raphael not play around with man.'

'You make me a better man Agnes, you make me realise my foolish ways. No woman has ever done dat for me before. *Mwen bizwen ou adan lavi mwen.* I need you in my life.' Agnes stood staring at Raphael, remembering she had to be strong, kind but not foolish. He did look lost, she missed him too, but she wasn't going to let him off easy.

'I don't have time for your *papicho*, foolishness. You have all the right words, but I find it hard to believe you. You let me down, Raphael.'

Agnes took a beat. 'I want to hear you say sorry again, like you really mean it.'

Raphael stood taller, and looked her straight in the eyes. 'I'm real sorry, Agnes. I have been a kind of a ways with myself since that day. I know I did you wrong. Please forgive me.' His pleading eyes spoke as much as his words. Agnes opened the door wider as an unspoken invitation for Raphael to come into the house. When he didn't move, she said boldly, '*Antwé!* Come in!'

A few hours later and everyone was sitting at the table with their bowls and plates licked clean. Raphael was quiet through most of the meal but as he sat back in his chair, she could tell he enjoyed it too. He caught her looking at him and smiled at her. Agnes looked away, but he could see that she blushed.

Vitalis leaned back and rubbed his stomach. 'Agnes you can make dat pumpkin soup again anytime and dat accra! Woi, dat was goood! All dat was missing was the hot sauce my mother used to make.'

Vitalis continued talking as he started to rise from his seat: 'I hope the next cousin I meet at Waterloo station they come wit a big bag of scotch bonnet for me so I can make some serious hot sauce.' He went to a cupboard and pulled out a large bottle of liquor. 'Dis bottle of rum travel with me over de seas from St Lucia and I fink this is a good occasion to have a shot or two.' At this point, Agnes expected Margaret to disapprove, but she just rose from the table and went to a cupboard to collect some shot glasses and placed them on the table in front of each person. 'Not every day you have friends from home at your table, let us raise a glass to ourselves for making it to England.' Agnes was not a drinker, but felt this was a moment to have a shot to celebrate and to show Raphael she was no prude, it was a special day, after all. 'Cheers, and as they say in England, bottoms up!'

Raphael only had the one shot of rum that evening, to show Agnes he meant business, and as he put his hat on and headed for the door, Agnes followed him. Linus, sensing they wanted a moment together, kissed Agnes on the side of her cheek.

'Tanks to you, Agnes, dat was a meal dat take me home for a few hours.'

He headed into the street, lighting a cigarette as he waited by the front garden wall for Raphael.

'You got a kiss for me Raphael?' Agnes said, and he moved to kiss her cheek too, but Agnes turned her face towards him and they fell into an embrace.

Pulling away, Raphael grinned. 'You my girl now, Agnes.'

She smiled, 'As long as there no more foolishness.'

As Raphael headed home with Linus, he wanted to run and jump with joy. Agnes was his girl and there would definitely be no more shenanigans, and he told himself he really meant it this time.

CHAPTER TWENTY

Raphael rang Agnes's doorbell at five o'clock on the dot a few days later. '*Raph mwé ca twavay!* Raph, I am working!'

Raphael didn't even get the chance to walk into the hallway, as Agnes was standing in front of him blocking his entrance. He felt instantly infected by her excitement. 'Hold on, what you say, did I hear you right? You have a job?'

'*Wi!* Yes! I have a job,' she said, in her best British accent making him smile. Agnes could get very animated and jovial once she let her guard down. It was one of the many things he loved about her.

'I am working at Maison Lyons Corner House in Marble Arch . . . *way papa!*' She clapped her hands in excitement. 'I went to the labour exchange this morning and they told me they are looking for kitchen staff for the tea house, so I went straight away. I tell them I can make tea, but for now they want me to be a dishwasher. The lady tell me it's an important job because, what was it she say . . . Oh yes, "We have hundreds of customers every day and clean dishes and teacups are essential for the smooth running of the service.'"

Raphael managed to finally make his way over the threshold and into the hallway and slipped passed Agnes, heading for the kitchen. She continued to chatter behind him.

'I have to start tomorrow!'

'Tomorrow?' Raphael said, stopping in his tracks. 'Who is going to make the food for me and Linus?'

'So Raphael dat's all you can say to me? Who's going to cook your food? Dat all I'm good for!'

Raphael could see the sparkle and excitement in Agnes's eyes. She looked beautiful. He hadn't meant to snap at her and sound so selfish.

'I am happy for you.' Raphael told himself he was happy for her, but he wanted to spend more time with her, and not just to collect the meals. His feelings for her had continued to grow over the past several weeks. But now that she was a working woman, this meant she would be more independent and less available for him. 'I know you have bin waiting to get a job. When you start making money, maybe you will forget about me?'

Agnes responded surprised.

'Eh eh Raph! You making out I going to another country. Yes, I will have to work hard and de money I'm making is not jus for me it's for my family. Eh eh Raph jus' be happy for me!' Agnes had told him that she wanted to work to become more independent, earning a wage so she could support Ella and her children in Canaries. It had been her main reason for leaving her family and coming to England, after all.

'Maybe you will forget me and meet another man? You a good woman, I don't want to lose you.'

'You will lose me where? As long as you are good to me, I'm good to you and I'm not going nowhere.'

He and Scottie had never discussed the night Raphael had spent with Annie, though he was sure Scottie knew. Scottie still kept inviting Raphael round for whisky and dominoes, but to avoid temptation, Raphael would only agree to go if there were no girls present. If there were, he would find a reason to politely decline the invitation.

He hoped that Agnes would see the change in him during their regular visits. He didn't want to be a player any more, he wanted to leave those easy, good-time girls alone, but he could not deny that a spark of wildness flickered inside him when he thought about them. He knew he had to learn to regulate his impulses and stick to the vow he made to himself. *'Awa,* no longer. *Pa ankò,* no more.

'So when will I see you? You on shift work? Let me take you out to celebrate. Let me take you to the cinema.'

'Well, Raph I don't know, I starting the job tomorrow so I will find out everything in the morning.' Raphael removed his cap and started scratching his head. He was searching for more questions to ask. 'What time you have to be at work? I fink the 36 bus pass Marble Arch, dat's my bus, I can walk with you to the bus stop in the morning, I get the 6.30.'

'All I know is, I have to be at the job for 7.30 and de rest of your questions I can't answer now.'

Raphael was aware of Agnes watching him and tried to look less vexed. But he must not have succeeded, because Agnes took a deep breath and softened her voice.

'I can see you're tired from your day's work, Raph. Take the food home while it's still warm. I will talk to a girl I know who might be able to cook the food for you and Linus. I will let you know in the morning when we catch the bus together, and you can show me the way. A trip to de cinema, would be nice, but I will let you know when, okay?'

Raphael smiled, this time for real. 'Okay. You know, Agnes, you are my kinda girl.'

It was still dark outside when Agnes made her way down to the kitchen the next morning to make some tea. It felt strange and quiet. As she sat listening to the kettle boil, she closed her eyes and prayed, 'Oh Lord, I thank you for this opportunity. I want to be the best at my job. Guide me oh Lord, and light my way towards good fortune so I can look after my family. And, oh Lord, keep me safe in dis big city called London.' She was awoken from her contemplation by the boiling kettle calling her back to the here and now.

Her mind wandered to the day before. She had been so happy to share the news of her new job with Raphael. But he hadn't responded the way she had hoped he would.

The truth was, she could not ignore that she had strong feelings for him. Nevertheless, she wanted to do things differently this time, she wanted to enjoy the independence of making her own money and not feeling obligated to anyone, like she had felt with Vince, who'd had all the right words but no commitment.

She dressed carefully, wanting to make a good impression on her first day at Lyons. She had decided to wear the navy-blue dress Ella had made for her, but she knew her flat black shoes let the whole look down. As she put the final touches to her hair, and added a little slick of lipstick, she decided that with her first wage packet, she would purchase more fashionable kitten-heeled shoes and a new overcoat. She had considered wearing her mother's coat that Ella had given her, but she wanted to keep it for special occasions.

She heard tapping on the glass door and could see Raphael moving around outside. Agnes opened the door. '*Bonjou*, good morning, Raph.'

'*Bonjou, Bonjou. Gadé belle,* looking beautiful, Agnes.'

'*Mèsi,* thank you, Raph.' Agnes felt her skin turn hot with nervous excitement.

'Let's go, let's go, I don't want to be late on my first day at work!' she said, barely able to contain her excitement.

Raphael seemed taken aback by Agnes's energy so early in the morning. He was never lively in the mornings.

As the bus moved briskly along the road, Raphael could see Agnes was wide-eyed as she took in the changing scenes from the bus. In her smart clothes, he thought she looked just as good, if not better, than some of the English girls heading to their office jobs.

'Okay, Agnes, your stop coming up. Don't forget to ring the bell.'

Agnes turned to Raphael with a knowing smile and responded in a hushed voice. 'Yes, I know, I've been to Edgware Road before.'

'Next stop Marble Arch!' the conductor announced, and Agnes stood up and pulled the string for the bell.

Raphael rose from his seat, allowing Agnes to pass and get off at her stop. He watched her walk quickly away, hoping that her first day was as good as she was dreaming it would be; she deserved it, but London had a habit of bringing disappointment.

Agnes felt she had got off to a bad start at the imposing Lyons Corner House. It was situated on the busy thoroughfare of Marble Arch, and even at this hour, the streets were thronged with workers and shoppers, all hustling and bustling to be somewhere.

The building itself, Maison Lyons, was much bigger than Agnes had expected, and had more than one entrance, which confused her. She entered through the main door at street level, only to be bustled out by a gentleman in a crisp white shirt and long black shirt-tailed jacket who told her in a hushed whisper to 'use the bloody staff entrance down the side, won't you!'

After following his directions, Agnes presented herself at the staff reception desk. The woman behind it looked over at her without smiling.

'Yes, what's your name?'

'Agnes Deterville, Ms, I've come to work, dey sent me from the labour exchange.'

The woman looked down at her ledger and this seemed to satisfy her. She spoke quickly: 'I'm Mrs Brown, and I'm in charge of all you new girls. Put a foot wrong and I'll find out about it. Don't be late, be polite and respectful, be fast and efficient and you and I will get along fine, now follow me.'

Agnes followed Mrs Brown, having to keep up with her through the maze of corridors, as she explained how the tea rooms operated. It seemed there were many floors, all decked out in different styles, and all with their own waiting staff and serving areas.

'You'll be in the kitchens where we make all the tea on this floor. It's always busy and you'll be run off your feet. I hope you're a fast learner.'

Agnes nodded, hoping she was too.

Mrs Brown showed her into a room that was full of lockers and benches for getting changed. 'There's your locker, Agnes. You will be sharing it with another girl on the next shift, so don't leave anything in there at the end of the day.'

'Yes, Ms Brown.'

'This is your staff uniform and your kitchen cap, which should be worn at all times back here in the staff area, and it's your responsibility to keep it clean. We deduct the payment for your uniform from your first wage packet. Get your bags in the locker, and you can put your uniform on over there. I'll be outside waiting so hurry along, won't you.'

Agnes removed her blue dress and folded it neatly on a chair. Slipping the white overall over her head she could smell the starched fabric. It was a little long, but that was something Agnes could fix. Despite the length, the dress fitted perfectly elsewhere and once she was dressed, she placed the white cap on her head as best she could, unsure how to keep it straight. She looked at herself in the mirror and found a different person looking back. She didn't have long to linger over her appearance however before Mrs Brown was calling to her from outside. 'Are you all right in there, Agnes, there's work to be done.'

She opened the door and presented herself for inspection.

'Turn around.' Mrs Brown looked Agnes up and down. 'Very good. I can see it fits you well. One of the girls will show you how to put your cap on properly so it doesn't fall off. You might need a few clips to keep it in place.'

Another woman entered the changing room and stood directly in front of Agnes, instantly scrutinising her in her uniform. She wore silver spectacles and stared at Agnes over the rim of her glasses. She seemed much older than Mrs Brown, and she had the manner of someone who had been at her job for a long time.

'This is Iris, your supervisor,' Mrs Brown said in the same brusque manner. 'She will take you to the tea station to show you your duties. It's a busy restaurant, so get to work. Chop chop!'

As Mrs Brown hurried off out of the changing area towards the restaurant, Iris turned to Agnes, regarding her with an interest that Mrs Brown didn't seem to have had for her new arrival. 'Hello, dear, follow me. What's your name?'

'Agnes, Agnes Deterville.'

'That's a lovely name. I had an aunt called Agnes. Unfortunately, she's no longer with us, bless her soul. I notice you have an accent, dear. Where are you from?'

'St Lucia,' Agnes replied.

'Is that somewhere in Spain?'

'No, Ms. It's in the West Indies.'

'That sounds very exotic. Do they drink tea there?'

'Yes, Ms, we drink tea. I used to make tea for Mr and Mrs Chestor. They are from Dorset.'

Iris arched her eyebrows. 'Dorset, oh my! You'll find the staff here a bit different, then. If I were you I'd leave your la-de-dah Dorset ideas at home, dearie.'

Agnes didn't know how to respond to the woman's sudden sharp words, and felt her mood slip further. 'Okay, Ms.'

Agnes followed Iris to the tea station, where there was a woman looking busy wiping teacups at the far end of one of the counters. 'Right, here we are, Agnes. Your job is to make sure the tea-urn is filled with piping hot water at all times. It only takes a few minutes to heat up the water, but you have to time it right so's you don't run out. Customers behind that door there in the restaurant drink gallons of tea all day long. Make sure you have your teapots lined up in a row, make sure you put two heaped spoons of the Maison Lyons Blend of tea in each pot, no more no less.'

Agnes surveyed the rows and rows of teapots along the gantry, and the giant urn that gave off clouds of steam that filled the air. 'I thought I was a dishwasher?'

'No, dear, you make tea. Now, if this tin of tea leaves starts to get low, ask me or one of the other girls to get you a fresh one from the storeroom. Place your pots here so they're easy to grab and fill at the urn. There will be a supply of clean teapots arriving from the downstairs kitchen about every fifteen minutes, depending on how busy it is. I'll keep my eyes on that.' Iris beckoned with her hand, calling forth the woman Agnes had seen working at the counter. She put her tea cloth down and made her way slowly over to them both. 'This is Katie. She's been holding the fort. You can't go wrong as long as you follow her instructions.' Katie gave Agnes a thin smile that soon disappeared into her plain face with grey eyes.

She looked sternly at Agnes as Agnes observed her. A few strands of dark brown hair had escaped from the back of her work cap, and were resting on her pearl-white neck. Her uniform was spotless and over her thin body, it looked as though it was wearing her. She wore no jewellery or make-up. Agnes found her hard to read, there was no friendly chat, she seemed aloof and cold.

It was overwhelming trying to take in all the information from Iris at once, especially when she had thought she would be washing dishes. She had never seen so many cups and saucers in one place and none of it had the delicacy of Mrs Chester's porcelain tea set, it was just plain white china painted with a gold rim.

With all the steam in the air she felt hot in her new uniform. The chiming of utensils, plates and glasses going into machines on the other side of the room was the soundtrack for the staff who were busy keeping the wheels of Lyons moving.

'The Nippies will pick up the teacups and trays from over there so no need to worry about that.'

'De Nippies? What is dat Ms?'

'They're the girls in the fancy waitress outfits, which I am sure one day you will want to wear. All the girls do, but without tea there's no tea house. This job is just as important. Ain't I right, Katie?'

'You're never wrong, Iris,' Katie said flatly. 'And who is this new arrival to the tea team, then?'

'This is Agnes from the West Indies, and I already know

she is going to fit in nicely. Don't she look pretty in her uniform. Though it looks like you need a few hair clips to keep your cap in place, Agnes. Katie, can you give Agnes a hand with that.'

Katie approached Agnes with two hair clips in hand, somewhat reluctantly. She arranged the cap on Agnes's head quickly and said, 'Now, that's better.' Katie stepped back and smiled. Agnes cautiously returned the smile, hopeful she might make her first friend at work. But as soon as Iris was out of earshot, Katie leaned in and whispered, 'I'm going to be a supervisor here soon, so you'd better keep on the right side of me, you understand?' There was a menacing tone to her voice, her words spoken so only Agnes could hear them.

Katie straightened, before raising her voice so Iris could hear. 'Don't she look a pretty picture, Iris?' She turned to Agnes with a smile that did not reach her eyes, which were hard and cold. 'Let's get to work, Agnes.'

Lyons Corner House had kept Agnes busy for her entire shift, she had no time to think about anything else other than the job at hand. Spooning tea leaves into pots, filling the teapots, and making sure the urns remained hot to create the perfect brew for the customers. Katie was responsible for taking the orders from the Nippy waitresses, making sure there were enough cups, saucers and teapots on the trays to take to the tables. Agnes completed every task put in front of her successfully, efficiently, and in no time she lost any feeling of being overwhelmed.

'Well done, Agnes, you worked very hard this morning. Now please wipe down the counters and make sure there are no wet areas on the floor.' Iris looked at her watch. 'It's now 10 o'clock and time for your break, make sure you are back at 10.15 so Katie can take hers. There's a clock in the staff canteen. Keep your eye on it and get back on time because we have to be ready for the busiest time of the day, lunchtime. You know where you're going?'

'Yes Ms Iris.'

Agnes managed to get a glimpse of the restaurant through the swing doors and it looked very busy already. This was more like the London that Mrs Chester had described to her. Table after table of paying customers eating and drinking from dainty teacups, served on white linen tablecloths in the elegant tea room; quite the contrast to the steamy back rooms where she was stationed.

The staff canteen was busy too, with Nippies drinking tea, smoking cigarettes and chatting, their laughter echoing up to the ceiling. Agnes decided to sit at a table on her own, and as she scanned the room was pleased to see a few brown faces amongst the staff.

She was soon interrupted by a friendly male voice behind her. 'Hello my dear, why you sitting on your own, you looking lonesome, can I join you?' Agnes had just taken a bite of her cheese sandwich and she had to swallow and take a swig of her water before she could answer.

'Um, yes, please sit if you want to.'

'Please don't choke yourself on my behalf. Plus ya mus' keep eating, you need to keep ya strength up to work in dis place. So, hello my dear, my name is Moses, I am de baker from Jamaica.'

Moses put his hand out to Agnes so they could shake hands. Agnes could feel his long slender fingers which were soft to the touch, his nails well-manicured.

'And who is dis pretty young lady I am talking to?'

'My name is Agnes Deterville and I am from St Lucia.'

'Ah St Lucia, I have been told dat de beautiful Josephine was born dere, de wife of de great conqueror Napoleon Bonaparte.'

'Really? My father told me she was born in Martinique, but had visited St Lucia many times.'

'Your farda might have been right but it don't matter, she was just lucky to have a powerful man at her side.' Agnes was amused by his comment. The man sitting opposite her had a long, elegant neck and held his head like nobility. His face looked fresh, but with a few grey hairs; it was hard for Agnes to tell how old he was. She enjoyed his air of playfulness. His elbow was resting on the table and his fingers were held in the air theatrically as if he was holding a cigarette.

'How long you bin working here Moses?'

Moses took in a deep breath before answering. 'Too long. I have been held captive to the Lyons oven as de baker for two whole years, but I do make de best buns, scones and bread rolls you will ever taste. If you meet me here at dis table tomorrow I will make sure I bring you some to try.' Agnes already looked forward to the next day's tea break, feeling sure she had just made a friend.

'Well, well look at de clock Ms Agnes, like you I have only a 15-minutes break. Now I have to get back to work and get my buns in the oven. So we have a date, same time, same place and don't you worry Ms Agnes I am after nothing other dan a friendly chat.' Moses was right, it was time to get a move on back to her tea station.

CHAPTER TWENTY-ONE

The cool evening breeze coming off the river was a welcome relief from the heat of the day. Ella sat on a bench at the back of the house. The cicadas and tree frogs were loudly chirping away in the trees. Tina and Charles were already in their beds. Ella was happy to have this moment alone to open the parcel from Agnes. It was getting dark out, so Ella adjusted the wick length of her trusty hurricane lamp so she could read the words under the warm glow. She admired her sibling's handwriting and the English stamps, which Ella had started to collect. Up until now, she had only received brief letters from Agnes, single sheets of airmail paper; this was the first parcel that had arrived from her sister.

Ella cut the string and pulled apart the brown paper. Within the package were three smaller parcels, one marked Ella, one Tina, and the other Charles. She squeezed the children's packages trying to guess what their gifts might be. She could definitely feel shoes in Tina's parcel and something soft. Charles's parcel rattled when she shook it. Maybe it was a toy wrapped in some other soft item. Ella looked forward to seeing the children's excited faces in the morning. She set their gifts aside and slowly unwrapped her own. Instantly, there was a sweet smell coming from inside the paper parcel. An envelope sat on top of a bundle of goodies, and before she delved in, she read Agnes's letter which contained three crisp British pound notes.

Agnes Deterville
63 Fernhead Road
London,
England.
31st July 1957

Dearest Ella,
I hope by the grace of God this letter finds you and the children happy and healthy. Thank you for your last letter and I am glad to know you are still working at the school and that the headmistress now has the money to pay you a little something each week. This is a blessing, as I know things remain hard in Canaries. I am happy to let you know my dear sister that I am working at the Lyons Corner House in Marble Arch. This is how I have managed to send you this parcel. This, too, is a blessing my sister.
The work is hard, the pay is good and I enjoy it. My manageress Mrs Brown told me I am doing a good job and Ms Iris, my supervisor she said I am a good addition to the tea team. The other girl I work with, her name is Katie, well I don't think she likes me because I do such a good job. I keep myself to myself and I try not to quarrel with her because I don't want to lose my job.
I am still living in the same house with Margaret and

Vitalis. They send their best wishes. I have a friend who you know from Canaries, Raphael Toussaint. He is a good man and he is working in construction.

Ella could not believe what she had just read. She had to glance over the words a second time, she was so stunned. *How did my sister get herself involved with Raphael Toussaint! Why she have to get herself tangled up with that man!* She continued to read.

Don't worry Ella he has changed his ways in England.

Ella stopped reading once again. 'Lord Jesus!' She quickly returned to the letter.

I won't make the same mistake I did with Vince. He is living with his brother Linus. I don't want you to worry. I wanted you to know this from me because I know how news travels fast to Canaries. We are nothing serious yet, but I like him and he has made it very clear that he likes me.
   You will be happy to know I have put money down on a sewing machine, it not as big as the one at home. Once I finish pay for it I want to buy cloth and make some dresses for Tina and a shirt for Charles, that is my wish. I am getting used to the weather, but at times the room I am in has a little damp and I catch a fwedee, a cold, but Margaret managed to get me a little ginger to make hot tea and it helps a lot. I go to church every Sunday now. The service is not the same as at home but the church is beautiful. Every Sunday, I pray and light a candle for you all. I have sent many letters to Mrs Chester, but so far I have not receive one back. I would so much like

to see her. I wrote to let her know I am now working. I know she would be happy for me.

I hope the children is not giving you too much trouble. I hope they like what I have sent them. Please write me and let me know if the shoes fit Tina and send me her shoe size for next time. I miss you all very much and I pray every day that it will not be long before I see you all again. Take care my sister, God is always on your side and I am so grateful for you. Please kiss Tina and Charles for me and tell them never to forget me.

Your sister,
Agnes

Ella set the letter aside and opened her parcel. The sweet smell that had met her when she opened the box was a bottle of Lily of the Valley talcum power. She had never received such a fragrant gift, in fact she had never received anything so indulgent that was just for her. Wrapped around the talcum powder was some cotton underwear and a pretty headscarf. All the items were doused in the sweet scent, but Ella could not deny the sour disappointment about Agnes's new friend Raphael Toussaint. Raphael, who had the reputation for being reckless and spoilt. 'How could dis be Agnes, you go so far and find dis man of all men!' Ella was furious with her sister on learning this, it overshadowed the joy of the parcel. She held the scarf to her nose and breathed deeply into the silky fabric in the hope of feeling her sister's presence. 'Oh Agnes!' Ella felt a growing familiar frustration about her sister, a concern about her which had been dormant, but which had emerged, once again, with this letter. Ella knew her sister was strong, but she could be naive and just as gullible as she herself had been with the schoolteacher, Byron.

* * *

At church the Sunday after Byron had kissed her and asked her if she would go away with him, the moment in the service came to turn and shake their neighbour's hand, and Ella was stunned but happy to find him directly behind her. Their shaking of hands went on longer than usual and their eyes shone, but they were soon interrupted by Father Thomas making an announcement.

'There are signs of a potential landslide close to Mrs Flora Deterville's house, and with the hurricane season soon upon us, we must assist her in moving her house to a small section of her family land in the village. A koudmen is being called for next Saturday to help with this important work.'

A koudmen was when the community would come together to assist another member of the community or a family in need. Father Thomas had told the congregation that 'koudmen' originated from the words 'a coupe de main', a French term meaning a 'helping hand'.

Ella had known this announcement was coming and had already started helping her aunt to pack up her belongings.

At the end of service, Ella turned to Byron. 'I hope you will be coming next Saturday.'

'For sure, Ella. I will be there and am most looking forward to it.'

Ella could barely contain her excitement that week. Before sunrise the following Saturday morning, when the air was still fresh from the rain that fell during the night, Father Thomas gathered with the villagers who would be taking part in the koudmen. After prayers, Ella opened her eyes and there Byron stood, shirt sleeves rolled up and ready for action. He acknowledged her with a nod and a warm smile. Even though Ella was aware of the curious eyes around her, she didn't care.

The work of dismantling the house took several hours.

The many hands made light work of the removal of the roof and timber frames. The rough-hewn timber boards all came apart once the wooden pegs that kept them together had been knocked or prised out, the whole house was stacked on the back of a cart and pulled by Mr Florentville's faithful donkey along the street the few hundred yards to its new location.

Under the breadfruit tree in the corner of the small plot, Mrs Deterville, Ella, Agnes and some of the ladies from the village had been busy cooking, cutting, slicing, stewing and boiling. Refreshing drinks of fresh fruit juices and coconut water were sitting in a vat of fresh river water awaiting the arrival of the koudmen crew.

Ella took a moment away from the boiling pot to watch Byron amongst the men. Her attention on her man didn't go unnoticed by Agnes. 'Eh eh Ella who you watching dere? I never seen you pay so much attention on de men hard at work.' The other women's laughter rang out in unison with Agnes. Ella only responded with a smile and went back to stirring her pot.

As the sun dropped to the sea in the west, and the long shadows stretched across the landscape, flambeaus were lit.

To celebrate the successful completion of their task, the drinks started to flow, a song started up, and the traditional drum beat, learned and passed down through the generations from Africa was set up. The women started to dance along with their raised voices in song. As the hymns were replaced by ancient African songs, the meaning of which had been lost, but whose spirit remained alive, Byron snuck a kiss on Ella's cheek. She took his hand, in the cool, dark of the evening. It had been a good day, and Ella's heart loosened another turn for Byron, she was in love.

Agnes was not totally convinced by Byron, but she could

see her sister was more talkative and happy than she had ever seen her.

'I ka palè twop, *he talks too much. You fink it's just talk Ella? You trus' him?*'

Ella would respond in defence of Byron. 'He is an educated man Agnes, he knows fings dat we may never experience.'

The nightmares that took over Ella's dreams and had tormented her for many years now seemed less vivid. The ache she had carried for years around her shoulders had fallen away from her muscles and she felt less worrisome.

Ella believed Byron was responsible for broadening her horizons; he told her she was part of his future and he made her feel alive and hopeful. There was no doubt that he was bringing her out of herself, contrary to her natural tendency of extreme caution. Such was the powerful and intoxicating feeling she had for him.

This did not go unnoticed, especially by the women in the village who would throw a comment at Ella in jest when they were down at the river.

'Eh eh, Ms Ella! I see you looking so happy these days, I wonder why?'

Ella would make no comment, showing only an enigmatic smile on her face.

Ella and Agnes were never sat down and told about the birds and bees. Yet, they knew about how babies were made and Ella had watched in awe as her sister brought her own babies into the world.

The crude conversation between the women at the river sometimes left no illusion for Ella about what was expected of women from their men.

'He come by me last night wanting me bad, he already hard in his pants. I tell him if dat's all he wants me for he bes' not come with nothin' in his hands; no money, no food for the children, nuttin'. I tell him you want to lay down with me? Well, come back when you have something for me and I will ride you all you want.'

The unspoken rule at the river was that whatever was spoken would never be repeated, just left to float away with the slow-moving waters out to the ocean. Still, everyone knew this was never the case, the juice was just too sweet not to share. 'You mean to tell me she walk in and find both dem lying in her bed? Way pa pa, he sure in trouble for true!'

The women would break down with laughter, and Ella would be astonished that the women were not expecting love, often using sex as a means of bartering, a requirement for survival and a way to feed their children.

She was not naive, but Ella didn't want to be dependent on a man just so she could feed her children. She wanted a husband to swear on the bible and make a vow to God Almighty, to make a life-long obligation. 'For richer, for poorer, in sickness and in health, to love and to cherish, till death do us part.'

Byron would often talk about his mother and how one day Ella would meet her in person. She never questioned his past pursuits with other women and all Ella knew about him was his hopes, dreams and desire for Ella to be part of the future he had planned.

One day she witnessed Mrs Francis, the headmistress, hand a letter to Byron during school break. She saw him reading the letter during break time, hunched over, with a look of concern on his face. She sensed it didn't bring good news. 'Everything okay with your mother Byron?'

'She has not been well, I might have to take another trip home.'

'Oh, I hope it's not too serious?'

He ventured no further details, but that evening he was subdued and not his usual talkative self. Byron had invited Ella to his place for a change.

'Dat would be nice Byron. I will bring some food.' She had cooked his favourite dish of fish bouillon, green bananas, breadfruit and homemade hot pepper sauce. She arrived carrying the warm pot, wrapped in a cloth, tied tight at the top. He arose from his chair on the balcony to assist her to the small kitchen area.

Byron had lit some candles which gave the plain room a romantic glow and Ella had noticed the scent of rum on Byron's breath as he spoke, an odour she knew all too well. The same fragrance her father carried and now Ella noticed a bottle of white rum, a quarter empty, on the dining room table, where they sat.

'Would you like a shot of rum, Ella? I don't make a habit of drinking as you know, but I thought it would be nice to make an exception this Friday evening, no school tomorrow!'

Ella would occasionally have a splash of rum mixed in some homemade juice, but it was a rare occurrence.

'Not dis evening, I will just have some of the tamarind juice I made.'

Byron looked a little disappointed.

'Byron, you seem worried about something this evening, what going on?'

'I do have a lot on my mind, Ella, nothing to worry yourself with. But with you here and the enjoyment of your delicious food and this shot of cheer in my glass, I am sure we will have a pleasurable evening.'

After Byron had finished eating and refilled his glass a good few times, she started to clear the plates.

'We can clear the dishes later,' he told her, his speech slurring.

Then he took her hand and guided her to sit on the edge of his bed, where he began to kiss her on her neck. She enjoyed the feeling it gave her and let out a giggle.

'Oh how I love when you laugh like dat Ella, it let me know that I make you happy.'

His kisses moved to her lips, and the taste of white rum and hot pepper sauce were still on his lips. He urged her to lie back on the bed, becoming insistent and forceful. Ella was filled suddenly with discomfort, her mood shifting from happy acceptance to concern and anxiety. He spoke, out of breath, heavy with emphasis.

'Ella, you must let me.'

He rolled on top of her, she could feel his obvious arousal. She froze as he pushed himself against her, moving to pleasure himself. Rolling off her he quickly unzipped his pants and took her hand roughly, placing it on his erect penis as he lay next to her.

'Pleasure me Ella.'

Ella was frozen with terror, unable to do what he wanted, or to run away, which her mind was telling her to do, but it seemed that Byron was caught up in his own needs and pushed her hand away, to pleasure himself vigorously. She remained frigid in fright as he moaned and groaned until the inescapable climax, then fell quiet. He lay still deep in his release and revelry. After some minutes Ella moved through her shock and embarrassment. She quickly rearranged her clothes, picked up her cooking pot and took one last look at Byron, who by now was asleep on his bed, his trouser zipper still undone and his flaccid penis between his thighs.

So this is what the women at the river talked about.

It had been easy to fall in love with Byron, but the reality was different from her dream. How could Agnes be fooled by a man such as Raphael Toussaint, the man they used to call a *kouyon*, idiot.

Pa gadé, don't be fooled.

Ella expressed her concerns with pen and paper, wiping her tears and wrote:

Ella Deterville
Canaries Post Office
St Lucia
West Indies.
21st August 1957

My dear sister Agnes,

Thank you so much for your parcel. It made us all so happy, and the money will be a great help. With the little I receive from the school and the help of cousin Johnnie we are all coping well. Every week Johnnie brings us fresh fish which we enjoy and your name is always mentioned as we sit by the river enjoying the food. You must not worry about us, we are doing well. The children pray for you every evening before bed so your name is mentioned each day without fail. I hope Mrs Chester writes to you soon.

I am so proud that you are working. You have always had so much courage, much more than me, but I am now worried, Agnes. Please do not let that man Raphael Toussaint turn your head. Can a man change by moving from one place to the next? From what I know of him, I don't think he can change just like that. Agnes, do not get yourself involved with him. Just concentrate on your work and make sure God is always present in your heart. Attend church each Sunday. This will help you when times are not so easy and keep you from harm. Remember why you are in England. You are there to better yourself and to look after your family. That is the promise you made.

We all miss you very much and by the grace of God please keep safe my sister. If I hear of anyone coming to England, I will send some spices and soft candle for you. Please, please be careful with that man.

Bless you my sister.
Ella

Ella took the letter to the post office, paying for the postage stamp that would take it all the way across the ocean to Fernhead Road in Paddington. She only wished she could talk to Agnes, that she could express the fear that was growing in her belly, not just that a man like Raphael was taking her sister away from good sense, but that England was taking Agnes from her family, and would not give her back.

CHAPTER TWENTY-TWO

The new contract was keeping Raphael busy at work, and when he wasn't working, he was spending time with Agnes. And he was drinking less and less now. Still, life in Britain, with its grey skies and damp cold, sometimes got Raphael down. So when he bumped into Scottie at the bus stop and was invited over for a drink and a round of dominoes that evening, Raphael didn't see the harm in it.

When Raphael reached Scottie's door, he almost turned round. He had vowed not to get tangled up with Scottie and partying, and wanted to stick to his resolve this evening, too. But before he could do that, Scottie, obviously hearing his tread on the landing, came to check who was there. 'Raphael,' Scottie said jovially as he patted him on the back and led him into the room.

'Hey, man. I can't stay too long—' Raphael began.

'I was hoping dat might be you. I ain't seen you for ages, where you bin hiding man?' Scottie was now sitting at the table with a cigarette hanging from his mouth, his hat perched on the side of his head and his hand on a bottle of whisky, ready to pour himself a drink.

'I ain't bin hiding, my brother. Just working and staying out of trouble,' Raphael answered, trying to think of a way to make his excuses and leave, when he had just arrived.

As if he had picked up on this thought, and keen to nip it in the bud, Scottie poured a shot glass of whisky. 'Here, take a shot.'

Raphael hesitated for a moment. But the amber liquid looked so good in the glass. And besides, one shot would only help warm him before he went back out into the cold grey streets. Maybe he could try to catch Agnes when she got off from work. Raphael took it, despite himself. 'Just the one, I gotta get on my way to see my girl.'

'Why you look like you in such a hurry?' Scottie asked as he turned a set of domino tiles out onto the table. 'Stay for one game, man.'

Raphael was about to answer when there was a knock on the door.

'I wonder who's dat now. Everyone must know I have a bottle of whisky on de table,' Scottie said, getting up from the table and walking to the door. Raphael stiffened when he heard Scottie say, 'Hey, beautiful ladies. Come in, come in.'

Raphael turned slowly in his chair and when he saw that one of the ladies in question was Annie, with Theresa right behind her, his heart sunk.

'Take a seat, ladies. Make yourself at home.' Scottie mimed a pouring motion with his hand. 'Raphael, get our guests a shot.'

Raphael could feel the sweat forming under his armpits, but he ignored his shirt's itchy fabric and the heat rising from under his jacket. This was the first time he had seen Annie since leaving her in bed at the big house in Bayswater without saying goodbye; he found it hard to look her in the eye.

Raphael hoped Annie would not make a scene and embarrass him in front of Scottie. He decided to speak first in an attempt to head off any bad feeling. 'Hey, Theresa, good to see you.' He hoped no one could see the sweat forming on his forehead.

Theresa grinned. 'This is Annie. You don't remember her? She was at the 101 that night.'

'Oh yes, that was a good night. We had a lot of fun.'

'So I heard,' Theresa said, with a sly smile before winking at Scottie.

So, Scottie did know. Before he could respond, Annie chimed in, with ice in her voice. 'Yes, you fellas certainly know how to have fun. You've got us girls dangling on a string.' Annie downed her whisky, but shot Raphael a sidelong dirty look as she pulled out a packet of cigarettes from her handbag.

Raphael leaned in to light it, trying to act as calm as possible. Inside, he was a mess. The last thing he wanted was for word of his night with Annie to get back to Agnes somehow, and he was also ashamed of how he had treated Annie, both of the women deserved better. It was clear Scottie knew about it, but would Scottie spill his secret?

Raphael made a show of looking at his watch and then stood up. 'Well, it's good to see you both,' he said to Annie and Theresa.

Scottie gave a chuckle. 'Well ladies, Raph got tings to do tonight and people to see, isn't dat right, Raph?'

Raphael made his way to the door quickly. He had just made it down the front steps of the house when he realised Scottie had followed him out. 'Don't be upset, man,' Scottie said, resting a hand on Raphael's shoulder and falling into step with him. 'Annie likes a good time, but you leave de woman and you never say goodbye. You know what she tell me, you make her feel cheap. She was real mad at you.'

'Look Scottie,' Raphael said, 'I did something I'm not proud of, but I don't want Agnes's feelings hurt.'

Scottie said, 'No need to get like dat. I jus' saying, she's Theresa's friend. And Theresa's my girl. Her father is a big man, a judge, and she likes me. And I like her too.'

'You be careful wit dem girls, Scottie. De fing is, I see where dey live in dat big house in Bayswater, but dey not like us, dey got money and dey all stick together. It all just fun for her, but English men don't like seeing us with dere girls. Be careful. You know how hard it already is for us, my brother.'

Scottie put a reassuring hand on Raphael's shoulder. 'Don't worry about me, Raph. I know who my friends are.'

Raphael hoped that was true.

CHAPTER TWENTY-THREE

1958

Agnes had been in Britain for more than a year, and on that early morning in May 1958, the sun was shining for the first time in what felt like months. She wanted to open the windows to allow the morning breeze in, and after prising the stiff wooden frames open, a refreshing chill blew in. Her hand-me-down curtains had a life of their own, waving and shaking dust off the fabric that now sparkled and danced in the light, resembling the gleam from a movie camera lens. Agnes just managed to cough out her words: 'I fink (cough cough) it's time to wash these curtains again (cough).' She vowed to do it at the weekend, but in her heart she wanted to make new ones.

Agnes had fallen in love with the 99K model Singer sewing machine the first time she had seen it in the Fletcher's haberdashery store window. When she asked to see it close up, the shop assistant emerged from the storeroom carrying what looked like a wooden dome. She unlocked the dome and lifted it, revealing a shining cast iron black sewing machine with the golden Singer logo. It took Agnes's breath away. She was tempted to secure the machine on hire purchase there and then, but she felt guilty knowing that some of the savings still in her wallet were already assigned to be sent home to Ella and the children.

The desire grew stronger day by day for her own Singer sewing machine and sometimes she would detour on her way home just to take another look at the machine in the window. Oh the beautiful clothes she would make with it! The day she made her first down payment Agnes knew she had to make sacrifices. 'I can't buy any more scarves, I will have to wait to buy new shoes for Tina and I will have to work overtime.' Agnes felt empowered knowing she could choose how she would raise the money to pay for it. It felt good to be working and to have regular money coming in.

Agnes leaned out of her window and looked onto the garden below. The sunshine made everything look so much less grim. The brightness gave her a sense of optimism that everything was right with the world, and she knew she had the courage to make life good. Her day-to-day existence had become mundane: work, sleep, work, sleep, but she felt grateful for it because it was better than struggling to make ends meet in Canaries, and she now had someone she loved, and could allow herself to dream of a future with, Raphael.

The letter from Ella, in which she'd shared her concerns regarding Raphael, had upset her deeply. Her sister showed no trust in him. Yet she knew she still had her suspicions about him herself, and that Ella's concerns were somewhat warranted. He still drank, and would sometimes arrive at her door tipsy at the weekends, jovial and playful, which wasn't so terrible. It's not like she had seen him falling over drunk, causing an embarrassment. He had let her down a few times, not turning up when he said he would, but Raphael had a way of making it up with Agnes with his sweet words and irresistible caresses. Agnes had let some of her boundaries slip, which was why Ella's letter had rattled her.

But being with Raphael was a far cry from being with Vince, she told herself, because she was now a different woman. She was not reliant on Raphael like she had been with Vince. She worked and earned her own money, which meant she was able to fulfil her responsibility and her promise to send funds to her family. For the first time in her life she felt independent, and it was nice to wake up some mornings alone and stretch out in her bed and then other times feel a warm body next to her when Raphael would stay the night. As Raphael would say, 'Why be lonely in London?' and Margaret and Vitalis didn't seem to mind. If it meant that every so often she would smell alcohol on Raphael's breath, she could handle that, especially since he never raised his hand to her or, as far as she knew, played around with other women. It was Margaret that had given her warning. 'Agnes you be careful with Raphael, he has hurt you once or twice already. It's good to forgive but remember you mus' stand your ground with him and remember why you are in England.'

As Agnes breathed in the cool, fresh air, she could feel the dirt from the window ledge on her hands. It encouraged her back into the room to wash the black soot off her palms before it got onto anything. When she was done, she looked at the clock. It was 7.45 a.m. She had better get a move on to catch the eight o'clock bus. Closing the windows took some effort, but again she managed it without breaking the rattling glass.

'Mrs Brown has been on the lookout for you,' Katie said. Agnes had barely just arrived and donned her uniform before Katie was snapping the words into Agnes's face. 'She wants you to go straight to her office. I wonder what that's about, Agnes?' Katie didn't attempt to disguise a nasty smile. Agnes had worked hard to ignore Katie's snide remarks and unpleasant digs, but it wasn't easy.

One day Agnes was in a cubicle in the ladies toilet, when she overheard one of the kitchen girls talking to another.

'You know Katie thinks Agnes is out for her job as section manager. I have told her that will never happen, she's been here longer than that coloured girl. Agnes is pretty, but she'll never get that job, I think it would be a disgrace if she did. My dad was effing and blinding last night, fed up with the foreigners taking our jobs . . . Katie said the same, it's not bloody right.'

Agnes didn't recognise the voices and the only time she had seen Katie with two women at her side was when she walked out of the Lyons building after their shift. The way they spoke sounded spiteful. Agnes stayed in her toilet cubicle and waited until the voices disappeared. Her blood was running cold in her veins at their comments. The wise words of Ella rang in her ears: 'It's good to know your enemies, you are wise to their actions.' But to think she was considered an enemy made her dejected because she knew her people came to England with goodwill in their hearts, not to harm or cause trouble, rather to work alongside the people of this island called England.

She knew now that Katie couldn't be trusted, but had no idea why Mrs Brown would want to see her, did Katie know something she didn't, something bad?

With Katie's words playing on her mind, Agnes knocked on the manager's door, feeling anxious. It was the first time since starting work at Lyons that she'd had cause to visit the manager's office. She was a good worker, kept her head down and did the work. *What had she done wrong?*

'Ah, Agnes. Come in dear.' Agnes walked into the office

Island Song

to find Iris, her Tea Station Supervisor, Mr Smith the Bakery Manager, and her Jamaican friend, Moses.

Agnes liked Moses, who still constantly referred to himself as the 'The Baker from Jamaica'. 'I bake to make your life sweet!' Agnes and Moses had become instant friends the day he approached her in the staff canteen. He would make her laugh when he did his impressions of some of their co-workers, and his Jamaican English accent made his imitation even funnier.

Moses always complimented Agnes on what she was wearing, adding his own fashion tips. 'Ms Agnes, why don't you get yourself a colourful neck scarf for when you wear dat purple jumper. It would look so nice against your skin and dat crown of your black shiny hair. You would look so beautiful, like Sarah Vaughan!' He would occasionally have a bag of pastries for her at the end of the day, the ones with the red jelly in the middle that Raphael liked.

Whenever she brought the pastries home, Raphael would say, 'I hope dat Jamaican fella not trying anything on wit you.'

Agnes always fell more in love with Raphael when he got a little jealous. It showed his vulnerability, that he wasn't as sure of himself as he led on. Confidence, this was the image he put out into the world. Raphael, the cool working guy. But he required her love, her reassurance. The truth was, Moses felt safe with her, enough to reveal a hidden part of himself and had told her he liked men, not women. Raphael was surprised and somewhat relieved at the discovery of Moses' true nature.

'*Eh eh, he a mal ma ma*, he is gay!' Agnes continued to explain how she found out about Moses. 'When I first meet him he told me I should not be worried because he jus' want to be friends with me. And den de other day we on de bus and he whisper to me and tell me he have his eyes on de bus conductor and I ask him what he mean by dat and he whisper again in my ears and tell me he prefer male company. We on de bus, it's not a place to talk about dem fings. So I hold his hand to let him know it's okay with me.'

Raphael looked thoughtful. 'My mother has a brother dat way, he now living in Martinique. It not safe for a man to be wit a man here in England, it not legal, same as St Lucia. Moses have to be careful because he could go to jail if he got caught wit another man.' Agnes was pleased to know Raphael wasn't offended by Moses being homosexual. 'At de end of de day everybody looking for someone to love!' Raphael held Agnes close. 'Ain't dat right, Agnes, and as long as he keep making dem cakes, I good wit dat.'

Mrs Brown's voice brought Agnes back to the present. 'Now you both must be wondering why you have been called to my office. Don't look so worried, Agnes, my dear. You're not in trouble!' Mrs Brown could still be stern and stiff, but she warmed up every now and then, Agnes had noticed. 'We just want to inform you that head office has requested that you both take part in the Empire Day—' Mrs Brown paused and quickly corrected herself. 'I mean the Commonwealth Day celebrations. This year's celebrations are going to be very special. Not only will it highlight the change of name, but we will be graced with the presence of her Royal Highness the Queen Mother on the 22nd May, two days before the official day. How does that sound to you both?'

'So she will be coming here, Ms, to Lyons?' Agnes asked, open-mouthed in surprise.

'Yes, Agnes, and because you are both from one of the Commonwealth Islands and such good staff members, head office felt it was appropriate for you both to be in the presentation line to meet her Royal Highness. Yes, they could have suggested some of the other staff members working here from the Commonwealth, since there are many of you working here now. However, we all agreed that you, Agnes and Moses, would be perfect for the job.'

Agnes and Moses looked at each other, almost not quite believing what they were being told.

Moses said proudly, 'It will be my honour to represent my country.'

'And represent Lyons, Moses.' It was the first time Mr Smith spoke, still with his arms crossed over his big belly.

'Are you happy to take part, Agnes?' Mrs Brown asked, nodding in encouragement. 'We will need to take you through the protocol and decorum for the day. We'll all have to be ready to show Maison Lyons at our very best!'

Agnes found it hard to speak, but she just managed to squeeze the word 'Yes' from her dry throat.

'So you mean to tell me you going to meet the Queen!'

'No, Raph, de Queen Mother.' Agnes could see that Raphael was finding it as hard to believe as she was.

'And it's just you an' dat Jamaican fella meeting her?'

'No, there will be other people in line to meet her. Because St Lucia and Jamaica in the Commonwealth we are representing our islands. There is a girl from Barbados working in the kitchen, she said she happy they choose me because she would be too nervous to do it. And since Katie hear de news she has stopped speaking to me.'

Agnes didn't tell Raphael that Katie had made her feelings known after the Commonwealth Day staff announcement. At the end of their shift, both women stood quietly at their lockers changing out of their work uniforms. As the other women left the changing room, chattering to each other, Katie closed her locker and approached Agnes.

She spoke quietly with venom in her voice. 'You lot come

here and take our jobs. And now you are going to be in the line-up to meet the Queen Mother. What is this country coming to? And just because you're allowed in this country, doesn't mean we all want you here.'

Agnes stood boldly in her shoes and looked squarely into Katie's face. When Katie had stopped speaking, Agnes summoned forth the courage she had always seen Margaret display, and spoke. 'I am sorry for you because you have such hate in your heart. I am just here doing my job just like you Katie, but you want to turn me into your enemy. I will pray for you.' Agnes picked up her bag and walked away, without waiting for a response from Katie. The next day a piece of paper was left inside the door of Agnes's shared locker which read 'WOG GO HOME.' Her hands shook as she stuffed the crumpled paper into her bag. She had no doubt that it was written by Katie.

The 22nd of May 1958 arrived soon enough, and Agnes was finally in line, wearing her new crisp and white uniform. She found it hard to control the shaking of her knees. There was a crowd of children waving flags in the air, each one representing the Commonwealth countries. Agnes had practised her curtsy a thousand times. All Moses had to do was nod his head, which he was disappointed about. 'Me fink I would give de Queen Mother a curtsy, watch.' As Moses bent his knees, Agnes howled with laughter.

The memory of the moment came into her mind as she stood waiting, and it made her smile and eased her nervousness. She was tempted to look along the line and wave to Moses but decided not to just in case he made her laugh out loud.

Now Agnes's moment had arrived. She performed the perfect bend to her knees, the single curtsy for the Queen Mother and also in honour of her sister. *See, Ella, I told you I would meet the Queen*. The camera bulbs went off. Agnes lowered herself perfectly and raised her head and stood straight.

The manager, Mrs Brown introduced the line-up to the Queen Mother. 'This is Agnes Detervile from the Island of Saint Lucia ma'am.'

'Are you enjoying your time here?' the Queen Mother enquired, her piercing blue eyes studying Agnes as she awaited a response.

'Yes, ma'am,' Agnes answered. There had been so much preparation for a heartbeat of a moment, but the excitement of the day stayed with Agnes for weeks. She had always hoped to meet Queen Elizabeth, but her mother would do.

The picture that made the *London Evening News* the next day was of the Queen Mother and Agnes giving her best curtsy. The headline read '*A Commonwealth Cuppa. The Queen Mother enjoys a cup of tea at Lyons Corner House and is welcomed by an exotic blend of her Commonwealth subjects from near and far.*'

The newspaper clipping was placed on the Lyons staff notice board. Weeks would pass and the edges of the paper would curl and fade, but in Agnes's home in the village of Canaries it was placed in a frame and hung next to the picture of the Queen of England. It made the radio news in St Lucia, and it was the talk of the village for months to come, and Agnes never tired of looking at it.

This was one in the eye for Katie, for sure.

CHAPTER TWENTY-FOUR

On the bank holiday Monday, Raphael, Agnes, Margaret and Vitalis were sitting at the kitchen table with empty plates in front of them. There were dirty pots and pans to wash, but no one was making the first move to the sink, everyone seated, enjoying the moment, chit-chatting about nothing important. The meal of boiled potatoes, carrots, cabbage and fried lamb chops was no replacement for the Caribbean delicacy of rice and peas, plantain, sweet potato pie, baked chicken, avocado salad, and fresh mango juice to wash it all down, but no one was complaining.

Margaret was still working at the hotel, and she made sure to make friends with the meat supplier who would often invite her to buy heavily discounted off-cuts from the back of his delivery van. Margaret had also made friends with one of the chambermaids from Jamaica who lived in Brixton, and she was very envious to discover that a market of exotic food was being established south of the river. Produce from the West Indies and India, native vegetables and fruits from home, were starting to arrive on the docks in London and were making their way to specialist vendors in key suburbs where Commonwealth immigrants had made a home. Next time she did a big lunch, she was determined to have her friend bring her some ground provisions and plantain to liven up their plates.

Vitalis was the first to move, but not towards the washing up. 'I have a surprise for you all. You will like this my love!'

Margaret looked at her husband unamused. 'You could never surprise me. I know your every move.'

Vitalis cast a mischievous grin her way as he walked with purpose out of the room and then quickly up the stairs. From the next floor he called out, 'WELL DIS TIME I FINK YOU MISS DIS MOVE!' Vitalis returned to the kitchen carrying a red leather box that looked like a square suitcase with a handle. 'Agnes, move de plates for me please, I need to use the electric plug behind de table.' Agnes leapt into action, quickly taking the empty plates, utensils and glasses off the table and placing them in the sink as instructed.

Raphael chuckled. 'I know what dis is. Where you get dis from, man?'

Vitalis placed the case in the middle of the table, unclipped the catches on either side and opened the cover to reveal the contents. On the inside of the lid was a picture of a dog sitting next to a gramophone underneath which were the words *His Master's Voice*.

'It's a record player!' Vitalis announced with obvious excitement and no small amount of pride. 'Dis fella at de hospital said it belong to his farda who recently passed. He told me he had no use for it, and he would sell it to me for next to nuttin', so I offer him three pounds, which was all I had to give right then, and I was surprised when he take the money! I ask him if he had some records for me to play on it. He left me three discs. But I know dis fella bringin' over the hottest new records from America, and he tell me he have some calypso tunes he can let me have too. For now let's take a listen to dis.'

Raphael started playing with the dials on the front of the record player. 'Vitalis, this fing looking new. I don't fink the old fella had a chance to use it. What kinda music he give you?'

'Well, he only give me three 45s. Let's tek a listen!' Vitalis carefully took the 45 discs out of their paper sleeves. 'Well, de fella show me to put all three discs here. You see how it hold all of dem, and dis arm just hold it in place. Den you flick dis switch. All right! You see de turntable starting to spin, hey, you hear dat, Margaret!'

The Everly Brothers hit came out of the speakers at full volume. 'Bye, Bye Love, Bye Happiness . . .' 'Yes! Ha ha we have music!' Vitalis took Margaret by the hand and encouraged her to dance with him. 'Come on, my girl. *Danśe épi mwen*, dance with me.' They took to the middle of the kitchen with the plastic black-and-white lino under their feet helping them slide easily to the beat of the music.

Next up on the turntable were two older songs from the big bands of Glen Miller, 'In the Mood' and 'Moon Light Serenade'. Both couples held each other close. Vitalis asked his wife what she thought of his surprise.

Margaret was very happy with the new addition to 63 Fernhead Road. 'Well, my *dou dou*, my darling, you did good. Money well spent, but I hope you can get us some calypso, De Mighty Sparrow, an Lord Kitchener and some Jim Reeves.'

It was the first time Agnes and Raphael had danced together. Wrapped in his arms, Agnes looked up at Raph. 'I used to see you in Canaries dancing so wild, but I'm glad to know you can slow dance as well.'

'Well, at least dis time you don't refuse me?' Raphael said.

Agnes slightly pulled away from his embrace. 'And dis time you not drunk doing your foolishness.'

Island Song

Raphael pulled her close again. 'And dis time you are all mine, and I have you in my arms.' He grinned from ear to ear.

Agnes smiled coyly. 'Raph, you so fresh.'

They played each song over and over again, dancing, their laughter loud and happy.

But over the sound of the music, Margaret could hear another sound. 'WHAT'S DAT KNOCKING?' she asked.

Everyone went quiet and Raphael turned the volume down. 'It must be de landlady, Ms Fletcher, telling us to turn the music down?'

Vitalis hurried to the front door and heard urgent voices, one was a voice Raphael recognised. 'Dat's Linus!' He rushed out to see what was going on.

All three men returned to the kitchen. Linus was sweating and panting heavily. 'Explain ya'self, man. Wha' goin on?' Raphael said, and then turned to Agnes. 'Get him some water.' Raphael tried to calm Linus down. 'Take your time, my brudda. Look, drink some water.' Linus put the glass to his mouth and drank, using both of his shaking hands to steady himself. 'Okay now talk to us Linus. What going on?' Raphael said, when Linus put the cup down, his hands still shaking.

When Linus finally spoke, his voice shook with emotion. 'Well, I come out of Westbourne Park station, and a whole lot of commotion going on. Next fing I know someone throw a bottle at me, and it smashed at my feet. I was shocked. Den I see Teddy Boys with pieces of wood in dey hands lookin' like dey ready to beat someone. One of dem sees me an' shout, "Look a darkie! Let's get the black bastard." I start to run, Raph. I never run so hard. Dey never catch me.' Linus paused, his face pained and took a deep breath before continuing. 'I fink dere is a madness goin' on in de Grove.'

Then everyone in the kitchen was stunned by an urgent

banging on the front door. Vitalis looked at Raphael with eyes of concern, Margaret and Agnes held their breath. Maybe it was it some of those Teddy Boys who had followed Linus to their door? Vitalis grabbed a knife from the sink, Raphael took the heavy fry pan off the cooker. Margaret asked for assistance, 'Lord Jesus help us.' Agnes stood by Linus who was now shaking even more. Vitalis and Raphael crept carefully into the hallway. Margaret and Agnes stared frightened at each other. Both men disappeared, making their way to the door. Agnes jumped at the sound of voices. Vitalis shouted out, 'It's Scottie, no one else, just Scottie!' There was relief knowing there was not going to be a riot in the house.

As he fell through the door and pushed past them through the corridor and into the kitchen, they saw Scottie had a bloodied handkerchief covering his hand, he was sweating and his clothes looked dishevelled on his body. He was taking deep breaths as if to calm the rage in his eyes. 'What you do to your hand man, what de hell is going on?' Raphael and everyone in the kitchen was shocked at the sight of Scottie. 'I'm all right man, I cut my han' on a glass bottle. It not serious.' Scottie touched Linus on the shoulder. 'It looked like you got caught up in the madness too.' Linus just shook his head, he found it hard to speak. Scottie explained what was going on in the Grove.

'Dere were bottles being thrown from all directions, glass shattered everywhere. Dey throw at us, we throw back. Lots of people hurt and bleeding on both sides. Dem Teddy Boys push us to dis. We can't take dere abuse no longer, we had to stand up to dem.

'De police right now are holding back a group of Teddy Boys in front of Ladbroke Grove train station, preventing them from moving further onto the streets. Me and some of de other fellas realise we had to move out of the area fas' so we don't get arrested. Dis is de only safe place I can fink to come. I'm sorry Ms Margaret for coming here and disturbing you all.'

Margaret approached Scottie. 'Let me clean up your han' for you Scottie.'

'No it's okay Ms Margaret, de bleeding stop already but I'll take another glass a water.'

Scottie continued to explain about why the fighting took place.

'Let me tell you, de White Defence national headquarters is located in Notting Hill Gate where our people living in squalor and dey say we coloured people invading dere country and dey afraid of mass interbreeding, dey don't want a mulatto race, dey want to maintain the purity of de culture of dere country!' Scottie was now standing in the centre of the kitchen as if he was preaching on a soap box, Raphael had never heard Scottie with such desperation in his voice. 'We fed up with de harassment from dem facists. The Caribbean community had to stand up. Enough is enough!'

The much-diminished jovial spirit in the kitchen was replaced with unease. Everyone was stunned to silence. Margaret managed to put together a plate of food for the still shaken Linus. 'Thank you, Ms Margaret. I sorry to disturb you all.' Raphael found it hard to respond, knowing what was going on in the streets, but he found the words to comfort his brother. 'Dis is your family. Where else you goin' to go? Eat your food, and we will make space for you to stay with us tonight. You all right wit dat, Agnes?'

'Of course, Raph, of course,' Agnes replied.

Scottie wasn't letting up. 'Everyone in dis room was invited and encouraged to come to dis country. We put up wit all de racist signs and de spitting in our faces. Dey ask us to come but dey keeping us down. What de hell man, we must fight for our rights!'

Agnes made herself busy at the sink scrubbing the pans and plates. The words WOG GO HOME on the note that had been left in her locker played on her mind and it was still at the bottom of her work bag. She had thought about taking it to Ms Iris, her supervisor, but Moses had put her off the idea. 'Agnes, me tink you best keep dat to yourself for now. Katie bin working at Lyons for a long time, and who you tink dey will throw out of a job? You! So you have to show her you're not afraid of her. Don't back down. Look her in de eye if she talk to you, it's de only way I have manoeuvred myself in dis place.'

Agnes was not afraid of Katie; she was afraid of losing her job. The thought of seeking out employment and maybe waiting weeks to get a position and not being able to send Ella any funds was a situation Agnes couldn't face. There was a time if anyone had cornered her like Katie had, Agnes would have cussed them out and would have been ready to fight and tear into her opponent like a cornered tiger, but not this time, she had to hold her tongue and keep her fists in her pockets.

Agnes could not sit still. She had to keep moving, cleaning the kitchen. The change of mood and hearing Scottie talk about the riots, seeing the fear in Linus's eyes also brought Katie's comment into her mind. 'You lot coming here taking our jobs . . .'

All Agnes wanted to do was to work hard and do a good job so she could continue to look after her family. Meeting the Queen Mother was a dream come true, one that she knew made her family in Canaries proud, but it had brought even more resentment from Katie. It seemed that resentment was everywhere and some people were prepared to use violence to show it.

* * *

Raphael sat at the table with his brother and watched him eat. Unresolved feelings began to bubble up inside him as he recalled when he and Bernard had to paint over the racist comment left on the walls for them at work. It had made him angry and powerless all at the same time because he could not take his vexation out on his abuser. But once calmed, he realised he didn't want violence, he just wanted to be accepted the same as any other worker.

Bernard had mentioned that racist comments had been shouted at him while walking down the street. Scottie had received abuse as well, but he gave the impression of being a fella who was strong enough to brush off stuff like that. Now, as Raphael absorbed the night's events, the fear and fury re-emerged in his belly. He needed a drink.

Margaret banged a kitchen cupboard closed and they all looked to her as she spoke, in tears. 'Why dey have to be so? Why people have to hate each other? For what? Because dey fink we so different from dem? All dat is different is the colour of our skin and de country we born, but we need de same tings. Oh Lord, help dease people understand, help dem Lord!'

Vitalis went to comfort his wife. 'I fink the best fing to ease our souls in the safety of dis house is a shot of rum!'

'Now you talkin'!' Raphael rubbed his hands together. Agnes shot him a nervous glance.

'Yes, yes dat's a good idea. Help to ease us up a bit.' Margaret wiped her eyes and went to her cupboard to pull out the shot glasses. 'Vitalis, where you got dat rum?'

Vitalis pulled out a large bottle of amber liquid from the back of one of the cupboards. 'Like I tell you, a husband got to keep some secrets from his dear wife.'

CHAPTER TWENTY-FIVE

It had been months since the Ladbroke Grove riots, and Raphael had stayed as close as he could to Agnes during that time. Eventually, it was Linus who encouraged Raphael to move in with her.

'Why you don't move in with Agnes, you living dere for most of de week. I'm doing good at work, I can afford de rent here. Ask her if she would be happy for you to share the rent with her. Beside, it will encourage me to make more effort with Cynthia, my girl upstairs!' Linus chuckled.

Raphael plucked up the courage to ask her. 'Agnes you can say no if you want, I will understand. Why don't I share dis place with you, help you with de rent. You can save a little more money to send down for your children? Plus, I stay here for most of de week and . . .' Agnes put up her hand to stop him mid-flow, telling him she would have to ask Mrs Fletcher the landlady if it was okay for Raphael to move in and share the rent.

A day later she confirmed it was okay. 'De landlady send you warning dat the rent must be paid each week on time and she say we mus' pay an extra twelve shilling on what we pay already. I know you are working so I know you can pay de extra.' Raphael responded enthusiastically. 'Sure, I can do dat.'

'Plus she say we mus' not bring any riff-raff into de property an keep de place clean as usual.'

'You don't know any riff-raff Agnes and I don't know any riff-raff, so we good right?'

'Yes, we good Raph.'

Agnes was confident that they could make living together work – he had been spending more time there than at home with Linus, and now it was official.

But it wasn't long before the cracks started to show.

'Raph, I need to talk to you about somethin'.'

Raphael pushed up on his elbows and looked down at Agnes. 'Oh? Don't tell me I've done something wrong again? You always use dat voice when I'm in trouble.'

'Well, I hope it's not trouble because de other day I find a quarter bottle of vodka at the back of my wardrobe, wrapped up in an old towel. Why you have to hide it from me? And don't tell me it wasn't yours, who else would put it there?'

Raphael could not sweet talk his way out of this. 'Oh.'

'Yes. Oh.'

Raphael shrugged. 'I know you don't like it when I drink, Agnes.'

'I don't mind you havin' a drink, Raph. My father used to take a drink every day, like most of de fellas in Canaries. But he didn't do *maji èvèk bétiz*, nonsense and foolishness in de village. Dat's what I'm worried about, you goin' back to drinking too much and losing yourself!'

'*Pa mélé*, don't worry, I promise you Agnes, I will not go

back to being like dat. Haven't I proved dat to you? Look, I like to have a drink Agnes, it help to ease me up and take away de pressure at de end of de day.'

'What pressure you have? You have no one depending on you, you have money to pay your bills and you have a roof over your head?'

'Okay, okay. Jus' calm yourself, I hear what you sayin'.'

Raphael usually enjoyed when Agnes got feisty. It made him want her more. But he didn't enjoy this interrogation.

He needed to change the subject.

'Agnes, let me take you to Piccadilly this Saturday. It's de end of the month, and I have a little extra cash in my pocket and I want to spend it on you.'

'Well, okay. But promise me no more hiding bottles!'

'All right! No more hiding bottles.'

Agnes took up the invitation. 'You sure you can afford that, Raph? You send de money to your mother this month?'

Raphael could feel the warmth from her breath on his chest as she spoke. He smiled. 'Agnes, you always caring for other people. I love you for dat, but sometimes you must fink about yourself. Let me take you!'

'Okay, what we going to do?'

'We can go and see the lights of Piccadilly and take a walk around, then we can go to the cinema.'

'There is a film Moses told me about called *South Pacific*. Moses wanted to take me, but you can take me instead.'

'Sure, I will take you.'

It was a cold November evening, when Agnes and Raphael got on the packed bus into Piccadilly for the cinema. Agnes had never seen the bus so full and buzzing. It was Saturday night after all, a night of fun and games.

She would usually avoid the top deck for fear of falling down the stairs while the bus was still moving, but with Raphael's persuasion, she made it to the top without incident. They sat in the middle seats; the front and backs seats were taken by other couples on their way to the West End.

It had taken her a long time to see the charms of London, through the gloom and grey, but the West End of the city was a place that came alive after dark and she loved seeing the bright neon lights of Piccadilly Circus and all the people dressed up in the latest fashions, all out for a good time at the theatres and the bars.

It was cold, and Raphael held Agnes close. Agnes felt excited about the evening ahead. It was the first time Raphael had ever seen Agnes wear red lipstick, she usually wore just a touch of the enticing colour – it looked stunning against her complexion. Her hair was hidden under a headscarf, the pattern on the silky cloth was understated with hints of red, the same colour as her lips. He was delighted to be with her. They were both aware that they were the only black couple on the upper level. They sat quietly enjoying the ride without drawing any attention to themselves.

Once off at their destination they stood still for a moment to get used to the pedestrians, black cabs, buses and cars all moving at pace. A multitude of moving adverts flickered brightly above their heads. It was five thirty and already dark, so the Bovril, Gordon's Gin and Coca Cola signs were flashing like fireworks bursting with colour, making Agnes giddy.

The movie started at seven at the Odeon Leicester Square, so Raphael decided they should take a walk into Soho and make their way around to the cinema. It was their first time out together in the heart of London, and he wanted her to enjoy the sights. They walked at a good pace, not stopping for very long. They saw boys and girls laughing as they walked; cafés, pubs, nightclubs and music made Soho just as exciting as

Piccadilly. They had almost made their way around to Rupert Street, and Raphael decided to take a turn down Lisle Street to take a short cut into Leicester Square. It would turn out to be one of the worst decisions he would ever make.

'Hey! Where you going, wog?' There was that word again, spat out with hate and venom. Agnes froze.

In front of them stood four Teddy Boys. They wore waistcoats and frock coats with velvet lapels, and their hair was styled in the high quiff which distinguished them from other teenagers their age. Their faces were twisted in hateful sneers.

'Agnes, keep walking,' Raphael said sternly, stepping around them on the pavement and clutching her closer to his side.

'You blackies taking our white girls, not so fast. Oy, coon, I'm talkin' to you! Where d'ya think you're going?' One of them shoved his arm out, almost knocking Raphael sideways.

His heart was pounding so hard now, he could hardly hear anything else. He started to run, pulling Agnes with him. He had to get her somewhere safe, but where in London would they be safe from this kind of anger, this kind of hatred? He thought back to the night of the riot, and the look on Linus's face when he'd shown up at their door. Fear, anger, pain, and a heavy sadness. Raphael fought all those emotions now as the gang, their quiffs slicked with Brylcreem and smelling of beer, ran after them. Before he knew what was happening, three of the Teddy Boys caught up with them and jumped Raphael, punching him as they took him down. Agnes screamed at the top of her lungs, the sound echoing and bouncing off the buildings. Raphael was being punched over and over again.

Raphael caught the light of a blade as one of the Teddy Boys pulled a switch blade from his coat. Agnes continued to scream.

One of the Teddy Boys yelled, 'Shut up you bitch! What you doing with this nigga? You *white whore!*' A hand came hard across Agnes's face in a brutal open-handed slap that spun her head cruelly to the side. The force of the strike burned like fire and she screamed louder.

'What's going on down there? Leave them alone!' The voice was coming from one of the buildings high above them. Raphael could hear Agnes, but no matter how hard he struggled, he couldn't beat the men off him. The blade glinted against a street lamp before his attacker cut through the cloth of his overcoat with it. Then he felt a sharp pain that turned warm, before falling to the ground.

'Look at her. Look! This bitch ain't white, she's coloured too, she just has less of the tar brush in her than him. Stan, you idiot, I told you, come on let's get out of here!'

'Leave them alone, leave them alone you vile bastards!' The voice was closer now.

Agnes screamed, 'Help him, help him!' and a man and a woman came running to their aid.

Raphael lay on the ground holding his side. Agnes, kneeling next to him, was badly shaken and traumatised. Raphael felt the tear in his coat, then reached inside, and felt blood oozing from the slit on his torso. His injuries could have been much worse if the coarse wool of his coat had not taken the brunt of the slash from the Teddy Boy's switch blade. One violent act of hatred towards a man they had never met or even seen before. Raphael was bewildered that such violence could be inflicted without so much as looking someone in the eyes. The cause: the dark colour of his skin and the mistaken assumption that because Agnes was so much lighter she was in fact white.

The man and woman appeared next to them, their faces full of concern. The man crouched down beside them both. 'You look like you need to go to the hospital. We must call the police.' The man handed him a handkerchief which Raphael held to his side to stem the blood.

'Nah, I'm okay, it's just a cut. I don't fink it's deep and we don't need no more trouble. The police they ask too many questions and next thing you know we are de troublemakers. Thank you for the handkerchief, this should be okay until we get home.'

Agnes held her own hand to her face, which was still burning from the wallop she'd received from one of the Teddy Boys. Raphael could still hear her screams ringing in his ears.

'My name is Robert and this is my wife Stella,' the man told them. 'We live on the third floor directly above. Our car is parked two streets over. We can give you a lift home. Where do you live?'

'Paddington, 63 Fernhead Road, off the Harrow Road.' It was the first time Agnes had spoken and she couldn't keep the tremor from her voice, and she was shivering all over.

'That's not far from my aunt's house in Maida Vale. We can certainly take you there, it's the least we can do. Not everyone here is like those bully-boy bastards.'

'I am Raphael, and this is Agnes.' When Raphael said her name, Agnes started to cry again.

The drive to Fernhead Road was a subdued one. Agnes and Raphael sat in silent shock on the back seat. Their night had turned from a joyous one to terror in the blink of an eye. Raphael's black skin made him a target for abuse. This was not why he had come to the Mother Country, to be beaten as he walked down the streets of London.

The couple in the front made constant apologies for the thugs' behaviour and spoke of how rough it could get in Soho on Saturday nights, when gangs of young men congregated around the Italian coffee bars. Bored, and with nothing better to do, they picked on innocent passersby, or failing that, fought amongst each other. So much aggression, the man explained, and it had to find its way out somewhere.

Raphael replied, insisting that he knew that not everyone

was like that and thanking them again for driving him and his girl home. It was a relief to not have to navigate the bus with such a strong pain in his side.

Once dropped off and after polite goodbyes, Raphael and Agnes retreated to their room. It was a hard climb, and they were relieved Vitalis and Margaret had gone out for the evening. Agnes tended Raphael's wound, washing it before applying a clean dressing of cotton wool; it was a nasty cut, but not deep enough to still be bleeding. She splashed her raw face with cold water from the kitchen sink to reduce the burning and swelling. It wasn't the night they had planned, but it was a moment that brought the two of them closer together than any pleasant evening of film and a stroll could have done. Raphael felt ashamed as he let Agnes tend to his wound. 'I should have protected you, Agnes.'

'Raphael I don't want you to speak, jus' res' yourself.' Agnes didn't want to talk and relive the horror of their evening. She turned off the light and lay down next to Raphael on the bed still in her clothes. The room had a slight spin to it, she felt drunk from the evening's events, the adrenaline still coursing through her body sizzled in her muscles. She closed her eyes and could feel her heart thumping, *thump thump thump*. She breathed deeply to help settle the pounding in her chest. She moved in as close as she could to Raphael and as she did, she could hear him crying.

'I'm sorry Agnes, I'm so sorry.'

CHAPTER TWENTY-SIX

Agnes woke with a stinging and grittiness in her right eye. She opened and closed her eyelids, and with every blink the horror of the night before flashed into her mind. This brought tears and much needed moisture to her eye sockets, but rather than relief, the tears only stung further. She put her hand to her mouth to stop the scream threatening to emerge from her throat. She didn't want to wake Raphael who was still asleep with his back to her, still holding on to his left side.

The room felt cold, and this was the encouragement Agnes needed to get out of bed. She wiped the tears from her face and lit the paraffin heater to warm the room.

'Agnes, you coming to church!?' Margaret called up from the floor below.

Agnes made her way to her bedroom door, peeped out, keeping most of her face hidden, and answered. 'No, Margaret, not this Sunday. I'm not feeling too good!' Agnes felt chilly as she stood at her bedroom door.

Margaret hesitated for a moment, as if she wanted to ask more, before answering, 'You sure? Any fing I can do for you?!'

'No, Margaret, don't worry. Raph is looking after me.'

'Oh I see. Well, if you need any fing, let me know. I will see you later!'

The raised voices woke Raphael, and he called out, 'Agnes where you? What's all dat noise?'

'I'm here. I was just telling Margaret I won't be going to church.'

Raphael tried to turn in the bed slowly to face Agnes, but he made an involuntary sound that confirmed he was still in pain. Agnes moved quickly to him. 'Raph, you moving too fast. Lift yourself on the side you are on first, then move your legs around to me.' He did as she said, and she helped him manoeuvre his feet to the floor.

He raised his head to look at Agnes and could not hide his emotion at seeing her face. 'Agnes, Agnes, what have dem bastard done to you!' Raphael began to sob again and through his weeping said, 'But your face, Agnes, I could not protect you. I so sorry.'

Agnes's face felt tender and sore when she touched it. She then found her handbag and pulled out her powder compact and looked at her image in the small mirror in the palm of her hand. Her eye was bloodshot red, her cheek bruised and swollen, branded by the hand that had clouted her, with the worst swelling on the point of her cheekbone. She could not hold back her horror at what she saw in the mirror. 'Oh, my! What am I going to do? I can't go to work looking like dis? But I have to go or they will fire me! *Bodie, Bodie*, oh God, oh God! What am I to do! Look what dey do to my face!'

Raphael felt hopeless tending to his own painful agony. Agnes focused and looked at her face again. She didn't recognise herself. Her red, puffed-up eye looked back at her in the mirror. Agnes took a deep breath. Now, as she looked at her reflection in the mirror, she saw that the terrifying attack had also summoned forth defiance. Those evil men would not bring her down. She had come too far, sacrificed too much. Agnes thought about Ella, and Tina, and Charles. Thought about how much she had risked to come to this country to ensure they all had better lives back home.

She sat up straighter and wiped her tears. She looked at the anguish on Raphael's face and her instant thought was to bring comfort to the moment and ease the distress. 'Raph, I know you fink it's your fault. It's not. We will heal and as God is my witness, they will not keep us down.'

The knife slash Raphael received from his attackers was stinging him sharply. He was lucky it had not penetrated his skin more deeply, but it still hurt. He now had to stand because he needed to use the bathroom and would have to grit his teeth.

Agnes managed to get him dressed and helped him walk down the flight of stairs. It was 10.30 in the morning and Margaret had left for Sunday Mass, so the only person they could run into would be Vitalis, who normally stayed in bed until Margaret returned.

It sounded quiet on the landing so they walked slowly, Raphael leaning heavily against Agnes. Unfortunately, Vitalis opened the door of the bathroom and they came face to face with him.

Unable to hide the surprise at what he saw, he cried out. 'What de hell? What happen to you two? Agnes, what happen to your face? Girl, what dis fella do to you! Hey, what you do to my cousin!?!'

'Vitalis, Vitalis!' Agnes said, shook her head. 'Raph done nothing to me. Some white fellas do dat to us last night. Now move out de way. Raph need the bathroom.'

Vitalis then noticed Raphael clutching his side, and his

drawn features, 'You mean to tell me you in the West End and fellas jump you in such a busy place?' Vitalis asked.

'We take a side road and dey catch us dere,' Raphael answered, wincing again at the pain in his side.

'Why dey hate us so?' Vitalis's face was a mask of anger and despair. 'The other day I hear a story about a Dominican fella jus' walking down the road minding his own business,' Vitalis went on. 'Dis white woman pass him on the street, and she spit in his face! And look what happen to Linus. Fings are getting bad, man. We have to watch our backs and not walk alone in the streets!'

Everyone had made their way down into the warm kitchen by the time Margaret returned from church. She too was shocked by Raphael and Agnes's wounds, but she immediately took control of the situation.

'I knew something going on dis morning when you don't come downstairs.' Margaret bustled around the room, organising them all. 'Vitalis, bring de box from de bottom of the wardrobe, and when you come back, put some heat under de pot of soup. But before you do dat, see dat pot dere at the back of the stove with the tea towel over it? I already shape the dough to make some bakes, fry dem for us and don't burn dem!'

Vitalis left the kitchen and re-emerged with an old biscuit tin. Margaret opened the tin and a fragrance of home rose up from within. Inside was a jar of homemade *fiksyon*, an ointment with a blend of ingredients: red lavender, eucalyptus, coconut oil and *chadèl mol*, soft wax, which would be rubbed into the body to relieve the symptoms of a cold. In the tin there were also dried herbs, a bottle of castor oil, and Bay Rum which helped to ease headaches or cool the body when used as a cologne. Some soft candles wrapped in paper completed the distinctive natural pharmacy of a West Indian home.

Margaret unwrapped the paper from a thin white candle and started rolling and warming it in her hands, before gently smoothing the oil in her palms onto Agnes's face.

'Dis will draw out the bruising and swelling. It won't all be gone by morning, but I promise you it will look much better.' Margaret's hands moved cautiously over Agnes's face. She had used the *pom canal* many times and knew its almost mythic power to heal.

Her hands had the tender touch of a mother's love, the tender touch Agnes would give to her own children. Tears rose in Agnes's eyes. 'You want me to stop, I'm hurting you?' Margaret asked, concern etched on her face.

'No, Margaret. I'm just so upset dat this could happen to us.' Despite Agnes's determination not to allow those wicked men to bring her down, she was still in pain, physically, and shocked.

'I don't understand it myself. Maybe dey are afraid of us. It jus' give dem power to beat us down. I can't explain it.'

'Dey thought I was a white woman. That Raphael was with one of "dere women", dat's what they thought.'

'Dat don't mean dey should try and kill you for dat.'

Vitalis spoke with his back to everyone at the cooker frying the bakes. 'Dey want to keep Britain white. Dey don't want us to mix wit dem. Dey bes' get dere story straight because we here to stay, we not going nowhere.'

They all murmured in agreement as Margaret went to work on Raphael's wound. She cleaned the cut with carbolic soap, dried it, and then smoothed over some dried leaves of the miracle leaf she had soaked in warm water. Miracle leaf was a cure-all plant that had healing properties as powerful and mystical as the soft candle. Margaret then dressed the area, applying tension to the bandage as she wrapped it around

Raphael's waist. There was healing energy in those hands. After working her magic a little longer, Margaret pulled out a bag of bright yellow powder from her tin. 'Turmeric tea will help to heal you too.'

Agnes and Raphael felt comforted and cared for by Margaret and Vitalis. The feeling of not being alone in suffering was therapeutic in itself. Raphael still found it hard to look into Agnes's eyes, feeling a deep shame that was hard to shake. Agnes sensed this, and knew his humiliation was driven by love, but she was unable to hide her face from him completely, the reminder making him feel worse, so she did the best she could, and stood with Vitalis at the cooker, making sure he didn't burn the lunch.

Before they ate their pumpkin soup with fresh fried bakes, Vitalis declared he wanted to say grace. He wasn't a church-going man, but he believed in the power of prayer.

'Oh Lord, we don't come to bring harm to nobody. Let us walk these streets with you at our side oh Lord. Let us enjoy this meal and heal the wrongdoing of dem evil bastard thugs. Amen.'

It was not an easy walk to the bus stop the next morning. Raphael walked with a slight limp, not at his usual quick pace, but he held himself up the best he could. Agnes held his arm to support him, but she was finding it difficult to keep her headscarf pulled close to her face to hide the remnants of her red eye and bruised cheek. Margaret had taken down some of the high colour of the bruising, but the shape of her attacker's middle and index finger could still be seen.

Agnes sat on the bus gazing out of the window so as to hide her face, trying to ignore the stares of commuters who passed her seat. Raphael sat still and would occasionally take a deep breath to ease the discomfort of sitting. Not much was said between them, they were each lost in their own thoughts, both knowing they would have to explain their injuries to their respective bosses at work.

When they got to Agnes's stop, Raphael put his hand on her thigh. Agnes knew what it meant. She put her hand on top of his, returning the gesture and the sentiment that came with it – be brave.

Once off the bus, Agnes turned to find Raphael's face. He waved to her gingerly, with a tight smile, and she waved back at him before turning her face to Lyons.

Inside, Agnes took a moment before knocking on the manager's door. She took in a deep breath and knocked. 'Come in, come in,' Mrs Brown answered.

'Good morning, Mrs Brown.'

'Good morning Agnes, what can I do for you?'

Agnes had kept her headscarf on, and as she approached Mrs Brown's desk, she slowly pulled it down.

Mrs Brown gasped. 'Agnes, what has happened to your face?'

Agnes did her best not to cry as she explained what had happened. When she finished speaking, it was Mrs Brown's kind words that brought the tears. 'Agnes, dear. Are you sure you want to work today? I know how important this job is to you, but will you be able to handle the tittle-tattle that will spread amongst the staff? They'll be twittering about it between themselves like a lot of birds. I could send you home on sick leave, but that means you will have to go to the doctors for an absence note or you won't get any pay. If you were working front of house, I would *have* to send you home.'

Agnes twisted her handkerchief between her fingers, silently, willing the tears to stop.

'I am so sorry this has happened to you, dear. I feel ashamed of some of my countrymen, very ashamed, but you do know we are not all like them, don't you?'

'Yes, Ms. I am happy to work today. If you could talk to Ms Iris I would be grateful.'

'Yes of course. Get your uniform on, and I will walk with you to your tea station.'

Agnes held her head down as she walked to the staff room. She was already getting stared at by other members of staff as she walked alongside Mrs Brown.

When Mrs Brown saw Iris, she motioned her over. 'Iris, may I have a word in my office.'

'Yes of course, right away.'

Iris and Mrs Brown made their way to the manager's office, and Agnes and Katie were left alone. Agnes did her best to keep her head down, arranging teapots and spooning in tea leaves.

'What's going on then? What trouble have you caused, now?' Katie asked, sounding even more cross with Agnes than she usually did. When Agnes raised her head, Katie gasped, and put her hand to her mouth, but Agnes could still see a malicious glint in her eye. 'Oh dear, it looks like that boyfriend of yours has been knocking you about. I can't believe they still want you to work with a face like that.'

Agnes looked Katie directly in the face and spoke quietly. 'No, it was not my boyfriend that do that to me, it was Teddy Boys who beat me and my boyfriend Raphael. You happy now?'

For once, Katie seemed dumbfounded.

'What, Katie, you don't fink English boys would do dis to a woman, you want to fink it was my man, and not your countrymen?

Agnes continued to speak in an icy whisper, looking directly at Katie. 'I know you have not liked me since the day I started working here. I have stayed out of your way because I don't want to get into trouble, even though every day I have wanted to give you a piece of my mind.' There was nothing that would hold back Agnes now. 'And I know it was you dat leave dat paper in my locker. What it say – "WOG GO HOME" – and yes, I still have de paper. It remind me every day how evil and wicked people can be and now, look at my face, I have more proof of dat.'

Katie's mouth had fallen open, whether in outrage or shock Agnes couldn't tell, but she wasn't finished with her yet.

'You are just like dem, Katie, yes you are de same, you might not be beating us with your fists but you are trying to destroy us with your words and your hatred, well I can tell you, you will not.'

This seemed to hit home, and Katie's face fell, she shook her head as if in disbelief. 'No, Agnes, I just find it hard to take in. I have cousins who are Teddy Boys, I just can't imagine them doing this, I would not want this on anyone, I am not like them Agnes, I am not . . .'

The force of Agnes's words seemed to have burst all Katie's confidence, the veneer of dominance she had held over Agnes was gone. Like many bullies, she had retreated in the face of strength. Now Agnes could see tears welling up in Katie's eyes, her face turning red trying to hold them back from falling on her flushed cheeks. Katie took in a deep sniff to pull back the snot building in her nose. She pulled out a hankie from her pocket, wiped her eyes and blew her nose a few times and then she spoke. 'I am sorry what happened to ya, Agnes, I really am, but I want you to know I am not an evil person, I'm not wicked. And I didn't write that note, it wasn't me.'

Agnes knew she was lying. 'I know you are not telling the truth.'

'Well, you can believe what you like, whatever I say you

Island Song

won't believe me, but I will say this Agnes, I never thought that this sort of thing would happen . . . not to someone I know anyway.'

Agnes felt as if her anger was like a cork that had come off a bottle; it was difficult to accept Katie's apology. Months of pent-up frustrations, months of putting up with Katie's snide remarks had given her vexation more force. Agnes wanted her colleague to know what kind of woman she was.

'Before I had dis job, I had another job. I used to work for a white lady from England, her name was Mrs Chestor, she was far away from her home, she came to my country, St Lucia. I cared for her, I looked after her and I was kind to her and to dis day I fink about her and hope she is happy. Why can't people in dis country do dat for me? Why can't you do dat for me Katie? I will pray for you because you need healing, your people need healing and I want you to know I am not going nowhere. England is my new home now. I am a decent person dat needs to be treated with respect, you hear me? Respect!'

Katie stood in front of Agnes stunned and the only action she took was to blow her nose some more and cough a few times as if to pull herself together.

'Agnes, I can see you are upset and you have good reason to feel the way you do. I can imagine it must have been very frightening, but I am *not* them. I will be honest and say, I get scared, scared that after all the years I have worked for Lyons, with new people coming, they will take away my chance for promotion and getting on in life. You're a good worker Agnes and well . . . I have been afraid that you would take away that chance from me.'

'I don't want your job, I just want to do the job I have, but I will not take your nastiness any more, you hear me?'

Katie did not respond, she just coughed again, as if to clear the air between them, her earlier emotions firmly put away once more. 'Why don't you take a quick break, I can see you are upset. I can hold the fort and start preparing for the lunchtime rush, be quick and don't be long, don't want Iris asking where you are. And like I say, I *am* sorry for what has happened to you Agnes. Now let's get going before we are both out of a job.'

Agnes could feel the fire in her belly subside, it felt good to speak her mind, she felt a weight come off her shoulders, a load she had carried for too long.

The bruise on Agnes's face hurt and it felt hot; she took some cold water from the bathroom tap, its cooling effect easing the discomfort. She stared back at herself in the mirror, proud to have finally stood up to Katie and showed her what kind of woman she was; a strong woman who would no longer tolerate bullying and abuse.

CHAPTER TWENTY-SEVEN

The news about Raphael and Agnes's attack spread like wildfire in the West Indian community in Paddington, and without doubt, the news would reach the ears of those back home in Canaries. As Agnes sat at the kitchen table, she thought about how Ella would react to hearing the news. She would have to write to her soon and explain in her own words. But how could she explain such a thing?

Agnes knew that Raphael would have preferred the news of their attack had stayed quiet, but even in Britain, in a West Indian community, your business was not your own. It was like living back home in the village of Canaries. Margaret's voice brought Agnes back to the present. 'What was that, Margaret?' Agnes asked, realising Margaret had said something.

'I said, *Pòdjab*, poor Raph, dey cut him up something bad.' Margaret shook her head as she stirred the mutton stew in the pot on the stove. 'Is good you two have each other and he serious about you.' When Agnes nodded, Margaret continued. 'You tell Ella about you seeing Raphael?'

Agnes sighed. 'Yes, and she not happy about it. But dis is my life, I'm working, sending money for her. My sister she ain't easy to please. I have to always prove to her with my actions an' when she see things working out, dat's when she trus' what I'm doing. I can't live like her and close off my heart just because Vince let me down. Dis is my business.' Before Agnes could continue, there was a knock at the door.

When Agnes opened the door, Scottie was standing there. 'Oh my.' Scottie was taken aback by the bruise on Agnes's face. 'What de hell dey do to your face man? I hear dere has been some trouble, but I never expect to see de damage dey do to you.'

'It's looking much better Scottie, de swelling has come down a lot,' Margaret said.

A look of anger passed across Scottie's face. 'I thought it was a made-up rumour and now I fin' out it's true. Le' me tell you none of us is safe. I ca' tell you how sorry I am dis happen to you. If you an' Raph plan to go out again let me know okay. Den we will be strength in numbers, okay?'

Agnes nodded at Scottie's suggestion, thinking it was a little late for that. 'Thank you Scottie, we will remember for next time. Raph is upstairs, he took it real bad. He will be happy to see you.'

Raphael heard someone coming up the stairs and he hoped it was Agnes to help him change his bandage and clean his wound. The boys at work had managed to cover for him and he was able to rest while they worked, only picking up his brush when they thought Mr Harrison was on the warpath, but he still felt very weak. He lifted his head at the knock on the door.

'Hey Raph, it's me Scottie.'

'Hey, Scottie, dat you?'

Scottie stood at the doorway, regarding his friend, before shaking his head.

Raphael gestured him inside. 'De news really get around.'

'What dey do to you boy?'

'It's a gash on my side; skin-deep but big, it's already healing up. Dey give me some licks with dey fists too. My ribs are all bruise up and it hard to breathe.' Raphael lifted his shirt to reveal his bandages and pointed to the wound.

Scottie inspected it, shaking his head the whole time. 'Tings are getting worse in de area, but some of us fellas not standing for it no more. I have a knife on me at all times, Raph. I an't taking chances. Look what happen in de Grove. Us coloured boys had to stand up and fight back. And if it happen again I will be right dere.'

Raphael was surprised to hear this. 'For real, Scottie? You want to put yourself in all of dat again, what if the police find you with dat?'

'Raph, I'm an easygoing fella, I just like working, earning money and spending it on my girl and having good times at de weekend. There are tings I can't brush off, that nobody should. You can call me all the names under de sun, but when you come at me with a weapon I have to defend myself. You ever hear of Eric Williams?'

'No, who is dat?'

'One day I tink he will be Prime Minister of Trinidad and Tobago. He is an educated man and a scholar on the topic of slavery and other tings. He said "Slavery was not born of racism; racism was the consequence of slavery." I read his book, *Capitalism and Slavery*. It was de first book I ever read outta the classroom at school. It was hard going but I got de gist. If it wasn't for emancipation, my brother, we would still be working on de sugar plantation! And as my name suggest, my father was a Scotsman and my beautiful mother was half black and half Indian. So I am all colours of de rainbow, but despite dat, I a proud black man and de Trinidadian culture is ingrained in me.'

Raphael remembered not being able to get off the ground as he was kicked and then stabbed; it was hard to defend himself and Agnes. What Scottie was saying was not realistic. 'Let me tell you Scottie, dease fellas beat me bad and to know dey put dere hand on Agnes... Man, I feel shame for letting her down, allowing dat to happen to her.'

Scottie nodded in understanding. 'Look right now you feeling bad, you were on de ground – if you were standing you would have beat dose evil bastards bad, you would have. I am sure she know dat. Dis has happen to you and now you know you mus' be ready to fight back if it happens again.'

Raphael believed that Scottie was a man that could change the world, but he didn't feel he was that kind of man, himself, he was a lover not a fighter. Scottie continued.

'My skin tone is what people see and I am judged on dat. First, hate is created and then de ignorant follow with fear. Dease white folks don't know who we are, Raph. Dey afraid of us. So you mus' learn to use dat, get educated man, know your rights and if anyone come at you again have something in your pocket to protect yourself.'

Raphael knew that when he was attacked he wouldn't have had a chance of pulling a weapon from his pocket, even if he'd had one. There were too many of them holding him down. But would he have retaliated by stabbing one of the Teddy Boys, potentially killing one of them? He didn't know if he had it in him.

Scottie could see by Raphael's face he was feeling discomfort at his wound. He eased up on his friend. 'Look, Raph, when you head out again with Agnes, let me know. There's force in numbers. We can double date, I already told Agnes dat.'

'Yes, man, dat would be a good idea. So you going wit Theresa?'

'Well, we bin spending more time together you know. She's a decent girl, she not just after a good time, Raph.'

'So when we plan our double date, what if she mention me and Annie? Man, I don't know if I can handle dat.'

'Don't you worry about dat, Raph. Theresa know how tings go, plus she know how serious you are wit Agnes. Everyting cool.'

On that note, Scottie made his exit. Raphael could hear Scottie mutter to himself as he made his way down the stairs, 'We gotta be ready, man.'

Later that evening on his way to his nightshift with British Rail, Linus dropped in on Agnes and Raphael. It had been a few weeks since the brothers had seen each other, and in that time, so much had happened.

'Well, my brother after what happen to you, I never thought dis would be on the cards for me, and the hardest fing to take was seeing Agnes get hurt. I could not protect her.'

Agnes was out of the room washing the dinner plates. Linus and Raphael spoke quietly.

'I know, my brother. Dat must have been hard, real hard. How you holding up?' Linus asked.

'I all right, it Agnes I worry about.'

Both men sat quietly for a moment, Linus frowning and shaking his head. When he spoke again, his voice was sombre. 'We have to look after each other, my brother. I wish I was there to defend you. At least I got away from dem hoodlums in the Grove, but dere have been some nights I wake up sweating tinking dey still runnin after me.'

Raphael put a hand on his brother's shoulders. 'Look, we all okay now. We experience someting dat will stay wit us for a long time, but we have to stay strong and remember not all white people like dat. We can't live in fear dat we going to get jump whenever we go out in London, you hear me?'

Linus had some other news for Raphael. 'Well, me and Cynthia have been getting serious, we bin spending a lot of time wit each other.'

Raphael was happy for his brother. 'Well, I tink it was de best fing I move out. Seems to me I was de one getting in your way. I happy for you my brother, good for you man!'

Linus chuckled at Raphael's praise. 'Well, you know what dey say about de quiet ones. She's a wonderful woman, Raph, and she look after me. Plus she can cook too, ha ha. We spending a lot of time wit each other since her roommate's fella come over from Trinidad.'

'Linus, I happy for you man. You know what, I happy for both of us, we lucky to have found two good women.'

'Raph, I understand. Agnes is a fine woman. Our mother will be proud of us, and our farda, I tink he will be surprised to know we making a life in England, despite all de challenges.'

Raphael nodded, but inside himself there was a cloud of doubt. Could he be the man his brother was? Linus had struggled and travelled so far, now he was creating the life he always wanted in a country not of his birth, with a good woman at his side and a job he enjoyed. Raphael knew his brother; he had no vices to hold him back. Linus was a man that made the world go around, working, paying his taxes.

Raphael had originally had grand plans for himself, making it big and achieving great wealth; he now realised all he really needed was the same as his brother, but his vices were ever-present, the drink and the lying to Agnes. Life without a drink to make him feel alive wasn't one he could look forward to. He still enjoyed dancing, throwing caution to the wind and stepping out of the daily grind. Agnes was the one who reminded him of his domestic responsibility, encouraging balance within himself and what it meant to be in a loving relationship. However, Raphael's demons were strong, and he found it hard to fight them and wasn't always sure he wanted to.

'Our father thought I would be back in St Lucia with my tail between my legs. Well I happy to prove him wrong,' he said, full of bravado for Linus's sake, but deep inside Raphael knew he had a long way to go in order to do that.

Agnes was becoming more and more concerned for Raphael since their assault. Sometimes he seemed to disappear inside himself, and he was drinking a lot more regularly. He had started to buy a quarter bottle of whisky at the beginning of the week and have a few shots before his evening meal, and then he would have a shot before bedtime, which had now become his routine. Agnes would look at him as he swigged his drink, unable to keep her feelings from showing on her face.

'Don't look at me like dat. I need it to help me sleep. Plus, I make de bottle last me de week.' Which was a lie. 'Don't worry yourself, I have it under control,' he would tell her. And without fail, when his head hit the pillow, Raphael would be fast asleep in minutes.

He required his nightly pacifier so he could close his eyes and rest, she told herself. But she could not deny that the days of Raphael only drinking at the weekends were now long gone. On Saturdays after his visits to Scottie and the betting shop, he would occasionally arrive home tipsy and sometimes argumentative. 'Why you giving me dat look again? Don't I treat you right? I'm a working man. I gotta have some release.'

Agnes would shout at Raphael in frustration. 'De bottle seem to be your good friend dease days! It seems to me you're going back to your old ways!'

'Old ways? What you talking about, woman? Dis is the new me! I'm a working man! I don't treat you bad do I?' Then he would stop mid-flow, exhausted at trying to defend himself, and switch to being amorous instead. 'Awww, Agnes, you know I love you, you know I do. Why you raising your voice to me so?'

If Agnes allowed him to get close enough to her, hold her around her waist, he would pull her even closer in a loving embrace. She would sometimes allow herself to let go and succumb to his advances, but at other times, she would push him away, not hiding her disappointment in him. He would fall back on their bed laughing and decide to stay where he had landed, quickly falling asleep. Raphael was never aggressive in any way towards Agnes, and he always returned home to be with her. He paid his part of the rent on time and when Agnes was on a weekend shift at Lyons he would be happy to do the grocery shopping and help to keep the place tidy. He never stayed out late, and he never had the scent of another woman on his body. She told herself she should feel grateful, 'No one is perfect. I should accept Raphael for what he is, as long as he treats me good and don't put his hand on me.' There were other benefits to living permanently with Raphael. They shared the rent and bills to which he was always willing and prepared to contribute. This meant Agnes had a little extra cash to send home and was able to make a small payment to her lay-away. She was determined to purchase her Singer sewing machine. One day she was going to start making her own dresses and had already started to collect a few Simplicity dress patterns and was keen to place them on fabric to cut and sew. Agnes was learning to take the small wins in life and not seek perfection, but she couldn't stop the voice of dissatisfaction from nagging at her, and she knew what her sister Ella would say if she could see Raphael sipping from his whisky bottle night after night.

Well Ella wasn't here, Agnes told herself, and she would just have to take what God was giving her in Raphael and make the best of it for now.

CHAPTER TWENTY-EIGHT

It was a week before Agnes's second Christmas in England, and she and Moses had just finished their day shift at Lyons Corner House. They stood close to each other, side by side at the bus stop doing their best to keep warm. The snow had fallen, and it was no longer a pretty white dusting but grimy, wet, and slippery on the pavement.

'Let me tell you, I nearly fall over de other mornin' coming outa me house. Ms Simpson, my landlady say she put salt on de ice to dissolve it. Den de dam ting nearly take me down. I tell her wit all dat snow and salt you trying to tenderise me for a stew! De landlady start laughing, telling me I funny. I tell her it's no laughin' matter, I could of bus' me ass!' Moses said.

By the time Moses finished his story, Agnes was laughing so hard, tears were rolling down her face. Moses was a tonic for Agnes. Even when he was being serious about the events that happened in his life, on many occasions he would have Agnes in fits of laughter standing waiting for their bus home. Since her attack in Piccadilly, Moses made an effort to walk with her to the bus stop whenever he could; he would stroll home with her if he wasn't on a late shift at the bakery. He had a room in Elgin Avenue, about a three-minute walk from Fernhead Road, so it wasn't too much of a detour.

Moses had a few days off work right after Agnes got hurt, so he never got to see the worst of her wounds from the Teddy Boy slap. But on his return to work, it was all the gossip in the bakery. 'Did you see that shiner? What was she doing walking around Soho late at night anyway. I heard it was her fella that duffed her up.'

Moses could not believe what he was hearing, and he was very upset everyone was talking about Agnes. 'If I hear anyone talking any more about my friend, I am going to go to de management and tell dem you giving Lyons a bad name.' That soon shut them up, for a little while anyway. Moses would later tell Agnes of his own experience with a violent assault. 'I know what it's like to be attacked, Agnes.'

'What you mean, Moses? Dem Teddy Boys get you too?'

'Well, no.' He closed his eyes as if he was reliving the moment and took a deep breath before he continued with his story.

'It was springtime, and let me tell you, all de flowers was out in de park looking beautiful. I was strolling in Holland Park, and I meet a gentleman . . .' he lowered his voice, his expression was unusually sombre, 'and next ting you know we find a hidden quiet spot, and we start to get amorous wit each other. And dis man do what he wanted wit me . . .'

Agnes understood what Moses meant, he didn't normally talk about the details of his sexual liaisons, and Agnes had never given any thought to how he met these other men. She let him continue, sensing his emotions.

Moses reached out for her hand. 'But den he turn into a

violent beast, and he beat me, right dere in de bushes, he tell me I ask him too many questions.' Moses took a deep breath, his face a mask of anguish as he recalled the details. 'I was just trying to build a little rapport, ya know. Den de man slap me in my face, and he wouldn't stop. I was in shock, Agnes, too slow to act quick, but I knew I had to defend myself. He den had me on de ground kicking me in me chest.'

Agnes had her hand over her mouth at the horror of what happened to her friend. 'Eh eh, Moses. Why he did that to you?'

'I know why he did it, he couldn't handle his own feelings so he take his shame out on me. I laid on the ground until dere was no light in de sky. I left dat park feeling broken. Most of de men I meet can't deal with who dey are Agnes. Dey feel shame about dem self. I had to accept myself a long time ago, but know now I have to be careful.'

'Moses, when dat happen?'

'A few years ago when I first arrive in England. I was foolish to tink every fing was free and easy here, but no! Just like my own country, it's illegal for me to be myself. And de fear dat some of my acquaintances have of getting caught in de arms of another man, terrifies dem into fury. De terror of going to prison and dere family finding out. I had to learn the rules the hard way. I can't help who I love. Thank god I wasn't working at the time, Agnes, because I had to stay home for weeks healing and recovering from de beating. Agnes, you must brush yourself off and hold your head up high and take it as a lesson. You are now wiser for it.'

Agnes took Moses' words and made them her own. She did feel wiser and stronger, and she never stopped hoping that one day, she and Raphael would to be able to walk the streets of London without watching their backs.

* * *

Island Song

After saying her goodbyes to Moses at the gate, Agnes walked in to 63 Fernhead Road and nearly trod on a few envelopes on the inside doormat. She quickly stepped aside so as not to wet the papers with her boots. It had taken a while for her to get used to the heavy footwear, but now she enjoyed wearing her winter booties cut off at the ankles. The leather, with a faux fur rim, hid the multiple socks she had to wear over her stockings to keep her toes warm. They were a blessing and worth the investment, and it wasn't the season for kitten heel shoes yet.

Agnes picked up four envelopes from the floor. One was from Ella and another was from Mrs Chester. She stood frozen to the spot taking in the sender's name and address: 'Mr & Mrs Chester, 42 Oak House, Holt, Norfolk.' She was sure she had addressed her letter to Mrs Chester to Dorset. Agnes was starting to feel cold standing in the doorway. She proceeded hastily up the stairs, wanting to get comfortable before reading the letter from Mrs Chester.

Agnes lit the paraffin heater, took off her gloves, boots and one of the two layers of socks. She put on her slippers but kept her coat on to retain some body heat in the cold, damp room which would take a while to warm up. Then she sat on the bed with Mrs Chester's letter in her hand. She always looked forward to Ella's letters, they were important to her, but this was the first time she had ever received a letter from Lillian.

Before opening the envelope Agnes held it to her chest and closed her eyes; she didn't know what to expect and hoped it was good news.

She opened it, slowly revealing a Christmas card depicting a traditional nativity scene. It was a beautiful card sprinkled with silver glitter on a star over a scene of the three wise men and baby Jesus in the manger. Agnes stroked the card to feel the grain of the silver dusted on the picture. She opened it to read what was inside. The greeting was printed, her name was hand-written:

To Agnes,
  Season's Greetings, from our home to yours.
  Wishing you a very Merry Christmas and Happy New Year.
  From The Chesters

Agnes opened the letter enclosed.

Dearest Agnes,
  I must apologise for taking so very long to respond to you. We have recently received a whole parcel of letters sent to our old address in Dorset. Our new address is written on the front of this envelope.
  We have now read all your letters and are overjoyed to learn you are now living in London. You made it, Agnes! What an adventure it must have been for you making that journey.
  We have so much to share with you. One piece of very important news is that Edward and I have become parents to our own little Agnes, and yes we named her after you!

Agnes had to re-read this section aloud to clearly understand this news. Agnes put her hand to her chest as if to hold herself together and then she touched her face and smiled.

  You were such an important part of our life in Saint Lucia, we felt it was right to name our daughter after such a dear and steadfast friend . . . One day I would like to visit you in London and enjoy a cup of tea with you at

Lyons. I do hope my instructions on making tea came in handy for you.
Until we see each other again, please do stay in touch and I promise to do the same.
With fondest regards,

And signed in ink, *Edward, Lillian and baby Agnes.*

Agnes sat on the edge of her bed and re-read the letter to allow Lillian's words to really sink in. She was overjoyed to learn that the Chesters were now parents. And to discover that she was not forgotten; and also very surprised and delighted to discover their child was named after her: 'Agnes'. She *was* still remembered by the Chesters and she was special enough that they named their firstborn after her. Agnes felt a thrill all the way down to her cold toes.

'Agnes you home?' Raphael called out from the hallway. She could hear him wiping his feet on the mat outside their door.

'Yes, I'm here.'

Raphael walked in to find Agnes sitting on their bed with her coat on. '*Eh eh Agnes, ki, ki sa ou ka fare la.* What are you doing there?' When Agnes looked up, Raphael could see she had been crying.

He walked over and sat on the bed next to her. 'You okay, Agnes? What's dat on your face?' Agnes touched her face and looked at her hands, it was the glitter from the Christmas card on her cheek. Raphael gently brushed the glitter dust off Agnes's face.

She showed Raphael what she had received. 'Look what came in de post, a Christmas card from Mrs Chestor.' She reached out her hand with the card and letter to show Raphael. Agnes had been waiting for some communication for so long, she was beginning to feel that Mrs Chester was a figment of her imagination, but this was proof that her feelings about Lillian were reciprocated.

'You have been waiting for dis for a long while. What she say dat make you cry?'

'Well, she name her daughter Agnes, after me. I can't believe she do dat.'

Raphael let out a relieved breath. 'Oh, dat's nice. It's not bad news den! I going to wash up, I can smell the food from the oven. I'm hungry.'

Agnes was feeling warmer. It was time to take her coat off and dish out the evening meal. Her sister's letter would have to wait for later, before bed.

Raphael stood at the bathroom sink and stared at himself in the mirror. He looked a little older than when he had first arrived in England, the lack of tropical sun dulling his complexion, but he still had his good looks, he told himself. He smiled at himself to see if his gold tooth cap had its sparkle and was reassured by the twinkling reflection from the mirror.

He enjoyed this part of the day, behind the locked door of the chilly bathroom when he was refreshing himself after a day working with his hands. It was quiet and still. It wasn't the best room in the house, with its damp walls and harsh light, but it was a space in which he could think and be with his own thoughts. When he splashed the warm water on his face it brought a calmness, as well as washing away the grime of the day.

The knife wound he received a few months ago had healed, but when he was feeling tired it ached. The boys at work had continued to cover for him, masking his weakness behind good cheer and chatter when the boss was around, and Raphael had gotten away with it, and was starting to pull his weight again.

The ache was a sign he needed to rest, but first he had to

Island Song

have his shot of rum to help him wind down and take him to sleep. He hoped it would keep him in a deep sleep until 6 a.m. and banish the recurring dream he had of being chased to the soundtrack of Agnes's screams. Some nights he could control the narrative of the nightmares and fight back against his attackers, but it was always the sound of her screaming that woke him up in a cold sweat.

Now the sound of someone coming up the stairs broke him out of his thoughts. It would be either Margaret or Vitalis, and they would need the bathroom at some point. He put his shaving soap and razor inside his towel, rolled it up, and moved towards the door, the ache on his left side slowing him down. He stopped, took a breath and unlocked the door.

Agnes called out from upstairs. 'Raph, your food is ready. Come and get it before it gets cold!'

'Okay, I comin'!'

Agnes had already put the meal of stewed mutton, potatoes and cabbage on a plate. A glass of water and an empty shot glass sat beside it. 'I don't know where you keep your whisky,' she said, looking at the empty glass. 'Raph, I don't want you to hide it from me.'

Raphael did not meet her gaze. 'I not hiding it from you,' he muttered, 'I just don't want to keep it out.'

He moved towards the small cupboard under the sink and pulled out the rubbish bin. Behind it was the quarter bottle of alcohol. He poured himself a glass and downed it in one. 'Now you know where it is.'

Agnes had known it was there all along. Only now, he knew she knew too.

Part Three

CHAPTER TWENTY-NINE

It was six o'clock in the morning and the sun was already high in the sky. The cockerels crowed, making sure to mark their territory and wake up the village in the process. Ella had been up and busy from 4.30 a.m.; it was the coolest part of the day. The winter trade-winds had the palm trees swaying elegantly in the breeze. Her white garments, hanging on the washing line and bleaching in the sun, swayed with the same rhythm. She did her best to avoid doing her laundry at the river, not enjoying the gossip and the crude jokes any more. A few weeks ago she had been washing Tina's school skirts when she overheard two women talking about an attack in London. Her ears immediately pricked up.

'I hear dey beat Raphael bad and Ms Agnes was with him, you know dey together now.'

The other washer woman responded in shock: '*Sa pa vwé*, No it's not true!'

'*Évwé*, its true.'

Ella had never been as confident as Agnes, who would have told them to shut up and mind their own affairs. She only listened in horror before the two women realised who she was, and lowered their voices to a whisper, or perhaps they had meant her to hear all along.

Ella was worried about Agnes, and upset with her for not letting her know about the attack. She couldn't believe she'd had to hear it from someone else. It should have been shared in her sister's last letter, privately. Ella knew that Agnes did not want to worry her, but to hear the news from a third party felt like the Deterville sisters were sharing their personal business in public. Tina was now eight and Charles six and both growing up fast. They spoke of their mother Agnes with interest and enthusiasm, always wanting to know when their next parcel would arrive. Ella could sense this dependence on their mother for money and gifts, and felt it didn't bode well for the future, especially while they lacked the direct physical expression of their mother's love. In her next letter she would advise Agnes not only to write to her, but to each of her children, and she would encourage them to respond with gratitude.

Ella felt lonely at times. She missed her sister, especially now in the Christmas season. When Agnes had been at home, the two sisters had enjoyed their preparations for it, and she remembered how Agnes would be eager to start mixing up the ingredients into the batter for their traditional Caribbean Black Cake. She would take great pleasure in opening the jars of preserved local fruit, green pawpaw, golden apple and carambola, or star fruit, stewed together then soaked in Ruby Rich wine and white rum.

The browning sugar would then be added to the cake batter, releasing the dark, sweet aroma which would permeate the air. The filled cake tin would be carried carefully to the baker in the village to place in his oven. The warm fruit cake would be returned home to cool and would entice anyone who would smell the aroma to take a slice.

The added scent of boiling red sorrel on the coalpot would add to the festive feeling. The juice would be sweetened to make it palatable and bring out the floral flavours. Freshly grated ginger soaked in water, with clove and cinnamon and a healthy dose of brown sugar and a squeeze of freshly picked lime were added to the mix and left to simmer. Once removed from the heat, it was cooled, then it was on to the brewing of alcohol-free ginger beer.

Now Ella had to face Christmas preparations without the bustle and vitality of her sister being busy around the house and she felt uninspired to keep up the tradition of the season. When would she see her Agnes again? Of this she was uncertain.

Ella's favourite aunt, Flora, had moved to the capital, Castries, to work with the Ministry of Education. It had been almost two years since she had left the village and now Flora's son Johnnie would visit Ella every week with fresh fish and ground provisions of yam and dasheen from the Deterville plot of land in Ravine Duval.

Every few weeks he would take the ferry to Castries to visit his mother and he would always return with a message: 'My mother has sent you some books for the children and she wants to know when you will visit her?'

Ella always found it hard to respond with a firm yes; she never searched her mind for a lie, as her excuse was, 'I have to be here for the children.' Which was true, but the real reason was because she was still afraid of the sea and the unfathomable ocean that had drowned the poor souls on the *Blue Belle*.

'Dere is talk dat de West Coast Road will be open soon, and

when it is, I will own a car of my own and I will take you to Castries myself,' Johnnie bragged to her.

Ella ignored him and changed the subject. 'You staying to eat with us?'

He responded without any hesitation. 'Of course, by law! You know I love your cooking.'

Ella loved to cook, and her favourite meal was green figs and saltfish, which Johnnie loved to eat. She had especially liked making it for Byron, but after that terrible episode, she never cooked for Byron again.

The day after his transgression, Byron arrived at her door before the sun had crested the deep verdant hills to the East of the village. He avoided meeting her eyes.

'Ella please forgive me. I know you have your principles. I have let myself down by debasing myself in front of you like that.'

Ella could not find the words to respond, she found it hard to look into his eyes as he spoke because she felt so embarrassed, remembering his face as it contorted in sexual gratification. But she also felt ashamed of herself, feeling that she had been the one to disappoint him through not knowing what to do. He stood in front of her waiting for her response, but Ella could only keep her head lowered to hold back her tears.

'Ella there is something I have to tell you. I have to go back to Barbados. The last letter I received was to inform me that my mother is seriously unwell, and I have other matters that I must take care of.'

Ella raised her head and finally found her voice, though it shook as she spoke.

'I can come with you and care for her. I will take to the ocean with you Byron. I will do what you want me to.'

Ella could see the perspiration beading on Byron's head; he took out his handkerchief to mop the sweat from his face. 'This is not the right time. I spoke with Ms Francis early this morning and we have agreed I will leave on Monday, the day after tomorrow. I should be away for two, maybe three weeks. I will write to you Ella.'

Ella did not see Byron again before he left. Her days and nights following his departure were wracked with sorrow and shame. Overwhelmed with such deep feelings of hurt, she would take herself to the river's edge at the back of their house underneath the broad canopy of the mango tree and there by the thick roots that intertwined with the rocks she would scrub her body with carbolic soap, then throw two buckets of fresh water over herself to wash the slime of Byron off her skin. She would watch the soapy mucus float away down the ever-flowing river. Her mind would continue to return to the shameful episode of Byron which made her feel sick to her stomach and any food she attempted to put into her mouth tasted sour.

But at night before a fitful sleep, she would pray that he would return to her, and with him the feelings of love and adoration that she wished she could still feel inside.

She found it was hard to eat. Tina and Charles would ask their mother, 'What is wrong with Auntie Ella?'

'She is not well, so be quiet in de house,' is the only way Agnes could answer; she found it hard to explain what it meant to be heartbroken. Maybe one day they would experience it for themselves.

Ella's dreams for her future had become intertwined with Byron and it was as if the world around her was shifting in a terrifying way.

When a letter did arrive from Byron, the contents did nothing to quiet her mind.

My Dearest Ella,

It is hard for me to write this, but I believe you deserve the truth. Ella, I am a married man. I have a wife and a son here in Barbados. They live with my mother. This is why you could not come. My wife has been caring for my ill mother but with a growing child it has been difficult for her to take on both responsibilities.

I know this will be a terrible shock to you, Ella. I had no intention of becoming romantically involved with anyone while I was in St Lucia. The truth is I could never marry you, but my dream of going to England with you was true. I still wish it could have been.

Please try not to hate me. In another lifetime, I would have lived a life of Shakespeare and adventure with you. I hope that through your faith in the Almighty, you can find it in your heart to one day forgive me.

Byron

What remained of Ella's heart shattered in that moment. Her body shook with shock and shame. Tears streaming down her face and with the little strength she had, Ella passed the letter to her sister, and Agnes fumed, declaring, 'I mantè, nom Sala MANTÈ! *He lied, that man LIED!*, E Salop la! *Nasty man!* Sakwé kouyon, *Damn fool!*'

The devastation forced Ella back inside her shell once more, but this time it was her words that were locked inside her too. A numbness overwhelmed her whole being. She could not summon forth any anger, she felt broken with sadness and disappointment and an overwhelming sense of shame for allowing Byron into her heart.

For many weeks, the only sounds that came forth from her mouth were the screams that accompanied the return of her night terrors. This time, before the bodies from the **Blue Belle** *dragged her down with them to their depths, she saw Byron, drifting away from her far out to sea, as she pleaded for him to rescue her.*

On laundry day, rather than soaking up the joy of the river, Agnes too now kept her head bent in silent mourning as the ladies whispered cruelly. 'She knew all about his family ya know! She want his money and was happy to be his Jabal, his woman on the side. Why she crying so? She a beautiful woman, an bèl fanm, *with her light skin an' good hair, she can get any man she want.*'

Agnes was often furious and wanted Ella to be too, but her sister had no strength left for anger. She took to her bed and didn't leave it for days at a time and when she did raise herself from her bed, her usual elegant stance was replaced with slow slumped movement; she hardly lifted her slippered feet, pushing herself along with whatever energy she could muster. Ella wanted the waters to take her and wash away all thoughts of Byron, of a future with a man she loved, and of an island she had briefly dreamed of leaving.

Agnes would tell her sister that it was Byron who should be shamed into silence, his lies showing his true colours.

When Ella's voice did return, it happened one morning when Agnes was sitting on her father's stool at the back of the house stirring their morning brew of cocoa tea on the coal pot. Agnes was singing a sweet melody, a heartfelt calling of an island song. A deep humming Ella could hear, willing her sister to speak again.

As Agnes handed her sister her morning cup of cocoa tea, she was about to turn away but Ella spoke after her first sip of the tea. 'Agnes you put too much bay leaf in this, you make it too strong, li bezwen plis sik, *it needs more sugar.*'

Without a word of response Agnes walked to the cupboard and reached for the sugar tin, with tears of relief that her island *song had worked its magic, she was just so happy to hear Ella's voice once again.* Agnes wiped her eyes wondering if her sister could finally be healed, or if Byron's betrayal had only imprisoned her sister deeper inside herself.

Ella dished up Johnnie's green figs and saltfish, to enthusiastic thank-yous from her cousin, and told herself she would get Tina and Charles to help her make the Christmas Black Cake – she would find the joy to do it and share it with them. She wondered if Agnes would have the ingredients to do it in England, and if she did, whether she would be humming her island song and thinking of home?

CHAPTER THIRTY

St George's Tavern was not as lively as Raphael had anticipated a couple of days before Christmas, the pub looked tired with worn out brown furniture, smoke-stained walls and some uninspiring rural landscapes and portraits of forgotten war heroes in dusty frames. There was a couple canoodling in one of the booths, a few fellas smoking at the far end of the bar nursing their drinks and some other solitary gents scattered across a few tables.

He had just finished Mr Harrison's latest project, and was not due back at work until after Christmas. Paddy and Olly Murphy, Irish brothers who had recently joined him and Bernard on the job, had convinced him to come out for a few drinks to celebrate the holidays.

'At lunch times it usually heaving in here, but no matter. Dere is still beer in the taps. Right, so what you having, Raphael? Olly, pint of your usual?' asked Paddy with his characteristic Irish lilt.

The latter was more of a statement than a question and without waiting on an answer Paddy went off to get their order of drinks while Raphael and Olly went to find an unoccupied table. Paddy returned with three pints of the black stuff, Guinness, accompanied with chasers, three shot glasses filled with golden liquor.

Raphael was surprised. 'Hey, boys, you trying to get me drunk?'

Paddy handed out the shots of whisky. 'Come on Raph, not every day you knock off for Christmas. And we have bin talking about having a jar with you for weeks. Cheers to our families and new friends.'

All three men raised their glasses. 'To family and new friends!'

Down the hatch it went. For Raphael it felt good, an instant burst of adrenalin, but he knew he had to be careful, and an egg sandwich at lunch was not enough to line his stomach for drinking. 'Dat's de last one for me, I'm going to enjoy my Guinness den get myself home.' He wanted to warn the Murphy brothers of his intentions.

'For sure, Raph. Is there a jukebox in here, we need to liven this place up.' Paddy got up to find the jukebox and before he'd returned, Harry Belafonte was singing 'Mary's Boy Child'.

Olly began to laugh. 'I tink he may have put dis on for you.'

'For me, what you mean?'

'Dis fella, singing dis island song, he's a Caribbean island fella like you. He sang "The Banana Boat Song", boy, I love dat song. You don't know it?'

Raphael looked at Olly bemused and shook his head.

'Right, I'll get Paddy to put it on.' Olly stood up from his seat and shouted to his brother with no concern for anyone else, 'Hey, Paddy put on "The Banana Boat Song"!'

Paddy responded from across from where the jukebox was. 'I don't tink dey have it! Oh no here it is!'

Island Song

The barman yelled from behind the bar for the brothers to keep their voices down. 'There are other customers trying to enjoy their drinks.'

Paddy apologised to the barman. 'Yes, sir, any ting you say, sir.'

A while later, four pints of Guinness and four shots of whisky were sloshing around Raphael's empty stomach, while the effects were swirling in his head accompanied by 'The Banana Boat Song'. The melody and the lyrics had penetrated his brain and he was losing his voice from singing the chorus with the Murphy brothers. *'DAYO, ME SAY DAY- AY-AY-OH, DAYLIGHT COME AND ME WAN' GO HOME . . .'*

Raphael was totally drunk and the Harry Belafonte hit was now egging him on to make his way home. 'Fellas . . . I got . . . to get . . . myself home . . . now . . . Agnes will not . . . be happy . . . an' she will be . . . worried.'

Olly was not having it. 'C'mon now Raph, one more for the road.'

Olly was usually the quiet one, but now with his singing and dancing, he had become the life and soul of the party. The pub had filled up with more revellers getting into the spirit of the season, and Olly was buying drinks for anyone who would take up his offer.

'Pat, make sure you have one for yourself.'

Pat, the barman, cheerfully obliged and no longer complained about the noise the Murphy brothers brought to his establishment. He was happy to put their wage packet in his till.

'Now I going to . . . take a slash . . . den I goin' home. It's bin good fellas but I have to go . . . !'

Raphael slowly moved towards the bathroom trying hard not to fall over a stool. Swaying back and forth in the stall, aiming into the urinal wasn't easy. But his overwhelming feeling was one of immense relief to be emptying his bladder. Making his way to the sink, zipping up his fly as he went, he leaned against it to wash his hands. He splashed some water onto his face and spoke into his palms.

He laughed at the hazy image of himself in the dirty bathroom mirror. It was time to get on the bus. '*Agnes e ka tjwe' mwen*, Agnes is going to kill me.'

'We will walk you to the bus stop, Raph. In fact, we can get the same bus. We will keep our word,' Paddy said when Raphael returned to their table. Paddy seemed to be the more sober one despite having consumed just as much as his brother.

Outside, Paddy stood in the middle between Olly and Raphael. They linked arms and Paddy pulled his comrades along the pavement, all barely able to put one foot in front of the other. Nonetheless, with Paddy steering the ship, they somehow made it to the bus stop. They leaned on each other, swaying, their backs supported by a shop window.

'Here we go. Here's our busss!'

They moved to the kerb as one, the bus stopped, bringing with it a chill winter breeze.

Paddy made his request. 'We would like to take dis fine bus to as close to home as possible Mr Con-duct-or.'

The conductor seemed amused by the scene of two Irishmen and a black fella. 'Okay, hop on.'

Raphael pulled off his cap and leaned his head on the cold window of the bus. He was enjoying the chill wet condensation on his cheeks and hoped it would sober him up. Soon, he started to drift into sleep.

'Next stop Shirland Road! Sir, sir this is your stop,' the conductor called out.

Raphael woke, thinking he was home in his own bed, so the conductor's words came as a rude surprise to his addled mind.

Island Song

'Okay . . . okay! Dis my stop? Where is dis?'

'Shirland Road and a few yards down the way there is Fernhead Road. So this, my good man, is your stop.'

Raphael looked behind him, only to find the Murphy brothers fast asleep. 'Conductor, make sure you get these friends of mine off at the right stop, okay, please and thank you . . . And a Merry Christmas to you!'

The bus conductor rolled his eyes as Raphael stepped off the bus into the frigid night air. Fortunately, he felt the blast of air was sobering him up a bit. Still swaying, he took a moment to get his bearings and put his cap back on his head. 'Okay, I know where I am.' Then he started to walk home singing his island song. 'Daylight come an me wan' go home . . .'

Agnes checked the clock again. It was eleven o'clock, and Raphael was still not home. She was in bed waiting for him, and it was agony. All sorts of images were running through her mind. Was he in some alleyway beaten up again? Was he in some kind of trouble? What should she do? Then she heard the front door slam and a rumbling on the stairs followed by Vitalis's voice.

'Take it easy, Raph.'

When she heard Raphael's name, she jumped out of bed and opened the bedroom door to discover Vitalis carrying a very drunk Raphael up the last set of stairs to their bedroom. 'Look like Raph had a few drink too many.'

Raphael raised his head and smiled at Agnes. 'Hey, baby, Merry Christmas.' His breath and clothes stank of booze.

Vitalis managed to get Raphael on the bed and turned to Agnes. 'I leave you to deal wit him,' he said, looking like he was trying to suppress a smirk.

Agnes, however, was not amused. Her face was pinched

with disgust at the sight of Raphael and the awful odour of his sweaty drunkenness.

Once Vitalis had left, Agnes started to remove his coat and shoes. When that was accomplished she stood over Raphael, who was sprawled out on the bed oblivious of her. Her hands on her hips, and shaking her head, she had to speak out loud to break the silence in the room; she spoke with disgust in her voice. 'I was worried about you, and all you were doing was drinking. You should have stayed out and not come back!'

Raphael mumbled something, but then promptly fell back against the covers and began snoring loudly. Agnes kept standing looking at him with no idea what to do other than push him to his side of the bed and try and sleep next to him with the sheet over her nose to shield her from his smokey, boozy body odour.

She turned her back to him and tried to shut out the sound of his snorting and muttering, but it seemed like an age before she eventually fell into a fitful and angry sleep.

Agnes awoke with the fumes of Raphael oozing out from under the sheets. She felt as though she had been in the pub with him the whole night herself as the cigarettes and alcohol reeking from his pores while he slept filled their bedroom. She was tired and unsure about how much sleep she had managed to get, but at least her anger had simmered down a little. Now her only goal was to concentrate on getting herself out of bed and off to work. She decided she was not going to creep around quietly while Raphael snored peacefully. It was six o'clock in the morning and the room was dark and cold, so the light had to be flicked on.

The harsh ceiling light illuminated the space and all its

flaws, especially the faded wallpaper and the shabby carpet underfoot. Agnes had done her best to make the room look inviting by placing a nice blanket on the bed and white netting on the windows, but this morning the drabness of the space weighed her down. Would she ever have a nice home with pretty ornaments and beautiful furniture?

Unapologetic about the possibility of waking her sleeping man, Agnes manoeuvred around the room, busy with her usual weekday morning routine of lighting the paraffin heater, boiling the kettle for a cup of coffee and using the rest of the warm water in a basin to wash. None of this banging and clattering disturbed Raphael who continued to be in a deep sleep, lightly snoring. This, frankly, annoyed Agnes no end. Despite her determined actions, she felt off balance and not centred. The drama of the night before kept replaying in her mind, the exhaustion of reliving the disappointment of seeing Raphael in his drunken state was enough to make her cry.

But no, she told herself, she would not shed a tear and feel sorry for herself.

She *was* starting to wonder, however, whether she may have made another bad choice in a man. Her sister's words came back to her again.

Can a man change by moving from one place to the next?

Was Ella right? Was she a fool? Agnes had given up her children and a sister who loved her for life in England, and what did she have to show for it? Battered and belittled, and now with a drunkard in her life too?

Agnes believed that he loved her, but still there was no denying he was easily led by the smell of alcohol. She felt despairing and confused, and didn't know who to turn to. The only thing she could think to do was to pray for hope and clarity. 'Oh Lord, give me the strength and courage to see this day through. Give me a sign that you are by my side, oh Lord, to know if Raph is the man to be at my side. Amen.'

Agnes gave Raphael a purposeful shake, bringing him out of his comatose state. 'Raph, Raph, *ou ka alé twavay*, you going to work today? Raph!' Agnes continued to shake him till he reluctantly sat up, rubbing his eyes and trying to focus.

'What? WHAT!' Raphael was finally conscious. 'Agnes, why you shaking me so!'

'You going to work today, Raph? I'm leaving now for work and you still sleeping like it's Sunday.'

'No! I off till next week.' He didn't turn round to look at Agnes. He knew she was upset, but he wasn't ready to face her yet.

'Oh, I see. Well, you know I have to work today but you still doing *dis papicho*, this foolishness. All I ask from you is dat you put the clean sheets on de bed and place the blanket how I like it. The sheets are in de wardrobe. Tidy dis room before I come from work and make sure you open the window to take out your nasty smell.' When Agnes walked out of the room and slammed the door, the whole house shook.

To bring further discomfort to Raphael, she had left the ceiling light on, throwing its harsh glow across the room. At some point he would have to put a shilling in the meter to make sure the electricity stayed on, but right now, he pulled the covers over his head to block out the light and went back to sleep for further respite from what would certainly be a crushing hangover.

Outside, the air was chilly, misty and dark. When Agnes had first experienced the clammy, thick, dark fog she had thought it was the end of the world. She quickly learned it was what Londoners called a pea-souper, the result of coal fumes causing the cold air to turn black. She prayed as she walked. 'Oh Lord, be in my every step to the bus stop, shine a light so I can see, and help me through the day ahead.'

A car passed with its headlights on, lighting her path for the briefest of moments before disappearing into the gloom. It was a dangerous thing to try and walk fast in the fog. She had heard stories of trains crashing into each other or coming off the rails by taking corners too fast. Taking it slow and steady was the thing to do.

The pavements were wet and Agnes was once again grateful for her boots, headscarf, coat, gloves and was relieved to have arrived at the bus stop intact. She boarded the bus, and took her seat. 'Is that Marble Arch dear?' Agnes nodded yes with her head, she was now a familiar face on the 7.30 a.m. number 36 bus. The conductor handed Agnes her ticket. The bus moved at a steady pace, and Agnes watched the Christmas decorations glowing in the foggy light from the shop windows, as they occasionally came into view through the mist. The pedestrians moved swiftly, making their way to work just as she was doing.

Ella came to mind, and Agnes wondered if her sister would be able to cope with the energy of London, the hard pavements, the gloomy fog and grey sky above, as if someone had turned out the light of the sun and replaced it with a weak lantern flame that the whole of London had to share between them. She also thought of her children's faces and how they would light up at the sight of the wonderful lights. Her heart ached.

The dreariness outside contrasted abruptly with the warm and inviting interior of Lyons Corner House. It was buzzing with the spirit of Christmas Eve even at this early hour. The restaurant was ornamented with baubles, tinsel and a large Christmas tree. The decorative festive theme made its way behind the double swing doors to the food stations and the kitchen for the staff to enjoy as well. A band played music in the restaurant foyer, and it sounded a little louder than usual so the customers and staff could enjoy the festive tunes as one.

The spirit of Christmas was definitely in the air, but this did nothing to lift her melancholy and only got Agnes thinking about her island home and the things she was missing. Back home this time of year, she would have been in the full swing of baking, cleaning and cooking. Her children would be making noise and running around her with Ella at the sewing machine humming away, finishing off orders for dresses to be worn on Old Year's Night.

Ella's words from her letter a few days before still rung in her head.

Please let me know you are okay. I am so worried. From what I understand somebody hit you? Please write and let me know how you are. I will not rest this Christmas until I get news you are okay.

The truth was she wouldn't rest this Christmas either. She was feeling out of sorts, and she knew the only cure was to write back to her sister and to have a serious conversation with Raphael about his drinking, no excuses.

Everyone was in a jubilant mood at work, even Katie, whose resentment towards Agnes had been kept in check since her Piccadilly attack. Ever since the day when Agnes had finally stood up to Katie, she had become more friendly towards her. They were not the best of friends, but Agnes gained the respect she wanted from Katie. Despite the fact she'd mellowed, she still managed a snide remark though. 'What you going to be up to for Christmas then? How do you and *your* people spend your Christmas?'

Agnes was surprised and annoyed at Katie's question. *What dis women fink we do at Christmas? We running around naked, swinging in de trees, like savages?* Agnes was still in a foul mood due to lack of sleep and her upset with Raphael. She had to be careful what came out of her mouth.

'Why you want to know, Katie? You never ask me about my life before. You fink we don't understand what Christmas is?'

Katie pursed her lips in a sulk. 'Well, if that's the way you feel, I don't give a toss what you do, I was just being friendly.' Agnes could see that her work colleague was rattled; she found it satisfying to see Katie in retreat, but then Ella's words came into her mind. 'Treat others how you wish to be treated.'

'Okay, Katie, if you want to know, I will tell you. I will be enjoying Christmas with my family at home just like you. I will go to midnight mass tonight. We will sing carols and give praise, it will be a joyful time, to celebrate the birth of the baby Jesus.'

'Midnight mass?' Katie pulled a face. 'Do you know what? I've never been to church. My family aren't churchgoers, they never had the time. Although, tell a lie, we did go to the funeral of my grandpa, that was in a church, but I couldn't tell you when that was, so many years back now, I'd almost forgotten it. My lot are either working or in the pub! The way you say it though it does sound like a nice thing to do.'

'Midnight mass is also a chance to ask for forgiveness.' Agnes thought of the way Katie had treated her.

'Forgiveness for what?'

'I have bin goin to church since I was a little girl – my mother took me. When we are dere, we ask forgiveness for all our wrongdoing, and forgive others for theirs.'

Katie continued lining up the teapots, not making eye contact. 'My dad always says you make your own way in life and don't need anyone, either in the heavens or on this Earth, telling you what to do.'

Agnes placed the teacups on their saucers. 'Well Katie, you can have your belief and I can have mine. As long as we don't fight with each other and cause each other harm, it's okay.'

'That's something good to believe in I suppose.'

'Yes, it is. And I wish you a very Merry Christmas Katie.'

'And a very Merry Christmas to you too Agnes.' Both women continued working with a subtle smile on their faces. Agnes knew this was the answer to her morning prayer, the knot in her belly had eased a little.

CHAPTER THIRTY-ONE

Raphael felt like a goods train had run over his head and his belly was rumbling loudly. He was hungry and had a hangover that would put anyone off drinking ever again. Well, for a while anyway.

He realised that the room was bright even though the curtains were closed; he turned his neck and looked up to be welcomed with the bare electric light bulb hitting his eyes and hurting his head.

'Agneeees,' he called out, remembering she had left the light on in a deliberate move to make him feel as uncomfortable as possible. He deserved her wrath. He recalled her last instructions: 'Change the sheets and open the windows to let out your nasty smell!'

Raphael made a move to get up but was stopped suddenly. He had been lying on his left side, and the pain was the reminder of his stab wound. Would the memory ever leave him? *Woi, dat ting still giving me gyp*. Raphael's belly rumbled again. *Man,*

I hungry, I gotta get me some food, but first, let me turn dat dam ting off.

He manoeuvred himself slowly out of the bed, still wearing his shirt and trousers from the day before. He sat on the edge of the bed, his head in his hands, and took a few breaths. He stank like a brewery. Head still pounding, he lifted himself up and moved towards the light switch. Click. Off. Relief.

The room went mercifully darker, with a few streams of light coming through the drapes. He made his way to the windows to open them as instructed. 'Dam, dis window hard to open.' But with a firm shove that made his head throb, it finally lifted, and the cold fresh breeze came in, making the netting dance in the wind. Raphael stood at the window and inhaled, but his mouth tasted foul, and he started to cough. It was the worst hangover he had experienced in many years. It was on another level compared to the boozy head he used to get after his drinking sessions with Linus and Scottie. Those sessions had always included sustenance, a good plate of solid food to help soak up the whisky. Drinking on an empty stomach with the Murphy brothers was not the way to go.

Raphael shuffled to the kitchen to see if there was anything he could eat. He opened the cupboard, nothing. Then he opened the oven door and found a covered plate, he assumed it was the meal that had been waiting for him from the night before. Without hesitation he found a spoon and started to devour the contents of the plate, a stew of meat and potatoes. It was cold but it still tasted so damn good to him, and at that moment, he felt love for Agnes and regret for his actions. She always made efforts to create home comforts, tasty food, a well-made bed to sleep in and a warm room. He appreciated all she did for him, but this morning Agnes had left for work disappointed and angry at him like so many times before.

Raphael had let himself be swayed by booze again, but he

could not deny that it was a great evening. It was hard for him to pull himself away from the fun. Allowing himself to put a glass to his mouth and not think about anything or anyone, just doing what he wanted to do. Drink. He could not deny at the time it had felt worth the hangover, but still he let Agnes down.

If only he had stuck to his original plan of one and home but then he would have missed out on a fun time with the Murphy brothers. *Boy dem boys can drink!* With the plate in one hand he grabbed the kettle and put it under the tap to make a cup of coffee. As the food hit his stomach, he started to feel better. He sat on the small stool in the kitchenette waiting for the kettle to boil, still amused by his flashbacks of Olly and Paddy. Raphael laughed out loud again, relishing the memory of the evening before, then coughed, patting his chest to help the food go down. He knew how to get around Agnes, he knew what he had to do. Just be loving and treat her to something nice, then he would be in her good books again, yes, that would do the trick. Then a giggle rose again in his throat, he was tickled and maybe still a little drunk. He was amused by an emerging recollection of the Murphy brothers singing 'The Banana Boat Song' at the top of their lungs. What a night!

Agnes had never wished 'a Merry Christmas' to so many people, even the staff on the late shift, employees who she had never spoken a word to.

Moses was not convinced by the season's well-wishing. 'Dat's how it go here. Dem polite, dey show dey have manners, but you don't know for sure if dey mean it; still, dey let us knock off a bit early. Come leh we go and see some of the Christmas lights,' he said, encouraging Agnes not to walk in the usual direction to the bus stop. 'Let me take your bag.' Moses had made Agnes a fruit cake for Christmas, and

Lyons had given all the staff a box of mince pies. 'No, it's not a meat pie Agnes but don't ask me why they call it dat but I know you and Raphael will enjoy them. It's an English tradition, I have bin told. We live here so let's do as they do, it's Christmas!'

It was almost four o clock in the afternoon and the skies were already dark. The Christmas street decorations strung from lamp post to lamp post were starting to sparkle. Agnes and Moses stopped to admire the Selfridges shop window with the moving Santa Claus and the cotton wool snow. The display of gift boxes, teddy bears and dolls made Agnes think of Tina and Charles. She hoped they enjoyed the gifts she had sent them, a doll for Tina and a Meccano set for Charles, as well as some books and clothes, with a beautiful rose-patterned scarf from Woolies for Ella.

'Look Agnes, dis window is so elegant.' The scene was of a family around the Christmas tree, with a fake roaring fire. Each mannequin was beautifully dressed.

'Look at dat dress Moses, look at the style. I like how dat neckline go so.' Agnes drew the shape with her gloved hand pointing at her chest.

'Dat would suit you Agnes and look at him wit his pipe. I tink I will get a pipe, it would make me look so distinguished.' They continued to look on, admiring the scenes from window to window. Nothing resembled their lives, no mannequins with brown faces.

'Moses, let's walk back to the bus stop, I tired and I have to rest before midnight mass.'

Moses didn't argue, but he could tell Agnes was not her usually bubbly self. He turned on his heels, grabbed Agnes by the arm and started to walk. The lights were twinkling even more brightly as the sky quickly dimmed to blackness. 'What's going on wit you, you don't seem yourself?'

Agnes was not in the mood to talk about Raphael, all day he had been her constant thought. *Shall I tell him to leave and go and live with his brother again?* Had Ella's warning been right? Would Raphael never change?

'I'm okay Moses, I'm just tired.'

'You know you can talk to me Agnes?'

'Yes I know. I just need to rest. I'm looking forward to the few days off work.' Moses decided not to probe any further and turned his focus to the moment. 'Agnes, look how pretty dis all is, I must bring my Auntie Paula to come and see it. I will be with her over Christmas, she not bin well Agnes. She de only family I have here. So I will cook for her and make her laugh, as you know laughter is a healer.'

Agnes smiled and wished for a moment that Moses was waiting at home for her with cooking and laughter later. No matter the weather or the mood he would always encourage her to see life in a positive way, but that would be hard this evening when she had to face Raphael.

Agnes's legs felt heavy as she climbed the steps to the house's front entrance. She was relieved that Margaret had decided to do the cooking for Christmas lunch at Fernhead Road. Margaret had requested that all the residents contribute financially so she could place an order from the hotel food suppliers at work for a turkey and a joint of ham with all the trimmings.

She was taken aback by Margaret's excited presence behind the front door. 'Agnes, I managed to get a large juicy chicken, not a turkey. The meat man say all run out, but I have de ham and my friend from Brixton bring me some sweet potato, green banana and some seasoning peppers!'

Agnes remembered she had the fruitcake in her bag. 'For true! Green banana, I cah wait to eat dat.' It was almost a year since Agnes had had green banana on her plate. 'And Moses from work make a nice fruit cake for us.' Agnes pulled out the cake box from her shopping bag and handed it to Margaret.

She lifted the box up and down as if to weigh it. 'Oh dat's feeling nice and heavy.'

Margaret's enthusiasm put a smile on Agnes's face. 'You going to come to midnight mass Margaret? I will go, but I have to rest first.'

'Of course, but first I have to season de chicken and boil de ham. I plan to put it in the oven early in de morning.'

'Okay, I will come down and see how you doing in a while.'

Agnes felt lighter walking up the stairs. Margaret was right, that fruitcake was really heavy. She kept the mince pies for Raphael and felt annoyed for thinking about his needs and enjoyment, he didn't deserve it after last night.

As she took the last few steps into her room, she could smell fish and chips. Raphael always put it next to the heater wrapped in newspaper to keep it warm. This did not amuse her because she knew this was his way of making amends. He would have to try harder this time. She opened the door and was welcomed with a well-made bed with the patchwork blanket placed how she liked it. Their lodgings felt warm and welcoming but there was no sign of Raphael. Where was he?

She sat on the bed to take off her boots, pulled off her headscarf and lifted herself up to put her coat on the hook on the door. She could hear quick footsteps coming up the stairs and knew it was him. 'Hey Agnes, you home? I have fish and chips for you and two bottles of Guinness.'

She looked at him surprised and sat back down on the bed. 'I can't drink Guinness, I told you I going to midnight mass.'

'You can have it later? You know Guinness is Good for You! It says so on the adverts.'

'You mean to tell me all dat drinking you do last night, you still want more!'

Island Song

Raphael sat next to Agnes. 'I'm sorry Agnes. I was only going to de pub for one drink and dem Irish fellas keep putting drink in front of me and next fing you know I can't stand up. Let me tell you I pay de price today! Wah my head was buss up.'

'Good! I'm glad you felt bad. My head bin hurting me all day, I didn't sleep last night. You are a selfish man Raphael,' she said wearily. 'You jus' thinking about yourself.'

'Eh eh Agnes dat's not true.'

'But it's not only dat Raph, you bin drinking every night. Okay I don't mind once in a while but every night! How you fink dat make me feel. I don't like it Raph.'

He took her hand. 'Agnes *ou sav mwen enmen'w*, you know I love you and I know you love me too. I sorry *dou dou*, darling.'

She pulled her hand away. 'Raph I don't come to England to play around, I come here to do good for my family. I had one man let me down and I can't take it if you let me down too.'

'Okay okay, I will do my bes' to always keep you happy. I promise you dat, I even have fish and chips for you.' Agnes was still not ready to accept his apology. Raphael had an idea which he hoped would get Agnes to forgive him. 'Why don't we just enjoy Christmas, Agnes, I will come to church with you dis evening and I will ask God for forgiveness as well, okay?'

'We can't go on like dis Raph. Promises and more promises. You have to fink of me before you do your *papicho,* your foolishness. I don't want my sister to be right about you.'

Raphael frowned. 'What your sister have to say about me?'

'She said you will never change.'

Raphael cursed under his breath, he was fed up with people's opinions of him; he stood and started to pace the room.

'All my life someone always have something to say about me. Ella don't know me. You know me. I'm not a bad fella, at de end of de day I treat you well. What's wrong wit me having some fun once in a while, I came home to you didn't I?'

Agnes was tired, she could not keep up the good fight any longer. But even if Raphael had made efforts to make amends, she wasn't ready to forgive. 'I'm tired Raph, if you carry on like dis, I can't be wit you.'

Raphael was shocked. 'Agnes, you mean to tell me because of last night you want me to leave.' Quickly he sat next to Agnes and took her hand. 'Agnes, please forgive me. I'm sorry. I don't care what people fink of me. I just want to be with you.'

'If you carry on so, I throwing you out.' She loved Raphael but she would be willing to end their relationship. She never had a chance to end her relationship with Vince, he just walked away, but this time she was willing to sacrifice what love she had in her heart for her own self-respect.

'Throw me out! You can't mean dat. Where am I going to go? Linus is now wit Cynthia, you will be putting me on de street. Don't do me dat Agnes.'

She had to hold her ground. 'So why you going to midnight mass? For me or for yourself?'

'For you, of course!'

'For me? You have to get on your knees and repent for yourself. For all de selfish wrongdoing you have done in your life.'

Raphael looked chastened. 'Okay I will walk with you to de church and I will get on my knees for forgiveness.' He grinned and spread his hands out widely.

Agnes felt riled by his flippancy. 'I should throw you out now! You don't deserve to walk with me!'

'Eh eh Agnes *pa de sa*, don't say dat.' Raphael moved towards Agnes.

She moved back. '*Pa touché mwen*, Don't touch me.'

'Agnes please, please don't talk about throwing me out, it's Christmas after all. Let me come to church with you. *Mwen enmen'w* Agnes, I love you Agnes. I am sorry Agnes.'

Agnes felt her resolve waver, she was tired. Her shoulders drooped. 'Well let's start from there, I will let you come to church with me. God is good, he will guide your way and my way. But, if ever you treat me so again, I throwing you out, you hear me Raphael.'

'Yes! I hear you Agnes and I will do my best to stay with you.'

Agnes found it hard to stay angry with Raphael for too long, she loved him, and arguing tired her out, and it was easier to forgive him.

They ate the fish and chips together in the kitchen; the hot food tasted good, and she looked forward to seeing Raphael on his knees in church.

CHAPTER THIRTY-TWO

'How much she owe on it?' Raphael asked the shop assistant as she checked her large green ledger. He was standing in Fletcher's Haberdashery shop, at three minutes past six on Christmas Eve. After he had shared his fish and chips with Agnes, he had slipped out to clear his head while she took a bath and he happened to pass Fletcher's. The shop sign was switched to closed, but he could see the young sales assistant still inside, picking up her coat and her bag and getting ready to switch the lights off.

The sight of all of the gleaming Singer sewing machines in the window had prompted him to think of a way he could make it up to Agnes.

The shop assistant had been quite firm, that they were shut, 'It's Christmas for me too, you know.' But when he told her she was his last hope of a happy Christmas, the young woman relented, letting him in and now he was standing there debating whether or not to make a purchase.

Island Song

The woman had opened her ledger and was checking the down payments on Agnes's sewing machine. 'According to this, there's still fifteen pounds left to pay.'

Raphael let out a low whistle. 'I thought she had been making payments every week on it?'

'She has sir and on a regular basis, she's very diligent, but sometimes it's just a few shillings at a time.'

The shop assistant was keen to hurry Raphael along. 'Would you be wanting to take the machine now?'

'Fifteen pounds you say.'

'Yes, sir.'

Raphael repeated to himself 'Fifteen pounds!' Almost two weeks' entire wage and most of the money Raphael had in his pocket. He remembered with rising frustration how much of his bonus and wages had gone towards buying drinks for Paddy and Olly. Oh, why could he not have had one pint and gone home?

'You'll have to hurry up, my husband and children are waiting at home for me, they love Christmas, you see, who doesn't!' She smiled, but he could tell she wasn't going to be kept waiting much longer.

'The price of the machine was reduced because it's an old model. The original price was forty pounds and ten shillings, so it's almost half price, you won't get a better deal.'

Raphael started to scratch his head, a habit he had when he was under pressure to make a decision. 'Okay, okay I'll take it.' He reached in his pocket and handed over the paper notes.

'A merry Christmas to you, sir,' the girl said as she turned the lights out and locked up the door behind them.

He wished her the same, and with the comforting weight wrapped in brown paper in his arms, he felt his anxiety subside. He had done the right thing. If this didn't get

Agnes back on side, nothing would. He felt relief and some excitement at giving her the gift. Raphael wanted to please Agnes not lose her. He meant it when he said he loved her, she was the only woman he had ever loved and maybe ever would.

The air was crisp and clear on this Christmas Eve night. Raphael looked up and could see some stars in the sky. He tried to take Agnes's hand on the way to midnight mass but she refused. Raphael had managed to slip back into 63 Fernhead Road and while Agnes was getting washed and ready for midnight mass in the bathroom he had glided up the stairs, hiding the sewing machine in the space above the airing cupboard.

Agnes and Raphael now sat with Margaret on her favourite bench, the three of them close together. Raphael had never been to a church that looked so beautiful. He had only taken the steps of the Canaries village church when he was a young boy and since being older he had not returned. Now as he sat next to Agnes he was graced by the spirit of the moment, a time to celebrate something bigger than himself. He felt small like a boy again. He put his hand on Agnes's knee but she moved his hand away.

He did want to do better, and he didn't want to keep disappointing Agnes.

He realised that this was the first Christmas Eve in many years that he would experience sober. In that moment he began to feel humbled by the service – the flickering of the candlelight, the strong aroma of the pungent incense, the voices raised as the hymns were sung with joyful abandon, and the solemnity of the prayers.

Christmas Eve in Canaries had been another opportunity for him to drink, dance and hopefully end up with a woman in his arms. Midnight mass had been for the old people. The rum shop had been the church he would roll out of on Jesus's birthday.

He looked up at the large crucifix above the altar and said a little prayer.

Please God, show me the way to be the man I know I can be.

He wondered if God would hear his prayer on this busy night for business, and chose to ignore the small voice in his head that asked him how badly he really wanted to change.

The following morning, Christmas Day 1958, Raphael had locked himself in the bedroom and was wrapping Agnes's present. Downstairs, Margaret and Agnes were in the kitchen preparing Christmas lunch.

He had just put the final piece of tape around the parcel when he heard Agnes's tread on the stair. She turned the handle, but the door wouldn't open.

'Raphael, you in dere? Why de door lock!' Agnes asked as she rapped on the bedroom door. 'What's going on, Raph? I don't want to come in dere and you up to no good trying to hide your rum bottle!' she called out behind the door.

'No Agnes, it's not like dat, trus' me. Agnes, I want you to close your eyes, you hear me,' Raphael answered. He opened the door, and after making sure Agnes's eyes were closed, guided her into the room.

He told her to take his arm, and led her further into the room.

When Agnes was standing right in front of the bed, Raphael said, 'Now, you can open dem.' Raphael stood to one side, at the corner of the bed, watching Agnes intently. Her hair was sticking up in all directions, and she was wearing an apron covered in food stains, but she looked beautiful.

'What is dat?'

'Agnes, it's a present, I want you to open it.'

Agnes smoothed a hand over her hair. 'Look at me, Raph. I need to wash my hands and make myself look nice.'

'You look nice already. Open your present.'

Agnes moved towards the box nervously and placed her palms on it. She took a deep breath in before removing the paper. 'It's nice paper. I don't want to tear it, we can use it again.'

Raphael bit his tongue. Would she just open it? She pulled at the ribbon and as she prised open the wrapping to reveal the box underneath, she caught sight of the lettering printed on the box and stepped back.

'Raph, no. No, Raph! I don't believe it.' She pulled off the paper completely to reveal her present in its full glory. Agnes screamed and then jumped for joy, shaking the old rickety furniture and tarnished mirror on the dresser. The floorboards creaked under her feet, and even the shilling tin near the gas meter started to rattle.

Raphael stood laughing with tears in his eyes. Agnes's response was even more joyful than he could have ever hoped for. He had done good!

The Singer sewing machine Agnes had hoped for was staring right at her. She never dreamed it would be hers so soon. She approached Raphael trying to catch her breath. 'Thank you, thank you, Raph . . . thank you! No one ever do anything like dat for me before.' She took him in her arms and kissed him with all the love she had.

Vitalis, Raphael and Agnes sat at the kitchen table taking in the bowls and dishes of food in front of them. Margaret placed a bottle of red wine on the table before she sat. 'Dis bottle come from, what dey call it? A Christmas hamper! It's a present from

Island Song

work. But before we eat and drink, Vitalis you want to say grace?'

Everyone bowed their heads and held hands and Vitalis led them in prayer. 'I call on you, my Lord, in thanks. I know der are many people who are not as blessed as we, so thank you oh Lord. We work hard for dis. My wife and Agnes work hard to make everyting look nice on dis table and my Lord we mus' eat now because we hungry, Amen and Merry Christmas.' Raphael and Agnes chuckled, but Margaret was not amused. 'Why you have to make everyting a joke?'

'What you mean? I hungry, God will understand dat. Come le' we eat.'

But Margaret had the last word. 'Thank you, our Lord, for dis beautiful meal. Please continue to bless all at dis table, our lord, Amen.'

'AMEN!'

Margaret stood to carve the chicken while Vitalis stood ready to pour the wine, but before he did, he checked with Agnes.

'So Agnes, after de other night you allowing Raph a drink?' Raphael gave an annoyed loud 'Chewps.'

Agnes put the glass in front of Raphael. 'He can have one or two and dat's all.'

'Well, you lucky Raph, to have my cousin's patience and forgiveness. I don't fink Margaret would allow me to sit at de table if I reach home in de mess you was in.' Agnes welcomed Vitalis's comment. Margaret added: 'My husband is right, I would have kick your ass out in de snow.' And with a smile Agnes continued to serve the roasted Irish potatoes and boiled sweet potatoes. Raphael did not try and defend himself. He picked up his glass and sipped his wine, slowly.

'Dat's lookin like *pon tè patat*, sweet potato?' Vitalis took a piece on his fork and put it in his mouth. 'Yes! Where you get dat, Margaret?'

'My Jamaican frien' from work. She visit a market stall in Brixton that have food from home.'

Raphael lifted a covered dish to discover stewed red beans, another surprise neither men expected. 'Dis the first time I having dat in Englan'.'

Margaret smiled, happy her efforts were being appreciated. She had moved on from the chicken and was now busy slicing the small joint of boiled ham.

Agnes noticed a dish missing from their feast. 'Margaret, you don't cook de green fig, de green banana?'

'No, I have a little salt fish dere, so I will cook it later dis week.'

'A good hot sauce we need for dat *èvèk konkonm*, with cucumber!' Raphael was ready to eat, with his knife and fork in his hands. 'Bon appetite *tout moun*, everyone!'

'BON APPETITE!'

After they had finished their delicious meal, Vitalis praised the feast.

'Now dat's the best meal I have since I bin in England!' Like Vitalis, everyone sat at the table with their bellies fit to burst.

Then Margaret spoke. 'You know what I miss. When family come to knock on your door in Canaries to say hello on Christmas Day.'

They all nodded, thinking of those they missed back home. Then Vitalis had an idea. 'I fink we should have an old New Year's Night party. It's bin awhile since I put my record player on. Raphael you can invite Scottie and Linus and anyone else who might want to come along.'

Margaret took a moment to respond. 'I can make some sandwiches and we can ask everyone to bring something. What you fink Agnes?'

'Yes, it's a good idea. I can make some food too,' she said, thinking already of what she was going to wear.

Island Song

Vitalis slammed the table, delighted that everyone agreed. 'De party will be on me, I will get Scottie to hook me up wit some bottles of whisky and I will make sure to put some extra cash in your hand my love so you can buy some more of dis delicious ham.'

Margaret was now looking at Vitalis suspiciously. 'Where you getting dis extra money from?'

'Don't look at me like dat,' he told her. 'Myself and some of my West Indian friends who work in de hospital, a few of the de nurses and de fellas I work with in maintenance, we come together, an we bin doing Pardner!'

The Pardner savings system was a simple scheme where a group of people could put money aside with a trusted individual, sometimes each weekly or monthly payday, and draw on it when needed.

'Fifteen of us all in all bin putting down few pounds a week for the past six months and it was my payout dis month.' He looked pleased, but Margaret still found reason to be vexed.

'Now you telling me dis, Vitalis? We need to save money for a rainy day, and you want to spend it on a party?'

'Don't worry Margaret I'm not being foolish. The party won't cost me much plus I get a little over a hundred pound, I will have enough left to put in our savings.'

Raphael's eyes opened wide at this point, as did as Margaret's. 'Vitalis you need to put me and Agnes in dat. Dat's good money my brother!'

Vitalis grinned at Raphael's enthusiasm. 'You an' Agnes can join the fresh round in January. It's a good way we can all help each other get ahead. You get out what you put in, but you get it easier than trying to get a loan from a bank. It's a way for us West Indians to look after ourselves, and there's no-one taking any fees out of our hard-earned money.'

Everyone nodded in agreement, Margaret saying that she wanted to join too. A plan was made. They took a drink to their success and the party that would see the new year in with a bang.

Agnes's joy at her sewing machine was tinged with sadness. The flavour of the food was overshadowed by the image of Ella and the children flashing through her mind. She hoped Tina and Charles were enjoying their presents; now that she had her sewing machine, there was no excuse not to make a dress or two for her daughter.

Thinking of Tina made her crave the moments of connection she'd had with her children, like combing her daughter's hair. She and Tina would sit by the river, and Agnes would rub castor oil into the partings on Tina's head and massage it into her scalp, encouraging nourishment and growth, a sign of love for any West Indian girl. Her hair was as luxuriant as her mother's and her tresses would shine and glisten with health. Agnes hoped Tina would be grateful for this in years to come, as her curls grew strong.

And her boy, Charles. Agnes smiled recalling watching Charles sleep while he sucked his thumb for comfort. He would look so peaceful and content, Agnes would feel the strong need to protect him and keep him safe with all her might. The memories brought tears to her eyes, and she reminded herself that these urges to protect and nurture her young children were what had brought her across the Atlantic Ocean to the place of 'gold paved streets'. She shook her head at the well-worn phrase that she now understood was a lie. Now she knew better. The real gold was in those who sought to transform their lives for the better, who sacrificed watching their family grow and in so doing brought new vitality to a country in dire need of brightening up. The golden ones were those who put their all in a spirit of solidarity and friendship but in return were treated at best sometimes with resentment, and at others with outright hatred. Her heart ached with the contemplation of it all.

While Vitalis and Raphael cleaned up and Margaret sat resting with her feet up, Agnes made her way upstairs to write to her sister, which she had promised herself to do.

Dearest Ella,
I am writing to you on this Christmas Day and hope it was a day of happiness, good health and peace for you and the children. Did they enjoy their presents? The weather here is cold and there has been white snow on the ground but not snowing today. I have never felt so cold, I have to wear stockings, socks and boots to keep my feet warm.
I think of you all every day especially when I am on the bus to work and I wish you could take in the sights I am seeing. Shop upon shop with Christmas decorations in all their windows, so many people rushing around. There is a road called Oxford Street not far from my work and they have lights hanging high up and it looks so nice when it gets dark. I think Tina and Charles would enjoy that. There are days I find it hard and wish I could be sitting with you by the river, Ella, watching the children enjoying the water, but I have to remind myself with every prayer, every day that I am not in England just for me, but for us all.
You all have been heavy on my mind and Christmas for me in England is not the same as in Canaries. I manage to go to midnight mass with Margaret and Raphael and I place a candle for you all.

I am sorry Ella for not letting you know about what happen to me and Raphael. I know you must have heard about it by now. I did not want to worry you. I am okay now with no scars. Raphael is still feeling the pain where the knife went in his side, but he is okay. I don't write to you Ella to worry you. I just want you to know I am doing my best and I do crave to see you all. Raphael buy me a tabletop Singer sewing machine. It is the best present I have ever received. He is a good man Ella. He look after me good. Things are expensive in England so hopefully I will buy some cloth when they have sales when things are sold cheaply in January and make some clothes to send for the children instead of buying them in the shop. So next time you write please send me their measurements.

I don't know when I will be back in Canaries Ella and I look forward for that day to see you all again. Please tell Tina and Charles I love them and I am here in England for them.

Please don't worry, we are all okay now and we do our best to stay out of harm's way.

May the Lord bless you all.

I miss you my sister.

Agnes

Agnes closed the envelope and looked forward to putting it in the post box. She lay down on her bed staring at her new sewing machine sitting on the only chair in the room. Her eyes traced the gold Singer logo on the machine's wooden cover. This would be her new friend, a gift she wished she could share with her sister.

Agnes was determined to make some clothes for her children with her new machine and with every stitch she would penetrate the item with her love for them. She knew it was Ella that had the ultimate sewing machine, the one that had belonged to their mother. The machine encased with their mother's love, which the sisters had dutifully cared for. Wiping away the dust, oiling the mechanism so the foot pedal would continue to spin, allowing the sewing wheel to hum and chime. With that thought Agnes closed her eyes and fell asleep peacefully.

CHAPTER THIRTY-THREE

Moses and Agnes had worked a four-day shift between Boxing Day and New Year's Eve and were now waiting for their usual carriage home, the 36 bus. It was five o'clock and the bus was late. The early morning shift was as busy as the afternoon, so it had been a long hard day, but Agnes welcomed the extra time-and-a-half pay in her wage packet. She felt tired behind her eyes, and her feet were sore from standing all day, but she was grateful for the comfy warm boots she had changed into.

Her mind drifted back to Boxing Day with Raphael. It had been two days of simple domestic pleasures: cooking, eating, doing laundry, moving around each other like a well-choreographed couple. He never got annoyed by the sound of the sewing machine as she made adjustments to a dress she was working on. It had been a hand-me-down from Margaret who could no longer get the zip closed. Margaret blamed it on the boiled potatoes which had a starring role on her plate at nearly every meal. There was ample fabric for Agnes to

Island Song

make adjustments for herself, and the bright red nylon satin dress had an embroidered bodice with a full skirt that would be perfect for the Old Year's Night party they were hosting at Fernhead Road.

As Agnes and Moses waited for the bus, the queue grew by the minute. 'Look at all dease people rushing to get home, Agnes, to see 1958 come to an end. I can't stand it when the bus get pack up and if you have to stand next to one of dem hoity-toity white ladies, giving you a look like she have a nasty smell up her nose.'

Agnes knew what Moses meant; she had experienced this herself. 'So you going to come?'

'Come where?'

'Moses, I told you yesterday, our Old Year's Night party?'

'Oh, of course I will be dere. I love a good party. Just try and stop me! It's been a while since I enjoy myself. And yes, I will bring a delicious cake creation for us to enjoy with a shot of whisky as we bring in the New Year at midnight, as requested.'

'Eh eh, look Moses, we bin waiting on one bus but now three comin.' They hopped aboard the third bus, which was only half full, taking seats towards the front, behind the driver, where they wouldn't cause offence to any hoity-toity types. The bus pulled away in convoy while they continued to chat about the evening to come. 'So, what you wearing, Agnes?'

'You will have to wait and see, Moses!'

Agnes had applied her red lipstick and with the final pursing of her lips, was ready to join the party. She took another look at herself in the wardrobe mirror, turning left and then right to see the full swing of the dress. She was happy with her handiwork. The only thing that let the outfit down were the shoes, the black ones she'd arrived at Waterloo station wearing, the same shoes she wore at work. Flat and plain with no style, but she had to live with them for this evening. 'De slingbacks would have been perfect wid de dress, but I will have to wait to buy dem.'

There was a time many moons ago when Agnes walked in Ravine Duval barefoot, enjoying the soft rainforest soil under her feet, but those days were long gone now. 'If I walked barefoot in the Harrow Road de policeman would arrest me.' She amused herself with the thought. Agnes stood still for a moment looking at herself in the mirror and wondered what 1959 would bring for her. Was it the year she would go back home? Was life going to get better or remain a struggle to make ends meet, as she continued to send funds to her family in Canaries?

Would Raphael still be her man?

'Agnes, you comin' down!?' Raphael shouted above the music. He sounded sober, and happy.

'Yes, I coming!' She took another look in the mirror and smiled at her reflection, reassuring herself that everything was going to be all right.

'Eh eh, Agnes you did good with dat dress. Very nice!' Margaret said as Agnes entered the kitchen.

'And you look lovely too, Ms Margaret. I like what you done with your hair.' Agnes felt petite looking up at Margaret, who usually had her hair pulled back while wearing slippers on her feet. But this evening, Margaret's mane was in full curl, which along with her heels, added a good few inches to her already imposing height. She was taller than most people in the room.

'Thank you, Agnes, I have been waiting to use my rollers. I'm glad you like it, but I not sure if I can keep dease shoes on my feet!' Margaret looked over at her husband and yelled, 'Vitalis turn dat music down, otherwise we upset Mrs Fletcher next door.'

Vitalis obeyed so Margaret's guests could hear themselves speak. Just then, Raphael approached and took Agnes's hand.

'Look at you,' he said, nodding approvingly. 'Dat dress look sweet on you, my love. Give me a spin, na!' Agnes was happy to oblige, allowing Raphael to twirl her on the spot. 'How about some punch for my girl?' Raphael asked and then went off to get her one before she even answered.

'Linus, dat you?!' Agnes said, smiling as Linus walked over with a young woman by his side. Linus's girl stood with an air of confidence in her high heels and purple-flower-pattern shift dress. Her hair was curled tight on her head and glistened with pomade. She wore blue eye shadow and pink lipstick which popped brightly against her brown skin. Linus was beautifully turned out in a suit and tie. Agnes was used to always seeing him in his work overalls. She could see he was sweating under his smart attire. 'Yes, Agnes, it's me!' Linus stretched out his arms and turned around so Agnes could take in his whole outfit. 'I wanted to look my best for dis evening you know. It's good to see you too, Agnes. Let me introduce you to Cynthia.'

'Nice to meet you, Agnes.'

'Lovely to meet you too, Cynthia. Linus tell me you are a nurse at de hospital.'

'Yes, I been dere for two years now.'

Agnes enjoyed hearing Cynthia's distinctive sing-song Trinidadian accent, so different from their own Lucian lilt.

'Okay, okay, what going on in here? Where you want me to put dis?' Scottie said, his loud, laughter-filled voice getting everyone's attention. He nodded towards the full crate of stout on his shoulder, and two white women at his side. 'Everyone, dease are my friends Theresa and Annie!' Margaret looked at Agnes from across the room. Both women stared at each other telepathically wondering, 'Who dease white women with Scottie?'

Scottie bellowed, 'What we doing wit dis bright light in here? Check my pocket!'

Vitalis laughed and reached into Scottie's coat pocket and pulled a red bulb out of it.

'Either you keep dis light off or put some more shillings in the meter for some red light.'

Vitalis, who didn't need to be told twice, pulled up a chair and exchanged the old bulb for the new red one. 'Now we talking, Scottie!' The new lighting transformed the kitchen, giving it a more intimate, playful feel. Agnes's dress glowed even more vibrantly in the ruby light.

Once everyone's attention had turned away from Scottie, Raphael grabbed his arm and quickly pulled him into the hallway. 'How you could bring Annie wit you, man? Of all de girls you have, you bring she wit you? What if she start speaking to Agnes?'

Scottie grinned and put his hand on Raphael's shoulder, he already smelled strongly of alcohol. 'No need to worry, man. Annie she cool. She know how tings are. So take it easy and get me a drink!'

Raphael gave him a stare, Scottie gave him a chuckle and both men went back into the kitchen.

Agnes could tell that something wasn't right. She watched Raphael pull Scottie into the hallway once he introduced his female friends and knew there was something up, so she approached Raphael with a question; the music was loud, despite Margaret's instruction, so she had to raise her voice for him to hear her. 'So Raph, what going on with you and Scottie?'

'Nothing going on my *dou dou*. Come, let's dance.'

Agnes was not convinced. 'You know dose women.'

'What women?'

Agnes was suspicious at his response. 'Oh you lose your

Island Song

sight, you ca' see now! De white women dat Scottie bring with him.'

'Agnes dere is no need to raise your voice.'

'Raise my voice! What de hell Raph? Dis is my house, I can raise my voice when I wish to.' Margaret walked over to Agnes and Raphael and encouraged them to take their argument elsewhere. 'Please take your upset outside. Dis is suppose to be party and not a time for *ro-ro*, drama.'

At this point Agnes felt the eyes of everyone in the kitchen on them. She stormed upstairs to their attic room with Raphael following behind her. 'Agnes, Agnes cool yourself.' Agnes's intuition was telling her that something wasn't right at all.

'So you know Theresa and Annie. Who are dey to you?'

'Theresa is Scottie's girl and Annie . . . is her friend.'

'Is Annie your friend too Raph?' Raphael didn't answer but Agnes was not letting up.

'Oh, so Theresa is Scottie's girl. So Annie must be your girl!'

'No Agnes, you my girl. Why you looking to cause trouble?'

'Trouble? TROUBLE! You mean to tell me you have your girlfriend downstairs in my house, and is me causing trouble?'

Raphael scraped his hand across his face, beads of sweat glistening on his brow. 'I used to know her.' Raphael now took a seat on their bed.

Agnes remained standing staring with fire in her eyes at Raphael. 'So all dose Saturdays you went to Scottie it was to meet your girlfriend. Now I see. When I was waiting for you to come home, waiting for you to come and eat the food I made for you and you leave me waiting, you disrespecting me again while you was with Annie! You treating me like a fool Raphael.' Agnes had Raphael under pressure, he now had his head in his hands. This small action confirmed everything for Agnes. It was a sign of guilt.

'Raphael how can you let Scottie bring dat woman here?'

'I didn't know he was going to bring her. When fings was serious with us I stop seeing her, dat's the truth.'

Agnes shook her head, her words icy, 'I know people have dere past, but for Scottie to bring dat girl here knowing you and her were together, it's disrespectful towards me. You have to tell her to leave de party, I am not coming back down to de party until she gone.'

'But I telling you dere is nothing for you to be worried about.'

Agnes gave Raphael a defiant stare. 'Either you tell her to leave or it's all over between us.'

'Eh eh Agnes dat's too much.'

'Too much? *Bava ou bava*, You're all talk no action. I am fed up with you men taking advantage of my good nature. You and Vince. You both call me a good woman, but you treat me bad.'

'I'm not treating you bad Agnes. I had no feelings for Annie. She meant nothing to me.'

'Then prove it and tell her to leave.' The music was now at full volume, the sound making its way to their bedroom was one of Agnes's favourites by Jim Reeves – 'I Can't Stop Loving You'. 'It's either that or I will bring in the New Year alone in my bed, and I'll never, ever see you again. That's a promise.'

Raphael stood up and stormed past Agnes before he turned and stared back at her. 'What de ass Agnes! You want me to go down dere and tell my friends to leave, you want me to shame myself Agnes?'

'Yes! Yes, Raph that's exactly what I want you to do.'

'Okay, I will do it for you Agnes, no one else but you!'

Agnes sat on her bed shaking with adrenaline, and began to laugh at her actions. Empowered tears welled up in her eyes. She could hear voices in the downstairs hallway, the volume of the music had been lowered. The front door closed loudly and then Raphael called out to her. 'Agnes dey gone! You happy now?' Yes, she was happy. Agnes wiped her watering eyes at the mirror, put on more lipstick and face powder, brushed down her dress and walked out of the room, proud of herself for taking a stand for her own respectability.

Raphael was waiting for Agnes at the bottom of the stairs. He watched her take every step and before they went back to the party he pulled her close to him and said to her softly in her ear, 'You see what I do for you?'

Agnes responded in the same way. 'Your foolishness makes me stronger.'

As midnight approached, the partygoers paused their dancing and eating and together shouted, '5,4,3,2,1! HAPPY NEW YEAR!'

Raphael pulled Agnes close, kissing her as they rang in the New Year.

As they brought in the New Year, Agnes was more confident that things would be okay with Raphael, but only if she stood her ground and respected herself. Raphael was relieved that he was able to make amends with Agnes. It was hard for him to tell his friends to leave the party but Scottie had many other parties to go to anyway, and this one would soon be forgotten about. Raphael had proved himself to Agnes tonight, he loved her, and she could not deny it, she loved him. They were bringing in the New Year together, in the same bed.

'Happy New Year, Agnes.'

'It had better be, Raph,' Agnes replied, saying goodbye to the old year, willing 1959 to be a fresh page and a fresh start.

CHAPTER THIRTY-FOUR

1959

My Dearest Sister,
Thank you for letting me know you are okay. I could not rest over the Christmas and now I am so glad to know you are well and fully recovered from what happened to you. I was so worried and upset, but God is good and I continue to pray for you every day.
Cousin Johnnie has been a good help with the children, taking them to the river and telling them stories about their family. Johnnie also had good news to share over Christmas. He is getting married to Rosa Mitchell, Ms Petro's daughter. They will get married in Canaries, so I am looking forward to seeing Auntie Flora, it has been so long since I have seen her.
Agnes, I wish you could be here with us. The children always ask if you are coming home, but I tell them you still have important business in England and that you are there for them to have a better life, so they must not think

badly of you for being gone so long. The children are growing fast Agnes. There will be a time soon that they will no longer be your babies. I worry for Tina especially because she is the oldest and will want to know your reasoning for leaving and when you are coming back. All the things you send for both of them, there will be a time it will not be enough. I give them care and love but they will need their mother's love and attention, after all they have never had that from their father. I am doing my best my sister and I miss you too, I miss hearing your voice and there have been times I hear you singing your songs as I am sitting by the river, this brings me comfort. I pray hard Agnes to be strong and replace my loneliness with hope that I see you someday soon.

I have been keeping myself busy making the wedding dress for Rosa and the bridesmaid dresses, one for Tina. I hope Johnnie will have someone take some pictures so you will see your daughter in her dress and how Rosa looks in the dress I make for her.

Please make good use of your machine because with everything you make, your sewing will get better and better. I hope Raphael is being good to you and not causing any trouble. I know you are a grown woman and I can't tell you what to do but you know I will always worry about you. If you have some castor oil you should rub Raphael's side with it to take down the inflammation.

I think Fredrickson, Sonsons's brother, is going to England in May. I will send with him a parcel for you with some herbs and spices from home.

And I will ask you again my sister to write to me first with your news and not let reports about you arrive at my door by someone else, you must promise me that.

We miss you my sister.
Take care, stay safe and may God bless you.
Your Sister,
Ella

Ella found it hard to work with the cloth Rosa had given her to make her wedding dress. It was a stiff white satin that had a bright glare which reflected the sunlight coming through the window, glistening in Ella's eyes. The softer satin baby-blue fabric for the bridesmaids' dresses would be easier to work with. The material was a gift from Rosa's sister who lived in America. Ella had been impressed and relieved that the parcel included matching thread for each cloth. She knew from experience the yarn available in Castries would have broken at the needle.

The thought of Agnes having her own sewing machine delighted Ella and she imagined them both side by side making dresses one day. Agnes was so much more creative with her designs. It would have been helpful to have had her sister's assistance with the intricate needlework and cutting and sewing of Tina's first bridesmaid outfit.

Thinking upon the last letter she had written to her sister, for as long as she could remember, she had always felt an underlying frustration at not being able to control Agnes. Agnes had her own rhythm. She had a beat to her own drum, a pace that Ella found hard to keep up with. There was also an element of envy, of Agnes's energy, Agnes's courage. However, Ella also knew there was a bond that went deeper, way beyond her insecurities. They had the same blood running through their veins, they had grown up looking after each other in a harsh and unforgiving world. Their support for each other was an unbreakable bond. They were sisters and they were survivors who still remained connected across the span of the

Island Song

Atlantic Ocean and Ella was determined that her love for her sister would never be diminished.

Ella had had to put aside her job at the school. It had been a hard decision to make. She felt she had found her purpose working with the children in the village, teaching them to read, watching their confidence grow as they began to understand and recite the words on the page, and even the small amount of extra money was welcome. But in her wisdom she realised she could not do it all. The dresses had to be finished in good time for Johnnie's April wedding, so she had to let go of her teaching responsibilities for now. She required more hours in the day to fit it around her chores and her life with Tina and Charles. Her existence in Canaries needed to remain very simple, one day much like the next, just how she liked it.

The highlights of her weeks were visits from Johnnie. It was her cousin who continued to encourage her to visit his mother, Auntie Flora, in Castries. There was nothing she wanted more, but it meant getting on a ferry and the fear of taking to the water was still too strong for her. Johnnie knew this.

'Ella, dere is talk of de building work on de road will be finished soon, it will be safe enough to drive all de way from here to Castries and aeroplanes now landing at the Vigie Field dat can take you to England. Maybe one day you will fly in de sky Ella!'

'Johnnie, *kouté mwen*. Listen to me.' Johnnie could usually make her smile, but her voice was firm. 'I will stay in de village and when you can take me by road to see my auntie, we will talk about it again. I am not going in no aeroplane!'

The only time Ella had had thoughts of leaving was when Byron Clarke had put them there, the teacher from Barbados who had spun a tale and twisted his words with the sonnets of Shakespeare and left a stain on her heart. The memory of him still lingered every day.

The sound and motion of her sewing machine helped to keep the recollection of him at bay. She would be in flow as she worked, lost with her foot moving the pedal, putting the wheel into action and the needle in the cloth.

It was her dreams that disturbed her. Byron's face would appear in them, gazing at her with longing. They would both be standing at the edge of the jetty, she would reach out to him, before he would be swallowed up by the ocean. Gone, as surely as he disappeared before.

CHAPTER THIRTY-FIVE

That night after reading Ella's letter Agnes found it hard to get to sleep. The thought of not being at a family event with her children brought her anguish. Not being there at such important events as family weddings, being the one missing from the family photographs and the fear of her children despising her for leaving them behind weighed on her.

She lay in the darkness listening to Raphael's breathing, trying to match her own breath to the rhythm of his – inhale and exhale – in the hope it would help take her mind off those thoughts and let her fall asleep. But her agony was too strong, and instead it bought tears.

The next morning her body ached as well as her head, and it was hard to get out of bed. Thank goodness it was Saturday, her day off. Still, she felt sick. She sat up, and as she did, Raphael came in with a cup in his hand.

'Morning, Agnes. I make some coffee for you.' Raphael frowned when Agnes waved it away. 'You okay?'

She shook her head. 'I'm not feeling so good. I didn't sleep well last night.'

'Well, no rush to get up. You want me to see if Margaret have some ginger to settle your stomach?'

'Yes, please ask her for me.'

A few minutes later, instead of Raphael returning with a cup of hot ginger tea, it was Margaret who delivered her the soothing brew. Margaret sat on the bed and handed Agnes the cup, studying her face. 'The pas' few days I could see you have been looking tired. What's going on with you?'

Agnes wrapped her hands around the mug, grateful for its warmth. 'I haven't been sleeping well. I just need to rest today. Raphael can do the shopping on the Harrow Road for me.'

Margaret, unconvinced by Agnes's answer, asked, 'When was your last period? You always ask me for sanitary pads but not dis month?'

Agnes looked at Margaret wide-eyed. In that moment she knew she was pregnant.

'Raphael, I can't stay in England with a baby and not be married.'

'And you sure you are pregnant?'

'Yes, Raph. I realise I have not had my period, and dease pas' few mornings I have not been well and I can't take the smell of the coffee. I put how I was feeling down to working hard and not sleeping. Not all women have morning sickness. I didn't have it with Charles or Tina.' Agnes rested her head in her hands. 'I jus' know I am pregnant, Raph, what we going to do?'

Raphael sat on the edge of the bed, scratching his head and rubbing his face, the crease on his forehead deep with concern. He took a moment to answer, leaving Agnes in bed under the covers shaking with dread at the thought of being left in the

Island Song

lurch to deal with a baby alone, once again, and this time without Ella to support her.

When Raphael finally spoke, Agnes peeked out from under the covers, her stomach in knots about what he might say. 'Agnes . . .' he patted her arm. 'I will do the right thing by you, don't worry. We will have to go to a doctor to make sure, but either way we . . .' Raphael hesitated for a second, 'we will get married. Okay?'

'Okay,' Agnes managed before sinking back under the covers and crying with relief as Raphael comforted her. It wasn't how she had expected to get a marriage proposal, but Agnes was relieved to know she would not be an unmarried mother yet again.

'Don't worry, Agnes. Everything will be fine,' Raphael promised. But he was not feeling fine, he was in shock. This unexpected news had shaken him to his core. Yet he couldn't let her know how he really felt.

Raphael held his wife-to-be until she fell asleep, and then peeled himself away, without waking her. Wanting to escape and be with his own thoughts, he made his way down to the chilly bathroom, his sanctuary, his quiet place, and sat on the lid of the toilet seat taking in deep breaths. As he breathed out, he could see a cloud of condensation leave his mouth; the disbelief he had felt was starting to slowly subside. Taking another deep breath to steady himself, he started to nod his head, as if saying 'Yes.' Yes, to the prospect of being a father for the first time. A father!

'Oh man, oh man. I never expected dat.' He laughed nervously at himself. 'It's only now I jus' start being a man, an jus' so I a papa, a daddy, a family man!' As the alarm wore off, he began to feel a sense of excitement at the thought of having his own child and making his mother and father into grandparents. But could he be a good father?

He already felt married to Agnes, they lived well together and asking her to make it official was not a hard decision for him. He loved her, and in hindsight, he now wished he had proposed in a more romantic setting, but in that very moment she needed commitment, and he had given it to her. He decided he would have to share this news with his brother. He needed his wisdom and calm encouragement.

Linus sat on a stool as his brother explained the situation from across the kitchen table. When Raphael was done, Linus finally said, 'Well, it take two to make a baby, my brother, and it look like you having an English born chil'! Plus, you will be daddy to Agnes' other two in Canaries, you will have to get more responsible my brother!' Linus was actually finding it amusing watching his brother pace the room.

'Agnes won't stop work straight away, right, and I will still be working, and we will be good.' Raphael was talking to himself as much as his brother, reassuring himself that he had everything in hand.

Cynthia, Linus's girlfriend, had come in a few minutes before and after watching Raphael pace the room nervously, decided to speak up to help bring him back to the present moment. 'Raph, jus' listen. First you must go to the doctor on Monday with Agnes and get a pregnancy test with Dr Garfield. Her surgery is not far from you, in fact it's just farther up your road. Dis is important because her workplace will want to see proof that she is pregnant so she can take time off for check-up appointments before the baby is due.'

'How she know all of dis, Linus?' Raphael asked.

'Don't forget, I am a nurse. I'm not a maternity nurse, but I know what needs to be done in dis situation. So calm yourself down, go and be with Agnes, and see the doctor on Monday, all right?'

Raphael sat down and leant forward, his elbows on his knees, his gaze aimed at the floor between his feet, rubbing his hands in front of his face. He never failed to remember that Agnes was already a mother to two children back in St Lucia. From early on in their relationship she made it clear that she had intentions of going back to Canaries to be with them. 'I am in England for my family, dat is de reason I am here. So if you want to be with me Raph you are with my children as well.'

Now they had their own baby on the way, too.

Mulling over the situation further, he was not sure if he could do what was required of him and take on the responsibilities of another man's children but then in that thought, in that moment, a spark of encouragement came. He was reminded what his mother had done for Linus, his half-brother. His mother took Linus into their home as a very young child after Linus's real mother had left him to fend for himself. The admiration he had for that decision began to fill Raphael with hope for himself. He raised his head and looked at his brother. 'Linus, you are proof dat someone can look after someone else's child. And to be a father to my own, I can do it, right?'

Linus gave Raphael the encouragement he needed. 'Of course you can do it, I believe in you, Raph, you have come so far. Now it's time to take yourself forward and have a family of your own. You get dere before me my brother, dat's what I want for me and Cynthia. *Félisitasyon frè mwen*, Congratulations my brother.'

The weekend had dragged on. Monday couldn't come soon enough for Agnes and it was a relief to finally be making their way to the doctor. She had made the necessary phone call from a red phone box on the street to Lyons to explain her absence: 'Ms Brown, I have been sick all weekend and I need to see a doctor.' Agnes apologised and also informed her manager that she would be coming into work, albeit late, as Agnes didn't want to lose a whole day's pay. She knew she couldn't say she was pregnant before it was confirmed, plus she didn't want her business getting around Lyons – if word got out it would spread like wildfire.

She would have preferred to have been getting on a bus making her way to Marble Arch, putting her uniform on and making tea. Instead, she was walking towards confirmation of another new chapter in her life, one that was not in her plans.

Another baby on the way, thank goodness Raphael had not suggested an abortion. Life was precious, a child was a blessing and as a Catholic it was against her religion.

Change once again, a life in England with a child. The vision she had for her life in England was diminishing, and that island song in her heart was beginning to lose some of its melody.

Would she be able to cope without Ella, she had always been there helping her raise Tina and Charles? Would Raphael be the one to make an honest woman of her? He promised, but promises could be broken.

Raphael was walking briskly and Agnes was finding it hard to keep up. They had not said much to each other all morning.

'Raph, slow down a little, *Ou ka alé twò vit!* You walking too fast!' She would usually be chatty and eager to get on with her day but there was a lump in her throat which held stuck emotion that would burst if she tried to say any more. She was getting irritated by Raphael's haste, but she understood it, he was as anxious as she was to know for sure if she really was pregnant. It was all well and good to make promises when she could still be just a little unwell, rather than pregnant. The truth could change everything, she knew that.

'Sorry, sorry, Agnes. It jus' I want to get there in good time.'

Island Song

Raphael could not get to the doctors soon enough. *Whether I'm a father or not, do I have it in me to be a good one?* he thought. If it was positive, he was going to be a father, and a stepfather to Tina and Charles. He was committed to marrying Agnes, he was not afraid of going to the altar with the love of his life, but to instantly become a father, this was still a struggle for him to reconcile with, was he ready?

When they arrived, Raphael took off his hat before opening the door and allowed Agnes to enter ahead of him. There were two other patients already seated quietly in the waiting room. The man had a newspaper open in his hands. He had lowered it to see who was entering but quickly covered his face as Raphael looked around. The woman held her handbag a little closer to her body, pinched her lips in disapproval and turned her gaze away from their brown faces. Raphael wasn't in the mood to take on the disapproving stare with his usual smile to show he came in friendship and Agnes had no time for the unwelcoming atmosphere, she just wanted to see the doctor to confirm whether or not she was pregnant.

Raphael and Agnes approached the receptionist, 'Morning, Ms, um we need to see the doctor for a pregnancy test.' Raphael felt it was best to get straight to the point, but Agnes nudged his elbow sharply in annoyance at his loose tongue.

'Have you been to see Dr Garfield before?'

'No Ms.'

'Okay. Here are some forms for you to fill in before you see the doctor.'

The receptionist handed them forms to complete, one for him and one for Agnes.

When he handed the completed forms back, the receptionist cast a quick glance across them both before looking down at the forms again. 'Mr Toussaint and Miss Deterville.' She now knew they weren't married to each other. 'Well, it looks like everything is in order . . .' The rest of the sentence was left unsaid.

'Tanks Ms.' Raphael was relieved she had chosen not to make a fuss about their different surnames.

On entering the doctor's office, Agnes was reminded that Dr Garfield was female.

'Good morning, please take a seat,' said Dr Garfield as she perused the two forms the receptionist had sent in ahead of them.

'We are here to have a pregnancy test, doctor. I have not had my period dis month and I have not bin feeling so well.'

'I see. Have you been pregnant before . . . Ms Deterville? You are not married?' The doctor looked at Agnes, her face stern. Agnes wondered how many other unmarried mothers had sat in the same chair as she was.

'Not yet but we plan to be. Very soon,' Raphael announced proudly. Finally feeling at home with his own words that matched his feelings.

Agnes felt a warm flush of pride when he said this, feeling grateful she wasn't alone. 'Yes, I have two children in St Lucia.'

Raphael was sent to wait outside while the doctor did some more tests and when Agnes was finally done, she approached the receptionist, looking around the busy waiting room for Raphael.

'You looking for the gentleman you came in with? I believe you will find that he is waiting outside.' When Agnes nodded, the receptionist continued talking. 'You will come back in a week to pick up your results. If your results are positive, I will inform you of your welfare benefits, for example dental care, family allowance and maternity support, as the government wishes to ensure that all babies have the best possible healthy start in life. You will be very fortunate to have your baby in

Island Song

England with all these advantages.' The tone with which the information was shared was lukewarm at best.

'Yes, Ms.' Agnes did understand that her third child would have benefits that Tina and Charles never had. Being born in England, this child would receive health check-ups, free schooling, and a good education, with work prospects. She was grateful for this, but conflicted, knowing her dreams and aspirations of returning home, the promise she made to Ella, would become a broken promise. Agnes could not deny this new child its British rights, this she could not just walk away from. Tina and Charles would have to make the journey to England, something Agnes had not considered before. She thought she was going to return to St Lucia, but now with this child on the way, everything would change.

The following week Raphael was still off work between jobs, which meant he was available to pick up the results of the pregnancy test. Agnes was back at work and glad of the distraction.

Waiting on the results made the days feel like an eternity.

Now, with the results in hand, Raphael was in a quandary. Should he open the envelope or wait for Agnes? The doctor's receptionist gave no hint as to what the results would be. Instead of heading back home, he went to the bus stop to meet Agnes. Fifteen minutes later, she was stepping off the bus. As she approached, Raphael could see her tired, worried eyes.

'You went to the doctor?' she asked.

He pulled out the letter from his pocket. 'Yes, I have it here. Let's get home, and we will open it together. Let me take your bag.'

Agnes walked heavily, her usual energetic steps were hard to muster. Her boots didn't help, despite how comfortable they were on her feet. When they arrived home, she put the key in the door, entered the house and walked up the stairs one step at a time, unhurried, knowing deep down the answer that the letter contained, and putting off the inevitable news just a few seconds longer.

It was never in Agnes's plans to have another baby, nor was it in her plans to meet someone in England and get married. Her plan had always been to work hard, look after her family back home, save money and return to Canaries, her island village in the sun.

But opening the letter from the doctors that day changed both their lives; Raphael was going to be a father, and that hadn't been in his plans either. But he knew he had better get used to the idea, fast. Now, here he and Agnes were, sitting in the kitchen at Fernhead Road with two people who would have changed places with them if they could. Agnes was desperate to share her news.

'I'm expecting a baby!'

'Eh eh, I'm an uncle again! Dat little bubba is going to have a lot of love.' Vitalis and Margaret were not blessed with children, however, they had decided many years ago to live a life of no regrets, despite never fulfilling their desire to become parents.

'I have lost many babies over the years. My body could not hold dem. So to know we will have a baby in de house will bring me a lot of joy,' Margaret added.

During the early youthful days of Margaret and Vitalis's relationship back home in Canaries, Margaret had yearned to become a mother. It was once a strong desire, but after three miscarriages she had lost hope. There were those in the village that had said, 'I fink someone put Obeah, *witchcraft* on her. Someone be envious of dem, so dey curse her. Dey don' wan' her to carry a child for Vitalis.'

Vitalis had been concerned that Margaret would lose her mind with the shame and anguish of not becoming a mother. But he had always told her, 'Margaret, as long as we are together, we can make our life beautiful, no matter what. You can be a mother to the children of our family and nurture yourself and others.'

Raphael decided to take the moment to share some more information: 'I have some other news to tell you all. Agnes and I will be getting married in de next month.'

Agnes was surprised yet pleased that Raphael decided to share the news of their wedding so soon, and to have decided on a date it seemed.

Margaret was delighted at the news though. 'Dat's true, Agnes?'

Agnes was pleased, as she had not had a conversation discussing their wedding dates with her husband-to-be yet; she decided to make another announcement of her own. 'Yes, yes! And we want you both to be *pawen èvèk nennenn*, godfather and godmother.'

This was a surprise to Raphael, however he knew it served him right for sharing wedding plans without talking to Agnes, but he couldn't help himself.

But Agnes had other concerns on her mind. From the moment she received the positive results, confirmation that she was going to be a mother again, the task of writing a letter to her sister was heavy on her mind. The letter had to be written soon before the news got back to Canaries, and she knew it would break her sister's heart.

CHAPTER THIRTY-SIX

My Dearest Sister,
 This letter is one of the hardest I have had to write. The news I share has come as a big surprise to me. It's something I had not planned but will change so much for me and our family. Ella, I am pregnant carrying Raphael's child . . .

Ella sat at the sewing machine slumped in her chair trying to make sense of what she had just read. She was numb with disappointment and anger at her sister. How could Agnes travel so far and make the same mistake, allowing a man to turn her head and become pregnant again? And of all the men to be involved with, Raphael Toussaint.

A breeze blew through the house, which helped to raise Ella out of the chair. She walked towards the family pictures on the wall and focused on the one of herself, her father and her sister. She so wished she had a picture of her mother, the person she was said to resemble.

Island Song

She felt a pain hit her heart. How could Agnes have got herself pregnant again, and now in England, while she, her dutiful sister, Ella, had been left here in Canaries to raise her first two children. She felt so let down by Agnes's carelessness with Raphael. The old emotion of worry that plagued her life in so many degrees, reached a new height now.

A fury began to emerge from the depth of her belly, rising in her throat before being thrown out of her mouth. She fell to her knees. 'Agnes! Agnes! *Oh bondyé, oh bondyé,* oh God, oh God.'

She held herself as if her mother was holding her as she crouched on the floor, her arms wrapped around herself. This was everything she had feared. The fear that Mrs Chester would lure her sister away never to return, that she would be left to rear Tina and Charles without the steadying hand of their mother. That she would be left alone, to grow old and wither away without the person she loved most in the world.

Tears did not come, but a deep moan rumbled in her throat. Her body rocked, her arms locked around herself, her head hanging heavily towards the ground.

Ella lost track of time, the moments lengthened until she had no idea how long she had been sitting that way.

A voice found its way through her consciousness. 'You okay?' Ella looked up at the figure silhouetted in the bright sunlight streaming in from the front door. 'You okay, Ms Ella?'

She found her voice though it cracked as if she was parched. 'Yes, I am all right. Who's dat?' Ella called out, still unable to make out the face.

'It's Rosa, Ms Ella,' Rosa said, walking into the house so Ella could finally make out her face. 'You told me to pass to pick up de wedding dress. Come, let me help.' Rosa helped Ella to stand.

'Thank you, Rosa.' Still shaking with emotion, Ella stood and took in a deep breath. Her hand was still on Rosa's shoulder, the leverage that helped her off the floor. 'I'm okay now. I just received a letter from Agnes . . .' Ella began, but trailed off. She wasn't ready to share what she had just read, plus she didn't want to burden Rosa with her news.

'Agnes is all right, Ms Ella?'

'I fink so, tell Johnnie to come and see me when he can.'

'Yes, Ms Ella.' Rosa was a lovely woman. She was a church-going young lady with aspirations to one day become a nurse. Her light grey eyes and constant smile gave her a sunny appearance, and her hair was thick, frizzy and tinged with copper. She was a real catch and Ella was glad Johnnie knew it.

'So you mean to tell me, Agnes went all de way to England to get pregnant again! Well, well. She will have three children to look after now.'

Ella and Johnnie sat at the back of the house talking in hushed voices so no one, especially the children, would hear their conversation. 'Yes Johnnie! She went all dat way to do de same fing again, I feel foolish in trusting her. Get pregnant knowing she has two other mouths to feed, I warned her not to get herself involved with Raphael, but she didn't tell me the whole truth about how serious they were with each other. I love Tina and Charles but I ca' look after dem forever. Dease children are growing fas'. All I can do is hope an pray dat Raphael will look after his child and be responsible for Tina and Charles, because Agnes can't rely on their father. I have not seen Vince for years.

'In de letter, she said that they will get married before the child come. So dis month there will be two weddings in de family. I jus' hope Raphael don't leave Agnes at de altar.' Ella felt as if Agnes had lied to her about her intention in wanting to go to England. Maybe all along she had never meant to come back.

Johnnie sighed and asked a question that had been on his mind since she gave him the news of Agnes's pregnancy. 'You fink you will go to England with the children now?'

Ella thought about Tina and Charles, knowing that one day they would *have* to be reunited with their mother. But as long as Agnes continued to support them with money from England, there was no need for Ella to make that journey out of St Lucia just yet. Ella shook her head. 'No, Johnnie, I am not going to England. I promise to look after de children here. I know my sister will find her way, she must.'

'Agnes is lucky to have you as her sister. She knows you will always look after dem, and I will always do my best to help you, my cousin.'

'Thank you, Johnnie. You have bin a great help wit de children. Make sure you are a good man to Rosa.'

'Eh eh, you don't have to tell me dat, and if I do wrong I will have you and my mother to deal with.'

The two shared a laugh and then Ella sighed. 'I'm looking forward to seeing Auntie Flora at your wedding.'

'Rosa's family have sent money down for her and de American dollar has taken care of everything, food, church service, *tout bagay*, everything.'

Ella wondered about her sister's wedding in London. Who would be there? And who would be making her sister's wedding dress?

She'd always imagined it would be her, but now she would have to put that dream away, everything had changed.

If not for the cash advance Raphael had received from Mr Harrison, Agnes would not have got her band of gold, her wedding outfit, corsage and a bouquet of flowers. The extra cash meant Raphael could splash out a little on himself with an off-the-hanger Italian suit and still have money left over to cover the rent and have shillings for the electricity and gas meter.

It was Bernard who had encouraged Raphael to ask his boss for an advance to buy the wedding rings. 'Ask Mr Harrison, Raph. He has help me out on a few occasions. Remember when my wife was sick? It was Mr Harrison that give me an advance to send to Grenada to pay for her health care. I already done pay him back. Ask him. Dis is important, and he will understand. Plus I tink we will be on dis job for more dan a few months.'

Raphael dreaded asking because it reminded him of the many times he had asked his father for money and the inquisition that would come with it. 'What you need de money for? When are you going to fend for yourself Raphael!'

However, he had a job now, and this time he could pay it back.

As it was, preparations for the wedding took longer than the month Raphael had envisaged, but the day came at last.

'Let everyone present here, on this day, Wednesday the 6th of May 1959, now recognise this marriage. May you treasure this trust and responsibility, may neither failure nor misfortune ever part you, and may you live full and rich lives together. On behalf of the City of Westminster, it gives me great pleasure to declare that you are now husband and wife. Congratulations, you may kiss the bride.'

The room had a sombre decor and the registrar's monotone voice did not summon forth a sense of celebration. He hardly looked up at Raphael and Agnes standing side by side in front of him.

Her pearl stud earrings and necklace were simple costume jewellery purchased from a stall on Church Street Market on

Island Song

the Edgware Road, but they made her look the part. Agnes purchased her dress suit from Whiteley's in Bayswater, preferring an off-the-peg dress for this special day. Her outfit was a baby blue polyester knee-length shift dress with a matching bolero jacket which she finished off with fashionable white heeled pumps. After so long it felt wonderful to be in new shoes and at her own wedding too.

As Agnes closed her eyes to kiss her husband, she felt a hint of disappointment. There were no bridesmaids, no meaningful prayers or quotes from the Bible. No white wedding dress, with a veil; and her biggest regret: Ella, Tina, and Charles were not present to witness the moment when she finally married the father of her unborn child.

The small gathering of friends was dwarfed by the dark panelled walls and the many empty chairs of the ceremony room at Marylebone registry office. Gathered at the front, to be as close to the bride and groom as possible, they did their best to fill the room with good cheer. However, the rest of the space simply absorbed their energy and gave nothing in return.

Once it was over, they were ushered out of the room. 'Please make your way out to the foyer now, to allow for the next wedding party to enter. You will be able to pick up your marriage certificate in a week's time.' The officiant turned on his heel and exited out a side door to collect the paperwork for the incoming group.

Margaret and Agnes walked towards the exit of the registry office, followed by Raphael, Linus, Scottie and Vitalis, the boys' boisterous laughter echoing around the halls and lobby. Scottie had accepted the invitation straight away. 'It would be an honour to be there my brother.' There was no disagreement between Scottie and Raphael, Scottie understood why Agnes wanted Theresa and Annie to leave the party. 'Raph, no woman likes to be in the room with their man's ex-girlfriend but how she fin' out?'

'I don't know Scottie, Agnes jus' sense it.'

Raphael had had to gently persuade Agnes to allow Scottie to attend. 'He is one o' my bes' frien' Agnes. I have known him since I arrive in England, I want him at de wedding. He is like a brother to me.' Agnes didn't want to argue with Raphael, but she had one request. 'Make sure he come on his own, not with his girlfriends.'

'How you feeling, Agnes?' Margaret asked as they approached the building's exit.

Agnes could not hide her feelings from Margaret. Her mood was not as upbeat as Raphael's. 'I wish my sister was here with the children.'

'Would she have come?'

'No. How could she come, there no money for dat, and especially with Johnnie's wedding on Saturday. I fink the whole of Canaries village will be at the church.' Agnes also knew that Ella would never have made the journey. Nor should she, Agnes reasoned to herself, the expense would have been too great. Their family had traditionally married in the small church in Canaries, but she was now in England and returning to her village to get married was a luxury she could not afford. A quiet, low-key ceremony was all that was required. She felt it was what she deserved after getting herself pregnant again so far from home.

'*I, sav ou gwo bouden?* She knows you are pregnant?'

'*Wi i sav*, yes she knows, I wrote her. And I told her we were getting married. I have not had her reply yet.'

Margaret regarded her with kind, understanding eyes, 'Agnes *pa mélé*, don't worry, she will understand, as long as Raph looks after you and de baby, dere is nothing for her, or you, to worry about. I am sure she is thinking of you both today.'

Island Song

'I hope so.' Despite the consoling chat with Margaret, Agnes still did not feel as happy as she should have. This was a moment she had been waiting for, her wedding day, and now it was here, she couldn't deny feeling deflated.

As they reached the top of the steps outside the offices, an English man with short back and sides, wearing a mackintosh and holding a camera approached them. 'Would you like me to capture your special day? They know me here. Here's my card with all my details. I'll take some pictures, and then you come into the studio and take a look at the contact sheet with all the shots on it. Let me know which you want printed and *voila*, one week later and they're ready. We can also frame them too for an additional fee. My studio is just up the road in Baker Street. How about it?'

Raphael stepped forward and took the photographer's business card. 'Yes, yes dat would be nice. How much?'

'Prices start at six shillings a print. That includes all my fees.'

'I don't have to pay you anyting now, right?'

'No, sir, you pay when you pick up your shots and you only pay for the ones you get printed.'

Raphael looked at Agnes. When she nodded with a little smile, Raphael and the man shook on it. 'You have a deal.'

The passersby on Marylebone Road could not help but look at the newly married couple and their friends on the steps of the registry office. Agnes was wearing the white gloves that Mrs Chester had gifted her and she held her bouquet of white roses in front of her growing tummy. The groom and the wedding party wore *boutonnières* of white carnations and baby's breath. Raphael looked dapper in his new dark blue Italian suit from Burton's, white shirt, tie and his polished shoes that glistened under the hem of his trousers. The clouds parted for a moment to allow some weak but welcome sunlight to grace the scene.

The photographer motioned for them to stand together. 'The

light is lovely right now. So can you all quickly stand closer together, wonderful!'

The camera shutter clicked, and then the photographer said, 'How about a smile from everyone? This is one of the happiest days of your lives.' Still no smiles. He didn't know that West Indians preferred to look distinguished without showing their teeth in photos. The photographer tried again. 'Now, how about a picture of the bride and groom, and this time how about a big smile for the camera, it is a wedding not a funeral after all eh?'

Margaret took out a small box of confetti from her handbag. 'Sir, maybe this will help?' She threw the colourful paper into the air over Agnes and Raphael.

This surprised them, and the photographer finally got his shot of the happy couple's big smiles. Raphael and Agnes loved each other. Raphael, for years to come would say, 'My wedding day, well dat was one of de happiest day of my life.' They were now bound by the vow they made to each other. 'For better, for worse, for richer, for poorer, in sickness and in health.'

As Agnes stood arm in arm with her new husband she could feel that indeed she was happy, she was pregnant, and her new baby would be born legitimate in the eyes of God and the law of England to married parents, this was a level of respectability she wished Tina and Charles could have enjoyed, and with the thought of them, despite the glow of the day, there was that hint of sadness, regret and guilt. 'I wish Ella and the children were here.'

CHAPTER THIRTY-SEVEN

Agnes insisted on six large prints, one each for Raphael's parents, her sister Ella, Mrs Chester and two for the family album into which baby pictures would soon be added.

Agnes wrote a letter that accompanied every wedding photograph sent by post and made sure Raphael also put his signature on each beside hers, as married couples do. This was her way of making sure everyone knew it was official; she was now Mrs Agnes Toussaint.

Now Agnes Toussaint closed the front door to be welcomed by the sound of Raphael calling out to her, 'Agnes, dat you? We in de kitchen, come!' She was not in the mood for being sociable. Her only desire after a busy day at work with her ongoing pregnancy, was to take off her shoes and lie down to rest before cooking the evening meal. She walked into the kitchen to discover Scottie standing with his back to the sink, his arms crossed in front of him, a rolled newspaper held tightly in one hand, with Linus and Raphael sitting at the kitchen table.

'Eh eh? You have company, Raph. All right, Linus, you okay, Scottie?' Raphael stood up to give her his seat and helped her out of her coat. 'Take a seat *dou dou*, my darling, you've had a long day. I'm so happy you're home safe.'

Agnes took off her headscarf and hung her handbag on the back of the chair. 'So, what going on here, you all look upset, so?' She turned to look at Raphael as she spoke, starting to feel nervous. 'What happen? Something happen to Vitalis? Where's Margaret?'

'Margaret is upstairs and Vitalis is still at work, dey okay,' Raphael assured her, but his face was serious.

'I hope and pray he makes it safely home tonight. We should walk to the bus stop to meet him.' The tension in Scottie's hand made the newspaper twitch.

The nervousness built within Agnes. 'Why you say dat, Scottie?'

'You hear about the fella dat get killed last night?' Scottie raised the newspaper in his hand.

'*At 2 a.m. on Monday morning of the 17th of May 1959, Kelso Cochrane, a 32-year-old Antiguan carpenter, was reported dead after being attacked and stabbed last night.*' Scottie was reading from the *West Indian Gazette*. They all leaned over to look at the article as he read it.

> *He was taken into Paddington General Hospital but did not recover from his wounds. A witness stated they saw a group of white men running after Mr Cochrane, who was alone. The unprovoked nature of the attack makes it a racist killing. A close friend said "Kelso was a keen boxer, strong fella but he could not beat off those hooligans." Mr Cochrane had lived in the United States before he made his way to England leaving behind two young daughters who still reside in America.*

Island Song

The name in print could have been any one of them sitting in the kitchen, or for that matter, anyone else with dark skin, it was an evil, senseless killing of an innocent man simply going about his business. Agnes held her tummy, feeling anxious her child within would be able to feel what she was feeling and the anguish of those sitting around her. She needed to go and rest, but before she climbed the stairs she wanted to know if justice was done. 'So dey catch de man who do dat, de police catch dem?'

Scottie read from the newspaper again.

'The police are investigating and will not stop until the culprits are apprehended and brought to justice. Until then they ask that the community of Ladbroke Grove and surrounding areas exercise caution when walking alone.'

Scottie rolled up the paper and as he spoke he used it like a batten that expressed more of his anger. 'Right now dease killers are walking de streets. And I bet you, dem police will not find the culprits. I doubt dey even look so hard in case it one of dere own brothers in de group. All dey concerned about is not having another riot like last year. But lemme tell you all, if there is, I will be right in de middle. Fighting for the right to walk safely on de streets of London.' Sitting in silence at the table, Linus remembered how he'd had to run from a group of rioters the year before. The fear he felt was still so raw within him. He was determined that the incident would not get the better of him. He had to encourage Scottie to compose himself. He could see it was frightening Agnes and causing Raphael to remember his own experience with those wicked Teddy Boys.

'My brother, you must calm yourself. Next fing you know we beating up every white man we see. Don't you see dey scared of us, dey don't know who we are. We are a peaceful people, we don't come here for trouble. Don't let dem push us in a corner and next fing you know we fighting like animals, dat's what dey want.'

Scottie heard what Linus was saying. These were words he had himself spoken. But he had also witnessed the hatred at one of his visits to the Sunday gatherings at Speakers' Corner in Hyde Park.

'You ever hear of de White Defence League?' Scottie now asked. 'Dis is a group of white men who already tink we are animals. Dey want rid of de black race in England. Dey want us gone, dey want to keep Britain white and dey will tak' any action necessary to keep it dat way. Linus and your brother here and Agnes all bin at de hand of dease evil fuckers. So you can't deny dere actions because you have experienced it yourselves. We were promised to be welcomed here but it seems to me some people here are not part of dat promise.'

Agnes knew she had to leave the kitchen, feeling overwhelmed by the emotions on display. Memories of the night she was attacked started to replay in her mind as she listened to the conversation around her. She sensed Raphael was feeling the same. The crease on his forehead was deep. She rose from her chair. 'I have to go and rest. Please, Scottie, don't do anything foolish.'

Sensing she wished them to leave, Scottie and Linus both soon made their exit. As the door closed, Agnes said a quiet prayer that they would be safe on the streets.

That night they ate in silence, haunted by the murder of a young man far away from home, just as they were too.

One week later, Linus, Scottie and Raphael stood outside St Michael's Church on Ladbroke Grove amongst more than a thousand mourners who had come to pay their respects at Kelso Cochrane's funeral.

After the funeral mass, the mourners filed out of the church sombrely and the casket was placed in the hearse. As the vehicle moved slowly off, the crowd filled in the street and walked behind it. Raphael had never experienced anything like it, so many people of different shades standing together, feeling the same pain, and like many around him, he could not hold back his tears. The procession walked in silence to Kensal Green Cemetery, many mourners openly expressing their grief. The senseless murder had shocked the community to their core, white and black stood shoulder to shoulder in respectful silence.

Once Kelso's coffin was interred in the ground and laid to rest, the three men walked to the gates of the cemetery and stood watching the crowd disperse.

'Let me buy you fellas a pint,' Raphael said, after a while, feeling the need to end the day in some way with the people he cared about. The others agreed and they walked to the nearest pub on the Harrow Road. When they opened the doors they were met with a packed bar of men and women who had attended the funeral. All having had the same idea.

'Barman, can we have three pints,' Raphael asked at the bar while the others found a place to sit. As he waited for the drinks, Raphael looked around the pub and observed everyone talking to each other, there was a solidarity in the air which was rare. Usually when he walked into a pub folks would keep themselves to themselves.

'That will be six shillings,' the barman said when he'd returned with the pints on a tray. He paused and then added, 'Everyone round 'ere has been upset by this fella's killing. I just wish we could all get on, no matter where we are from . . .' The barman was clearly making a point of letting Raphael know he and his friends were welcome and would have no trouble in his pub. Not on this day.

Raphael picked up the tray and the barman continued to

serve his customers. Scottie paused, seemingly lost in thought, then he took his pint and raised his glass.

'To Kelso Cochrane. We should never forget him. I have been told he was a good man, a father and a son. May he rest in peace and dey find de killers dat take his life.'

His friends raised their glasses solemnly too, their voices joined by others in the pub who did the same.

'To Kelso Cochrane.'

Agnes eventually received a letter from Ella in early August. It was, however, a more substantial envelope than the usual thin single sheet of airmail paper she was used to. Enclosed was a photograph mounted on stiff cardboard of Johnnie and Rosa's wedding party. Agnes felt it was a return gesture for the picture of her own wedding party on the steps of the registry office that she had sent. Tina had grown taller than Agnes had realised, she stood upright and proud with a pretty smile that Agnes imagined was just for her. Both the bride's and the bridesmaids' dresses were perfect, Ella had done a beautiful job. The photograph was in black and white, but the satin fabric shone through. Johnnie had put on weight, and it suited him. Ella and Charles were absent from the photograph. Agnes was disappointed as she had so very much wanted to see their faces, the sister and son that she missed so much.

Agnes was comforted that Ella sent her blessing but still she knew her sister was disappointed, as there were no kind words of love and encouragement to accompany the photograph.

CHAPTER THIRTY-EIGHT

Agnes's ankles were swollen, her lower back ached and her belly felt huge, sticking out in front of her. She could just about do up her overcoat. It was now October, and she was 8 months pregnant. It was her last day of work. As Agnes took her time gathering her belongings from her locker, she was overwhelmed with sadness but also gratitude. Lyons was so much more than just a job and wage packet at the end of the week – she had grown to love it. It had given her independence, the confidence to interact with a wide variety of people, and the courage to stand up for herself. She had also met Moses who had become a great and trusted friend, who made her laugh in times of adversity. As she closed her locker for the last time she turned round and was surprised to see Katie, and with her, Iris, her supervisor.

'You all packed up Agnes?'

'Yes, Ms Iris. I will wash my uniform and make sure I bring it back.'

'I really do hope you come back to us Agnes, you have been an excellent worker. We wish you all the best. You're going to make a lovely mum.'

Iris gave Katie an encouraging nudge to step forward with what looked like a gift-wrapped package for Agnes.

Katie spoke gruffly. 'This is a present from Iris and me. My Auntie Vera made this for yer baby. She's a wonderful knitter. You can open it now if yer like.'

Agnes took the gift and slowly began to open the wrapping. Inside was a set of white woollen baby items: a pair of white booties, gloves and a baby cap. 'Thank you so much Katie and thank you Ms Iris. Dis is very kind of you. Please tell your auntie from me, they are lovely, it's so, so nice for the baby.' Agnes put the gift down on the bench in front of her locker. Katie had treated her badly, but now she was offering an olive branch. Agnes had gained strength and courage despite Katie, not because of her. But instinctively, Agnes reached out and gave Katie a hug of thanks. Katie did not respond in kind, but stood rigidly and awkwardly, unable to fully return the gesture, whether through reluctance or embarrassment Agnes couldn't tell.

It didn't discourage Agnes, because within her embrace was hope, to be an example of kindness, and as they stood in the locker room on Agnes's final day at Lyons, Katie could surely feel some of that hope too.

'Well, thank you again.'

As Agnes walked towards the staff exit, farewells and best wishes were showered upon her by various members of the staff. Some she knew well, but the goodwill she received seemed genuine from all of them. 'Good luck Agnes, don't forget to come by with the baby!'

She walked to the bus stop with Moses as usual. 'Why you looking so sad Mrs? You don't have to come back to dis place.

You now married and having a baby. It's time to put your feet up and let others look after you! And don't worry, I will visit you at home.'

They walked side by side up the alleyway to the main road and headed for the bus stop as their conversation continued.

'But I love my job, Moses.'

'I tink you will love being a housewife and mother even more, but if you still want to work here I am sure Lyons will always take you back.' Agnes liked the thought of that.

Raphael was relieved that Agnes had stopped working. Getting up in the morning and making her way to work was so tiring for her, and he felt somewhat guilty because as her husband, he should be taking care of the finances and allowing her to focus on the coming of their first child.

A week later, Agnes was delighted to receive a letter from the Chesters which was filled with Lillian's own news.

My Dear Agnes,
 Congratulations on your marriage to Raphael, what wonderful news. Edward and I are overjoyed, the double blessing that you are due to have a baby is just marvellous . . .
 Little Agnes is now nearly two years old and a bright little button. She is so full of mischief, wanting to explore every little thing that she comes across. But her enthusiasm for life is so endearing I cannot bear to chastise her for this curiosity.
 Edward is now headmaster of his school and he has taken to the role very well. I am very much enjoying my voluntary work with the Women's Institute in the village. It keeps me busy and engaged with the comings and

goings of the villagers. These days my life is filled with joy since having my little Agnes who has given me so much strength . . .
We plan on coming to London in the spring, I will be sure to come and visit you.
Congratulations once again and send my best wishes to your husband Raphael, I look forward to meeting him.
Until the spring!
Lillian, Edward and Little Agnes

Margaret was proving to be a great help. Agnes welcomed her nurturing nature and support with the cooking, grocery shopping and prenatal care. Every Friday Margaret would encourage Agnes to drink a Guinness punch with her fish and chips: one bottle of Guinness with condensed milk, which masked the bitterness – it was thick and sweet. 'Dis is good for you Agnes. It has a lot of iron and vitamins, it will make you and the baby strong!'

Agnes had come to rely on Margaret, as she came back from her hospital appointments praising the nurses for their care and expertise. Margaret was the one who took the time to read all the leaflets that explained the state benefits Agnes would receive once the baby was born. 'It say here you receive free orange juice, cod liver oil tablets and baby formula and once a month you visit de nurse so she can make sure de baby is doing well, dat baby is lucky baby.'

When Agnes gave birth to Tina and Charles, it had been at home in the bed they slept in. It was Ella that assisted the village nurse at the birth, there were no aftercare visits. It was Ella that cleaned, washed and fed the family while Agnes breastfed. The benefits of the NHS were not available in the village of Canaries. Babies were born and natural home remedies were made to ease any and all ailments. When the

Island Song

baby had colic the whole family would take turns to rub its back to bring up the wind and ease the child's discomfort and stop the crying, but when a baby ailed and took sick, sometimes there was no money for doctors and hospitals, and occasionally no help beyond that which the village could provide. She was glad that was one thing she would never have to worry about in Britain.

In the early hours of the morning on the 5th December 1959, baby Helena Toussaint was finally ready to be in the world, weighing in at a healthy eight pounds and five ounces. Agnes's waters had broken at eight thirty the night before, and she had been in labour for five and a half hours. It was a straightforward birth without complications. Agnes's relief to learn that her new baby was fit and healthy brought on a mix of exhaustion and tears.

The brisk efficiency of the delivery team calmly busying around her was a real contrast to the basic home births of Tina and Charles, where Agnes had been reliant on the experience of the local *fanmchay,* midwife and the kindness of her neighbours.

Before she knew it Helena had been cleaned up and wrapped in fresh linens while Agnes was assessed for any possible issues caused by the delivery. A nurse explained to the fatigued Agnes that she could spend a short while bonding with her baby before she would be moved into the nursery. In a dreamy state of bliss, Agnes cuddled the tightly swaddled bundle in her arms. She took a long moment to study every aspect of baby Helena's face and introduced herself. 'Hello my *dou dou,* my love, I am your mummy, you are God's blessing.' Helena stirred briefly in acknowledgement of her mother's voice, but did not wake. Agnes felt a loving relief which brought tears that fell on her baby's blanket. 'This is tears of joy Helena dat you are here.'

Helena's name was chosen only days before the birth. Their daughter would be named after their beautiful island's nickname 'The Helen of the West'. As legend had it, in honour of Helen of Troy, the most beautiful woman to have ever lived. Agnes added an 'A' to the end, after herself, and to give the name a more exotic ring. Helena.

A little later on, Raphael was allowed in to see his wife and new daughter, albeit under strict guidance. 'Mr Toussaint, please keep as calm as possible causing no stress or making any noise for mother and baby.' It was a welcome warning because Raphael had a strong desire to jump in the air shouting out with all his might, 'We did it Agnes, Helena is here!'

Raphael approached the hospital bed, and Agnes gently introduced him to his daughter. He took Helena tenderly in his arms and peered into the bundle to gaze upon Helena's face. '*Bon jou Helena*, Hello Helena. I am your papa.' He spoke reverently to her in the quietest voice he could muster. Agnes was overwhelmed by how happy Raphael was to meet his daughter. So happy that he cried like a baby himself when he first held his daughter. As she watched him hold Helena in his arms, gently cooing and whispering endearments of love and promises of the future, Agnes knew he loved Helena as much as she did.

With a deep sense of love and gratitude for watching such a beautiful moment she closed her tired eyes and drifted off into a deep and serene sleep.

Vitalis was the first to visit his cousin, arriving at the ward before his mid-morning shift at the hospital. Agnes was settled upright in bed breastfeeding her baby when he entered the room.

'I come at a wrong time Agnes?' he asked quietly.

'No, no, it's good to see you. She soon done.'

'Margaret gave me this for you.' It was a bottle of Lucozade wrapped in orange see-through plastic. 'She said it will ease your stomach and give you energy.' Agnes had noticed the same bottle on some of the other mothers' side tables and wondered what it was for. Now she had her own bottle of the fizzy drink to sample.

'Margaret say she will pass and see you later. Before I left the house I saw Raph, he say he got in a little after five o'clock. He looked real tired but he say he was too happy and excited to sleep just yet.'

Agnes could feel Helena's lips slipping from her nipple, her belly was filled with milk. She lifted the baby away from herself, covered her chest with her blanket and wiped Helena's little mouth with the edge of the sheet. Helena's eyes were tightly closed in deep contentment as she was raised to her Uncle Vitalis so he could hold her.

'Eh eh you heavy my *dou dou*, my love. *Ou bèl Helena*, you are beautiful Helena. Your Auntie Margaret is so looking forward to meeting you.' Vitalis kissed his goddaughter on her forehead and then gently handed her back to her mother. He said his goodbyes and took himself off to the busy maintenance department at the hospital to start his shift.

Agnes loved the milky scent of her newborn. Her feet and her hands were perfect. She had long fingers and toes like her father, with the complexion of her mother, and when she opened her eyes she would stare right back at Agnes with a knowingness that convinced Agnes that Helena was an old and wise soul. When Helena was taken away to the nursery, Agnes missed her bundle of joy terribly but it gave her a few hours to close her eyes and sleep.

Agnes believed in her dreams, she took them as messages from God. She dreamed that Tina and Charles stood either side of her hospital bed looking at Helena in her arms; they were not speaking, but then a voice from across the ward called out, 'When are you coming home Agnes?' It was Ella in the opposite bed. Agnes woke suddenly, breathing heavily with eyes wide open staring at a nurse looking at her medical chart. 'Looks like you had a bad dream there Mrs Toussaint.'

'Yes, I fink I did nurse.' The nurse approached Agnes and took her arm to read her pulse.

'This tends to happen to new mothers, all their senses are heightened and after going through giving birth, you are tired and rest is the best cure.' Agnes thought on what the nurse had said as she sat up in bed with a thermometer in her mouth and her arm in the nurse's hand. *I am not a new mother, I am a mother of three children and I miss them terribly.* The nurse deflated the cuffs on Agnes's arm. 'Now Mrs Toussaint, looks like your blood pressure is up, so take this opportunity to rest, you don't want to stay in hospital longer than you should. You will want get home, won't you?'

'Yes nurse, I want to go home.' But she still wasn't sure which home she wanted.

The next day, entering through the door of 63 Fernhead Road with baby Helena in her arms and Raphael by her side gave Agnes a deep sense of relief. If Tina and Charles had been there her family unit would have been complete. She had no idea when it would happen, but her prayers were steeped in the possibility of all her children under the same roof.

Raphael was quiet on the journey by taxi back to Fernhead Road. After the dream, Agnes had spoken to Raphael about the possibility of bringing Tina and Charles to England, and he had given her a considered response. 'Agnes, I don't know when or how it will happen. We have to raise de money to do dat, I know it's what you want so don't put pressure on me yet. Let us get Helena home and take it from there, okay.'

At least Raphael seemed to be onboard with idea. She decided not to push the conversation any further.

As they climbed the creaky stairs to their attic room they were welcomed by Margaret and Vitalis at the top of the stairs.

Margaret took every effort to make sure Agnes and her newborn were comfortable. 'So nice to have you both home. It was cold so I put on the heater in your room.'

When Raphael opened the door for Agnes in their one-room home she discovered a crib at the foot of their bed, a comfy lounge chair and a standing lamp on the opposite side of the room by the window.

Vitalis shared where all the items came from. 'Mrs Fletcher said there was no use keeping it in storage, best make use of it. And the chair she said was for when you feed the baby. And she has a pushchair for you.' Margaret and Vitalis remained standing at the door eagerly watching Agnes's reaction to the generosity of their landlady Mrs Fletcher.

Agnes stood for a moment with baby Helena in her arms looking around the now much improved and cosy room. 'I will thank her in the morning, she is a generous woman.' Agnes took Helena to the crib and placed her inside. She looked so petite within the wooden frame, her chubby face peeking out from the white blanket in which she was so comfortably wrapped. 'And Margaret buy the blankets for de crib for you.' The generosity of friends and family moved Agnes deeply, Helena was bringing out the beauty of those around her.

As Raphael stood with Agnes looking down on their baby Helena, he made a vow. 'I promise to keep you safe our little English girl, welcome home.'

CHAPTER THIRTY-NINE

Raphael stayed in bed for as long as he could. He was enjoying the quiet while Agnes was out shopping with the baby. It was Saturday after all, no need to rush to get to work. But he had a lot on his mind. It was a pleasure having his family around him but it was nice to have the place to himself. He adored his baby girl, little Helena, and it was wonderful watching Agnes enjoying being her mother.

However, it was easier to accept the responsibility of another man's children from a distance. He could manage putting a little extra cash in an envelope for Agnes to send home, now that Agnes was a stay-at-home mum no longer on a wage. However, reality had struck a few nights previously, when Agnes talked about Tina and Charles coming to live with them in England. It was something that had never crossed his mind before, but it was a natural wish for any loving parent to be reunited with their children.

'If I stay, Tina and Charles would have to come to join me, I can't leave them with Ella forever, can I?'

Agnes had heard Raphael say many times before that he had no intention of going back to St Lucia any time soon, but it came as a shock to her that she now had no intention of going back either, her plans had changed.

She had to break her promise to Ella. The promise of her return to St Lucia. 'I am leaving to come back.' That was over.

'And now we have a chil' born in England, she should go to school here. Why take her back to St Lucia where there is not much opportunity for her?' It surprised Agnes how easy it was for her to make this decision, nonetheless, it was true. They had both paid their taxes, working for the benefit of themselves and the country, it was what they were entitled to. Agnes also knew what her reality would be like if she went back to St Lucia, depending on Raphael from a distance and the anguish of not knowing what he was up to, and maybe losing touch with her husband completely.

She had to do what she had to do and stay for the sake of her peace of mind and survival. Plans would now have to be made to bring Tina and Charles to England. She could not expect Ella to look after them forever. Ella would surely expect this too, mother and children finally together, but she dreaded having to tell Ella of her change of heart. She knew it would be hard for her sister to bear.

Raphael's mother had recently written back to him, not the usual letter of a few words of thanks for the funds he would send, but with the firm instruction to use the money to look after his new family. *'Keep the money and save it for your wife and daughter. You are now a father and it would make me happy to know you can look after them.'* He took his mother's instruction to heart, but now with the looming possibility of having more mouths to feed, two more children felt a heavy burden to carry. He knew they had to start saving; for airline tickets for Tina and Charles, for a bigger house, for greater weekly expenses, and now with Agnes not working, and with her small maternity allowance only lasting a few months, he was fully responsible for earning the weekly wage to look after the family. He was grateful to have worked for the same company for almost two years. Not only had he learned a trade, but the work had helped him to discover what kind of man he was, a man that could be relied upon.

Raphael sat on his favourite stool in the kitchen, sipping his coffee and looking around. Baby clothes were soaking in a bowl on the sink drainer. A big metal pot was on the stove for boiling nappies and a wooden drying rack took up much of the room. They could not live like this forever.

He decided it was time to head out and get some fresh air and enjoy a little more of that peace before Agnes returned with the baby.

Raphael realised he was getting used to the cold in England, in fact he enjoyed feeling the bite of the breeze on his face, it woke him up, cleared his head. Whenever he passed by his old home on Bravington Road, the place he'd shared with Linus when he first arrived in London, it always brought back memories of how lost he'd felt in those first days. The crushing disappointment at not seeing the pavements lined with gold; a fantasy he had desperately wanted to believe was true. What he'd thought he'd find in London was an easy life, a rich life, without doing much in the way of actual hard work. He could just reach out his hand and take, with no hard knocks. But as Bernard always said, 'You need to be knocked down so you can stand up again!'

Agnes was not ignorant of how he had lived his life before,

she knew of his reputation, but she had the benefit of seeing him in a new light, not in the warm glow of the tropical sun but the dimmer reality of him trying to do better in a new harsh landscape. Raphael understood her motivation for coming to England, unlike his, was not a selfish act. Her family in St Lucia were what she had been striving for, and now little Helena too. Her decision for stepping beyond the bounds of her village and into uncharted waters, braving the Atlantic, not knowing where she would land, was a truly courageous one. He was more proud of her than of himself. She remained his compass, that pointed him to a better path.

CHAPTER FORTY

1960

The first year Agnes was gone, it felt like a cavern had been left in the centre of the house, one that would sometimes echo Agnes's voice. Ella would turn from what she was doing and imagine that she heard her sister call her name. As the months moved on, the void seemed less deep and wide, but there was still an empty space where Agnes used to be.

It had now been three years since Agnes had left for England. The children would sometimes pine for her, especially at night when they missed their mother's bedtime rituals, but with gentle words from their Auntie Ella and their nightly prayers, they would ease into slumber. They would wake the next morning with buoyancy and eagerness to get to school, without a thought of their mother, until the next night.

The children were sprouting up fast and outgrowing the clothes and shoes their mother had sent them from England. Now that Agnes had another child to feed, Ella knew that money would be tight. These extra stresses caused Ella concern. How would she manage to look after the children's growing needs herself? She knew she would have to express these concerns in a letter to her sister, but she would have to find the words to voice her disappointment and the turmoil she felt within herself first. They were so far away from each other, she could not look her sister in the eye and say, 'You let me down Agnes.' It was so hard for Ella to get a grasp on the situation and let go of the promises Agnes had made, that she would return to their family unit.

Once the children were at school Ella would spend her days tending to her usual domestic activities of de-weeding her vegetable garden, and when in season, checking the fruit trees for mangoes and golden apples. She also kept an eye on the breadfruit tree so no ripe fruit would go wasted, sharing her pickings with some of the villagers in exchange for fish or any produce they would be growing on their family land. If she had time to spare she would take herself to the church to meditate, and on occasion would have an opportunity to chat with Father Thomas. And she would never leave the church without lighting a candle for her family. Her skill as a seamstress helped pay the bills, but it was only sporadic work, so she was grateful for the two days she worked at the school, for which she now received a wage. It was nice to be teaching the children to read, even though it paid very little. But it was regular, and doing it brought her joy. Her cousin Johnnie would visit once a week with some fresh fish and dried provisions of rice and beans, for which Ella was always grateful.

One afternoon, Johnnie was sitting at the back of the house, taking some breeze off the river while Ella cleaned the fish.

'How is your mother, Johnnie, you gave her the wax candle I send for her?'

'I gave it to her, but she keeps asking after you. She is still sick.'

'I'm sorry to hear that. I pray for her every day,' Ella answered, sensing there was more to come with this conversation.

'She wants to see you, Ella, the time you saw each other at the wedding was not enough, it has been so long, it's time you paid her a proper visit.'

Without looking up from the bloody fish water, Ella said, 'You know how fings are here, I don't like being far from home and I have the children to look after, and when she moved to Castries to work at the Ministry of Education, it wasn't easy for me.'

Johnnie was not going to give in this time. 'Well, de road from Canaries to Castries is now open. What if I tak' you to see your auntie, and Rosa will look after Tina and Charles?'

Ella stood and threw the fish water into the river. 'How you going to tak' me, you don't hav' a vehicle?' she said, unwilling to comply easily.

Johnnie, who had been prepared for her evasion, answered, 'I have been sharing Ton-Ton's car dese pas' couple of months and taking people down to Castries. It's bigger and busier than ever, Ella. You mus' see it, and you mus' see your Auntie Flora too.'

Ella attempted another of her hard stares, but she could tell that this time Johnnie was not going to back down.

'My mother was de one dat gave you her time, remember how she used to sit wit' you and read when you was small? It's still one of the tings you love to do,' Johnnie said.

Ella searched for arguments and excuses to throw back at him, but she knew she had none. Charles and Tina were getting bigger, and Ella was wise enough to know that they would soon outgrow the village, and that their mother could send for them any day.

Island Song

The thought chilled her. Agnes was making a new life for herself, and deep down inside, Ella had started to doubt that her sister was ever coming home, but it was a fear she pushed away, frightened by what it meant.

Ella's reluctance to step out of her village remained strong, but her Aunt Flora had been the closest thing to a mother they'd had after they'd lost their own. If there was one reason for her to venture out, it was Flora.

A few days later, after more of Johnnie's gentle persuasion, Ella agreed to go and visit Auntie Flora in Castries by road for the first time.

Johnnie guided Ella to the car, a dark blue Russian Lada, imported from Cuba, and into her seat. The paint job was highly polished to be as smart as it could be and was reflecting brightly in the early morning sun. Ella could tell Johnnie was feeling nervous and wanted to impress her as her chauffeur for the day, he had been promising to do it for long enough.

'You comfortable, Ella?' She was startled to discover the seats were stuffed with straw, a couple of stray pieces had worked their way out of a seam that scratched Ella's leg. She pulled the offending stalks out abruptly and threw them from the window.

'Yes, Johnnie I'm good.'

Ella looked out of the passenger window, her breaths visible in the morning air. She was surprised to see how small the village looked nestled in the deep green chasm of the Canaries River valley when viewed from the winding thread of dark black tarmac road. The new paved road that wound all the way to the capital of Castries, through the village of Anse La Raye and Roseau.

As they reached the top of the incline, just before the turn that would drop the village from view, she had a strong desire to stop. 'Johnnie, can you stop the car?'

'You haven't changed your mind, have you?' was Johnnie's quick reply.

'No, Johnnie, I'm okay, I just want you to stop for a moment.' Ella stepped out of the car and looked down below her to take in the glistening river running behind her home and the immense expanse of the beautiful turquoise Caribbean Sea. It lifted her heart to see the once bright red, now faded to pastel pink, corrugated roof of her family home.

Now, it seemed foolish to her that she wouldn't want to see the village this way, from outside. It seemed obvious to her now that nothing could take it away, no matter where she went, or where Agnes, or Tina or Charles would be, Canaries would remain, somewhere always to return to, not just on the island but in their hearts too.

'The Lord has truly given us a beautiful day!'

Ella returned to her seat in the car and Johnnie turned to her, grinning.

'He sure did, can we go now, cousin?'

As they drove through the Roseau valley, the banana plantation on either side of the road was very impressive with its abundant crop of bananas hanging off every tree and the trimmed-off stems and leaves lying fermenting and fragrant on the fertile soil.

As they descended from Morne Fortune, the hill that overlooked the city, and down into Castries, they were met with the majestic view of the deep-water harbour. Looming over the landscape, due to its sheer size in comparison with the storage sheds along the dockside, was the hulking steel side of the Geest Line banana boat that shipped the 'green gold' to England each week. Trailing out of the shed on the dockside, up the gangplank and into the hull of the ship was a continuous line of women all of whom had balanced on their heads a whole stem of green unripened bananas. They moved gracefully back and forth like a human conveyor belt in their flowing skirts and cloth-wrapped hair, passing the tallyman who would give each woman a token for each trip.

Ella's eyes were wide open, taking in the hustle and bustle of Castries. It was a shock to her system. She held on to the car handle for dear life as she watched hordes of shoppers, ladies with their market stalls selling an abundance of vegetables and fruit, and men with baskets on their heads selling their wares filling the streets.

She was happy to leave the city excitement behind, as they finally arrived at Flora's house in a quiet suburb just north of the city. Auntie Flora's traditional Caribbean wooden chattel house was painted in pretty light blue with the intricate gingerbread trellising around the roof and doorway, a remnant of the French Creole style.

Auntie Flora was at the door leaning on two walking sticks, not looking as upright as Ella remembered when she last saw her at Johnnie and Rosa's wedding. She was smiling as she welcomed Ella into her home. 'Ella, Ella, *wo gade' belle*, you're looking beautiful.'

'Auntie!' Ella responded with tears in her eyes and kissed both her cheeks and held her tight, not wanting to let go, chastising herself for denying herself this loving feeling for so long. Flora radiated the familiar smell of the coconut oil she used; Ella used to watch her aunt combing it through her abundant black hair that was now thinning and grey.

'Eh eh, Ella you going to take my breath away.' Flora was so happy to see Ella but could see the years had left some sadness in her eyes. 'Come inside, come inside.'

They entered the sitting room where a large dresser took up most of the walled space that divided the room from the rest of the rooms at the back of the house. The dresser cabinet displayed ornaments, pretty drinking glasses, plates and cups and saucers for special occasions. Ella noticed some gaps in the items on display – they had been placed on the dining table in anticipation of her visit.

All the windows were opened and draped in clean white netting. The breeze blew in, dancing and ruffling some of the house plants that sat beneath.

After using the washroom, which Ella was delighted to find had a flushing toilet, not like the bucket, the river or the communal toilet she would have to use in the village. This was one luxury item on the top of her wish list. Ella rejoined her aunt in her comfortable living room with the small sofa and the green crocheted cushions. Auntie Flora always kept a lovely home, and her job as an administrator at the Ministry of Education had given her a consistent salary and now a pension. Flora was living in well-deserved comfort.

'Come, sit down and eat.'

'Yes Auntie.' Ella pulled her own chair out and sat opposite her beloved aunt.

Flora had already set the table with a feast of fried fish, salad, rice and beans, ground provisions of breadfruit, sweet potato, yam, cucumber salad, lettuce leaves and a large jug of fresh green mango juice. They said grace after which Johnnie poured everyone a glass of juice.

'So, tell me Ella, how is Agnes enjoying England? Does she write to you often?' Ella took a bite of food before she answered. She knew Johnnie had told his mother about Agnes's baby and hoped he didn't mention the anguish she had felt when she received that letter. Ella wanted to keep the afternoon upbeat and not share the concerns she had about her sister.

'Every month she send me a little money, which I am very grateful for. As you know, she has a baby, her name is Helena and in her last letter she said Raphael is now looking for a new

Island Song

job, but she promise to keeping sending things for the children. She doesn't share much about how she is doing but I am sure she is okay Auntie.'

Flora sat a little taller in her chair, voicing a slight disappointment in the vague correspondence from Agnes on how she was coping. 'I don't know what happens to our people when they go to England, I feel they keep so much from us.'

'I suppose they don't want to worry us, Auntie.'

'I suppose you are right, Ella, no news is good news,' Johnnie added to the conversation, 'which reminds me . . .'

They exchanged news, both from Castries and wider afield. Johnnie told them about his friend in London who had won some money on the Littlewoods Pools and had spent it on a big house in Ladbroke Grove.

'What is the Littlewoods Pools?'

'Mama, I told you about it!' Johnnie sighed.

'Well, remind me again.'

The three of them laughed as Johnnie tried to explain the English football lottery to his mother, then they ate and talked at length before Flora encouraged Johnnie to go and rest in her bedroom before the drive back to Canaries.

While Johnnie was taking his siesta the two women sat close together on the sofa.

'It has been so wonderful having you here, Ella. What joy it has brought me to see you! Please don't leave it so long in future. I love you and Agnes like you are my own daughters.'

Being with her aunt again, leaving the village, the exciting drive, all of these things had opened up Ella's emotions. There was so much she wanted to tell her aunt, about her secret fears, her worries for Agnes and the children's future, but she didn't know where to start.

'I know Auntie.' Ella hesitated for a moment as the tears started to come. 'But, life has not been easy on me, I have been scared, Auntie, and I don't fink Agnes is coming home.' Not only did the floodgates begin to open, but the words she wanted to hold back started to flow out of Ella's mouth. 'Agnes now has a chil' with Raphael. He is a man I cah trus'. Agnes says he change but I cah believe it Auntie. Agnes fooled again by another man.' It was the first time she had admitted this to anyone, and she couldn't hold her emotions from her aunt any longer. 'I fin' it hard to fink of Raphael as a responsible man. I cah forget how de women at de river used to talk about him, womanising and drinking. Can a selfish, irresponsible man change his ways Auntie?'

'Anyone can change for de better if they want to and we all have to face de consequences of our actions, even you Ella. Agnes is not bringing shame on de family, she is getting on with her life and from what I understand from Johnnie, Agnes send you money for de children, parcels and letters, she still cares for you all. She is not takin' advantage of you, I believe she is doing her bes' and who would she leave her children with, a stranger? We cah control everything Ella but we can always give love. You cah control Agnes but you can always love her, dat's all you can do.' Ella listened to her aunt's reasoning; it wasn't easy to agree with all her aunt had said but it felt good to share what she had been holding inside herself for so long.

'Ella, take dis and wipe your face. I know life can be hard sometimes, but I believe Agnes is doing her bes'. Keep supporting your sister and look after her children the bes' you can. You are lucky to have each other despite being so far apart. And in times of trouble you mus' support each other.' Auntie Flora moved closer to Ella and put her arm around her shoulders and spoke even more softly so Ella could be soothed by her voice. 'Ella, ever since you were a little girl you never wanted to leave your mother's side. You have been alone a long time without your parents, but you have allowed loss to cripple you. Byron was not de man you thought he was, it is good that he left. Agnes leaving to make a better life for her family, I believe is not a selfish act. And now you are here to fend for yourself and the children, are they not fed each day? Clean clothes on their bodies and sent to school? This is because of you Ella and the little money Agnes is sending you is more dan a help, am I right Ella?'

'Yes Auntie.' Ella felt like a small child in her aunt's arms, it had been a long time since anyone had held her so close. Auntie Flora continued to soothe Ella.

'I am so sorry I wasn't there for you enough when you needed support.' Tears sparkled in Flora's eyes too.

'I have tried to be brave, but Byron broke my heart, I believed that with him beside me I would be stronger.'

'Ella, I have loved and lost, I have grieved the death of your mother and father, and my own mother and father, too. When my husband decided to leave me for another woman, I had to raise Johnnie on my own. I educated myself, and with the Lord at my side, I vowed to live with purpose and serve him and look where I am now. I didn't stop and allow pain to hold me back, I used it to push me forward.'

'You have the courage that I just don't have,' Ella said softly.

'I tried my best, but I didn't show you how to be a woman in the world, when you needed me most, I was looking to find my own way.' Flora took her niece's smooth hand in her own lined, wrinkled one. 'Ella, you and your sister, must find your *own* way in the world. Agnes is doing it her way, and you must find the courage to find your path too.'

Ella dried her tears with her free hand. 'Auntie you gave me your time, and I will never forget dat.'

'After what you just said, this may seem cruel of me to say, but I must do so. I am telling you because despite what you fink about yourself, I know you are a strong woman, and dat is what I need you to be for me when I tell you what I must tell you.' Flora stopped to draw breath and pulled slowly and gently away from Ella, and as she did so, she gripped Ella's hand tightly, holding her gaze, her words filled with emotion. '*Mwen maladi*, I am sick, Ella, my health is not good. Johnnie is a good and dutiful son, but I don't share everyfing with him.'

Ella felt fear grip her at these words. 'What are you saying, Auntie? *De Mwen*, Tell me.'

'I have cancer. It started in my stomach but is now slowly spreading to my other organs.'

Ella had to hold herself back from wailing, she held the hankie over her mouth. Auntie Flora held her close again.

'I am at peace, child, I am at peace.'

Ella's courage failed her in the moment. She wasn't able to ask the ultimate question, the question of how long Auntie Flora had left. 'I am in good hands, under de care of Dr Sylvester, his family live in Castries. He trained in America, and is a good doctor, I am taking a day at a time, but now . . . it's just a matter of time.' Ella felt in awe of how gentle and strong her aunt was, to know that she might die at any moment, yet still living with such calm and grace. At that moment Ella realised she had to pull herself together, her worries and problems seemed less important now that she knew her aunt was so sick, it instantly put her woes into perspective.

'Ella, go to the bathroom and wash your face and come straight back. I have something for you.' Ella did as she was instructed. She looked at herself in the bathroom mirror – her eyes were puffy from the tears. She asked for courage, she asked to be fearless, if not for herself, then for her aunt.

When Ella returned, Flora was sitting at the table awaiting her. She had a large envelope in her hand, and Ella could see her name written on it.

'Ella, sit down, I must give you this before Johnnie wakes up.

I have an envelope for him too, but this is yours. It's for you to do with as you wish, this is my gift to you.'

'Shall I open it now?'

'No, wait till you get home.' Ella folded the envelope and placed it in her handbag. Under normal circumstances, she would have been impatient to open it to reveal its contents. But the shock of Flora's news was still too fresh and raw. Nothing else mattered at that moment but the love between Ella and her beloved auntie.

Auntie Flora made Ella a cup of tea and some coffee for Johnnie ahead of their return journey. 'To keep your eyes sharp,' she told her son.

'You have any cake Mama?'

'Yes, here's some black cake, I made sure I didn't put too much rum in it though.'

'That's the best part!' Johnnie put a smile on their faces.

'Auntie Flora it has been so good to see you,' Ella said, holding her aunt's hand and insisting she not stand from her chair again. 'I promise to come and see you again very VERY soon, I love you, Auntie.' Ella was now bent down looking up at her aunt at a familiar angle, the way she used to at her reading lessons with her aunt. Tears welled in Ella's eyes, but she managed to wipe them away so Johnnie could not see. 'We must get back before the roads turn dark,' Johnnie urged Ella.

CHAPTER FORTY-ONE

The weather started to change as Johnnie and Ella left the capital behind them and headed down into the Cul-De-Sac Valley. 'The road will be a lot quieter, so we should make it in good time back to Canaries.'

'Yes, but take your time, drive carefully,' Ella said.

'Of course. Safety first,' Johnnie reassured her. Ella wasn't in a talkative mood, she felt guilty knowing the news about her aunt before Johnnie, but his time to know would soon come. Johnnie could sense this, so he asked if he could put the radio on.

'Okay, but not too loud.'

The hustle and bustle of the morning had taken on a new kind of energy as the market stall owners and commuters looked up to the skies and moved in haste knowing rain was coming. The rain arrived like a wall of water, instantly soaking anyone unlucky enough to be caught out as the calypsonian Mighty Sparrow sang out from the car radio. '*When a country girl comes to town . . .*' The song seemed to ease some of the travel tension Ella was feeling and it helped Johnnie to concentrate on the road, so why not allow the calypso song to drift over her.

The torrential downpour only lasted about ten minutes but left the road surface slick, while small waterfalls cascaded down the hillsides and onto the road, the deep guttering overflowing where it had got clogged by fallen vegetation and branches.

Only three miles from home, their journey almost completed, the car was starting to struggle up the winding road out of Anse La Verdure. Ella saw Johnnie look at the temperature gauge, and she could see sweat was pouring off his brow.

'Johnnie, is the car okay?' Ella asked as the car struggled.

'The engine is overheating, and this car always takes its time uphill,' Johnnie said, trying to sound calm, but Ella saw the steering wheel twist, suddenly.

Ella screamed as Johnnie lost control as the car, which picked up speed as they approached a sharp bend in the road. Veering into the bush, the car careered through it and tipped off the steep verge, juddering down into the ravine. The only thing that stopped them tipping over and crashing headfirst to the bottom was the abrupt and violent collision with the upper branches of a giant silk cotton tree.

According to Caribbean folklore, the tree had supernatural powers and would never be cut for fear of releasing spirits and now it had prevented the car and its passengers from plummeting into the deep dark, lush green ravine below, and certain death. Any sudden move from either of them could do the same now, dislodging the car from its precarious resting place.

Without a seatbelt on, Johnnie had hit his head on the steering wheel. Blood oozed down his face, while both of them slumped unconscious in their seats. Silence descended across the ravine for a few moments, before the cicadas and tree frogs came to life again. As night fell, badly shaken, concussed, and confused, Ella awakened and her screaming began again.

'Johnnie, Johnnie? You awake, stay with me, *Bondyé ap ede nou*, God help us, *nou dwe priye pou li ede nou*, we have to pray for him to help us.'

Johnnie groaned, 'I'm sorry, Ella, *padon Ella*, sorry Ella . . .'

'*Se pa fòt ou*, It not your fault, Johnnie, the rain and the car. *Se pa fòt ou*, It's not your fault. *Repoze tèt ou*, Rest yourself. God is good, *èd ap vini*, help will come. You got to stay with me Johnnie, okay?'

Johnnie groaned, drifting into unconsciousness once more.

Ella had soon realised the futility of her screams; there was no one on the road at night in the pitch darkness, but she had to believe someone would come to their aid. She knew she would have to preserve her strength to get her through what the night would bring.

'Please God save us . . . *Pa kite Johnnie mawé*, Don't let Johnnie die,' she prayed as she shivered with the shock and the cold of the night air. The night that followed seemed the longest that she had ever experienced. For once she wasn't afraid of the shadows in the dark or the spirits that might present themselves from the silk cotton tree. Her only thoughts were for Johnnie and his survival; she kept talking to him gently, telling him stories from their youth and singing him the island songs she remembered from her childhood; anything to keep the silence and the cold at bay.

As the sun rose over the ravine, she looked at him slumped in the driver's seat. His head had stopped bleeding, but Ella was worried about his long silences, and his eyes were still closed. She took one hand and touched the side of his neck, relieved to still feel his pulse and the warmth of his skin.

Her eyes dropped to her feet and her handbag containing

the large envelope that Auntie Flora had given her. Ella pulled carefully at the seatbelt to loosen it so she could stretch to pick it up, but as she did, the car creaked and shuddered, and she froze in place, scared to breathe. Slowly, she leaned forward again.

The belt loosened slightly, allowing her to pinch the envelope between two fingertips, carefully drawing it towards her, before clasping it to her chest. She held it tightly and took a breath.

Looking down at the envelope and her name inscribed in Auntie Flora's neat script, she decided to open it. Before she did so, she looked over at Johnnie. His eyes were still closed, and his chest was rising and falling steadily. As Ella opened the envelope, the sweet smell of her aunt's coconut oil hit her nose, and she started to cry. Unable to stop the tears, she put her hand deep into the envelope, pulling out a small, wrapped parcel with a letter tucked under its string which read 'For Ella'. She wiped her face with the back of her hand before opening it up fully.

My Dearest Ella,

This is a gift for you. I wish I was able to give it to you long ago, but I had to be patient and save a little at a time. Use it well. Allow it to free you from the confines of the walls you have created for yourself. I hope it helps you live with a new purpose. I will love you always, and God and I will always be at your side.

Your loving auntie.
Flora

She slowly opened the parcel to reveal a thick handful of Eastern Caribbean 100-dollar notes, some of which fell into her lap. She could not make out how much it was, but it seemed like thousands, and all she did know was that she had never seen so much money in her entire life.

Ella sobbed quietly, and in that moment a prayer rose from deep within her. 'Oh Lord, when I am saved from this, I promise to serve you, be your disciple and always walk in your shadow as your faithful servant, and to be as strong and brave as my Auntie Flora. Oh Lord, I promise you this.' Ella collected the wayward notes and then placed the letter and sheaf of money into the envelope, folded it and placed it in the waistband of her skirt, close to her skin.

Johnnie started to cough from the seat in front.

'Ella, you okay? I'm sorry, I'm so sorry.' His eyes slowly closed again as he passed out once more. He was, thankfully, still breathing.

'Johnnie, Johnnie, help is coming. The Lord will ensure we are saved.'

It was now that she started shouting for help, and this time instead of tears, she put all of her strength into her voice. Their lives depended on it.

Father Thomas had been awoken late the previous night by Johnnie's wife Rosa. He had opened the door of the vestry half asleep, blinking into the darkness as his eyes adjusted to focus on who was addressing him with a high-pitched gabble of words. 'Is that Rosa Deterville?'

'I am sorry for calling on you so late, Father, but Johnnie took Ella to visit his mother today, and they are not yet home! I'm worried. With all that rain on the road . . .' her voice trailed off and tears started to well up in Rosa's eyes. 'Father, you're the only place with a telephone in Canaries. Can you make a call to Ms Flora's neighbour, he has a phone and can go next door to ask her if they are still there?'

After a lengthy game of relay on the phone to Castries, it

was confirmed that Ella and Johnnie had departed for their destination but had not returned home.

It had been an impossible search in the dark and wet night, but as the sun rose over the valley, Father Thomas and a contingent of villagers in their vehicles had scoured the roads for any sign of the missing car. After making several twists and turns, they came across two fresh skid marks in the road that led straight towards a mess of broken soil and snapped branches. Rosa saw it first.

'Stop!' she shouted. They came to a halt next to the evidence of the mishap.

'Ssh, listen.' Rosa silenced the murmurings with a wave of her hand.

'You hear that?' Rosa exclaimed as a hoarse shouting travelled up the valley.

'HELP US LORD, HELP US!'

'That's Ella voice. Lord be praised, we've found them.'

After many hours, two men with ropes tied around their waists attached to a large truck above them, snaked down the hill.

A rope was placed around Ella's body underneath her armpits and tied off with a big knot to secure her. She tried not to look down.

Johnnie was distressed and less able to help himself than Ella and his rescue took longer, but once all were back to safety, a loud cheer went up. The victims' injuries were not as severe as they first seemed, and both could be tended by the local nurse from the village health centre, and their rescuers were treated like royalty by the villagers who plied them with a few too many shots of strong white rum.

The following Sunday Father Thomas took to the pews at mass and gave thanks and shared his pride in how the villagers came out in support in action and prayer for the safe recovery of Ella and Johnnie.

Ella was in church despite her cuts and bruises, sitting in her usual seat as Father Thomas gave his thanks.

She thought back to the people who had died in the *Blue Belle* disaster. Those poor folk had perished. Ella and Johnnie could have been killed too, but instead they had been spared.

It fuelled her determination. Ella felt strongly that she had been saved for a reason, and she wanted to live with purpose like her aunt. She wanted to be there for the villagers, as they had been there for her.

But first she had to talk with her sister and let her know of the incident before the news travelled to England. She also wanted to let Agnes know that she understood why she had not returned. Her sister needed to know that Ella would still be prepared to look after Tina and Charles for as long as she could, as long as one day they would be reunited with their mother. She had to make a phone call and the only telephone number she had belonged to a Mrs Fletcher.

'Agnes dear your sister just called from St Lu-char and I told her to call back in ten minutes, so make haste to be sure you're at the phone when she calls back.' Mrs Fletcher was out of breath as she shouted from the bottom of the stairs up to Agnes after letting herself in the front door at 63 Fernhead Road. Mrs Fletcher's unprecedented entry into her tenants' property and the news that Ella was going to call, made Agnes jump into action. It was five o'clock on a Sunday afternoon, and Raphael was home. Agnes quickly laid Helena in his surprised arms, and the house shook as Agnes descended the stairs at speed.

Margaret came out of her room concerned. 'What all da commotion, *Sa ka fete*, What happening Agnes?'

'*Mwen pa sav* Margaret, I don't know. All I know is Ella is on the telephone!'

Agnes stood by the phone with Mrs Fletcher at her side. Neither of them spoke as they waited for it to ring. Agnes had all kinds of things going through her mind, the wait seemed to take forever. *What if something happened to the children, what is wrong with Ella, who died?*

The phone rang. 'Ella, Ella dat's you! What happen?' Agnes held the phone tightly to her ear and listened to Ella, a voice she had not heard in so long, the voice she missed so much. Agnes was relieved to hear her sister's calm voice on the other end of the phone.

'My sister, it's so good to hear your voice.' Agnes found it hard to respond through her choked tears. Ella could hear Agnes crying from the other side of the world.

'Agnes, I have cried so much too, I miss you more than you know.' Ella had to hurry the call along.

'I'm calling from Father Thomas's telephone at the church, so I can't speak for long, but I will send you a letter soon and tell you more. For now I want you to know everyone is okay. I just want to let you know Johnnie and I had a bad accident, but we are okay. Johnnie was driving, and we came off the road. I didn't want you to hear the story from anyone else. You know how news travel and it always sounds worse than it is.'

Ella outlined what had happened as briefly and as best she could about how the community came out to their rescue. 'Agnes, I thought I would not make it. God saved me.' Ella had to take a breath and hold back her own tears. Agnes was overwhelmed with tears but she finally found space between her emotions and took a breath so she could speak.

'Ella, thank you, thank you for your patience. Thank you for all you have done for me and my children. I want you to know I am doing my best, I will come home one day, but not right now.'

'I know,' Ella said. 'I will still be here, my sister, always for you and your children, as long as you need me.'

They said their goodbyes quickly and tearfully, and as Agnes placed the receiver back on the cradle, she felt a strange kind of longing.

That night, Agnes, looking at Helena sleeping soundly in her crib felt fireworks of unconditional love burst in her heart; she wanted Helena to have the very best life possible. And with this thought her mind turned to her family in Canaries – Tina and Charles growing so tall and strong; but what of their future, what would they do? She felt her determination build. It was time to bring her children together here in London, where they could pursue whatever dreams they may have and in so doing her sister would be freed to achieve her own goals in life. Different to her own as they were. The Deterville sisters were connected across the ocean with an unbreakable bond. Despite having their own voices, they sang the same island song.

Auntie Flora lived for another year after the accident. Ella did visit her aunt as often as she could, travelling on the bus to Castries, and with every journey Ella became braver. And before Auntie Flora passed away she put an idea into Ella's head. 'Why not use dat money for you Ella, educate yourself. Maybe fink about becoming a teacher? Go to the Ministry of Education, they might be able to help you wit' a scholarship? And dis money help you go to where you need to go to college.' Ella had thought about becoming a teacher many moons ago. It was once her heart's desire, which had drifted out of her life with the daily grind of living hand to mouth. Her lack of confidence and lack of funds had diminished the idea. 'Could I become a teacher?' She began to make enquiries and discovered the St Lucian Ministry of Education was affiliated with a teacher training college in Trinidad; the idea of an indoor toilet and running water with an indoor tap would now have to take a back seat. As she watched her Auntie Flora fade away, her aunt's words took on new significance. 'Live your life Ella, don't give up on your dreams.'

The car accident became a true revelation for Ella, she felt empowered and blessed to be alive. This revelation became a call to action, and Ella vowed to become a pillar of her community by becoming a teacher, and to make her simple life in her home village a much more fulfilled and rewarding one. Not everyone was supposed to yearn to make a new life across the Atlantic Ocean like her sister Agnes. She was exactly where she needed to be, with her people in her village of Canaries.

CHAPTER FORTY-TWO

'Agnes, I start on Monday!' With the recommendation of Bernard and the request for a reference from Mr Harrison at Morton Construction he was positive that after the three months' probation they would confirm that he would officially be a full-time staff member working for Marlborough Housing Association. The association had purchased properties in the Paddington area, and the houses would be turned into self-contained flats for people on low income and for families in need. 'And you know what she said Agnes? Because we are living in Paddington we can put our name on de waiting list for a flat of our own!'

'Even before dey take you on full time?'

'Yes! Because we are a family in need. We can't live like dis forever, I told her about our situation, living in one room wit a baby.'

Agnes sat with Helena on her lap while Raphael moved around the room with excitement, an energy she had not seen in him for a while. She was relieved by this news, it gave her faith in their coming future. The thought of having their own place, with their own front door, their own doorbell . . .

It had been a blessing living with Margaret and Vitalis, she would always be grateful for their generosity. At times she'd had her doubts about her choices and there were days when she did feel confused, 'Is England for me? Have I done de right fing leaving my family behind?' And in the same breath she would say, 'I always wanted to come to England and here I am. At times it has been hard but here I still am.' The England Mrs Chester described was very different from what she had experienced, that picture was now shattered. Some of its people were judgemental, not everyone was friendly as Mrs Chester said; some were even outwardly aggressive, yet Agnes still felt hopeful. Hopeful, because everyone she knew was struggling with the same issues, everyone was in the same boat, everyone struggling to make a better life. Raphael, Linus, Margaret, Vitalis, Moses, Bernard and even Scottie with his radical ways were trying to make sense of their new home, discovering ways to survive this other island. Knowing that there was a community of friends for support who had travelled so far for the same reasons brought comfort to Agnes. Her island song still chimed in her heart, the melody yearning for a better life still had volume – it had become louder and stronger as she overcame every adversity. This was Agnes's revelation.

There were more St Lucians moving into Paddington, along with an influx of other islanders, who were making their new homes from Maida Vale to Harrow Road, through to Ladbroke Grove and all the way into Shephard's Bush. Food imported from the Caribbean, Africa, spices were transforming the marketplace on Portobello Road; their part of West London was now a little St Lucia.

Occasionally someone would make the journey back home and Bernard was one of them. His island song was still calling him back to Grenada and he had said as much to Raphael.

'I have to go back to my island Raph, be with my wife, go fishing in my boat. I save enough money to get my hardware store going. Plus, I ca stay here no more. England is a two-face country. Dey make you come but dey treat you bad, it's time to leave dat bullshit behind.'

With every passing week, month and year they had been on this not so sunny isle, Agnes had seen a change in those who took the journey. Doing her Saturday shop on the Harrow Road she would hear news of West Indians now buying houses and becoming their own landlords. There was more resilience and understanding of how to navigate the changing tides, and the new arrivals were less naive about what England promised; the path for new arrivals was eased by those who had come before, and their faces and their culture had started to become part of the fabric of life in London.

Monday morning didn't come soon enough for Raphael, he was up and out of the house by seven o'clock. 'I can't be late on my first day.'

Agnes was so happy for him, for them. Relieved that her husband had found a better paying job, and that as soon as they could, a parcel would be sent to St Lucia for the children and Ella. Agnes could only imagine what it must have been like for Ella to be stuck in a tree holding on for dear life. The thought of losing her sister brought a sickly feeling to her stomach, like having the air kicked out of her. To help the feeling subside she had to focus on the reality, her sister was still alive. She had to give gratitude. 'Thank you, Lord, for not taking my Ella.'

The house was quiet after Raphael left, everyone else was at work too. She heard the post box rattle against the front door. She hoped she would finally receive a letter from her sister. She would check it after she was done feeding Helena, who was enjoying sucking on her milk bottle and staring up at her mother. Her daughter was growing fast and she seemed to enjoy the free powdered baby milk she was given at the health centre instead of being breast fed.

Her beloved daughter had changed everything; she had the same love for all her children and she wanted Tina and Charles to experience the benefits that Helena would have too. To wear shoes and not endure bare feet, full bellies without worrying where the next meal was coming from, money for necessities, as well as the occasional treat, or a day out. Agnes sighed as she looked down at her baby girl, she didn't know when that would happen.

Agnes put her sleeping baby in her cot, then walked quietly down the stairs to the front door to see what letters might have arrived for her. She picked up four letters. Not one from Ella, she was disappointed to see, but she was pleasantly surprised to see one from Mrs Chester.

Eager to see what she had to say, she opened the thick ivory envelope straight away, deciding not to walk up the stairs to sit down but read the letter where she stood. She started to read the neat writing, in a deep royal blue that sat beautifully upon the cream-coloured paper.

My Dear Agnes,
 We have finally made plans to come to London and visit my aunt. We will be in London for a week in May, and I am hoping we could visit you and your family on Sunday the 15th of May? Edward will not be joining us, so it will be myself and little Agnes. We will be staying with my aunt in Putney and the next day we will be returning to Norfolk.

Please write back, or you can call us on our telephone number, Holt 265 to confirm our visit.

I so look forward to meeting everyone and seeing you after so long.

Best wishes,
Lillian Chester

At the first opportunity Agnes showed Barbara Fletcher the note from Mrs Chester. It had been so long since Agnes had seen Lillian, the prospect of seeing her filled her with an instant jolt of excitement. She looked forward to the opportunity to demonstrate to her old employer how far she had come since last they saw one another in Canaries four years before. Although a prickle of anxiety built within her as she contemplated how to entertain Mrs Chester and her daughter within the confined and basic surroundings of her accommodations. 'Barbara, I remember dat Mrs Chestor like fings a certain way. I don't even have a teapot to brew the tea how she likes it.'

Barbara looked delighted. 'You go ahead and make the call; you forget Agnes, I promised you that should this day come, you could welcome your guest for tea here. I can pull out my best china and we can put together a good feast, fit for the Queen, how about it, let's show her how we entertain in our part of town.'

'That would be wonderful, Barbara. I will ask her to come to your house. Thank you!'

This was the second time Agnes had been invited to use the telephone in Mrs Fletcher's sitting room, but she understood that the little box next to it was where she would be expected to drop a shilling to pay for the call. Telephones were expensive to use after all. The phone was placed on top of a dedicated telephone table with a shelf underneath for the directory, which

Mrs Fletcher pulled out to look up the code. 'Now let's have a look. Holt! There it is 0263 and what's the number?' Agnes looked at the note from Mrs Chester to check. '265.'

'Go on Agnes, dial it.' Agnes was filled with nervous excitement; she put her finger in the hole of the 0 and gave the dial a full turn, waiting patiently for it to rattle back to its stop, completing the dialling process as briskly and smoothly as possible. At the end of the last turn she held the handset to her ear, listening to the clicks and whirs as the call was connected to a house hundreds of miles away in rural Norfolk.

On the fifth ring the voice at the other end came through with a clipped clear delivery. Mrs Chester was using her very best telephone voice. 'Good morning, this is Holt 265, the Chester residence. Lillian Chester here, to whom am I speaking?' The airs and graces of Middle England phone etiquette were unmistakable and brought a smile to Agnes's lips.

'Hello Mrs Chestor, It's Agnes.'

'My apologies, there was a crackle in the line and I didn't catch that, could you please repeat yourself?'

Agnes cleared her throat with a cough and used her best English accent. Mrs Fletcher stood by egging Agnes on with a grin.

'Mrs Chestor, dis is Agnes Deterville speaking, Agnes from St Lucia.'

'Agnes! My dear is that really you?' All of Mrs Chester's formality instantly fell away from her voice. 'It's so good to hear your voice Agnes, where are you calling from? The line went terribly fuzzy there for a second, I could believe you were calling me all the way from Saint Lucia!'

'Oh no Mrs Chestor I am calling from London.' Agnes explained about Mrs Fletcher's phone, 'She is my landlady and she lives next door, she very kind and let me use it to speak to you.'

'Oh how lovely, that is so kind of her, please thank her for me. I won't keep you on the phone any longer than I should then. So, can we visit you on the fifteenth?' Mrs Fletcher was avidly moving her head up and down mouthing 'yes'.

'Yes Mrs Chestor, you can come to Mrs Fletcher's house. She is the house right next door.' Agnes confirmed the address, surprised by how nervous she felt speaking to Mrs Chester.

'Okay, I have made a note. Most likely we will come by taxi, three o'clock it is. I'm thrilled by this news and am so looking forward to meeting you all and introducing you to our little Agnes!'

It was Sunday the 15th May 1960; Agnes had been in London for a little over three years and this would be the first time she had seen Lillian Chester in all that time. So much had changed. They both had daughters, lived in England and had dramatically different lives to the one they shared together at Sweet Cinnamon Cottage. Agnes stood in Mrs Fletcher's kitchen with Helena on her hip watching Moses and Margaret fussing over the table setting for the tea party. She was happy to see the abundance on display, a true banquet. An abundance of food was, after all, how a West Indian family expressed their love and respect for visitors. Moses had created an impressive two-tiered marzipan-coated fruit cake, the top of which was covered with an artistic display of delicately carved marzipan fruit pieces. It stood in pride of place at the middle of the table.

Margaret had arrived with a large tin of assorted McVitie's biscuits that she laid out in concentric circles on a plate, placing it next to the cake, either side of which were plates laden with the egg and cress sandwiches and freshly made accras she had spent time that morning making. She was keen to let everyone know she had done some research regarding her offering. 'Well, de chef at my work said egg and cress is a very traditional sandwich that English people do love to eat with their tea. He says it's fit for Her Majesty de Queen, so I fink Mrs Chestor will like dem. She is a special guest of yours Agnes and you have not seen her in a long while, am I not right?'

'Yes, you are right. Thank you Margaret so much for all your help.'

Margaret gave her own efforts some further praise. 'Plus, I made the accras to remind her of St Lucia, I know she will enjoy dat.' At this Margaret took a step back and surveyed her handiwork, happily anticipating the glowing compliments that would surely be coming her way in the hours ahead.

Mrs Fletcher's Red Rose tea set sat prettily against her starched white tablecloth. 'Thank goodness I have enough cups and saucers to serve everyone.' She lifted one of the cups to show Agnes. 'You see these roses, they always remind me of my husband Bob, he would have loved this.'

Raphael was in the garden having a cigarette and would have preferred to stay with Vitalis next door. 'Why we treating her like she de queen? Anyway, she don't wan to see me?'

'Awa! No way Raphael Toussaint, you will be sitting right there with me, I want you to meet my friend, Lillian Chestor,' Agnes had said. So, as instructed, he put on his best shirt and trousers and was present, although sat as far as possible from the centre of the action.

At 2.55 p.m. everyone was sitting in their assigned spot, waiting on the doorbell to ring. The kettle had been boiled, but would need to be reheated briefly to bring the water to a rolling boil again. There would be no stewed tea served today.

At 3.15 everyone was starting to get fidgety. Agnes stood up and walked into the hallway to check the front door and peer into the street, anticipating seeing a black London cab pull up any second. But the street was empty.

Mrs Fletcher's clock chimed at four o'clock and Mrs Chester was now an hour late. The rumblings within the room had grown into a combination of deflation and outright frustration. Agnes felt an acute sense of embarrassment looking at the faces of her friends sitting around the kitchen table overladen with food.

It was Moses who spoke up. 'Well Agnes, I must say dat dis lady is rude for being so late, I thought you told me she had manners.'

Had Lillian had another one of her funny turns, Agnes wondered? Maybe coming back to England wasn't the answer for her after all? However, she felt the need to keep up her loyal stance. 'She does have manners Moses. Something must had happened to her. She would never just be this late without a reason.'

'Well, the telephone was invented for such occasions,' was Mrs Fletcher's retort. Agnes knew she was right. She was so disappointed and didn't know where to look or what to say.

Margaret lifted up her plate of sandwiches. 'Agnes, we can't sit around looking at dis food, soon de bread will go stale.' Raphael spoke up from his position at the garden door. 'De lady let you down Agnes, maybe she had a better offer? I fink we should eat up and pack up.' At this moment the doorbell rang, saving Agnes from having to reply in defence of Lillian Chester. It was two minutes past four. Everyone stopped talking and looked directly at Agnes. Raphael threw up his arms in surrender, knowing that he would now have to play the role of dutiful husband and host to this white lady he had never met after all.

Helena, who had been snoozing quietly in Agnes's lap up

to this point, was brought abruptly awake by the immediate change in mood and the jolt of energy that ran through Agnes as she stood quickly with the relief obvious on her face, and started to cry. In one movement Helena was lifted to her hip, which settled her crying. Agnes looked down at her and quickly wiped her face with her bib and rearranged her pretty dress so she looked presentable and made her way into the hallway to open the front door. She could see Mrs Chester's shadow through the glass; she stood for a second and took a breath to calm herself and then opened the door.

There stood Lillian, red in the face and obviously very flustered. 'My dear Agnes. Hello! I am so dreadfully sorry I am late. We've had a terrible time getting here. There was a terrific accident ahead of us as we were crossing the Putney Bridge. It took the police an age to sort everything out. We were simply stuck there, no going forwards or turning round, it was solid in seconds and utter bedlam. I begged the taxi driver to do something, but in the end we just had to wait for the police to clear the mess up and reopen the road. Fortunately no one was badly hurt, but there was debris all over the pavement as we passed and a truck had its bumper lodged in the railing. Heaven knows what happened to cause such a mess. Anyway, I'm rambling now, I do apologise, you must think me terribly rude. But honestly there was nothing to be done. I couldn't even use a telephone to let you know what was happening. Little Agnes has been such a treasure, she was so patient, quiet and I'm sure she will need the bathroom very soon.' Mrs Chester took a breath from making her explanation.

'Agnes, I feel terrible, I hope I haven't ruined your day. I thought I had left in plenty of time. It is so good to see you and this must be your baby Helena.' She took a gloved hand and gave baby Helena's face a gentle stroke to get her attention.

At this point Agnes finally got a chance to respond.

'Hello, Lillian it's so good to see you too. I was getting so worried about you.'

The two women stood facing each other, both so different in so many ways, brought together in the fishing village of Canaries, on the rugged west coast of Saint Lucia, and now reunited on the well-polished doorstep of Mrs Fletcher's home at 61 Fernhead Road in West London.

Agnes took in how Mrs Chester was dressed. She looked as stylish as ever in a dark teal fitted coat and jaunty hat of the same colour placed elegantly on the side of her head, revealing her blonde hair tucked up neatly at the back. She looked a little older, the hint of a few crow's feet at the corners of her eyes, a slight crease each side of her mouth, but it was still very much the Lillian Chester that Agnes remembered so vividly.

'Agnes let me introduce to you, your namesake, my most prized possession on this Earth my own little Agnes . . . And Agnes, this is the nice lady I told you about, who looked after Mummy so well, when I lived with Daddy in St Lucia, on the other side of the ocean. The lady Mummy was so grateful for that I named you after her.' The two Agneses smiled at each other.

Little Agnes was a miniature version of her mother, yet with the same high cheekbones as her father. She held on to her mother's hand, enveloped as much as was possible in the pleats of her skirt, a little shy, yet still she was polite and confident enough to say, 'Hello, my name is Agnes, nice to meet you.' She looked at Helena and said to her mother. 'Mummy, do you think Mrs Agnes will let me play with her baby?'

Agnes didn't wait for Lillian to reply, 'Of course you can, please come in. Everyone is very excited to meet you.' Agnes turned and ushered the visitors into the hallway and through to the kitchen and the welcoming party. Lillian Chester composed herself and politely stated to the room: 'Goodness, I can see you have made every effort to welcome me and I am intolerably late. Can you ever forgive me?'

The frustrations and disappointment of the last hour were quickly forgotten as the noise level increased with a lively response of greetings and welcomes.

'Let's have some tea!' Agnes said, Helena still bouncing on her hip.

'Shall I be mother, Agnes?' Lillian said, offering to take over the serving duties. 'You rather have your hands full.'

Agnes caught Raphael's eye, and he reached out and took Helena from her mother.

'It's all right, Lillian,' Agnes said. 'I'll pour.'

EPILOGUE

'Look Tina, look Charles, dere's Johnnie and Rosa waving to us!'

As the passenger ship pulled away from the quay, Ella, dressed in a bright green dress with a full skirt she had made in the latest fashion, could see the bright figure of Rosa in her large purple hat waving furiously from the jetty.

'I'll wear dis big hat, so you can see us amongst all de other people saying their goodbyes,' Rosa had told Ella, as they drove the Deterville trio from Canaries to the port in Castries. She was right, and now Ella could also see Johnnie next to her jumping up and down, waving goodbye madly.

Tina and Charles were so excited at going to England, and seeing their mother again, that Ella didn't know how she was going to keep them calm for the next two weeks at sea. In her luggage she had brought them books and games to keep them occupied and she only hoped that the terrible seasickness she had heard about would leave them all alone.

Island Song

For herself, Ella felt slightly dazed as she listened to the captain telling them over the tannoy that this would be their last view of St Lucia. Ella knew that wasn't true for her, she would definitely be coming back very soon.

Her sister Agnes had finally been able to send enough money for Tina and Charles to come to England, but there was no way on earth Ella would have let them make the journey without her. So here she was, doing the one thing that she never imagined she would, or could do. The money that her aunt Flora gave her had paid for her fare, and made a difference to her everyday life, no more struggle and hardships for a while thank goodness. The best news was that the Ministry of Education had recognised her work with the schoolchildren and were offering to support her with a teaching scholarship that would start in September.

She almost felt as excited as Tina and Charles at the prospect of seeing her sister and her new niece; and as for Raphael Touissaint . . . well, he'd have to work hard to impress Ella, but she was prepared to let him try his best.

Ella screwed her eyes up and imagined for a moment that she could see the memorial to the *Blue Belle* in the distance, sitting silently as a testament to the vanished travellers, and she thought briefly again of those lost souls and the fears that had trapped her for so long.

Their ghosts no longer haunted her dreams. Their fate was not going to be her fate – she believed that with a certainty that almost scared her, but that also sent a thrill of anticipation through her veins.

Her nightmares were gone, her fears were silenced, and in their place she could hear her island song loud and clear, its tune filling her heart with hope and with courage.

Agnes's song had taken her to another island, and another life. Ella's song would bring her back home.

ACKNOWLEDGEMENTS

Island Song was written in celebration of those who crossed the Atlantic Ocean for a better life in England from the Commonwealth countries in the Caribbean – and for any immigrant who took a journey into the unknown for the betterment of themselves and their families.

I would also like to recognize all my cheerleaders who encouraged me to take my journey in writing this book.

Thank you, Titi Fawn, for always taking time out to share memories with me of times gone by, of your life in St Lucia, your own journey across the waters, how to pronounce Kwéyòl words and how important it is to keep using this expressive language.

My mother-in-law, Mary, I read to you my first draft and you cried with pride and joy, this was a sure sign I was on to something. Thank you for your happy tears.

Shirlie Kemp for asking the question, 'Why did your mum leave the St Lucian sunshine, Peps?' You made me realize *Island Song* was a story worth telling.

Many, many thanks to Ajda Vucicevic for seeing my potential and championing me.

To my fabulous team at HarperFiction, especially Kate Bradley, my editor, who held my hand every step of the way. When I had doubt, you gave me reason to continue and to get the words on the page!

My agent, Tim Bates, for taking me on and giving me the confidence to call myself an author.

This is also for you my brothers, David, Max, Robbie and Charleston. My sister, Tecia, for braving the journey across the waters as a young child, and for her husband, Maurice, for caring for her until the end.

Thanks to my aunts and uncles, especially Titi Rose, who helped to raise us all.

Big up to my cousins, especially Mullin and her children, Keira and Galton, Lindel, Sylvia, Pearl, Pat, Maurice and Luke.

My nephews and nieces, especially Mark, Louis, Jon Pierre, Michelle, Christian, Alicia, Cesar and Kiara. I hope this book stays on your bookshelves, so you remember how far your family have come.

I would also like to acknowledge Kelso Cochrane and his family. The killing of Kelso in Notting Hill's Golborne Road in 1959 brought a community together, if just for a moment. Unfortunately, his killers have never been brought to justice. My wish is that they will one day be identified in order to bring closure to this senseless hate-crime.

Last, but never, ever least, thank you to my husband, James, for being my support throughout and for inspiring me to tell this story in honour of my parents, Agatha and Roger. With you I found my home, my island song.

KWÉYÒL GLOSSARY

Kwéyòl is a language which I have used throughout *Island Song*. It's a melting pot of French with some African dialect thrown into the mix. My mother would talk to me in Kwéyòl and I would answer her in English. Somehow my London accent didn't give me the confidence to respond back to her in Kwéyòl but now because of her, I understand every word and I'm proud to say I can pull together a sentence or two. Kwéyòl is a language related to other Creole languages throughout the Caribbean and is not only spoken in St Lucia but also in Dominica, Guadeloupe, Haiti, Martinique, and even Mauritius and if you wanted to seek further you would find this expressive language spoken in other parts of the world.

Here is a small sample of words and phrases to pique your interest and if you would like to learn more, check out @twossaints or @kweyolsentlisi on Instagram. Google Translate even has Haitian Kwéyòl as a language option!

Island Song

Apwézan! – Now!
Asiz – Sit down / have a sit
Bondyé – God
Bonjou – Hello / good day
Di sa ankò souplé – Say that again, please
Doudou – Sweetheart
Li Cho! – It's hot!
Ki mannyè ou ka di an Kwéyòl? – How do you say in Kwéyòl?
Konmen pou li? – How much does it cost?
Kouman ou yé? – How are you?
Mwen byen, mèsi – I am good, thanks
Mwen faché – I'm angry
Mwen pa kopwann – I don't understand
Ou paka tann! – You don't hear!
Pasé an bon jouné – Have a good day
Pa fè sa – Don't do that
Pé la – Shut up
Sa ka fèt? – What's happening?
Sa ki sa? – What is that?
Titi – Auntie

Scan the QR code below to hear Pepsi's selection of her favourite island songs.